DAY ZERO

The sound was like a hammer striking an apple. There was a whisper of air, and a wet crunch. The man jerked and spun as if he'd been struck. Something hot and red caught Olly on the cheek as the man tumbled down onto the pavement with boneless finality.

The world slowed and finally stuttered to a halt as Olly stared down, in shock. His first instinct was to try and staunch the wound in the man's chest. He'd seen it on television and in films a thousand times. You reached out and pressed your hands to the wound and it stopped pumping. Only it didn't. The blood just kept coming, and it was on his hands and his trousers and in his nose and – oh God, it was everywhere.

The shot had come from out of nowhere – a sniper? That sort of thing didn't happen in London – in the UK. The scene replayed in his head over and over again. The man climbing to his feet, cursing him out, then jerking around, falling. The blood…

WATCHDOGS®
L E G I O N

DAY ZERO

JAMES SWALLOW &
JOSH REYNOLDS

ACONYTE

First published by Aconyte Books in 2020

ISBN 978 1 83908 048 7

Ebook ISBN 978 1 83908 049 4

Cover art by Stonehouse

Distributed in North America by Simon & Schuster Inc, New York, USA

Printed in the United States of America

9 8 7 6 5 4 3 2 1

ACONYTE BOOKS

An imprint of Asmodee Entertainment Ltd

Mercury House, Shipstones Business Centre

North Gate, Nottingham NG7 7FN, UK

aconytebooks.com // twitter.com/aconytebooks

DAY FIVE

SUNDAY

Bagley-bytes 13654-9: Things are popping in old London town, gang. To whit the following events of note: Skye Larsen, futurist and weirdo de jour, has published yet another TOAN-deaf essay in the Grauniad, arguing that really, you'll all be better off if you just let her stick a cTOS chip in your brains. It is to laugh. Oh wait, another thing I can't do. Sad. Fake news.

+++

Here's something that's not news — CCTV feeds have clocked a white transit van at multiple unscheduled, unlogged stops across the city, including Blackfriars Bridge. Nothing suspicious there. On an unrelated note, there's a lot of internal chatter up and down the Albion frequencies. I wonder what our favourite paramilitary contractor is up to, hmmm? Does anyone recognise the term LIBRA? No? Moving on.

+++

And something familiar — the Met is getting a lot of reports of foul doings and black deeds in the Whitechapel Terminus. Show of hands, who's surprised? Please put your hand down, Terry. You're embarrassing us both. Possible involvement of Clan Kelley has been mentioned. Sergei, be a chum and get on that.

+++

Speaking of Whitechapel, our favourite Labour MP, Sarah Lincoln, is giving an unnecessary speech on community unity at Lister House later today, when everyone would much rather be watching the footie. Be sure to give the crowd a scan, Hannah. You never know who might prove sufficiently disaffected and useful.

+++

And finally, we have the best for last. According to our Dalton, it looks as if MI5 is experiencing some political blowback from the Newcastle incident. My heart would bleed, if I had one.

1: BRICK LANE

Olly Soames hit Brick Lane at top speed, letting the bicycle's momentum carry him along. He wove through the midday market crowd with an ease that was down to experience and a total lack of concern for traffic safety laws. As he pedalled, he reached into his pocket and thumbed the screen of his Optik AR, waking it up. Linked to a tiny electronic device implanted just in front of his ear, the handset was networked to GPS, and through it he called up a retinal overlay of the borough.

The digital map unspooled across his field of vision. He barely noticed it these days, though it had taken some practice to get used to riding with it. He blink-scrolled through the pop-up advertisements, tapping in his destination as he skidded and thumped along the pavement, leaving a trail of startled curses in his wake.

Not everyone appreciated Olly's skilful navigation and more than one piece of fruit bounced off the back of the canvas bag slung across his back. He ignored them. He had bigger worries than a badly-aimed satsuma.

He was late. Not the fashionable kind of late either, but the other kind.

The one that meant that he'd screwed up. *Again.*

It wasn't his fault. He had an excuse, but excuses only counted if the other person was willing to listen. Olly doubted his handler was the understanding sort, given their encounters to date. He bent low over the handlebars, urging the bike to greater speed.

The Optik handset in his pocket hummed, and a congestion warning flashed on his display. He veered down a blind alley, hoping to avoid the traffic jam. He bounced off the pavement and along a parallel road, seeking the path of least resistance.

Newsfeeds flickered at the corner of his eye. London was playing host to a big technology conference this week. That explained all the security drones in the air overhead. Olly had it on good authority that most of them were run by a pair of bored plods in an air-conditioned box at New Scotland Yard.

A Bogen saloon pulled out of a side-street, horn blaring as he arrowed towards it. He kicked the front wheel up and went up and over the hood of the car. He nearly bit his tongue as he came down hard on the pavement. He kept the bike upright, but only just.

From behind Olly came a cry of "Wanker!" There was no way he hadn't scratched the paint. Olly couldn't bring himself to feel too bad about it. What did the guy expect, driving in London on a Sunday? He tossed two fingers over his shoulder, but kept his face forward.

Olly knew CCTV cameras were tracking him, but that didn't mean much if no one was paying attention on the other end of the feed. As far as they knew, he was just another arsehole delivery driver. That was fine by him. And if he needed to, there were a few tricks he could play to make identification all but impossible. Electronic eyes could be fooled as easily as flesh and blood ones, if you knew the trick. He flicked the Optik screen again, activating a pre-set command. It sent out a coded data-stream, scrambling the CCTV feeds in his immediate area for a few seconds.

A rainbow of curry houses and fashionable graffiti streaked past on either side of him. He angled the bike, skidding around a corner, startling a dog-walker and nearly tagging a concrete bollard. Barks and yelps pursued him down the street.

His Optik was buzzing, but he ignored it. Whatever it was, it could wait. He was close. Maybe close enough. Maybe he wasn't late after all. *Maybe, maybe, maybe* – the mantra went around and around in his head.

This was his last chance. If he screwed up this time, that was it. He was done. The thought made him queasy. The feeling only got worse when he reached his destination.

The alley was a little hook of space, caught between two buildings. A piece of old London, folded into the new city and forgotten – like a scar you barely remembered getting. A gloomy stretch of cobbles and pavement, lined with rubbish. The walls were plastered with old theatre handbills, posters for funk bands and decades of overlapping tags. Neon swirls of spray paint intersected with mimeographed flyers and tattered advertisements for loft shares.

He hadn't bothered to ask why the hand-off was taking place here. There was probably a good reason, but they weren't going to tell him. Answers only came with trust, and he was all too aware that he hadn't earned either yet. And anyway, a good delivery driver knew better than to ask about things like that. It didn't matter what was in the package, so long as it got where it was going on time and intact.

He brought the bike to a screeching stop. A rat pelted into the rubbish, its squeaks echoing against the bricks. Daylight sifted down past the edges of the rooftops above. He climbed off the bike and wheeled it towards the end of the alley, heart thumping. If she'd already left, he'd never hear the end of it.

"You're late," a voice said, to his left. The voice – and its owner – were posh. Too posh for this part of London, but he kept that to himself.

"Traffic, yeah?" He turned. She was young, his age, maybe a little older. Dressed professionally, black hijab and an Optik audio-bud in her ear. Cute. She reminded him of someone famous – a TV chef, he thought, though he couldn't bring a name to mind. He considered doing an image search, then thought better of it. "Hannah Shah?"

She quirked an eyebrow. "If I wasn't, I wouldn't tell you."

He shrugged. "Fair enough." They'd warned him that she'd be nervous. In her shoes, he'd be bloody terrified. Data crawled across his vision. The hacked facial recognition software installed in his Optik gave him everything about her, including shoe size. Gave new meaning to the phrase "open book". His feed pinged, and he knew she was trying the same. Olly wished her luck. He'd spent several long, sleepless nights online shaping his data profile into something innocuous and uninformative. Hers was far more interesting.

Hannah Shah. Third generation British Bengali. Personal assistant to Sarah Lincoln, newly-elected Labour MP for Tower Hamlets South. "Bit off your patch, aren't you?" he asked, with a smile and made a vague gesture. "Limehouse is over that way, Ms Shah."

She frowned. "It's a free city. For the moment, at least."

"That's why we're here," he said. "Got the whatsit?"

"How do I know you're the one I'm supposed to hand it over to?"

"If I wasn't, I wouldn't tell you," he said. He tried for a cheeky grin, but from her expression he could tell it hadn't worked. She stared at him, and he restrained the urge to squirm. "Look, I'm not Albion, if that's what you're worried about."

"I wasn't, but I'm starting to." Her stare didn't waver.

He stared back, and suddenly remembered the passphrase. He slapped his forehead in embarrassment. "Bugger. Redqueen says *off with their heads.*"

"A bit late for that," she said, her tone dubious.

He didn't blame her, but even so, he was annoyed. It wasn't his fault, was it? He wasn't the one who'd insisted on meeting in a dark alley like something out of a bad movie. He wasn't the one who'd insisted on bullshit codes, when they could have just sent encrypted pings to each other's Optiks.

"I forgot," he said, defensively. When she didn't reply, he turned his bike about. "I'll leave then, shall I?" He tried to sound unconcerned. "No skin off mine," he added. Which wasn't strictly true. But no need for her to know that.

"Wait," she began. He paused, saying nothing. After a moment, she sighed. "Here."

She extended a folded A5 envelope. Inside was something small. A flash drive, he thought. But he wasn't so new at this as to open it and check. Not in front of her. Even so, he hesitated. He knew enough about this sort of thing to know what she was probably risking, meeting him like this. "You know you might get in big trouble for this."

"Only if *you* get caught," she said, softly. "So for both our sakes, don't get caught."

"Wasn't planning on it." He stuffed the envelope into his vest for safe-keeping. "Ta, love. Be seeing you." He was on his bike a moment later and gone three seconds after that.

He didn't look back.

Hannah Shah aimed herself towards Whitechapel, flicking through urgent emails on her Optik display as she walked. It was Sunday, but that didn't mean the work stopped coming. Besides, it was a good distraction.

A police car sped past, siren blaring. There were more police on the streets than she could ever recall seeing before. Something was in the air. She thought it might have to do with the TOAN conference, later in the week. The Technology of All Nations conference was big news. A sign of London's resurgence, some claimed. Privately, Hannah had her doubts.

Around her, boutique shops and hipster joints stretched for what seemed like miles. Tradition warred with gentrification in Tower Hamlets, and the latter was winning. There was no money for anything these days, but work was being done nonetheless, mostly by foreign concerns. London had been sliding towards international irrelevance for years, and no one wanted to admit it. And if that meant inviting in certain elements… so be it.

Elements like Albion.

She still felt queasy about handing off the data. Krish had vouched for the courier, and he'd matched the profile in her face-recognition program, but only just. It was as if he'd never used social media or had a photo taken.

Other than an e-fit she'd managed to dig up on her own initiative. It wasn't a good likeness, but it was close enough. The suspect had briefly hacked the systems of several newly-deployed automated shelf-stacking robots in an upmarket grocery store, turning them into thieves – two for the shelf, one for the 'bot. There was no information on what happened to the stolen items, though there was an attached note that implied the items had been distributed to several local foodbanks by anonymous donors.

Oliver Soames – Olly to his mates – had been questioned during the course of the investigation, but nothing had come of it. That was the extent of his history: one brief mention in a police file, now closed and forgotten.

Hannah could practically smell the industrial strength bleach. Someone had scrubbed Olly from the system. It was that lack of information that had decided her in the end. If Olly Soames wasn't DedSec, he was doing a good impression.

Suddenly nervous, she adjusted her hijab. Maybe he wasn't DedSec. Maybe he was Albion. An illicit tracker program alerted her to the presence of numerous security drones overhead. More than one might normally see for a Sunday morning. Maybe they were cracking down on unlicensed stalls at the market – or maybe they were following her.

She wove along the pavement, instinctively avoiding the drone-sweeps as best she could. Her record was spotless but there was no sense taking any more chances. Especially if someone found out what she'd done. It had been a calculated risk, but what else could she have done? Albion was dangerous.

Not everyone agreed, her boss for one. She saw Albion as "an opportunity". As such, she'd ordered Hannah to construct a complete dossier on the company – everything from hiring practices to financials. Whatever she could find, however seemingly insignificant. Unfortunately, there wasn't much available. But what was there, was terrifying.

One of the world's leading private military contractors, Albion was looking to expand into privatized law enforcement. They wanted the UK to be their test market for long-term urban deployment and pacification, starting with London. A foothold in the city was as good as a boot on the throat of the rest of the country.

If they succeeded in getting the contract, they'd have no accountability and little-to-no oversight. A paramilitary force, occupying what was left of the United Kingdom. The thought wasn't a pleasant one.

Luckily for Hannah, DedSec agreed. Or at least she hoped they did. It was hard to tell from the outside what DedSec actually wanted at any given time. At first, she'd thought they were just one more hacker collective, out to cause trouble. These days, she knew better.

DedSec had a plan. But what that plan was, she wasn't sure, save that it was aimed at making life a bit better for everyone. And that including stopping Albion from setting up shop in London. Or so Krish had assured her.

She smiled at the thought. When she'd known him, he'd been just another kid, looking to play rap artist. Now he was – what? A hacktivist? Part of the Resistance, power to the people and all that.

And today so was she.

Her proximity alerts flashed, and she looked up. News-drones were circling like carrion birds. Whitechapel had become a focal point of interest lately. Albion had been given limited remit to ply their trade in Tower Hamlets while the government debated the merits of extending and expanding their current contract.

That, in turn, had the locals more agitated than ever. Especially when word got out that Albion was looking to buy up properties and convert them into operations centres for their London spearhead.

Whitechapel's council estates had been on the cusp of demolition for years – including Lister House, the one her boss was visiting today, and the one earmarked to be the first Albion barracks. Lister House had escaped the council's plans for gentrification more than once over the years, and you could practically set your watch by the protests. Hannah didn't blame them. There wasn't anywhere for them to go if the estate got bulldozed.

Unfortunately for them, despite her public image, Sarah Lincoln couldn't have cared less. In fact, Hannah suspected that she was all in favour of her current constituency being replaced with a lighter coloured, well-heeled variety. Sarah would have denied it, but after several years together, Hannah knew how Sarah's mind worked.

Sarah Lincoln had a plan, too. And she would happily step over anyone and everyone to make sure that plan went off without a hitch. Not that the MP for Tower Hamlets South hadn't done some good on her climb to the top. But it was all incidental – the equivalent of a queen dispensing sweetmeats to her pets. A generous queen, but a queen nonetheless.

Hannah hadn't noticed it at first. She'd been too busy. Being a PA for a Member of Parliament, even a junior member, meant she was on call all hours. And Sarah could be very charming, even friendly, when she wanted to be.

But there was steel under the silk. For all that she'd been born in the borough, she didn't seem to care what happened to the people that lived there, so long as it didn't make her look bad. And the people had started to notice.

That was why they'd come out today – why she'd had the chance to make the drop-off. A recall petition was doing the rounds and Sarah had been on it like a tiger on a tethered goat. She'd arranged for an ad hoc town hall meeting to quiet the grumblers. To reassure them that they weren't going to be forcibly ejected from their homes – at least not yet.

The real issue, from Hannah's point of view, was that Sarah hadn't yet made up her mind about whether she was supporting the Albion deal or not. If she did, the borough – and her constituency – would see major changes, and perhaps a great deal of economic growth. In return, they only had to sell their soul.

Her Optik buzzed as it automatically synched with that of her employer. She looked up. The council flats of Lister House and its neighbour, Treves House, were modernist buildings rising out of a sad patch of green space. One was a long row of terraces, the other a tall block with clean lines and proportions, but both were looking decidedly shabby these days. The local council wavered between benign neglect and outright hostility, and tenants and leaseholders had been facing imminent eviction for almost thirty years.

Trees and hedges set behind black iron fences marked the

boundaries of the estate, and cars lined the streets. People were already gathering in the common area between the blocks of flats, waiting to hear what their MP had to say for herself.

Sarah's black Brubeck town car was parked just off-site, and out of range. Hannah skirted the crowd, threaded through an unobtrusive security cordon and made her way to the vehicle. She climbed in to the back, where Lincoln sat in air conditioned comfort, flicking through feeds on her high-end rose-gold Optik.

"You're late," the MP said, not looking up from her device. "I thought I was going to have to do this without you."

"I'm sorry." Hannah paused. "That must have been traumatic for you."

Sarah snorted, but didn't look up. "Careful. I might take offence and fire you."

Hannah wasn't unduly worried. "You won't. Five personal assistants in as many years. People might draw the wrong conclusions."

"Fair point. What do you think of this TOAN business?"

"We haven't RSVP'd."

"Good. I can't think of anything more stultifying than attending a technology conference." Her eyes flicked up and she shifted subjects again. "What was so important you had to go all the way to Brick Lane?"

"Meeting a friend," Hannah said. She was used to Sarah's abrupt switches of tack. Her boss did it intentionally, so as to discomfit people. Knowing this, Hannah had rehearsed the story in front of a mirror. Before Sarah could ask, she added, "She works for Natha."

Lincoln's eyes flicked up. "And why, pray tell, were you

talking to someone who works for the... honourable representative... of Tower Hamlets North?" she purred.

Hannah hid a smile. She'd known mentioning the other MP's name would provoke the right reaction. Winston Natha was second generation, like Sarah, though his parents were from Calcutta rather than Dusmareb. Despite that, they had more in common than not, something Sarah didn't like to be reminded of. "Word is, Natha is throwing his weight behind the Albion deal," she said.

Sarah sat up, nearly colliding with the roof of the town car. She was a tall woman, taller than Hannah. Taller than most men, especially when wearing heels – which she did as often as possible. Lean and honed, wearing clothes that cost more than most of her constituency made in a year, she could have been a runway model in her youth. Her hair was tightly bound in a bun at the back of her head. She slid her Optik into her jacket pocket and looked down her nose at her assistant. "What did he say?"

"He thinks they're doing a – and I quote – 'sterling bloody job' in Tower Hamlets."

Sarah frowned. "You know that for sure?"

"Seventy per cent," Hannah said. She had to be careful. Sarah wasn't stupid – even if she wanted to believe the worst of Natha, she'd be looking for independent confirmation.

"Not good enough," Sarah said, with a slight smile. "Though I wouldn't put it past the little weasel. He'd privatise oxygen if he could get away with it." She paused, one hand on the door release. "Still, it might be something to keep in mind. If Natha's for it, that means all the wrong people will be gunning for him."

Hannah relaxed. "I thought you'd want to know."

Sarah laughed softly. "If politics doesn't work out, you might have a career in espionage." She opened the door and slid out of the town car. "Come on. I can hear our constituents growling. Let's get this *wacal* of a day started."

2: WHITECHAPEL

Olly was moving quick, keeping one eye on his display. According to his Optik it was twelve minutes to Limehouse. Experience told him it was more like twenty, depending on traffic on Vallance Road. He veered onto the pavement. Away from the cramped confines of Brick Lane, he could see the Parcel Fox courier-drones swooping like clumsy pigeons.

The drones were the reason he was barely holding onto his job at the moment. They accomplished the same tasks he could in half the time, and didn't need paying. Soon enough, everyone would be using the damn things and then were would he be? Right back where he had been, before he'd lucked into this job. Before DedSec.

He thought about Hannah. Was she DedSec too? Impossible to know. He could ask, but he could just imagine the answer. Best not to risk it. Hard not to be curious, though. He'd always been curious, taking things apart to see how they worked. Phones, computers, televisions. As a kid, he'd fancied being a repairman.

Times changed. And you had to change with them – or get buried.

London was learning that the hard way.

Olly braked hard, narrowly avoiding a barricade. Lots of barricades in Tower Hamlets these days, after the Redundancy Riots. Lots of protests, mostly about immigration. The city – the country – was like a pot left too long on a lit hob. It hadn't boiled over yet, but it wouldn't be long.

He wasn't looking forward to it. He'd been in nappies when things started unravelling, and it hadn't gotten any better since. When it came time to divvy up the haves and the have-nots, he was definitely the latter. But when things got bad, it was always the have-nots who got the wrong end of the stick. Money was tight – and getting tighter.

Crappy as his job was, he was lucky to have it. Most of his peers couldn't say the same. The ones who weren't dealing for Clan Kelley or one of the smaller syndicates were working part time at the local chippie or on the dole.

He hopped the bike over a cracked kerb, scattering pedestrians. A courier-drone shot past him, waggling its fans in an almost taunting manner. He longed to catch up with it and knock it out of the air, but that would only attract the wrong type of attention, no matter how good it might feel. Then, it was that sort of thing that had gotten DedSec to notice him in the first place. Thankfully, they'd gotten to him before the police.

Sometimes, he wondered if there'd even been police on him – or if that was just what he'd been told. DedSec needed recruits, and they weren't shy about playing dirty to get them. Maybe that was just the way of it. If you weren't on one side, you were on the other. Whether you knew it or not. All in all, he preferred to be on his bike.

He took a turn, weaving along a cut-across. He was fairly certain he wasn't being followed, but you could never be too careful. He'd been around long enough to know that sometimes the Filth let a suspect run to the end of their tether, hoping the little fish would lead them to the big ones. But none of his security programs were pinging. As far as the drones overhead were concerned, he was nothing special. Even so, that didn't mean he wasn't being watched.

He hopped a kerb and pedalled through a car park, weaving around the vehicles. He tapped the Optik and activated a mirror program. It would clone the GPS signals of the cars he passed, and substitute them for his own. It wouldn't fool a dedicated trace for long, but it would make it harder for the casual observer to follow his trail.

Given what he was carrying, a bit of pre-emptive evasive action seemed only sensible. And Olly was nothing if not sensible, these days. He liked to think that he'd come a long way from the kid who'd cracked shelf-stacking bots, or made cash machines spit notes.

Only time would tell whether any of it mattered at all. When DedSec had offered him a way out, he'd taken it. A chance to purge his record, stay out of nick and maybe, just maybe, do something important for once. Even if he wasn't sure what that was, just yet.

Oliver Soames. What is my favourite trainee up to today?

Olly blinked, startled. The voice in his ear was light, the accent smooth RP – like polished chrome. A newscaster or a telemarketer. Friendly, open and sociable.

"Heading home, Bagley," he murmured. "Unless something's up…?"

By home, I assume you mean Limehouse?

"Where else would I mean?"

Fair point. Do you have it?

"If I didn't, I sure as fuck wouldn't be coming home, now would I?"

Language, Oliver. I'm very sensitive. Besides, you never know who might be listening.

"Hopefully nobody," Olly said, sharply. "This is a secure channel, right?"

Safe as houses. The channel has been piggybacked, cloned and reversed.

"None of that means anything."

A silly question deserved a silly answer.

Olly bit back a retort. There was no use arguing with Bagley. You might as well argue with a toaster. His personality was a mirror – you saw what you expected. A pre-packaged rudimentary AI personal assistant, available to anyone who owned a Blume Optik.

I can hear you grinding your teeth, Oliver. Remember, life's better with Bagley.

Olly grunted. The consumer model version of Bagley was only as smart as his parameters allowed him to be. DedSec had discovered a number of constraints on his programming, no doubt put in place by Blume. Removing those constraints had a few unfortunate side-effects. Standard Bagley was pleasant. DedSec Bagley was an annoying sod. If that was the original intent of the program's creator, Olly considered him due a punch or three in the gob.

I recommend you take a short cut through Lister House.

"What?"

It'll cut your time by five minutes. It might interest you to know that both it and Treves House were designed in 1956 by the architect, Count Ralph Smorczewski-

"Fine," Olly interjected quickly. If anything went wrong, he could always just blame Bagley. He swept through the narrow footpaths of the council estate, moving quickly. His alerts were chiming, feeding him data on the crowd that was gathering in the common area.

Someone had set up a low stage and a microphone. Chairs had been set out, but not enough. He thought he spied Hannah Shah, next to a tall woman in professional attire, on the stage, along with representatives of the local council. Shah didn't look happy. Then, given the mood of the crowd, she probably wished she was anywhere else. He skirted the edges of the crowd, trawling for faces and names, to be stored for later perusal.

Information was better than money, especially given the current exchange rate. Like the thing in his pocket. An envelope – she'd put it in an envelope. Who did that? You could buy signal blockers in any phone shop on the high street.

"Amateurs," he muttered.

You're one to talk. You still have training wheels on.

"You don't even know what I'm talking about!"

I can crunch cryptocurrency algorithms and write a focus-grouped bestselling novel simultaneously. Extrapolating what you're muttering about is child's play. I – hang on.

"What is it?"

There's something –

Olly didn't hear the rest. He was too busy going face-first over the handlebars into the gravel. The idiot who'd collided with him slammed into a parked car and bounced onto the street. The man was older, lean and hollow-looking, like a strong wind would send him sailing out over the Thames.

"Watch where the fuck you're going," the man growled, clambering to his feet. Spitting gravel, Olly rolled to his feet, ready to fight.

"You're the one who ran into me, mate."

"Fuck you, I–"

The sound was like a hammer striking an apple. There was a whisper of air, and a wet crunch. The man jerked and spun as if he'd been struck. Something hot and red caught Olly on the cheek as the man tumbled down onto the pavement with boneless finality.

The world slowed and finally stuttered to a halt as Olly stared down, in shock. His first instinct was to try and staunch the wound in the man's chest. He'd seen it on television and in films a thousand times. You reached out and pressed your hands to the wound and it stopped pumping. Only it didn't. The blood just kept coming, and it was on his hands and his trousers and in his nose and – oh God, it was everywhere.

"Bagley – call an ambulance, or divert one or something – this guy, I think he's been shot, Jesus, oh Jesus, somebody shot him…"

Even as he babbled, a part of his mind was analysing what he'd seen. The shot had come from out of nowhere – a sniper? Was there some lunatic on a roof somewhere? That sort of thing didn't happen in London – in the UK. It wasn't America. The local crazies used Stanley knives and screwdrivers, not rifles.

The scene replayed in his head over and over again. The

man climbing to his feet, cursing him out, then jerking around, falling. The blood…

Oliver.

Bagley's voice was cool in his ear. He ignored the AI. Why was there so much blood? He looked at his hands. Completely red. His thoughts stuttered to a halt. It was so red. Why was it so red? Wasn't there some reason – arterial blood, maybe… his mind began to wander through fields of trivia until Bagley brought him back.

Oliver. You need to leave. Lincoln's security detail is closing in on you.

Olly shook his head. "I can't, I can't, he's–"

Dead. Flatlined. Function terminated. I can't help him, but I can help you. Get up.

Olly looked down. The man looked like a wax dummy, all slack and shrunken. As if everything that had been him had been yanked out, leaving only an empty husk behind. He sat back on his heels, trying to think. People were screaming. Running. Human instinct was to get as far away from trouble as possible – at least initially. But not all of them. Plainclothes security people, probably plods in civvies, were hurrying towards him, fighting through the crowd. They did not look friendly.

His Optik hummed, alerting him to nearby recording devices. News-drones, Optik-cameras, all of them zeroing in on him. Worse, the sound of sirens, drawing nearer, pierced the fog of panic.

"Fuck. Fuck, fuck, *fuck.*"

I couldn't have put it better myself. Get thee hence, young Oliver.

"Going," he said, hoarsely. He stumbled to his feet, blood-stained finger tapping at his Optik even as he wrenched his bike upright. His mind was moving faster than his body, isolating the problems and solving them one by one. An old girlfriend training to be a psych nurse had called it reflexive compartmentalization, whatever that meant.

First, the news-drones. All the agencies used the same network these days – everyone used the same network these days – hack one drone, hack 'em all. So he did, initiating a feed wipe of five minutes. The Optiks were next. They were easier. DedSec had perfected the art of making Optiks see what they wanted them to see. The facial recognition software wouldn't get a match, or, rather too many matches. He was the next best thing to invisible – one more pasty yob in a ratty hoodie and tracksuit bottoms.

Officers en route from Bethnal Green. Eight seconds.

The police would be a different matter. They wouldn't be so easy to fool. He had to move. Get to Limehouse. Hide out until he could do a full scrub of the local feeds. A different sort of panic settled on him now – not blind, but urgent.

You have six seconds until the police arrive. Make them count.

Limehouse. He was on his bike a moment later, and gone three seconds after that. By the time the first police car arrived, Olly was on the other side of the estate, heading east as fast as he could pedal.

"What was that?" he hissed, as he took a sharp corner. "What happened back there?"

Unknown. I've piggybacked onto the scrambled feeds – quick work, by the way – and I'm analysing the data as we speak. There was something odd about the shot.

"What does that mean?"

Nothing yet. Keep moving. Let me worry about it.

"Gladly."

Oh – you still have the package, don't you?

A tremor ran through him, and he desperately swatted at his jacket. He found the shape of the envelope and what it contained. He sighed in relief. "Still got it," he said. At least he hadn't screwed that up.

Good man. Pick up the pace, Oliver. Things are popping.

Sarah Lincoln was three minutes into a tight five minute speech on the need for unity and the proud, if somewhat chequered, history of the Vallance Road community when she heard the screams. Unruffled, she managed another thirty seconds before all hell broke loose and her carefully orchestrated public gathering devolved into chaos.

The sound didn't register at first. She thought it was a car backfiring. Only when she saw a man at the edge of the crowd twist and spin and fall did she realize what had happened. Or at least what she thought had happened. Someone bent over him – had they shot him? Impossible to tell from where she was, buried under several members of her security detail. "Off – get off of me," she snarled, trying to get to her feet.

"Stay down mum," one of them snarled back, pushing her down. Or trying to.

"If they'd wanted to bloody hit me, they would've. Now get off!" She forced her way upright, over their protests and looked around. It was chaos – people scattering, her people trying to force their way towards the action.

"I think we – we need to get out of here," Hannah said, grabbing at her arm. Her eyes were wide, her voice brittle with fear. "Someone's shooting!"

Sarah shook her off. "But not at me. Call an ambulance." She snatched the microphone and raised her hand. "Everyone, calm down – calm down!" No one was listening, but she wasn't doing it for their benefit. And the news-drones circling overhead were capturing it all.

She heard the first sirens moments later. She kept her eyes on the body, on the man kneeling over him – going through his pockets? No. Trying to help. A concerned citizen. Her people were closing in on him, whoever he was.

It had been going so well, too. That was the annoying part. The speech was one of her best, she thought – simultaneously comforting, informative but lacking in any real substance. An anodyne quote was a safe quote, perfect for contextless soundbites.

Early in her career, she'd made the mistake of playing the firebrand. She'd been too young, too inexperienced, to think about the optics of a tall, second-generation Somali woman berating her peers. When she realized how it was being spun, she'd been forced to re-evaluate her idealism – to hone it into something more politically expedient. It hadn't been difficult. She'd always been pragmatic.

Idealists got into power. Politicians *stayed* in power. And Sarah Lincoln had decided there and then that she'd rather be a politician. And as a politician, she knew an image was worth a thousand words. And the image of an MP, trying desperately to calm a panicked crowd – well… two thousand words at least.

Her people reached the body even as the first police car squealed to a stop, blue lights flashing. More arrived moments later. The concerned citizen was long gone. She wondered where, then dismissed the thought. Fewer people to share the spotlight with was a good thing. At least, that was what she told herself as one of her security detail knelt beside the body. Sarah started over, despite Hannah's protests.

The security man had stripped off his jacket, folded it up and slid it beneath the victim's head. Her father's stories about the civil war came rushing back, even as she tried to recall the lessons of a long ago first aid course.

It was clear to her that the poor bastard was already dead. The hole was too big, there was too much blood. She felt a moment's nausea, before pushing it down and walling it off. Had he lived here? She thought she'd seen him in the crowd. He didn't look like the sort of man who got shot on the street. She couldn't help but wonder why he was dead.

Several uniformed officers had gathered. One was speaking hurriedly into his radio, while another – a woman, part of the uniformed detail provided for her speech – joined her. "You okay, Ms Lincoln?" the officer asked, gently.

"Quite well, thank you. It's just – I've never seen someone die before." She took a deep breath. "I guess it wasn't a heart attack, was it? I thought it was, at first, but…"

"The crime scene unit is on the way–"

"Officer, there's a bloody great hole in his chest."

The officer looked away. Sarah studied the body. A part of her wanted nothing more than to get away as quickly as possible, now that she'd done her bit for the cameras. But another part was curious. This wasn't the sort of thing that happened here. Tower Hamlets – the East End – was no stranger to violence. But it was always a very specific sort of violence. This seemed appallingly random.

The police went about their business efficiently. A cordon was set up, witnesses questioned. Sarah watched and made sure she was seen to watch. Hannah brought her a cup of coffee and tried again to get her to leave.

"What if it was meant for you?" Hannah said. "You wouldn't be the first MP to be attacked by some lunatic…"

Sarah took a sip of the coffee. It was terrible. Milk and sugar couldn't hide the taste of burnt beans. She grimaced, but kept drinking. "If it had been meant for me, they would have hit me. Or you. We were on stage, after all."

"Even so…"

"Even so, we're perfectly safe now." Sarah looked at her assistant. After a moment's hesitation, she asked, "Are you alright?"

Hannah looked at her, startled. "I think so. Just a bit shaken."

Sarah patted her on the arm. "Good girl. Stiff upper lip, as the old white men are fond of saying. Now, come on. I want to know what's going on." She strode towards the largest knot of police officers, Hannah trailing diffidently in her wake.

They nodded respectfully, but were less than forthcoming. A Labour politician couldn't be seen to be too chummy with the Met, else the usual suspects in her own party would start whispering. Law and order was for the Tories.

She turned to Hannah. "Go out and get coffees for everyone. Or tea, or whatever they'd prefer. And be quick."

To her credit, Hannah didn't argue. She simply started making the rounds, taking everyone's order. Sarah looked back at the body, under its white sheet, surrounded by anonymous technicians in their clean suits. One of them was using a laser pointer to calculate trajectory. Others were looking for the bullet that had killed… she paused. "What was his name?" she asked, out loud.

The officer who'd talked to her before turned. "We don't have a confirmed ID yet, but we think he was a local." She spoke in low tones.

"He lived here?"

"Possibly."

Sarah looked at her. "What's your name?" She could have simply asked her Optik, but there was something to be said for the human touch.

"Jenks, ma'am. PC Jenks."

"Thank you. For earlier, I mean, PC Jenks. Checking on me."

Jenks was about to reply, when the sound of a heavy engine rumbled through the air. They turned, and the policewoman frowned. "What are they doing here?" she muttered. Sarah saw a blocky vehicle with the yellow Albion logo stencilled on its reinforced hull pull into a nearby car park.

It was an ugly thing, meant for driving through demilitarized zones and urban battlefields. The doors opened and two men climbed out. A moment later, the rear hatch disgorged half-a-dozen Albion security personnel in their black fatigues and combat gear. One of them was disappointingly familiar. "Faulkner," Sarah said.

Hannah tugged on her arm. "We should go."

"No," Sarah said, watching as several officers moved to intercept the newcomers. "I don't think so. This is my patch, and I'll not be hurried off by a bunch of jackbooted thugs looking to play copper." She caught sight of Jenks trading glances with another officer at her words. The looks were approving, she thought. The Met weren't yet on board with the government's plan to turn over their brief to Albion. Neither was she, come to that. Not unless someone made it worth her while.

Ordinarily, she wouldn't care. But Albion liked to throw around its weight in Tower Hamlets. And that irked her considerably.

She moved towards the burgeoning confrontation, hoping to reach it before it boiled over. The relationship between the officers on the street and Albion's personnel was hostile at best. She had dozens of reports of altercations between the two, mostly verbal but some physical. Faulkner, Albion's man in East London, frequently tested the limits of his authority. He'd been reprimanded twice, but it didn't seem to concern him or his employers all that much. Then, maybe he was doing exactly what he'd been ordered to do.

Faulkner was a soldier – ex-soldier, rather. Her dossier on him was incomplete, mostly redacted. Albion liked to protect the privacy of its employees. Even the little fish like Faulkner. He was short and barrel-chested, with close-cropped salt and pepper hair, and a face that had been on the wrong end of a few too many punches. But his eyes were sharp and he had the air of a man who was constantly taking stock of his surroundings.

"Albion can go where it wants, mate," he was saying, as she arrived. He almost, but not quite, poked one of the officers in the chest with a blunt finger. "Tower Hamlets is our patch. You don't like it, take it up with your bosses."

"Whose patch?" she asked, brightly.

Faulkner turned – and frowned. "So nice to see you again, Mr Faulkner," Sarah said, before he could speak. He had an issue with minorities, she knew. He wasn't a full blown bigot, but rather more presentably condescending. Bigots were less annoying.

"Sergeant Faulkner," he corrected.

"Mr. Faulkner," she continued, as if he hadn't spoken. "This is a matter for the police, surely." She put herself between him and the officers. It would no doubt make for a powerful image and the news-drones were circling overhead, cameras whirring.

"As I was informing these officers, Albion has jurisdiction–"

"For now," she interjected. "You have jurisdiction for now. And what jurisdiction you have is singularly limited in scope. Active crime scenes are not part of it, I believe."

"Maybe we were just being concerned citizens."

"And I'm sure the police will be happy to take your statements, as part of their ongoing investigations. Until that time, perhaps you might – oh, let's say, bugger off?"

Faulkner blinked. He wasn't used to being talked to in that way. Sarah allowed herself a thin smile. Most men hated that smile and Faulkner was no different. He didn't reply. Instead he turned stiffly on his heel and marched back to his men. They retreated to their vehicle, and Sarah watched in satisfaction as the police moved to ensure that they stayed there. She glanced at Jenks, who'd joined them. "Carry on then, PC Jenks."

Hannah fell into step beside her as she made her way back to her town car. If Albion were here, it was time to go. If the police wanted to ask questions, they could come find her at her office. "Are you certain that was wise?" Hannah asked, softly.

"No. But I find him repulsive and it pleases me to antagonize him." She glanced at Hannah. "I want to know why he's here. Albion aren't an investigative body."

"Maybe they were just trying it on. You know they've been trying to muscle in on the Met's brief for months now. To show they can do a better job" Hannah seemed nervous. Then, maybe that wasn't a surprise, given the way men like Faulkner looked at her.

She looked back. Faulkner was watching them go. She was tempted to blow him a kiss, but decided against it. There was a fine line between justification and provocation.

"Maybe," she said. "But I still want to know."

3: TOWER HAMLETS SOUTH

Olly had achieved something close to calm by the time he reached Limehouse, and the garage. He'd stopped to strip off his bloodstained hoodie and stuffed it into a handy bin, leaving him in shirt sleeves, but noticeably cleaner. He'd gotten it from a Salvation Army donation box in the first place, so it wasn't a big loss. DNA evidence worried him some, but there were ways around that, if he was smart.

He twigged his newsfeed to scan for any updates on the shooting – and it had been a shooting, he was sure of it. Even if he hadn't seen where the shot had come from. Conflicting reports danced across his display. The video-feed of the shooting replayed itself over and over again, impossible to ignore.

He thought of the look on the dead man's face. That sudden cessation – like a light going out, only not quite. A brief moment of horrible realization, followed by a slackness as everything in the human machine stuttered to a halt. He'd never seen anyone die before. And he was certain he didn't want to see it again.

The garage was shuttered and dark. Cast iron window frames, now boarded over, glared blindly at the street. Loading doors on the opposite side opened onto the Limehouse Cut, though he couldn't remember anyone ever opening them.

The building hadn't always been a garage. Olly's feed filled with local colour as he approached it. It had started as a sailmaker and chandler's stores – whatever those were – before transitioning into various sorts of warehouse, and finally, a garage.

It had been vacant since before Olly had been in short pants, though it still had a faded sign declaring itself a MOT centre. Oil stains marked the broken, weed-choked parking area in front of the bay doors and the iron fencing was plastered with signs offering a cheap sale, if one contacted the estate agent.

Olly knew for a fact that the agent had also gone out of business. Nor were they the only ones. The housing market had tanked a few years ago and never quite recovered. Even so, every few months, some firm or other would come sniffing around, looking to knock everything down and build luxury flats, the way they had with the neighbouring derelict shops and units. They always went away disappointed. DedSec made certain of it.

He slipped through a gap in the chained gate, and squeezed his bike through. Bits of unidentifiable rusted machinery littered the lot, like the detritus of a losing battle. Some of it was rigged with motion sensors keyed to send a silent alert to the Optiks of every DedSec member in the area. Closed-loop recording devices would be tracking his every step. Not that they would see much, in his case.

There were drones whizzing by overhead, but the garage

had a concealed baffle-unit attached to the spine of the roof. The device inserted regular three second interruptions into the feed of any recording device in range, making the garage – and anyone coming in and out – as good as invisible.

Of course, if someone were watching from one of the cars across the street, it wouldn't matter. But Olly wasn't getting any pings from unknown Optiks, so he was reasonably confident in not being spotted. That didn't mean he wanted to linger outside any longer than necessary.

The shutters were always locked, unless someone needed to hide a car in a hurry. He wheeled his bike around to the side entrance, waving to the concealed security cameras, and pressed his Optik to the front of the lock. A hidden sensor trilled, and the lock released with a click. Olly pushed the door closed behind him once he'd gotten his bike inside. The lock, and the alarm system attached to it, rearmed themselves. If you didn't have the right app installed on your Optik, the alarm went off and a reinforced security shutter slid into place behind the plain old wooden door.

If someone were determined to get in, it wouldn't really keep them out. But it would buy everyone inside a few extra minutes to escape. That was DedSec standard operating procedure in a nutshell – *observe, harass, delay* – run away to fight another day.

Olly had never been a big fan of running away. Even as a kid, he'd tried to slug it out with the bigger boys. It never worked out well, but that'd only made him try harder the next time. He'd gotten beaten up a lot, but he'd learned how to roll with it. And how to hit back without getting caught.

That was what the stunt with the shelf-stacking robots had

been – hitting back. Or at least that was what he told himself. It was an old British tradition, wasn't it? Stealing from the rich, and all. Proper Robin Hood, he was. Only instead of a bow and arrows, he'd used a cloned Optik and a cracker-app. He'd been proud of himself and wetting his pants all at the same time. Waiting for the police to knock on his door. But it hadn't been the police.

DedSec had come calling, and Olly had gone with them without too much hesitation. He liked to think he'd impressed them, but he knew they were pulling in anyone with the necessary skills. DedSec weren't the only hacktivist hive in London, but they were the best organized. That was the claim, at least. Sometimes, Olly thought it was anything but. You never knew who you'd be talking to one day to the next, and sometimes you got asked to do contradictory shit. There was no one to complain, even if he'd been brave enough to do so.

Screw-ups didn't get to complain, and Olly was a screw-up. He'd fucked up twice – once more, and he was out in the cold. Maybe banged up in Pentonville, if his handlers were feeling vindictive. The first time had been an honest mistake – he'd handed a package to the wrong person. The second time, he'd almost gotten himself and few others arrested.

Olly touched his jacket, and felt the envelope. No screw-up this time though. Despite the universe's best efforts. He took a deep breath, inhaling dust and the smell of mildew. The interior of the building was just as dodgy as the exterior. The roof was mostly glass, set into an iron frame that was being eaten up by rust and bird shit.

Walkways ran along the upper reaches of the interior, largely inaccessible from the ground floor. Heavy winches and loading hooks hung from a track along the underside of the roof. Rusted out generators and other bits of obsolete industrial equipment sat abandoned along the walls. Patches of green mould ran along the brickwork in the corners closest to the river and the loading doors. The broken floor was dotted by pools of rainwater or runoff, all of it smelling vaguely of the river.

Taking it all in, Olly wondered if this was what people meant when they said "urban decay". He stored his bike in a concealed rack behind a broken section of wall. There were two others already there, both better than his. Somebody was home, then.

He went into what had been an office. Forgotten filing cabinets, covered in black mould and rust stains, sat like lonely sentries in the corners, and a shabby desk, now mostly rotten, occupied the centre of the room. Over the desk was a broken light fixture, and inside it was a hidden fibre-optic sensor. Condensation proof, like every other bit of kit installed in the building. Had to be, otherwise it'd spark out every few days.

He called up another app on his Optik, and waved it over his head. A tiny flash of green told him they hadn't changed the locks. There was a muffled click, and he felt the floor shift under his feet. He knelt and reached down, feeling at the mouldy carpet squares that littered the floor. When he found the access panel, he pushed down on it with all of his weight, and scrambled back as the concealed hatch rose slowly on its pneumatic hinges.

The hatch was barely big enough for one person. A set of metal steps wound down into a dimly lit space below the garage. The property had a cellar of sorts, and it had still been there when DedSec had bought the property.

It wasn't a cellar anymore, though. Now it was a den for all kinds of troublemakers.

He took the stairs carefully, the LED lighting providing him just enough illumination to put one foot in front of the other. As he descended, the hatch sealed itself with a hiss of air. There was a reinforced door with a keypad lock at the bottom, and he quickly punched in the current code. It changed weekly, and sometimes daily, depending.

He closed the door behind him and looked around. The cellar wasn't much, but it was home. Olly had a flat, but he didn't stay there often. It was depressing. Here wasn't much better, but at least the hob worked and there was stuff happening.

The place had been reinforced and extended over the years, growing from a single space to a warren of brick tunnels and small rooms. There was even access to the river somewhere, though Olly had never seen it.

Camp beds and couches dotted what space wasn't taken up by a jury-rigged set up of computer screens and equipment. Power cabling ran across the floor like jungle vines and hung in electrical taped bunches from the walls and ceiling. It ran across the central space and down along short corridors into the half dozen smaller rooms that jutted in all directions like the spokes of a wheel. Most of these rooms were crash-pads, but one was the showers, and another, the armoury, with its whirring 3D printers and racks of pre-printed caseless ammunition.

Televisions locked on the 24-hour news channels flashed mute images from the corners, and music played softly in the background. The air smelled wet and electric and it made Olly's skin tingle.

Bagley's voice thrummed from his Optik. Home again, home again, jiggety-jog. Welcome back. Safe as houses now.

Olly looked around. There were a few others here, but no one he knew. They weren't a friendly lot, on the whole. Hackers and deadheads mostly, eyes glued to screens and fingers stuck to keyboards. They fought the good fight from the safety of their sofas.

A few were like Olly – pranksters and wannabe folk heroes who'd wandered into the wrong alley. Others had been looting cryptocurrency accounts or scamming benefit grants for years before the idea of the Resistance had even been a gleam in somebody's eye. And then there were the hard cases.

There were more and more of them around every day. Men with prison tats and scars on their knuckles. Women who carried shooters in their handbags. That one old bat who could walk you through an emergency tracheotomy with a ballpoint pen and some hand sanitizer. Not Olly's sort of people at all.

Most of the newsfeeds were keyed on the TOAN conference. But one showed a familiar scene – somebody's shaky cam recording of the shooting at Lister House. And there was Olly, scrambling to his feet, blood on his hands, running.

They don't have your face. Your prints and DNA are a different matter, of course.

"That don't make me feel better," Olly said. "Where's Krish? I need to hand this off and then find some place to lay low."

"Too bloody right," a familiar voice said. Olly turned. Krish strode towards him, a sour look on his face. It was a comfort, in its way. Krish always looked like that. He was tall and lanky, and dressed like he'd wandered away an unlicensed rave and wasn't happy about it. "Where the fuck where you, fam? I was expecting you ten minutes ago. I thought you'd been nicked. There's police everywhere. We're on lockdown."

"Where the fuck was I? You watched the news?" Olly snapped. He tossed the package to Krish and gestured to the televisions. Heads were turning now, as the others listened. A good blow-up was better than canned entertainment any day.

"Of course. Some fool got shot over at..." Krish trailed off as he looked Olly up and down. Stopped. Looked at him again. "Is that blood on your trainers?"

"It ain't mine," Olly said.

"What happened?" Krish demanded. "What have you done?"

"That's what I'd like to know." The voice was unfamiliar – a woman's voice, and behind him. Before he could turn around, it was followed by the distinctive sound – the click of a pistol being readied.

Sarah Lincoln tapped the flashing alert and brought up a news story. She'd keyed her Optik to bring all mentions of her name to her attention in a daily digest. She scanned the afternoon newsfeed with a mixture of satisfaction and annoyance. As she'd hoped, she'd gotten top billing despite only being a glorified bystander – but nothing at all was mentioned of her face-off with Albion. She sucked on her bottom lip and dismissed the alert. Slightly annoyed, she leaned back in her chair and looked out the window.

Whitechapel was part of her fiefdom these days, such as it

was. Tower Hamlets had been gerrymandered and reshuffled to within an inch of its life over the past decade, and the constituencies renamed for the second time in twenty years. The district had once belonged to what was now Tower Hamlets North, and its reapportioning was still something of a sore spot. She smiled. Not that it wasn't something of a poisoned chalice.

Whitechapel was within spitting distance of the heart of London, but it was nonetheless one of the most deprived areas of the city. Even the planned revitalization of the Whitechapel Terminus had been brought to a stumbling halt by ham-fisted austerity measures.

Deprived though it was, Whitechapel was also the administrative heart of Tower Hamlets. Everything went through the district, and Sarah had duly set herself up in offices overlooking the site of the former Royal London Hospital.

The site had been earmarked for a proposed town hall, but, as with the Terminus, construction had ground to a halt a few years ago when the economy had plunged off the proverbial cliff. Now it was now nothing more than an eyesore. The abandoned scaffolding and faded signage of the site reminded her that what seemed a sure thing one moment was counted as a mistake the next.

A lesson every politician had to learn, if they wanted to remain a politician. And Sarah Lincoln desperately, determinedly, wanted to remain a politician. Even if that meant bowing to pressure and signing off on the Albion deal.

Her gaze fell to the stack of newly printed papers on her desk. She preferred hard copy, when feasible. Easier to read, easier to get rid of. She leaned forward and started scanning the pages. She made notes in the margins as she worked, to remind herself of questions she needed to ask later.

Every transaction had some grit to it, no matter how smooth the deal seemed. The Albion deal had more grit than most. She'd met Nigel Cass, the current head of Albion and the son of its founder, a grand total of twice. She'd come away unimpressed both times. He always came across as a thug playing at being charming. A mercenary looking to buy himself a war.

She knew something about war, despite having never experienced it herself. Her parents had been part of a Christian minority in Somalia. They'd fled to escape persecution during the civil war, and come to London looking for a new start. What they'd found was a different sort of conflict – not as violent, perhaps, but no less dangerous.

Thankfully, they'd had some money, and her father had made more. He'd worked hard, and taught his daughter to do the same. Her mother had taught her different sorts of tricks. The right way to sit, to breathe, to look interested. Her father had given her a work ethic, and her mother had given her the skills she needed to make best use of it.

Sometimes, looking out the window, she thought of her parents' stories about the civil war. About how quickly everything fell apart. When things started to go wrong, you had to move fast to keep from being overwhelmed by the chaos. Resignation killed as surely as a bullet. She did not intend to resign herself to the current state of affairs.

She made a note to repeat her request for a tour of the temporary Albion facility in Limehouse Basin. She'd made the same request three times since her last meeting with

Cass, and had been studiously ignored every time. She tapped her papers with a biro, thinking. She activated her Optik. "Hannah?"

Hannah stuck her head in the door. Sarah sat back. "Anything yet on why our paramilitary friends were snooping about the scene of the shooting?"

"Not yet. Everyone is being very close-mouthed of late."

"Mmm. Probably worried about botching the deal." Sarah leaned even further back and studied the old water stains on the ceiling tiles. If Albion were getting nervous, so much the better. Cass was desperate to get the deal done. And desperate men were often amenable to compromise. "Send another request for a tour of their local facilities. Emphasize that the press will be excluded." She paused. "Has Winston called yet?"

"Twice in the past hour."

Sarah smiled. "Good. When he calls again, tell him to book us a table somewhere nice – but local. Neutral ground, preferably."

Hannah frowned. "You want to have lunch with him? In public?"

"I need to gauge his mood. I want to see if he'll back my request for the tour. I know he's been itching to get in there himself. If we pooled influence, we might actually get somewhere." Sarah balanced the biro on her index finger, before tossing it up and catching it. "And make an appointment to go to Bethnal Green station. I want to give my statement in person, and see how the investigation is going."

"May I ask why?"

Sarah set her pen down and turned back to the window. "Call it curiosity."

4: REDQUEEN

Liz Burton watched the man calling himself Alex Dempsey die for the third time in as many minutes. He turned, twisted and fell, a red crater opening in his chest. Twist and fall, twist and fall. Again and again. Every time he hit the ground, she replayed the scene, hoping, praying that it might turn out different. That this time, he might not fall.

The day had been going well. Things were tickety-boo on her end. Irons in the fire, and all that. The harvested data of half a dozen potential recruits slid across her display in a wash of mundanity. A disenfranchised anarcho-socialist with radical views and an attitude problem. A sad-eyed bouncer who read Voltaire and liked to punch fascists. A paranoid genius who could build an RFID implant out of spit and wire when he wasn't yelling about the Royals being reptoids. Even a former Spetsnaz officer in search of moral clarity.

DedSec would welcome them all. Sooner or later, everyone with a conscience or an axe to grind would be a member of the Resistance. That was how Liz saw it. A grab-bag army of the unheard and the unwashed. Enough, even, to bring down Hobbes' leviathan.

But she wasn't thinking about any of that now. Right now, she was thinking of killing someone. Which was why she was currently pressing the barrel of her Px4 to the back of the new boy's head. Not hard; just enough to let him know it was there. "Olly, right?" she said, her voice mild. "Turn around."

"Liz," Krish began. He sounded scared. Krish liked to play gangster, but violence – real violence – freaked him out. Most of the others in the room were the same. Of them all, only Liz had ever fired a real weapon. And she was angry enough to do so again.

Her gaze flicked to the younger man. "Do shut up, Krish. I want to have a chat with our new recruit. Turn around, Olly."

Olly turned slowly, hands raised. He was younger than she'd thought. Practically a kid. Lean and narrow, like he'd missed more than a few meals. Dressed for comfort, no obvious tattoos or scars. Just another chav, playing hard man.

Just looking at him made her feel old. She was pushing forty, and though she kept herself in shape, there were some days she could feel the weight of all that experience pressing down on her, like the hand of God. Today was one of those days.

She looked Olly up and down and snorted. "How old are you?" she asked derisively.

An unimpressive specimen, I admit. But that is no reason to shoot him, Elizabeth.

"When I want your opinion, Bagley, I'll ask for it." The AI annoyed her. The faux-friendliness of its personality grated on her for reasons she found hard to articulate. She was too old to trust something based on the cTOS network.

Touchy today, aren't we?

"Quiet," she said, harshly. "I just saw a friend of mine get gunned down on the street." Even as she said it, she wondered about it. Alex hadn't been a friend, not exactly. Something more, something less. It wasn't the sort of thing she'd ever thought to quantify – and now it was too late.

Alex hadn't been DedSec material, not really. A petty thief, who'd never had a political thought in his life. The sort of person who thought of protests as good for business – which they were, when your business was picking pockets and identity theft.

But he'd had good ears, and a good memory. He listened and passed on what he'd heard, when she asked. All it cost was the price of a drink, maybe a meal. There were worse people to have dinner with. Alex could be – had been – funny when he wanted to be.

No more jokes, though. Nothing left but a bit more anger to add to the pile. She twitched the Px4, making Olly's eyes widen. "You were there. I want to know why."

"I didn't do it!"

Liz smiled thinly. "If I thought you had, I'd have already shot you." She glanced at Kris. "Is this tit the one you sent on the Albion pick-up?"

Kris nodded. "He's good, Liz."

Liz turned her attentions back to Olly, calling up her Optik display. She scrolled through a crawl of information, most of it redacted in an efficient, if ham-fisted, fashion. She wondered if he'd done it himself. "Oliver Soames. Early twenties, favourite flavour of ice cream is rum and raisin. You once dressed in drag for a mate's stag do…"

Olly flushed. "We was all doing it," he protested. Muted laughter rose from the others. Liz silenced them with a gesture. She was the oldest one here, the de facto authority. The others were scared shitless of her, and she played on it for all she was worth. Hacktivists and code crackers were about as biddable as cats. The old ones were stubborn, the young ones self-righteous, and some of them were just plain psychopaths.

Liz considered herself a little of all three. That was why she was left to babysit Tower Hamlets, and keep things ticking along on an even keel. Sometimes that meant talking soft, sometimes it meant she had to flash a shooter.

A gun was a good way to get everyone's attention, and convince them you were serious, all in one go. But now that she had it, no reason to keep swinging about. She lowered the semi-automatic, and peered at Olly. "So what happened? And make it quick."

Olly swallowed and cut his eyes to Krish, who nodded. "I was – I'd just made the pick-up and I was cutting through Lister House…"

"Why?"

I told him to. It would have cut his travel time by –

She kept her eyes on Olly. "Fine. You cut through and…?"

"He – he ran out in front of me. Crashed right into me!"

"Crashed – he was running?"

"I – I don't know." Olly gesticulated. "I got up, we had words and then – boom. He was down." She could read the fear and horror in his eyes. It mirrored her own. Whatever part he might have played, she was sure he hadn't pulled the trigger.

"His name was Alex," she said, softly. She slid the Px4 back into its concealed holster at the small of her back, and looked at Krish. "That drive – the Albion info?"

Krish nodded. "Should be."

"Good. Scan it and start disseminating it to the usual suspects. Bagley, analyse the images of the incident." She looked around. "I want to know everything there is to know about the moment Alex died. I want the velocity of the shot, I want the make and model of the weapon. Everything."

I have already begun.

She looked at Olly. "I want you to tell me every move you made today. From the moment you took your morning shit, to just now. Come on."

"Where are we going?"

"Downstairs."

Olly blinked. "I thought we were downstairs."

Liz laughed. "This is just the fucking lobby, kiddo. Now come on."

Olly looked at Krish. The other man raised his hands in surrender. Liz outranked him. Olly knew she'd been a crackerjack hacker, back in the bad old days – they'd called her "Redqueen", though he didn't know why. Maybe she just liked the sound of it.

What he did know was that she'd never so much as spoken two words to him since Krish had brought him in. She was older than him, her thick, braided hair gone the colour of gunmetal, and her frame shaved and sculpted by age. She wore battered motorcycle trousers, combat boots and a t-shirt emblazoned with the logo of a band that hadn't been popular in a decade. Her arms were lean and muscled, with a pagan crawl of ink on the biceps. There were scars as well – not just on her arms, but on her face too – and her eyes were pale and sharp.

She scared the shit out of him. Not just because of the gun – though that was a large part of it – but because of her whole look and what it meant. She wasn't playing quiet. She was a fucking freedom fighter and didn't care who knew it.

He'd only started breathing again when she'd lowered her gun. Now he was expected to follow her down… where? "We're already under the building," he protested. "Any lower we'll be in the river."

Liz laughed. "Think so? Then where does that door lead?" She pointed to the far wall and Olly turned. He'd never noticed a door there. Perhaps because it was hidden behind a diagonal of cheap shelving, full of hard drives and cabling. Or maybe because it didn't actually look like a door, so much as a piece of riveted steel, set flush to the wall.

Liz led him past the shelving and he spied a thumbprint scanner installed in the wall. It was small, and easy to miss. Not concealed, but no obvious either. Liz slid her thumb into the slot. There was a hollow hum, and a brief flash of green. Then the sound of tumblers turning. The door swung inwards. A set of stone steps went down. Unlike the rest of the place, the walls were clean, smelling of anti-mould spray.

Liz saw the look on his face. "Limehouse's roots go deep. Smugglers used – still use – the Cut for transport. There are hidey-holes all along the canal. Most aren't much bigger than an allotment shed, but with some sweat and elbow grease, you can make anything liveable. Down we go."

Olly swallowed and followed her down. Fibre-optic cabling ran along the brickwork, descending in bunches. Motion sensors and other security devices littered the walls. They turned green as Liz passed them, and then flicked red again. "I'm getting the feeling I don't know nothing about nothing," he said.

"That's the first smart thing you've said."

"Why are you showing me all of this?"

"I'm not showing you anything you wouldn't have seen eventually." At the bottom of the steps was another door – heavier than the first. Reinforced steel hinges. Bullet-proof too, Olly wagered. Maybe bomb proof, even. DedSec weren't playing around. This one had a retinal scanner installed in the centre of the door. Liz leaned close and the door opened with a hiss of escaping air. "Welcome to the cellar, Olly. The real one."

Lights flickered on automatically as they entered. The room was small and not quite square. Like a folded ribbon of white-washed brick, insulated and sealed. There was a cheap, circular table at the centre of the room, and a few chairs scattered about. A battered couch, covered in duct tape, sagged against the wall. "This room doesn't exist on any plans, or schematic. Only three people can get in, and two of them aren't here."

"So it's a secret base in a secret base," Olly said, looking around. The walls were covered in more cables and machinery, some of which Olly didn't recognize. All of it looked important. He could practically feel the information flowing through it all.

"Think of it more like a post office," Liz said. "Upstairs is just the front counter. This is the sorting room."

"Sorting room. Right." Screens were mounted at regular intervals, showing feeds from what Olly realized were hijacked drones. He stopped and stared, somewhat taken aback. "You've got the whole city under surveillance."

"Not the city, no." Liz sat down at the table. "What do you know about us, Olly?"

He felt like a student put on the spot. "Uh – well..."

"I mean, what do you know about DedSec operations?" She studied him. "It's been three months since you were recruited. What have you learned?"

He stared at her blankly, uncertain as to what she was getting at. "I know enough, I guess. I mean, I know what I've been told. Resistance, innit?"

"And what have you been told?" Liz gestured. "Never mind. Here's a crash course, new boy. DedSec is decentralized. You know what that means?"

"I'm not an idiot."

"You didn't answer my question."

"It means nobody is in charge – or maybe everybody is. There's no leader. No guidelines. We're making it up as we go, and hoping we don't fuck up too badly."

"Concise and correct. Maybe there's hope for you yet." Liz turned. "But decentralized doesn't mean anarchic. Black bloc cells work together, often at a remove. Mostly when it comes to information."

Olly frowned. "Like whatever it was I picked up for Krish."

"Exactly." Liz paused. "Information is power. we collect it. We hoard it. But not everybody we get it from is a DedSec operative. Most of them aren't, in fact."

She pulled out her Optik and tapped it. One of the screens

glitched and showed an e-fit. Olly recognized the man who'd been shot. Alex, she'd called him.

"Alex Dempsey. He was a … friend. But more than that, he was a set of eyes and ears."

"But not one of us."

She frowned. "Neither are you, not yet."

Olly sat. "Then why'd you bring me down here?"

"Because I wanted to talk in private. About what happened."

He swallowed. "I didn't kill him."

"I know. But someone did. And I need to know why."

Olly stiffened, as a thought occurred to him. "What if they were trying to kill me, and not him?" He imagined the bullet tearing through him, knocking him down. He shuddered.

Liz nodded. "Another reason to get you down here. This is as close to a safe house as we've got at the moment." She leaned back. "Either way, we need to figure it out soonest. So tell me about your day, Olly. Run me through the whole thing. And for your own sake… leave nothing out."

5: SCENE OF THE CRIME

Danny Hayes shifted in the weight of his tactical vest, and watched the Old Bill work. Scene-of-Crime officers in blue noddy suits scuttled around a field of little yellow flags – evidence markers, probably. Lights were being set up, as the sun rode low in the sky. Danny suspected he was in for a long night. Not the end of the world, but he'd promised his mum he'd be home for dinner – a promise he'd broken twice last week alone.

Uniformed plods watched the proceedings from the sidelines, thumbs hooked into the straps of their lowest bidder stab-vests. One or two of them met his gaze, and looked away, as if he were invisible. He wasn't sure whether or not he preferred that to the glares.

Albion wasn't making any friends in East London, that was for sure. Danny wasn't sure how he felt about that either. He'd been born and raised in a Tower Hamlets council flat. As a kid, he'd wanted nothing more than to leave. And now here he was, patrolling the streets he'd grown up on. Except they weren't really patrolling, were they?

More standing around, looking menacing. Easy to do, in his tac gear, with his Vector .45 ACP submachine gun and his helmet. He might as well have been on sentry duty back in Fallujah. His Optik display flickered across the interior of his helmet. Targeting data danced over his eyes, reducing his surroundings to a series of threat assessments and obstacles.

In the sandbox, that had been something of a comfort. Here it was annoying – and a bit disturbing. The program didn't distinguish between jihadis looking to cut off his balls and the officers who he was theoretically working in support of. For now, at least.

Word was, Albion was positioning itself to replace the Met. Danny didn't even want to think about how such a thing might work. Tower Hamlets was giving them enough trouble. The thought of trying to do the same with the entire city – hell, the country – was mindboggling. He was just a soldier. He followed orders and kept his head down.

"How long are they just going to let him sit there?" Hattersley said. He stood beside Danny. The two of them were stationed outside the armoured patrol carrier. Faulkner was inside, on the comms, checking in. The rest of the squad had been sent to kick around the nearby streets and make themselves seen.

Danny glanced at the other man. Hattersley was shorter than him, and built like a rugby fullback. He'd rolled up his sleeves, exposing tattooed arms. Some of the ink was downright obscene, and Danny often found himself staring. "Until they finish, I guess."

"They must've taken a hundred pictures. How many pictures do you need?"

"As many as it takes," Danny said, smiling slightly. Hattersley was a champion grumbler. He complained about everything, from the weather to the consistency of fried egg sandwiches. He could keep it up for hours, even on a yomp.

"I think he's starting to smell."

"That's probably you."

Hattersley gave himself a discrete sniff. "So it is. Cheers."

"It's that shitty oatmeal soap you use. Makes you smell like a bowl of porridge."

"My bird gave it to me."

"Which one?"

"Sasha – no, wait, Dionna." Hattersley hesitated. "I think."

Danny bit back a laugh. That was the one thing Hattersley didn't complain about. "You should probably figure it out. Before you send a thank you note to the wrong one."

"I'll take it under consideration," Hattersley said. He was silent for a moment. Then, he said, "This is bone. Waste of our fucking time."

"Could be worse," Danny said, not looking at him. He'd caught the eye of one the plods – a woman. Young, his age. Fit, too. She worked out. He could tell from the way she bounced on the balls of her feet. Weightlifter? Maybe. That was interesting. Danny preferred a more all-round work out. Big muscles were fine, but endurance and speed were more important when you were ducking shrapnel.

"How?"

"They could be shooting at us." His admirer was talking to one of the other officers, but her eyes kept straying back his way. Dark hair. Dyed, he thought. Blonde, probably. Was she interested? Or maybe she was just wondering why they were still standing there. In her place, he would be.

Hattersley snorted. "At least we'd have something to do."

"We are doing something. We're showing the flag."

Hattersley looked at him. "Now you sound like a fucking Rupert."

"Faulkner said it, not me."

Hattersley grimaced. Faulkner was a lot of things, but not that. "Of course he bloody did. Got a saying for every occasion, does the Sarge."

"How else is he supposed to motivate us?"

"Money," Hattersley said. "We're not soldiers anymore. We're private contractors. I don't need speeches. I need paying."

"From your lips to God's ear," Danny murmured. He held out his fist, and they bumped knuckles. Money was why he'd stayed in uniform, when his stint was up. Albion was on a hiring spree – anybody with training was getting offered a contract. They needed boots on the ground. That implied something big was in the works.

"Tell you what, though… I wouldn't mind hearing a speech or three from the tasty honourable member from earlier. There's something about an older woman who knows what she wants, know what I mean? What's her name again?"

"Lincoln," Danny said. "Sarah Lincoln." He recalled that his mother had voted for her, though she claimed to regret it. "She's a looker, yeah." He paused. "Scary, though. There's a woman who doesn't take shit."

Hattersley nodded. "Just my type. What's the gen on her anyway? Faulkner looked like he'd swallowed a mouthful of glass when she got done with him."

Danny shrugged. "Just a local MP, innit?"

"So another civvy who knows bugger all, looking to screw us over. Wonderful."

"Dunno. She had some good points, I thought." Danny didn't consider himself political. One politician was much like another, as far as he was concerned. Sometimes he felt like he ought to pay more attention, but who had the time?

"Don't let Faulkner here you say that. He'll rip your bollocks off and hang 'em in his office." Hattersley made a vicious twisting motion. Danny winced.

"Yeah, yeah. She was right though. This shit here? It ain't working."

"What would you suggest then, Hayes?" Faulkner's voice cut in. Danny and Hattersley stiffened as Faulkner stepped down out of the back of the personnel carrier. "Should we put it to a vote maybe? See what the locals have to say?"

Danny turned. "No, Sarge. Sorry, Sarge."

"Sorry? For what? Sharing an opinion?" Faulkner ambled around them, an easy smile on his craggy face. The smile didn't reach his eyes, though. "That's what squaddies do. They gripe and moan, until the orders come down. And then they do their bloody job, like it or not."

"Yes, Sarge," Danny and Hattersley said, in unison. Faulkner held them with his gaze for a few moments, then turned towards the crime scene.

"When they're finished, I want you two to move in. Cordon off the scene so we can bring our own people in." Faulkner scratched his chin. "Not that it'll do much good, but orders are orders, and we have ours." He turned to Danny. "Walk with me, lad."

Danny glanced at Hattersley, and then followed Faulkner as he prowled closer to the scene. Without looking at him, Faulkner said, "This is your manor, isn't it?"

"Sarge?"

"You were born in East London, weren't you?"

"Yes, Sarge."

"Must be like old times, being back here. See many friends – family?"

"My mum – a few others."

"Your sister?"

Danny hesitated. "Don't talk to her much, Sarge."

Faulkner patted him on the shoulder. "That's all right lad, I don't much like my siblings either. Can't choose your blood. You can choose your loyalties, though."

"Yes Sarge?" Danny hadn't meant it to come out as a question, but it had nonetheless.

"You like working in the private sector, Danny?"

"I like it all right."

"Me too. Money's good. And it's bound to get better, once Nigel Cass gets things up and running. Something to keep in mind, perhaps." Faulkner looked towards the police cordon. "Think she likes you, eh?" he murmured. "Man looks his best in a bit of kit. Stand up straight, Danny my lad. Chin up, dick out."

Danny blinked. "Sarge?"

"Figure of speech," Faulkner said, clearly amused. He tapped Danny's visor. "Squad feed, remember? We see what you see. And you were observing her closely, I noticed." He turned. "Do me a favour, chat her up for me, would you?"

Danny looked at him. Faulkner's bonhomie evaporated.

"You heard me. Go talk to the bint and be as fucking charming as you can manage."

Danny hesitated, but only for a moment. Faulkner's patience wasn't infinite. When he said jump, you jumped or you spent the day square bashing, at best. Danny nodded and ambled towards the knot of constables. Once, he'd have done anything to avoid getting anywhere near the Filth. He was the wrong colour, wrong class, wrong everything for friendly interactions with the authorities.

Or he had been, at any rate. These days, he had a certain cachet. He was a hard man, a rock solid operator in his black tac gear and urban fatigues, with the weight of Albion backing him up. It was a good feeling, in a way.

Even so, it made him uncomfortable at times. Some of the others, like Hattersley, seemed to regard East London as foreign soil, full of enemies. They picked fights, instigated conflict – and Faulkner egged them on. Sometimes Danny wondered if he were following orders the rest of them weren't aware of.

He pushed all that aside as he drew close to the police. Heads turned, stares steady. He felt as if he were looking down gunsights. He cleared his throat. "Lovely day for it," he said, plastering on his best smile. His mother assured him it was his best feature.

The woman laughed. Danny flushed. "Yeah, fine," he said, making as if to turn away.

She waved a hand. "Wait, wait – steady on, mate. It's just... did you hear yourself?"

Danny paused. Then chuckled. "Yeah. Sounded like a right tit, didn't I?"

She nodded and stepped away from the others. "Can I help you with something?"

"Bit of chat," he said, hopefully. "It's boring, just standing there, watching you watch me." He turned. "This place hasn't changed."

She raised an eyebrow. "You local?"

"Was. Am again, I suppose."

"Where from?"

"Locksley Estate." He shifted the weight of the Vector on its sling. "You?"

"Hackney Road."

He grinned. "And look at us now. Both coppers."

She frowned. "*I'm* a copper. I don't what you are."

Danny paused. "A soldier, I suppose."

"You don't sound sure."

He gestured. "Whitechapel is lot of things. Not really a warzone, though."

"Tell your boss that."

Danny laughed. "I'm a grunt. Nobody listens to me." He peered at her. Then, hesitantly, he stuck out his hand. "Danny. Danny Hayes."

"Hello Danny-Danny Hayes. I'm Moira Jenks."

"Moira?"

She fixed him with a level look. "You have something against 'Moira'?"

"No, no. It's a pretty name…" He hesitated. Faulkner was sidling towards the crime scene techs – no, towards the evidence bags. What was he doing? He hurriedly looked back at Jenks, a sudden uneasy sensation churning in his gut.

"So why are you still here, Danny?"

"Orders, innit?" he said. "They say stand here, I stand here."

"Sounds dull."

"Seems to me you were doing much the same." He glanced back towards Hattersley, and the other operative gave him a thumbs-up. Jenks saw it and snorted.

"This has been interesting, but maybe you ought to – *hoi!*" Jenks turned, and Danny did as well. Faulkner was going through the evidence. He stepped back quickly, hands raised as Jenks stalked towards him. More plods swarmed in, drawn by her shout. The tension, on a low simmer, suddenly ratcheted up. Hattersley hurried over.

Danny, torn for a moment, hesitated. Then training took over and moved to Faulkner's side. He kept his weapon aimed at the ground, and signalled Hattersley to do the same. The last thing they needed was for this to become a standoff.

"Ease up," Faulkner was saying. "Honest mistake, that's all."

"There's such a thing as chain of evidence, mate," Jenks said. "That means you keep your mitts off it, right?"

"Why not just let me have a look, eh? Bit of professional co-operation?" Faulkner was smiling, but it wasn't friendly. "We'll get our hands on it eventually."

"'Eventually' is a problem for someone else," Jenks said. "Right now, you're mine. Back up." Her eyes flicked towards Danny. Hard now, not friendly at all. "You too, Danny-Danny Hayes. Back on your side of the line."

"This is a mistake, love," Faulkner said. "You plods are on the way out. Clever girl like you might want to make sure she's got friends. Albion is always looking for experienced people, and we're an equal opportunity employer…"

"Shut it," Jenks said. She had her back up now, and Danny realized that she wasn't the only one. The other plods were pressing in from all sides, bumping them back from the evidence. Hattersley was looking nervous. They were armed but, that didn't mean much at the moment. Danny waved Hattersley back.

Faulkner kept smiling, but it was strained now. "Fine. Like I said, misunderstanding. No need to get bent out of shape. We're going." He pointed at Jenks. "But I'll be speaking to your superiors about this." He turned. "Come on. Nothing more to be gained here."

Danny and Hattersley followed him. Faulkner glanced back at Danny. "Good job, lad. Though I doubt you'll get a second look in. Shame too… she seemed to like you."

Danny glanced back. Jenks was watching them, a hard look on her face. Uncomfortable, he turned away. "What were you looking for, Sarge?"

Faulkner chuckled harshly. "Never you mind, Danny Hayes. Keep your head down and follow orders, and all will be well." He looked back, and there was a warning in his eyes. "Big things come to those who keep their mouths shut, eh?"

Danny swallowed. "Yes Sarge," he said.

Wakey-wakey, young Oliver.

Bagley's voice was an insistent purr. Hard to ignore. Olly blinked and stirred. A dull pain radiated along his back and shoulders. Trying to nap on the couch had been a bad idea. He groaned softly and checked the time.

"You awake then?"

Olly peered over at Liz, still standing where he'd last seen her, watching the news feeds. He wondered whether she'd even moved. "Coffee," he moaned.

"Later. Bagley?"

My calculations are complete.

Liz sat and swung her legs up onto the table. "Good. Bring up the map."

Olly watched in fascination as pixels coalesced in the air over the centre of the table, shaping themselves into a digital map of East London and its environs. He whistled appreciatively. Liz smiled. "Military tech," she said. "Cracked it myself. And synched it to the GPS apps on every DedSec Optik." Her smile faded. "Can't trust off the peg GPS these days. Too many fingers in that particular pie. This way we get a more accurate picture of the city." She looked up. "Bagley? Tighten in on Lister House."

Shall I add the new data as well?

"Yes," Liz said, somewhat impatiently.

"New data?" Olly asked, somewhat muzzily.

Liz glanced at him. "Bagley took a peek at what the Filth have been up to. We've folded their data into ours for a more complete analysis." She gestured. "Look."

The image changed – it was sketchy, primitive, but Olly recognized it as Lister House. A formless blob – the crowd – appeared. A moving shape he took to be himself raced along its fringes, colliding with Alex. Even as impersonal as the images were, he couldn't help but feel his stomach tighten at the sight. He knew what was coming next. He cut his eyes towards Liz, and wondered if she were feeling the same. It was hard to tell.

I ran every possible scenario. Only one makes sense, given the evidence.

A red line reached down to intercept the Alex-figure. Down, not across. Olly huffed in surprise. "Bloody Nora. A sniper?"

Indeed. And not just a sniper. The shot was incredibly precise, and given the velocity and force of impact – it did not come from either of the nearby structures. Rather farther away, in fact.

The red line rose at a steep angle. Olly blinked. "That don't look possible."

"Shows what you know," Liz said. She was leaning forward, chin resting on her clenched fists as she studied the image. "What type of weapon?"

I will know as soon as the police do. Bagley paused. *I should inform you that I am not the only one attempting to discover that information.*

Liz looked up. "Someone else is trying to hack the Old Bill?"

Several someones, by the looks of things. It seems we are not alone in our suspicions.

"What was he involved in?" Olly blurted.

Liz sat back, her arms crossed. "And why did it get him killed?"

I may have an answer to that. I detected an unexpected data-pulse moments before the shot occurred...

Olly snapped his fingers. "I remember that. What was it?"

A GPS ping.

"His Optik," Olly said. He leaned forward, mind racing. "They determined his position through his GPS signal. Holy shit – that's fucking clever. Evil as fuck, but clever."

"That's impossible," Liz said.

Olly looked at her, bewildered. "Nah, dead easy innit? I could do it – not that I want to shoot anybody, but–"

"That's not what I meant," Liz said. "Alex didn't have an Optik."

Olly shook his head. "Everybody has an Optik."

"He didn't even have a phone." She tapped the side of her head. "He had a thing about invisible waves and cellular frequencies and that sort of shit."

"You mean he was crazy."

She glared at him. "No." She hesitated. "Well, maybe. A little bit. Either way, he didn't have an Optik." She stared at the digital map. "Unless… oh, Alex you absolute *twat*."

"What?" Olly asked.

Liz gave a rueful laugh. "He swiped it."

"He stole an Optik? What's the point of that? They give the damn things away free."

"I don't know why, but I know that's what he did. Alex is – was – a thief. Little stuff, mostly. A wallet here, a bit of identity fraud there. He must have stolen an Optik… and then… shit." She sat back, her face gone pale.

Olly caught up with her a second later. "Oh bugger. The shot wasn't meant for him."

"No. So who the fuck was it meant for?"

6: HAYES FAMILY DINNER

The sky was the colour of ripe plums when Danny finally got to the Locksley Estate. He was still thinking about Jenks and Faulkner and whatever it was Faulkner had been trying to pinch when he reached his mum's flat. But all that was washed away by the smell of the chicken cooking on the other side of the door.

For a moment he was fifteen again, and hurrying home from practice. He'd wanted to be a footballer then, like every other kid his age. He wasn't sure when that had changed. He paused and turned, momentarily at a loss.

The estate was much as he remembered it. He could still see the Pinnacle on St Mary Axe from where he stood outside his mother's door. The glassy corporate tower was lit up like a Christmas tree, with some looping bank logo glowing along its flanks. The estate, in contrast, was mostly dark, save for a few sputtering lights on the walkways or bleeding through cracked curtains.

He could hear the murmur of televisions and radios. Voices

on the levels below. Mum lived on the top floor. He craned his neck, curious. Idle youth in the courtyard. Probably dealing. He stopped himself even as the thought occurred to him and turned away.

Whatever they were doing, it was none of his business. He wasn't in uniform. No sense bringing trouble to mum's door. Ro did enough of that, if what he'd heard was correct. It was hard to tell with Ro. You never knew how much of it was just trash talk, and how much was truth.

That thought was foremost on his mind when he finally knocked. He'd never gotten along with his younger sister. They'd fought from the first, competing for attention. He loved her, he supposed, but he'd never much liked her. He expected that she felt the same. If she was here tonight…

The door opened. Ro glared at him and sucked her teeth. His sister was shorter than him, but muscular. She was still in her workout gear; he'd rarely seen her in anything but sweats and trainers. She'd shaved the sides of her head, and added purple highlights to what was left. "About time," she said. "You been standing out there for an hour."

"What happened to your hair?"

She frowned. "Stylish, yeah?"

"Do it yourself?"

"Maybe."

"Looks like it." He stretched out a questing finger. "I thought mohawks were supposed to stand up, like."

"Don't *touch*." Ro balled her fist, and Danny tensed. Ro had a mean left hook – infamous, even. She'd had aspirations of mixed martial arts stardom, but as with many of Ro's big ideas, it hadn't worked out. From the look of her, she hadn't let her training regimen slip, at least.

"Wouldn't dream of it." He paused. "Can I come in?"

"I'm thinking about it."

"Think quick, or I'm going through you."

Ro frowned and made a show of looking around. "Oh? Got some backup, then? Brought some of your Albion pals? I'll kick their arses too."

Danny shook his head. "Big talk, from such a tiny person."

Ro bared her teeth. "That just means I'm close enough to punch you in the nuts."

Danny took a step back. It wasn't an idle threat. "Don't think I won't thump you."

Ro made to retort, but was interrupted by the rattle of pots and pans inside. "Who that at the door, girl?" a woman's voice called out. Ro stepped aside with a sigh.

"Just Danny, Mum. Nobody important."

"Ta," Danny said, as he squeezed past her into the flat.

"Fuck off and die."

"Rosemary, language." Cece Hayes was short and round and never seemed to get any older, no matter the length of time between visits. Unlike her children, she spoke with a strong Trinidadian accent. She bustled into the hall, wiping her hands on her apron. "Oh my days, Daniel. The prodigal son, he comes home!"

"Hello Mum, give us a kiss?" Danny bent, and his mother clasped him in a bone-crushing hug. "How are you?"

"I'm gone tru, love," she said. "Been running around all day, awa?" She stepped back. "You look thin. You not eating?"

"Not as good as I used to."

"We'll change that soon enough. Inside, inside." She pulled

him along. "Rosemary, close the door, you letting gnats in."

"Yeah Rosemary, close the door," Danny said.

Ro flipped him the finger and slammed the door. Danny grinned. The kitchen was smaller than he'd remembered. It was barely there at all, most of the space occupied by the oven and the small, chipped Formica table that nestled flush to the wall. A window looked out over the courtyard on the opposite side of the building, and under it a battered radiator sagged beneath the weight of drying clothes – Ro's, by the look of them.

"You brought your laundry," he said, as his mother guided him to a seat.

"Mum offered," Ro said, claiming another chair for herself. There were only three around the small table. Just enough, no more, no less.

Cece turned from the stove, ladle in hand. She had a pot on the bob, simmering away. "If I hadn't, you'd be wearing them nasty clothes in here, making my kitchen smell like sweat. Like your flat, I might add."

"You moved out?" Danny asked, somewhat surprised.

"About time." Ro knocked on the wall above her head. "Need my own space."

"More room to hide contraband, huh?"

Ro's eyes narrowed. Before she could speak, Cece said, "None of that now. Your sister has a good job. She's not running with them no account wide boys no more."

"A job? Doing what?"

"Courier, innit?"

The way she said it caused him to prick up his ears. He leaned towards her and pitched his voice low. "For whom?"

He already knew the answer, but he wanted to hear it from her.

"For whom?" she mimicked. "None of your business."

"Wrong," Danny said. "I'm an officer of the law, remember?"

"You ain't nothing." Ro leaned forward belligerently.

Danny sat back in his seat. "Some things never change."

Ro reached for him and he slapped her grasping hands aside. She didn't relent, and his chair rocked back on its back legs. She was stronger than he remembered, but so was he. The problem was, Ro fought dirty. The table squeaked between them as they struggled.

"Allyuh be quiet!" Mum stormed in, ladle whipping left and right. "Danny, you let go your behen right now or I give you bois!" Danny recoiled. The ladle was still hot. Ro scrambled aside, jeering at him until their mother rounded on her. "An you," she said, in a low voice. "You wajang…"

"Mum," Ro protested. "He provoked me. He's always provoking me."

"You ain't seen him in three years girl." She snorted dismissively. "Talking about always. Behave, chile." She glanced at Danny, and he raised his hands in surrender. "Goes for bloody both of you, awa? Now sit down. It is time to eat."

"Gladly," Danny said, carefully taking his seat. Order restored, Cece ladled out plates of chicken pelau. Danny's mouth watered. Chicken browned in sugar, cooked with peppers, fresh herbs and coconut milk. He tucked in eagerly.

As he ate, he eyed his sister over his plate. She returned his glare with one of her own. She stuck her tongue out. He bit back the urge to respond in kind. Five minutes together, and they were kids again. It might have been comforting, if it wasn't so annoying.

They ate in silence, their mother doing enough talking for all three of them. Finally, she poked him. "What about that today, then?"

He looked up from his food. "What?"

"The shooting!" She slapped her hands on the table, causing it to wobble. "I saw you on the news getting yelled at by the police, didn't I?"

"They filmed that?" Danny paused. Of course they had. They filmed everything these days. "It was nothing, Mum. A jurisdictional misunderstanding is all."

Ro snorted, and Danny glared at her.

"Somebody trying to shoot that Lincoln woman, no doubt," Cece continued, ignoring their byplay. "Doesn't surprise me. She got no care, that woman. Vikey vike, like your father. Doesn't care about no one but herself."

"Mum, didn't you vote for her?" Ro said, innocently. Cece turned, squinting.

"A woman can't change her mind, then?"

"It wasn't her they were after," Danny said, picking at his food. His mother and sister turned, and he immediately regretted saying anything. Ro frowned and poked at him with her fork. He batted it away. "What?"

"Not her, then who?"

"Some rando. Local bloke."

"Who shot him?"

"Why do you care?"

Ro looked down at her plate. "Just curious."

Danny studied her. He'd always been good at reading Ro's face, or maybe she was just bad at hiding things. But it seemed like she'd learned how, over the last three years. Her expression told him nothing, and that worried him.

The conversation drifted away from the shooting and onto local topics. Gossip, mostly. Cece Hayes was a fine, upstanding Christian woman, but she had her flaws. She took an inordinate amount of pleasure in recounting the travails of her friends and neighbours, and always had. Danny wondered why companies like Blume bothered to craft data-gathering software, when they could just plant people in the kitchens and barber shops of East London. They'd have more information than they knew what to do with in a fortnight.

"Mum, have you ever heard the term *schadenfreude*?" he asked, finally, interrupting a story about the unwed mother one level down, and her dating habits. He stood and stretched.

"Don't you get smart with me, Daniel Benjamin Hayes," she said. She rose as well. "And where do you think you are going?"

"Home. Sleep. Early roll call." He grimaced slightly as he said it. Faulkner wanted to roll up to Bethnal Green police station in the morning, make a show of force and get a look at the evidence. Danny had been under the impression that they were supposed to be keeping a low profile – maybe new orders had come down. Either way, he wasn't looking forward to it – or the possibility of running into PC Moira Jenks.

Ro stood as well. "Me too. Deliveries all day tomorrow."

"Oh, look at you both. Hard workers. You make me proud." Cece kissed them both, and followed them out, still talking. When she'd finally closed the door, Danny turned to his sister. "I heard you been running with the Kelleys."

Ro turned and started walking away.

Danny hurried after her. "Am I right then?" he asked.

"What's it to you?"

"I'm your brother."

She stopped. Turned. "Three years you been gone. You call once in a while, maybe send an email to Mum. Not much of a brother."

"I offered to help you get a job… Albion's looking–"

She laughed. "How is that any different to the Kelleys?" She poked him in the chest. "From where I stand, they're pretty much the same thing. Just your lot is better armed."

Danny didn't reply. Ro shook her head and turned away. She waved dismissively as she left him staring after her.

"See you in another three years, bruv. Or better yet, make it five."

Ro Hayes made her way across the street, ignoring traffic. She was still angry. She was always angry, but this was different. Danny hadn't changed. Three years without a word, and he thought he could come back to their ends, pick up where he'd left off, easy as that. Her fists clenched in the pockets of her hoodie.

She wanted to knock his block off. Take him down a peg or six. It wouldn't do any good. He'd been trying to run her life since she was a kid. He thought a stint with the army made him the big man, but she knew he was just another tosser in a fancy uniform. Doubly so now that he was working for Albion.

She'd almost laughed when her mum had told her about his offer. Like she wanted to be manning a call centre or arranging files for a crap outfit like Albion. Because that was what he meant by job – something safe and boring.

She'd tried it, and didn't like it. She needed something different. She'd always been a fighter, and she liked that. She'd tried wrestling, but playing at fighting wasn't what she wanted. She wanted a real fight.

Mixed martial arts had seemed to promise that, but she'd made some bad decisions early on – trusted the wrong people – and her career had ended before it had even begun. She'd needed her brother then. But he hadn't been there. Too busy playing soldier.

Thankfully, she'd had friends. And those friends had introduced her to other friends and acquaintances and she'd done some favours for some quick cash and then…

She stopped, waiting for a light. Just a few favours. And then, before she knew it, she was a proper villain. Nothing big. Mostly she hit people who needed hitting. Sometimes she just threatened to hit them. Either way, she got paid for it and that was the important part.

She didn't think about being a criminal. She doubted Danny thought about being a soldier. It was what he was. And she was this. She pulled her hands out of her pockets and studied the faint scars that ran along her knuckles and fingers. She made fists and stuffed them back into her pockets.

The light changed, traffic slowed, and she crossed the road, heading for the pub on the other side of the roundabout. It was a small building, old fashioned, crouched securely in the shadows of more modern neighbours.

The pub – and its owners – were resisting gentrification with commendable fortitude. It had been a hole in the wall since before the Blitz, and would remain so even after it was surrounded by gourmet cake shops and boutique clothing retailers. The white exterior was smudged with decades of soot and grime, and the red trim was faded and peeling. The golden lettering on the red sign was tarnished, but still legible – *The Wolfe Tone.*

Light and music tumbled out of the open door and a pair of hard lads stood on the stoop, pints in hand, cigarettes dribbling ash into the street. Ro peered up at them. "Reggie. Saul."

"Ro," Saul said. Or maybe Reggie. It was hard to tell them apart. Reggie and Saul Godfrey were both heavyset builder-types, with blunt features and thick necks. Which was appropriate, given that they were builders, on occasion. When they weren't collecting dosh on behalf of the Kelley bookmakers. Ro did some collecting herself, when needed.

"Didn't think we'd see you tonight," Saul – or Reggie – continued. "Weren't you having dinner with your old mum?" His brother snickered, as if he'd said something dirty.

"Weren't a euphemism, Saul," Ro said.

"I'm Reggie."

"Allow it." Ro made to go inside, but Reggie flung out an arm. Ro looked at the arm, and then at him. "Got something to say, Saul?"

"Reggie. And I heard your bruvver got himself a cushy gig with them Albion tossers. That true? He working with the filth now?"

"And?" Ro tensed, looking back and forth between them. Ordinarily, she had no problem with the Godfreys. Not nowadays at least. Not after she'd nearly drowned Reggie in the gents that one time. "I'm not his keeper."

"That's not what we hear."

"What do you hear, Reggie?" Ro asked, leaning into his space. He twitched back, probably remembering her hand on the back of his head, pushing him down into the toilet. "And who told you, anyway?"

"Word gets around, Ro," Saul mumbled. She rounded on him, backing him up against the doorframe. Saul had been on the floor, puking up his guts, while she gave his brother a thorough flushing. "Looks bad, your brother…"

Ro frowned. "Albion are just another gang."

"Yeah, but way we hear it, not for long."

"Oh, well, that's different." Ro snorted. "But I'll take your concerns under advisement. Now, I want a pint. You going to move, or I do need to move you?"

The Godfreys shuffled aside, and Ro squeezed past and headed for the bar. The public bar and the saloon were both crowded, but that was nothing new. There wasn't much to do these days but drink.

The Wolfe Tone was owned lock, stock and barrel by the Kelleys. Nor was it the only one. They'd been buying up pubs, garages and the like for years. Diversifying, they called it. Owning a business made it easier to launder cash through it. It also made it easier to move product out the back. And if the plods started sniffing around, well – pubs burned down all the time. Shame, but the insurance money made up for it.

Of course, laundering money was getting harder and harder these days. Hardly anyone was using cash. The pound was in free fall. Cryptocurrency was filling the void. ETOs, mostly – E-tokens. ETO was anonymous and untraceable. It had become the new coin of the realm, at least when it came to the black market.

Ro bellied up to the bar and ordered a lager. As she waited, she surveyed the room, picking out familiar faces. She didn't need an Optik for that, though she had one. She knew everyone and everyone knew her. Some smiled, a few frowned. One or two ignored her entirely. She wasn't exactly high up in the hierarchy, which was a blessing at times.

Things were changing. Something was in the wind. Every wide boy, lag and hustler in East London was on alert. Not just the riots or the paramilitary wankers on the streets, but something closer to home. The Kelleys were on the prowl. They were gobbling up bits of turf left, right and centre and there wasn't much anyone could do about it. Even so, there'd be blood on the streets before it was done.

Ro felt a tingle of anticipation. She hadn't been called on to do anything too bad yet, but that day was fast coming. There'd come a moment some fool would decide not to stay down, or she'd be ordered to make an example of someone – and then what? She looked at her hands again, wondering if she'd have the minerals to do what needed doing.

"Pensive," a familiar voice said.

Ro turned. "What?"

The man standing beside her was shorter than her, but not by much. He was stocky, a lad's lad, with a shaved scalp and three lions tattooed on one forearm. He grinned, showing off a gold tooth. "New word-a-day app the missus got me. Bloody brilliant. Today's word is 'pensive'. Means thoughtful, innit?"

"Shut up Colin." Ro smiled as she said it, turning back to the bar. She'd known Colin longer than she liked to admit. He wasn't a friend, exactly, but he was friendly. Her pint arrived, head rolling down the sides of the glass. She took a sip. Colin didn't shut up. She didn't mind, as she hadn't expected him to. Colin liked the sound of his own voice.

"Looks like everyone's in here tonight. Something must be going down."

"Not that I heard," she said.

"Billy sent word round." He was talking about Billy Bricks. William Brickland to the Old Bill. Billy had been a boxer once, before he'd started taking money to lose fights rather than win them. Now he was a top dog for the Kelleys, seeing that things got done when they needed doing. Ro was scared shitless of him. Billy Bricks was a wrong 'un, and not afraid to mix it up with anyone – except possibly Mary Kelley. Then, even the feds stepped light around the matriarch of the Kelley Clan.

"Did he say why?" she asked.

"Does he ever?" Colin looked at her. "Haven't seen you around much these days, Ro." He signalled the barman and ordered a pint of Guinness. "Keeping busy?"

"Busy enough. You?"

"You know me, luv. Always something on." Colin was tapping on his Optik as he spoke, eyes on the screen. He was shaped like a brawler, but he'd never thrown a sober punch in his life. He was a white van man by trade, though that was mostly just a side hustle. He made his real money driving for the Kelleys. When something needed moving in a hurry, there was Colin. He grinned. "Been running some new routes, you know."

Ro frowned. "What sort of new routes?" Colin's routes had to be authorized. Since his van was mostly owned by the

Kelleys, that was only fair to Ro's way of thinking.

Colin frowned, as if he'd said something he hadn't meant to. "Just new ones," he said, by way of explanation. She heard the hesitation and straightened. Colin wasn't the sharpest knife in the rack. He'd gotten dinged a time or two for wandering off his patch, making off-the-books deliveries.

The first time they caught you, that got you a warning, maybe a beating depending on how you took the former. Sometimes, if the money was right and you offered to pay a percentage, they even let you keep doing it. But the second time...

"Colin," she began. He looked past her, and then pushed away from the bar.

"Sorry luv, got to take a piss. Talk later." He hurried towards the gents, glancing over his shoulder as he went. Ro was about to call after him when a heavy hand fell on her shoulder, startling her.

"Rosemary. Just in time." She knew the hand and the voice, and didn't turn. She cursed Colin for not warning her.

"Billy," she said.

"Was that Colin I saw scuttling away?" Billy Bricks asked as he leaned against the bar beside her. He was an old villain, grey and weathered by violence, but still hard with muscle. His nose had been broken and reset at least twice. Eyes like polished stones looked her over. She didn't meet his gaze. Billy didn't like people looking at him.

"Yeah. He had to take a piss."

"Bet he did." He smiled. "Thought you weren't going to make it tonight,"

"I wanted a pint."

"Well, it saves me having to run you down later, don't it?"

"Something up?"

"Why would you ask that?"

Ro took a swallow of her beer, playing for time. Something was on Billy's mind. That made her nervous. "No reason. It's just… you don't usually talk to me."

Billy smiled. He had an ugly smile. "I usually don't need to, do I?" He turned to the bartender and knocked on the wood. "Pint of Best please, Harry." He looked back at Ro. "We're having a meeting later, in the back. That's why everyone is here."

"I didn't know about it."

"But you're here anyway. Lucky you." Billy leaned close, and she could smell his aftershave. Like him, it was out of date.

"What's the meeting for?" she asked.

He was silent for a moment. Then, he chuckled softly. "Someone's being cheeky again. Running a side-deal without permission. One of our vans got spotted down near Blackfriars Bridge this morning. Only we didn't want no one making any deliveries over that way today, did we? Like I said, cheeky."

"Maybe they were running a personal errand," she said, and immediately regretted it.

"On company time? Heaven forefend, Rosemary." He shook his head in mock-disappointment. "That's why the place is packed tonight. I'm spreading the word that if anybody hears so much as a whistle about someone taking side-jobs without our say-so, they need to tell me, post haste. And if they don't… well." He drained his pint and set the glass down with a thump. "Put it on the tab, Harry, there's a good lad."

Billy pushed away from the bar, but paused. "You don't

know anything about it, do you Rosemary? Anything you want to share?"

Ro thought of Colin, and shook her head. "I don't know nothing, Billy."

Billy nodded. "Good. But keep an ear out, eh?" He ambled off, calling out to some other unlucky bastard. Ro watched him and then determinedly finished her drink. She needed to talk to Colin. She left the bar, hurrying out back towards the lavatories.

Colin was hanging around near the side-door that faced the gents, face glued to his Optik. She didn't wait for him to notice her. "Are you an idiot?" she hissed, catching his arm and bending it up behind his back. Colin yelped.

"Hey, let go," he began, and she shoved him against the wall, her forearm pressed against his throat. Not hard, but hard enough to make breathing difficult. His eyes widened and he clawed at her arm.

"Stop it, stop it," she said, in a low voice. "Settle down and answer the fucking question. Are you an idiot?"

"N-no," he gurgled. "Why?"

"Then what are you up to?"

"Nothing."

She frowned and pressed her weight against his throat. His eyes bulged. "C-can't breathe," he whined.

"Stop whining. If you couldn't breathe, you couldn't talk." Ro leaned close, eyes narrowed. "Earlier, you said you had a new gig. And the way you scarpered when Billy Bricks showed up... what are you into, Colin?"

"Nothing, I swear. Just some deliveries." He squirmed out of her grip. "Look, come outside. We'll talk out there." He took a quick look around and headed for the side-door. Ro hesitated, and then followed.

The side-door opened onto a narrow alley, barely wide enough for two people. It was full of rubbish and crates of empties, and the smell of rotting veg and stale beer was so heavy she had to breathe through her mouth. She could hear rats scrabbling in the dark, but to her relief she couldn't see them. She hated rats. Always had. "So spill," she said, impatiently.

Colin lit a cigarette. Not an e-cigarette, but a real one. Silk Cut. He was old fashioned that way. He didn't offer her one, but she wasn't that broken up about it. "I'm just moving some stuff around, right?"

"Like down Blackfriars?"

He hesitated, and she read the truth in his eyes. "You absolute plonker."

He looked away. "It's just a bit of work on the side, nothing to get so bloody upset about."

"It's not me you should be worried about," she said. "What if Billy Bricks finds out?"

"And how's he going to do that, then? You going to grass me up?"

Ro paused, considering. If she didn't tell someone, and they found out, she'd get whatever Colin got, but worse. The Kelleys only prized loyalty when it benefited them.

Colin frowned. "I thought we were mates," he said.

"What was it?" she asked, after a moment.

"What was what?"

"What were you delivering that was worth this aggro?" Her hands clenched. She knew she ought to go back in, ought to find Billy. But then what? Turn Colin over? The thought made her stomach do flip-flops. Billy would kill him – or as good as.

Colin finished his cigarette and tossed it away into the dark. "Didn't ask. I – hang on a sec." His Optik chimed, and he reached for it. An instant later, there was an echoing crack. Colin's head jerked backwards, and he toppled without a sound, his Optik clattering to the ground seconds before his body followed suit.

Ro stared in shock. There was something hot and wet on her face. Colin's body spasmed as it shut down. His Optik flashed and went black.

Behind her, she heard voices. The door opened. Shouts. All of it seemed to be occurring far away. The only thing of importance was the body in front of her, twitching out its final moments in the rubbish-strewn alley.

And then, at last, going still.

DAY FOUR

MONDAY

Bagley-bytes 13658-2: This just in, someone else is dead, but more on that later. According to our man at the ministry (hi, Dalton) Her Majesty's Snoops are thinking of a rebrand. There's talk of a new team charged with the dubious strategy of "intelligence response" or something similar. Everyone stay tuned to update your contacts. I prefer the first name myself, but what do I know? I'm just an unfettered AI with access to the sum of all human knowledge.

+++

RE: sum of all human knowledge. It's not as much as you might think.

+++

Onto more cheerful topics. The pro-Albion PR campaign is heating up as Nigel Cass kisses the right rings and twists the right arms. Somebody make a note to find out which is which, so we know who to recruit and who to blackmail. Or vice versa. Up to you, really!

+++

Speaking of recruits, underground DJ Adam Logan is throwing another one of his bashes at an old warehouse on Park Street in Southwark. Might be the sort of place to meet new faces, as they say. Someone crash the party, please. And by someone, I mean anyone other than Terry.

+++

Sergei reports that the notorious Clan Kelley dive, the Wolfe Tone, is full of plods. No, it's not being raided. Apparently someone got shot out back. Quelle surprise, as the French say. Remember that bit earlier? Seems our friendly sniper has been busy. A double-header.

+++

Finally, Albion definitely have a bug up their bum about something called LIBRA. If anyone has any information, please share it with the class. I'm all ears. Not literally of course, but you get the picture. If not, please ask Sabine to explain it to you in words of one syllable or less, as I can't be bothered.

7: PERFIDIOUS ALBION

The showers at the hideout were shit. But the water was hot, and Olly needed to feel clean. He stood under the scalding spray, letting the heat seep into his aching muscles. He'd tried to sleep again, but hadn't gotten much. Every time he closed his eyes, he saw the moment of Alex Dempsey's death – the instant the life had gone out of the man's eyes replayed over and over again in Olly's brain.

He wanted to move past it. Needed to move past it. Couldn't. So instead he stood in the shower and tried to wash it away. Eventually, the water started to cool, and he got out. Someone had brought him new clothes, and he dressed quickly. The shower room was small, badly tiled and smelt of damp. Repurposed lockers had been arranged along one wall, and benches sat in front of them. It reminded Olly of a changing room in some low-rent gym.

As he was lacing up his trainers, Krish came in. "You okay?"

"No." Olly didn't look at him.

"Liz shouldn't have done that, fam. No call for it."

Olly shook his head. "It's not that."

Krish fell silent. Olly could almost hear the questions rattling in his head. He spoke up before Krish could gather his courage. "Why'd you bring me in?"

"What?"

"DedSec. Why you'd bring me in?" Olly looked up at him.

Krish smiled. "You got style, bruv. Like me."

Olly laughed. Krish was all about style. He DJed for a pirate broadcast, streaming an eclectic mix of breakbeat hardcore, grime, old soul rarities and Asian dub, in between delivering fervent political or anti-corporate screeds. Olly had listened to Krish's show a few times before he'd hooked up with DedSec.

"Proper resistance, man. That's what you were. I saw that right off." Krish puffed his chest out. "And you ain't never let me down. Except for those other times, I mean."

Olly shook his head. "It's like the pigeons were out to get me." He gestured. "Like I was... what's her name? In that film. You know the one. With the seagulls."

"Yeah, but twice?" Krish grinned. "You got some serious bad luck, bruv."

"Cheers." Olly looked down at the floor, trying not to think about birds. He decided to change the subject. "Did you know him?"

"Who?"

"Dempsey. Guy that got topped."

Krish looked away. "Not really. He wasn't one of us, you know?"

"That's what Liz said."

Krish nodded. "He was a thief, yeah? Liked to lift people's

wallets, steal their identities, that sort of thing. Never been big on that myself." He smiled. "I prefer to make up my own. Less hassle."

"He was old school. Like Liz."

"Don't let her hear you say that, man. She'll pop your plums like it was nothing." Krish shivered. "Liz don't fuck around. That's why she's in charge."

"I thought nobody was in charge."

"Well, she's nobody." Krish banged on a locker. "She's the original model, you know. DedSec one point oh."

"So she's out of date and buggy?"

"Why else would she stick a skeng in your face, you dozy bastard?" Krish shook his head. "She is *not* to be messed about, ya get me?"

Olly bobbed his head. "Trust me, I am well aware of that."

"DedSec – it used to be easy, you know?" Krish sat down beside him. "Decrypt some shit, drop some information on the dark web, clap some cash from a bank machine and 'ting. Hacktivism, bruv. Non-violent."

"Liz didn't seem like the non-violent type to me."

"Changing, innit?" Krish scratched his chin. "Now we got people talking about drone warfare and guerrilla resistance shit, you know? Like proper freedom fighters."

Olly looked at him. "I don't want to shoot nobody."

"No choice, bruv. Day's coming, you know? Everybody sees it."

Olly nodded and looked away. He and Krish sat in silence for a time. "Sometimes, I see all this shit and think maybe the best thing to do would be to cut the signal, you know?" Olly said, after a time. "Crash everything and begin again."

"What, like – everything-everything?"

Olly nodded. "Everything, bruv. All of it. Start over from the zero point, right?"

"Lot of people would die."

"Lot of people going to die anyway." Olly looked up. "Shit. I don't know."

"Lucky we ain't in charge," Krish said, and slapped him on the back. "Liz sent me to look for you, by the way. She thinks she found something."

"Why does she want me?"

"You belong to her now. I don't make the rules."

"Cheers," Olly said, drily. He stood. "Let's go see what she's after."

Olly followed Krish out into the cellar. Things were humming. The shooting had everyone on edge, and they were all trying to look busy and stay out of Liz's way. Heads bent, fingers tapping at keyboards, virtual or otherwise. Stock information and exchange rates danced across the closest screens. "Payday," Krish murmured. Olly nodded.

DedSec, or at least the London hive, seemed to get most of its funding through peer-to-peer transactions. ETO accounts were regularly set up for people who didn't exist, except on paper, or in cyberspace, rather. Generative network software could create composite facial images for bogus social media accounts, bot algorithms could be tweaked to post regularly and semi-coherently. Olly had done some of it himself – he had a handful of sock puppets set up, and often used them as camouflage for his DedSec runs.

The hard currency – the seed money for everything – came from government and corporate accounts. Nothing big, nothing flashy: quiet programs designed to divert fractions of a penny into ghost-accounts on a regular basis. That sort of pittance was hardly noticed by company accounting, and it snowballed quickly, if you knew how to invest it.

If a lot of money was needed very quickly, there were always smash and grabs – a virus attack on corporate systems and a quick snatch of everything you could get in the window the virus opened for you. But that attracted attention. It was easier to hit a local villain in the wallet, and not the digital kind.

Olly had never participated in a raid like that. The thought of waving a gun around in a betting shop after hours, or busting up an illegal counting house, left him feeling cold. It was too much like being an actual criminal. But some of the others enjoyed that sort of thing. They liked a bit of the old ultra-violence to break up the monotony. Olly preferred to steal ones and zeroes from the safety of the hideout. He wished he were doing it right now.

Krish led him towards the far corner of the central room, where a team sat hunched on their couches and leaky beanbag chairs, diligently scrubbing the cTOS surveillance grid of any images of Olly. Liz was hovering over them, arms crossed, expression unreadable as she watched them work.

Olly felt a flush of pride as he noticed how few there were and how scrambled the ones that did exist were. Liz saw his smile and nodded. "You do good work, Olly. Bit sloppy around the edges, though. A few drones spotted you disposing of your hoodie."

"Shit," he said, smile fading.

"Already handled it," Liz said. "Hoodie's already gone, anyway."

Olly nodded. He'd figured someone – a street person, or just someone bin-diving, would have claimed it. "It was good gear – you know, except for the blood."

Liz turned away. "Smart getting rid of it, though the DNA might have bitten you in the arse, if the plods had found it. Never leave anything behind, and if you have to, don't leave it intact. Burn it, bleach it, chuck it in the canal. Something, anything."

"I wasn't really thinking about it."

"Well, learn to think about it. We have to be lucky every time – they only have to be lucky once. Remember that." She checked her Optik. "Right. Time to go."

"Where?"

"Downstairs."

"Oh good. I was missing that sofa."

"Not to sleep. To talk." Liz started to walk.

"I thought you had everything," Olly said, as he hurried to catch up to her.

They're ready for you. Chin up. Straighten your shoulders. The elite awaits.

Bagley sounded inordinately pleased, and Olly felt a tremor of anxiety. "Who's he talking about? Who's here?"

"Never mind. Just answer their questions, be helpful." Liz led him back downstairs. The lights were already on, the screens full of data, servers humming. There were voices as well, distorted by electronic interference or scratchy from pirated frequencies, but understandable. They overlapped one another, as if several conversations were going on at once.

Olly stopped dead when he saw the floating heads. The holographic projections were crude things – a pig with a monocle, a gas mask, a knight's helmet, half a dozen others.

They spun in a slow circle over the table, projected by Bagley from multiple sources. As the owner of each projection spoke, their image was limned by light. The conversations had clearly been going on for some time.

"...managed to install a sneak and peek sub-routine into the new Battersea surveillance systems. As soon as they're operational ..."

"...Malik is definitely buddying up to Cass. His mob may be angling on working with Albion..."

"...so we need eyes on the Parcel Fox distribution centre..."

"...any photos of the AWY Imports warehouse across from the Tate Modern..."

"...MI5 is on the way out. My contacts..."

"...Kelleys are operating in the Whitechapel Terminus, I'm sure of it..."

"Who...?" Olly began.

Hush, Oliver, Bagley chided. The adults are speaking.

Liz lifted her Optik and activated an app. The holographic image of a crowned skull, glowing crimson, joined the discussion circle. "Redqueen reporting in," Liz said. At her words, all conversation ceased.

The knight's helm lit up. "Any more on the shooting?"

"We're working on it. I've got the witness here. I've already uploaded his statement, but if you want to ask him any questions, now's the time."

"Not necessary, Liz."

Liz frowned. "No names, Dalton. Jesus. Remember our discussion?"

"If you say so. This stuff isn't my sort of thing. I prefer the material to the virtual."

"Hard to punch someone who isn't there, you mean," another voice piped up. An ovoid mask, with an animated dragon crawling across its surface.

"Ah, you know me, Sabine."

"Names," Liz reiterated, with an air of resigned frustration. She rolled her eyes. "What's the point of enacting security protocols if you lot never follow them?"

Indeed. Though I have already encrypted this session, and scrambled the frequency.

"Good job, Bagley," the knight's helm – Dalton – said. "Sorry, Redqueen. I'm slacking off in my enforced retirement. But like I said, I trust your report. My only question is whether or not this incident is connected to the others?"

Olly silently mouthed the word "others?" at Liz. She ignored him. "Unknown as yet. I suggest we keep an open mind in that regard. Not everything is connected."

"And yet, we find ourselves with a pattern nonetheless," the ovoid – Sabine – murmured. "Unrest is already brewing in the emigration centres. There was an anti-tech riot at the site of the TOAN conference last week. And there's chatter on the crypto-boards… someone is moving money to all the wrong places."

A cartoon character – a wolf with a wide grin, lolling tongue and big eyes – lit up. "I still say the Kelleys are behind it," it said. The accent was foreign, Eastern European. It reminded Olly of one of his neighbours, an old Albanian. "That witch is sinking her claws into every rotten pie she can reach – she's up to something. I can smell it."

"Maybe so," Dalton said. "But in my experience, this has all the hallmarks of a false flag operation. Fake trails, double blinds, the lot. And while we chase leads all over London, the threat in question is free to do whatever they want."

"Which means what?" Liz asked.

"Which means, your highness, that we have to pull on every strand until the whole thing unravels. Proceed as planned, until told otherwise."

"I'm starting to see why MI5 gave you the sack, Dalton," Liz growled.

Dalton chuckled. "Names, Liz – remember?"

"Fuck off, Dalton."

"And cheerio to you as well."

That was that. One by one, the images blinked out until only two remained – Liz's and Sabine's. "He has his own way of doing things, Liz," the latter said. "You know that."

"I know that he's not taking any of this seriously," Liz said. "He thinks it's just smoke and mirrors – old school spy craft, James Bond bullshit."

"You're wrong. He takes it seriously. We all do. But he's used to this sort of thing, and we're not. Not all of us, at any rate." Sabine paused. "How are you, by the way?"

"Tired."

"I know Alex was a friend of yours. I'm sorry."

Liz was silent for a moment. Then, "Thank you."

"Dalton is right, however. We have to keep pulling threads until we get the right one. And that means you need to keep following this one, wherever it might lead. Even if it's a dead end. Do you understand?"

"Yes, I know." Liz looked at Olly. "I might need help."

"All that we can give." Sabine paused again. "Things are coming to a head here, I can feel it. So can Dalton, for that matter. There's something brewing, just out of sight. The sooner we find out what it is, the sooner we can stop it."

"Agreed," Liz said. "Be seeing you."

Sabine's image blinked out. After a few moments of quiet thought, Liz regarded Olly again. "I figured they weren't going to ask you any questions, but I thought you should see it."

"What was that?"

"DedSec London. A good chunk of it, anyway. Sometimes there are more of us, sometimes less. It depends on the day, what's going on, that sort of thing." She ran her hand through her hair and studied him, as if considering how best to approach a problem. "There was another shooting last night."

"What? Where?"

"The Wolfe Tone."

Olly raised his eyebrows. "That's a Clan Kelley pub."

Liz nodded. "Good chance whoever got topped was working for the Kelleys…"

"Or they wanted him dead."

Liz shook her head. "They wouldn't do it right on their own doorstep. Not so publicly, at least. Mary Kelley is a bloody-minded old hag, but she's smarter than that."

"So does that mean the Kelleys are mixed up in all this?"

"I don't know. It's hard to imagine Mary Kelley *not* being at the centre of something so vicious." She paused. "What do you know about Albion?"

The question surprised Olly. "Just what I see on the news – or in the street." Albion had become a definite presence in East London. They were on practically every other corner in Tower Hamlets, swaggering around in full military kit like they were in bombed-out Baghdad or somewhere. "Bunch of wankers playing toy soldiers, innit?"

"Dangerous, though. Do you know what it is Krish sent you to pick up yesterday?"

Olly shook his head. "Didn't ask."

"You're smarter than you look." She paused. "It was a dossier on Albion. Most of it we probably already know, but…"

"Information is information," Olly said.

She nodded. "Albion are positioning themselves for… something. They're not the only opportunistic bastards on the board, but they're here now, and they're the ones I'm worried about." She tapped her Optik. "Yesterday, they had a bit of a set-to with the local coppers."

An image – a drone-feed, Olly knew – popped up on his display. He saw the cops swarm towards a trio of Albion goons. No guns were drawn, but the tension was evident, even from high above. "What set that off?"

"According to the report of one PC Moira Jenks, one of the goons tried to walk off with some evidence." Liz looked at him. "Like maybe an Optik that was used in the commission of a targeted assassination, for instance."

"Shitting hell," Olly murmured. "Albion did it? Why?"

"That's what I'm planning to find out." Liz smiled. "And that means we need to pay a visit to Bethnal Green police station."

Olly stared at her. "You what?"

The restaurant was new. Chic, scruffy-trendy, the sort of place that wouldn't last a year in the current economic climate. Sarah threaded her way through the tables, letting nothing of her disdain show on her face. Instead, she put her best smile as Winston Natha rose from his seat to greet her with genteel enthusiasm.

Winston was short and round and genial. The sort of man designed to run a corner shop and chase street urchins on the rob with a broom. He dressed well, but not too well, and his grey hair was slicked back against his skull. He stood as she drew close, and took her hands in his. "Sarah, it is ever a delight to see you."

"Winston. You're getting fat."

"I prefer the term 'sleek'. Like a sealion." They sat and he looked her over. "You, on the other hand, look as statuesque as ever. How many times a week do you go to the gym? Six – or seven?"

"Once a day, work permitting. You should try it."

"No, I prefer to invoke my privilege in this instance. As a man, my gravitas is only enhanced by a bit of patriarchal pudge. I'm told it lends me a grandfatherly air."

"You do look a bit like Father Christmas, I confess."

Winston smiled. "Then it is working. You've succumbed to my charms already." He continued to smile as a waitress swooped down and took Sarah's order. "I was surprised to receive your invitation. We haven't spoken much since the election."

"I've been busy, as have you."

"Indeed, busy days, busy days. Much to do." He paused. "What do you think about this TOAN conference business?" He took a sip of coffee. "You got an invitation, I'm sure."

"I did. And you?"

"Of course. Are you going?"

"I'm debating it."

Winston smirked. "That means no."

Sarah smiled. "What about you?"

"Tempting," Winston said. "We've spent enough on it. I feel somewhat obliged."

"How much was it, at last count?" Sarah asked, as the waitress brought her coffee. She took a sip and regretted it. Burnt beans again, and way too much cinnamon. "We've spent tens of millions we don't have, bringing in financial and tech-elites from all over the world. Just to remind people that Britain still exists and matters."

Winston raised an eyebrow. "I'd say that's fairly important, wouldn't you?"

"At the moment, I can think of any number of better places for that money than paying for Skye Larsen's glorified ego-trip. Oh, she says it's about discussing the issues of the day – the housing crisis, the wage gap, all of that – but we both know it's just an excuse for the new elite to mingle and network."

"Now you sound like a conspiracy theorist. Maybe you should start a blog."

Sarah laughed. "No one *blogs* these days, Winston. Even you should know that."

"So I take it you'll be out front with the protestors, then?"

"Mmm. Perhaps not that far." There were any number of protests going on these days. Most were concerned with the ongoing deportee crisis. The European Union had made clear that it intended to refuse all deportation claims unless they were settled on British soil before arriving on the continent.

Temporary emigration offices had been set up in Southwark and elsewhere, but word was they were already overwhelmed. Some people were protesting the EU, others on behalf of the deportees and a few for issues only tangentially related to the crisis. She sat back. "At least not until I see what our Right Honourable Prime Minister has up his sleeve."

It was Winston's turn to laugh. "Pragmatic as ever, Sarah."

"One does what one must for one's constituency, Winston. Speaking of which..."

"Albion," he said.

"Indeed. I hear you're thinking of swinging your weight behind them."

"And who told you that?"

"A little bird."

"Gossipy things, birds. Because I'd heard the same thing about you."

Sarah paused. "Did you now?"

Winston nodded. "Oh yes. Sarah Lincoln and law-and-order go hand in hand. Forgive me for saying so, but there's always been a strong whiff of New Labour about you. People remember these things."

Sarah considered this. "I admit, I've always had a soft spot for market economics, but I don't know that I'd go that far. And you're hardly one to talk, Winston."

"Fair dues," he said. He sipped his coffee, watching her over the rim. "But I think we both have the best interests of Tower Hamlets at heart, don't you?"

"I hope so."

"Good." Winston smiled again. "By the way, I invited Nigel Cass. To join us today."

Sarah didn't give him the satisfaction of reacting. "How lovely, I wanted to speak to him as well. Thank you, Winston. You've saved me a trip."

"Not even a twitch," Winston said, with some disappointment. "Am I that predictable, Sarah? Or are you merely that devious?"

"A little of both, I think." Sarah folded her menu and set it aside. The waitress was closing in, an anxious look on her face. "Have you eaten here before?"

"Once or twice."

"Order for me."

Winston smirked, but did as she asked. She turned her attentions to the rest of the clientele. They were all of a type: young, professional, well-off… the exact sort of people one wanted in one's borough.

"They all look a bit like shop dummies, don't they?" Winston murmured.

Sarah looked at him. "I wouldn't say that. Not in public, at any rate. When is Cass supposed to be here?"

"Any minute now. I– ah, speak of the devil." Winston stood, and Sarah followed his example. Nigel Cass prowled through the tables, moving like a man awaiting enemy fire. He was accompanied by four other men – hard-faced, well-dressed, but uncomfortable in their suits, obviously bodyguards – and a young woman. The woman was pretty, in a cool sort of way. Another Oxbridge clone, Sarah thought, somewhat uncharitably. She had her Optik in hand, and was talking softly to someone. A PA, then.

The bodyguards peeled off, taking up unobtrusive positions across the room, where they could watch Cass without being obvious about it. The PA stayed glued to his side, still talking. Cass didn't so much as look at her.

"Ah, Nigel," Winston said, arms spread in welcome. "We're

pleased you could make it. I trust we're not taking you away from anything important?"

"Nothing that can't be rescheduled," Cass said. He nodded to Winston, and looked at Sarah. "Ms Lincoln. A pleasure to see you again." He looked at his PA. "Go get a drink. Leave us to it."

The woman hesitated. Cass made a sharp gesture. "I said go." She went, visibly reluctant. He smiled apologetically as they sat. "Danielle is in public relations. She's working to… rehabilitate my image for the public."

"And does it need rehabilitation?" Sarah asked, innocently.

Cass grinned mirthlessly. "I wouldn't know. Not my area. But it is yours, isn't it? I saw you on the news, standing firm against my man, Faulkner. He had quite a bit to say about it, in this morning's briefing."

Sarah allowed herself a smile. "I'm sure he did. And how is Mr Faulkner?"

"Sergeant," Cass corrected.

"Hmm?"

"It's *Sergeant* Faulkner."

Sarah gestured aimlessly. "I trust he wasn't too put out by that bit of theatre?"

Cass frowned. "Saying he's put out is putting it mildly. You dressed him down in front of the lower ranks *and* the locals."

"Winston and I are locals as well," she said.

Winston nodded and joined in. "The fact is, your man has been throwing his weight around a bit. He was due a bollocking, and Sarah gave him one. Trifle more public than I myself might have done in her place, but it was overdue." He shrugged apologetically. "I'm sorry, but there it is."

Cass stared at them for a moment. Then he nodded and

looked at his menu. "Is that why you invited me to lunch in the mess? To complain about the conduct of my men?"

"Not at all. We merely wished to get better acquainted."

"And to pump me for information." Cass smiled. "Fine. I'm always open to answering questions. I have a – well – what you might call a reductionist view of the world. Good versus evil, that sort of thing. As politicians, you don't have the luxury of that sort of view, I know, but I'm not a politician."

"Oh, except you are, now," Sarah said. "Of sorts, at least."

Cass grimaced. "Don't remind me."

Sarah and Winston laughed politely.

"But you are," she pressed. "Otherwise you wouldn't have come for lunch."

"I was taught to seize opportunities when they present themselves," he said, studying her. She could read the interest in his eyes. "You're a perceptive woman. You two are my biggest opponents at the moment. If I can flip you, it solves most of my immediate problems."

Sarah had a sudden thought: Cass was only pretending to be uncomfortable, the old soldier struggling to know how to fit back in polite society. She wondered how many times this act had got him exactly what he wanted.

"A *trifle* blunt," Winston murmured.

"Accurate, though," Cass said, not looking at him. "And you invited me – why? To feel me out. See what I have planned?"

"Call it… reconnaissance," Sarah said. Cass was smart, but she'd known that already.

"And that's exactly why I wanted to start with East London," Cass said. "The natives are getting restless. And a good deal of that restlessness is concentrated here."

"Yes, because unemployment is spiking. We're at a hundred-year high. The modern British workplace is almost wholly automated, and human workers are made redundant at a ridiculous rate. Anti-tech protests are becoming common." Sarah watched his eyes as she spoke. Cass was… bored. "Is it any wonder there's unrest?"

"I'm not here to debate the causes," Cass said. "Regardless of the reasons, the populace is restive – aggressively so. And my intelligence tells me that there are those looking to exploit that unrest. DedSec, for instance."

"DedSec?" Winston said.

Sarah sat back. "Intelligence? *Spies*, you mean."

Cass looked at her. "Yes," he said, bluntly. "Eyes on the ground are integral part of any operation. Both to watch the enemy – and your allies." He paused, still looking at Sarah. "You don't seem surprised."

"Well I bloody am," Winston said. "I thought DedSec was an American problem."

"Terrorism has a habit of spilling across national borders."

Sarah cleared her throat. "Strong word. They were just 'hacktivists', last I heard." Not that she'd heard much. DedSec wasn't something on her radar, though it was impossible to avoid hearing about them, these days.

"A pretty word hiding an ugly reality. Like 'freedom fighter'. They're terrorists, plain and simple." He sat back. "Like most insurgent organizations, they're broken into cells. And those cells are broken down into smaller cells, and so on and so forth. I have it on good authority that the London cell is bigger than anyone realizes. They're as dangerous as any other insurgent element. Maybe more so, given their method of operation."

"Computers, you mean." Winston glanced at Sarah, and she knew he was playing the fool. The out-of-touch politico was a mask they'd all donned once or twice in their careers. Cass's eyes narrowed. Sarah wasn't sure he'd bought it, but he seemed willing to elaborate.

"Among other things. Instead of bombs, they plant malware." He paused. "If anything, it's more dangerous. Bombs kill people. Malware kills systems. And they're not the only ones using such methods. London is rife with factionalism. Maybe you don't see it – maybe you're trying not to see it – but it's evident to me."

"And you think Albion has the resources to combat this… problem?"

"Boots on the ground, drones in the air. Give me three months, and I can knock East London into shape. With six, I could bring the whole city to heel." He spread his hands. "Force is the great leveller. Enough force and even the strongest rock breaks."

"We're not talking about rocks, though."

"No, but the principle is the same. A decade or more of budget cuts have rendered the Metropolitan Police Service toothless. They cannot effectively maintain law and order on a city-wide scale. Albion can, for a fraction of the cost." Cass gestured. "Tower Hamlets is the first step. With your support, we can get permission to step up patrols and take on investigative duties, thus freeing up the Met to get on with their paperwork."

"Is that why Faulkner was out at Lister House yesterday?" Sarah asked.

Cass scratched his chin. "He just wanted to lend a hand."

"He wanted to take over the scene. I was curious as to why." Sarah tilted her head. "As you said, Albion's remit does not extend to investigative work." She paused. "Curious as well that he got there so quickly."

"We have access to the police frequencies."

"And drones in the air," Winston said, drily.

Cass glanced at him. "That is part of Albion standard operational procedure, yes." He took a sip of coffee, watching them.

"Operational procedure for enemy territory, I believe," Sarah said, seizing on the opening. "Is Tower Hamlets 'enemy territory'?"

Cass studied her over the rim of his cup. "You don't agree?"

"I grew up in Tower Hamlets, Mr Cass."

He put down his cup and favoured her with a warmer smile. "Nigel, please."

"Nigel, then. This is my home. I still reside here."

"I imagine in a nicer house."

Sarah bared her teeth in a smile of her own. "Oh definitely. Indoor WCs and track lighting. Very posh. The borough has its issues – it always has – but the answer to those problems is not armed patrols. It is money. More money for schools, more money for council housing, a universal basic income…"

Cass chuckled. "That's your answer for everything isn't it? You people–"

Sarah fixed him with a look. Cass paused, aware of what he'd just said. He frowned. "I meant politicians," he explained.

"Of course you did," Winston said, smoothly. "Though possibly we can be forgiven for thinking otherwise, given your men's propensity for – ehm – a certain inequality of applied force, shall we say?"

"Say what you want to say," Cass said, flatly. "Don't shilly-shally."

Sarah leaned forward. "I don't think you're a bigot, Mr Cass. But it's not what I think that matters. You haven't thought things through. You see the borough as foreign territory, to be subdued. I see it as my constituency. The people who elected me to represent them. I'm sure Winston feels the same."

Winston looked uncomfortable, but nodded.

Sarah tapped the table with an expertly manicured nail. "I speak with their voice, even if you'd rather not hear what they have to say. And what they want me to say is that Albion – in its current form – is unwelcome."

Cass was silent for long moments. Then he gave a grunt and made as if to rise. "Thank you for lunch. It was… an edifying experience."

"For us too. Farewell then," Sarah said. She sat back and watched him go. He hadn't shaken hands.

Winston gave her a slow clap. "Oh, well done. You do have a talent for pissing off all the right people." He dabbed at his lips with his napkin. "I thought it was going so well, too."

"Oh, climb down off the cross, Winston." Sarah fixed him with a basilisk stare. "You set us both up. Wanted to see us go at it, did you?"

"A bit. Mostly I wanted to see what you thought about Albion."

"And here I thought that's why I invited you." Sarah gnawed her lower lip. "He's a smarmy creep and having his jumped-up stormtroopers in my territory irks my sensibilities."

"Mine as well. But that's the way the wind is blowing,

dear heart. It's a new world, with a new way of doing things. Including policing, it seems."

Sarah sighed. "You sound as if you're leaning towards the Prime Minister's view on the matter. I expected better of you, Winston."

"No you didn't." Winston smiled. "And I haven't decided anything yet. Neither have you, unless I miss my guess."

"I'm still pondering the variables."

Winston laughed. "Polite way of saying you're trying to grab what you can." He waved her protestations aside. "And what was that little speech about growing up here? Trying out some new material?"

She didn't reply. They sat in awkward silence for a few moments, and then Sarah said, "I want to view that facility. I want to know what they're getting up to in Limehouse." Her eyes flicked towards her fellow MP. "And I want you with me."

"Limehouse is your problem, not mine."

"Limehouse is in Tower Hamlets. It's *our* problem. Besides, I can tell you're dying to know what Cass is hiding."

Winston shrugged. "You have me there. Fine. We'll issue a joint request, put some pressure on him. I doubt we'll get the full tour, but… we'll see something at least." He paused. "What was that about Faulkner and the shooting?"

"As I said, I was curious. Still am, in fact. Faulkner showed up far too quickly for my liking, police wavebands or no."

"You think they were – what? – expecting it?"

Sarah frowned. "I don't know. And what's more, I don't like not knowing."

8: INVESTIGATIONS

The locker room was crowded when Danny arrived at headquarters for his shift. Leave had been cancelled, and everyone was gearing up. Word had come down that a show of force was scheduled today, boots on the streets and Albion operatives on every corner.

Danny knew why. They all did. Faulkner was planning to make a scene at Bethnal Green police station during the handover of the evidence from the shooting. The Sarge was going to show up in full tac-kit to make a statement, and that statement was "do not fuck with us sunshine, we are not in the mood."

Danny wasn't sure that was a good idea, but no one had asked his opinion. Such decisions were far above his pay grade. He was just glad that the handover was now happening in the afternoon, rather than the morning. The change had come down from on high, for reasons that weren't especially clear. Danny figured it had to do with the press. Faulkner wanted a strong showing to make up for the clusterfuck the previous day.

He looked around. The room was really just a stretch of lockers isolated by particle board walls from the rest of the facility. The building had been a warehouse at one time. Now it was centre of operations for Albion efforts in Tower Hamlets.

Albion had three such facilities in Tower Hamlets – or at least three that were common knowledge. One was the drone facility on Limehouse Basin. The other two, of which this building was one, were temporary deployment sites – one in Tower Hamlets North, and this one, in Tower Hamlets South.

Danny got his gear down and pulled on his kit without thinking about it. His mind was still on the night before. On Ro and his mother. Worry simmered at the back of his head. If Ro wasn't in trouble now, she soon would be. She couldn't help it – it was just her nature.

She'd always been that way. Even as a kid. He'd broken up so many fights and listened to so many excuses over the years. The worry he felt wasn't so much about her as what she might bring to their mother's doorstep. Ro could take care of herself.

Even so, he wondered whether he should push a bit – maybe see what the files had on the Kelleys. There was bound to be something of use, even if it wasn't immediately apparent. He was still thinking about it when someone slammed the locker beside his, startling him.

"She called you yet?" Hattersley asked, grinning.

Danny looked up. "Who?"

"The plod. Jenks – that was her name, right?" Hattersley sat down on the bench beside him. "She called you?"

"Don't be daft."

"Fair enough. Ready for today?" Hattersley asked.

"Ready enough. You?"

"Easy, innit?" Hattersley grinned. "We show up, give the plods a bit of a tweak, and roll out, reputation restored. Textbook."

"That'd make for a nice change."

"Danny boy, oh Danny boy – come to me, my blue-eyed Danny boy," Faulkner mock-sang from the doorway of the locker room, interrupting Hattersley's reply. Danny reluctantly looked up.

"Got brown eyes, Sarge," he said, as he stood. Hattersley turned back to his locker, trying to look busy. Danny wondered what Faulkner wanted. Nothing good, most likely. He was set to be a part of the handover squad, though he wasn't especially looking forward to it.

"Have you, lad? To tell the truth, I never noticed. Come here." Faulkner gestured. Danny moved briskly. Something in Faulkner's voice told him hesitation wouldn't be looked on fondly. Faulkner was already in full kit, his helmet dangling from one hand.

"Sarge?"

Faulkner grinned in a friendly fashion and clapped him on the shoulder. "Smile lad, it's good news – you've been volunteered."

Danny frowned. "For what, Sarge?"

"Special assignment. You and your mate, Hattersley. You're off handover. I've got something else for you." Faulkner leaned close. "No need to worry about any awkwardness with PC Jenks this way. You're welcome."

"Thanks, Sarge," Danny said, without enthusiasm.

Faulkner chuckled. "That's my keen lad." His good humour faded. "Walk with me." Danny dutifully fell into step with Faulkner. "I like you lad," Faulkner continued. "You know how to follow orders – that's a rare thing, these days. Most of the operators we employ these days are good at interpreting orders, but piss-poor at actually following them. When I tell a man to do something, I want him to bloody well do it, no questions asked."

"Yes, Sarge."

Faulkner looked at him. "But you're not an idiot, either. You've got a brain in that head. Another rarity. That's why you volunteered."

"Yes, Sarge."

"There's a great future ahead of us, Danny. So long as we walk the path of the righteous, as laid out by our lord and master, Mr Nigel Cass." Faulkner smiled as he said it. "Albion is the pre-eminent private military contractor in the western hemisphere. We took what others did, and did it better." He paused. "A bit like curry, innit?"

"Sarge?"

"Never mind. There was a shooting last night."

"Another one?" Danny said. "Where?"

"Out back of some dingy boozer. Same MO. One shot. Clean. Precise. The plods are all over it, but we're going to stick our oar in." He stopped. "The victim's name was Colin Wilson. Know anyone by that name?"

"No, Sarge."

Faulkner studied him for a moment before replying. "You sure? It was practically on your patch. The pub was over near the Locksley Estate."

Danny felt a chill. "Which pub?"

"The Wolfe Tone."

Danny grunted, careful not to let his sudden unease show on his face. Was that where Ro had gone last night, after she'd stormed off? "That's a Kelley pub."

Faulkner frowned. He knew who the Kelleys were. Albion operatives had produced stacks of dossiers on the Kelley Clan and the other criminal gangs who'd divvied up East London between them. The order hadn't come down to move against the Kelleys or any of the others thus far, but privately Danny figured it was only a matter of time. The only real way to get the East End under control was to remove the gangs from the equation.

"So you do know it," Faulkner said.

"Even my mum knows it, Sarge. Everyone does. The Kelleys don't exactly hide it." Danny paused. "Do we think they're are involved?"

Faulkner scratched his chin. "Good question, my lad. I want you to find out."

Danny looked at him in confusion. "Sarge?"

"You and Hattersley. I want you to look into this. You'll start with the poor sod who got slotted last night." Faulkner turned away. "Come with me."

"Sarge, I'm not an investigator," Danny said, as he hurried to keep up with Faulkner. "Come to that, are we are even allowed to investigate crimes in the borough?"

"Better to ask forgiveness than permission," Faulkner said, not looking at him. "Tower Hamlets is our forward fire support base. And these shootings are making the natives restless. The plods won't solve it, so we need to – and fast. If that means a few politicians get their noses out of joint, well fuck 'em sideways, says I."

"Yeah, but–" Danny began.

Faulkner glanced at him. "Danny, shut it and screw the cap tight, eh? Orders is orders, and I expect you to do as you're told. Can you do that for me, lad?"

Danny nodded. "Yes, Sarge."

"Good lad. Now, there's someone you need to talk to."

"Yeah, who?"

"A guest in the custody suites."

The custody suite was a small block of a dozen temporary cells at the back of the warehouse. Each of the cells was soundproofed, with a steel door and a viewing slot. All were currently empty, insofar as Danny knew. Albion didn't yet have official permission to hold suspects. But when they did, they would be ready.

"I thought we weren't allowed to detain suspects yet," Danny said, as Faulkner led him down the row of cells. "Or is this another one of those forgiveness permission things?"

Faulkner snorted. "Don't play the clever clogs, Danny, it don't suit you." He led Danny to the cell on the end, tapped a code into the digital lock, and swung the door open. Inside, a man sat on the cell's bench, looking very nervous and very tired. "I need to take a piss," he said, as he stood. Faulkner hit him in the gut.

"What you need to do is tell young Danny here what you told me," he growled. He shoved the prisoner back against the bench and turned. "This is Gary. Gary was at *The Wolfe Tone* last night, weren't you, Gary?"

Gary wheezed and nodded, one arm pressed to his stomach.

Faulkner sat down beside him, and put a companionable arm over the man's hunched shoulders. "Gary got picked up for having a slash in public. Not exactly a criminal genius." Faulkner looked at Gary. "Tell him what you told me, Gary."

"If I do, are you going to let me go?"

"We'll consider it. Now talk."

Gary talked. He hadn't witnessed the shooting, but he'd known the victim. Wilson had been a white van man, which Danny mentally translated as a courier for the Kelleys. He also knew where Wilson lived.

Faulkner patted Gary on the shoulder when he'd finished, and rose to his feet. "I want you to start with the flat. See if there's anything there that'll tell us what we need to know."

"The plods will have picked it clean by now."

Faulkner smiled. "Gary, tell young Danny what happened after the shooting."

Gary looked away. "The Kelleys stripped the body. Took his Optik, his wallet, his keys. Everything that could identify him." He paused. "They told us to keep quiet about it, until they say otherwise."

Danny grunted. That was fairly standard for the Kelleys. The shooting would bring the police right to their doorstep. They'd be doing everything in their power to keep any investigation to a minimum. He was surprised they hadn't moved the body – then, that might only have made the police more suspicious.

He wondered if Ro had been involved. He hoped not, but knew there was a vanishingly small chance of that if she'd been there that night. Part of him wanted to ask Gary about it, but not with Faulkner standing right there, nodding.

"The police will figure it out soon enough, but until then, we've got some time," Faulkner said. "Which is why you and Hattersley are going to get there first, and take a look around the flat before the plods stomp all over it."

Danny hesitated. It didn't sound entirely legal. But orders were orders. "What are we looking for exactly?" He thought about the Optik Faulkner had tried to snatch yesterday – was there a connection between the two victims? And if so, what did Faulkner know that he wasn't saying?"

Faulkner gestured to the door, and Danny left the cell. "Anything and everything, my lad. Starting with anything related to who might have shot him." Faulkner followed him out. "Not to mention why."

"Oi, what about me?" Gary began. "You said I could go?"

"Danny, did I say that?" Faulkner asked, innocently.

"You might have implied it, Sarge," Danny said, hesitantly.

"But I never said the words, did I?" Faulkner looked back at Gary and shrugged in mock-helplessness. "Shame, but there you have it, my son. Rest easy." He shut the door on the rest of Gary's protests.

"Are you going to let him go, Sarge?" Danny asked.

Faulkner looked at him. "Eventually. When we're done with him. Now, don't you have some place to be?" He gestured. "Hop to it."

Danny went.

Billy Bricks hauled open the loading bay door and ushered Ro inside the grimy warehouse just off the Mile End Road. "Tell me again," he said, as he closed the door behind them.

"I've told you five times already," Ro said, resignedly. She was tired. She hadn't slept. Billy had kept her awake all night, and her head was starting to pound. Too much caffeine, not enough food.

The Godfreys had stripped Colin – the corpse – on Billy's orders. They'd taken every bit of identification on Colin's body, and Billy had put the frighteners on all the punters, including Ro herself. No one was to talk to the Filth, if they knew what was good for them. Billy's word carried a lot of weight. He spoke for Clan Kelley, and everyone knew it.

The plods had shown up that morning, looking peeved. Two shootings in forty-eight hours was a bad job. They weren't happy. Neither was Billy. Ro rubbed her face, the lack of sleep catching up with her.

Billy shoved her. Not in a friendly way. "And you'll tell me a fucking sixth, love."

Ro spun, fists raised. Billy didn't so much as twitch. Ro lowered her hands, forcing herself to relax. She was in enough trouble as it was. A flicker of a smile crossed his face. "You're tired, so I'll forgive that, Rosemary."

"Don't call me Rosemary."

"It's your name, innit? Rosemary Hayes. Daughter of Desmond and Cece Hayes. Sister of Daniel Hayes. Last person to see Colin Wilson alive."

"Wilson?" Ro asked, without thinking.

Billy peered at her. "Yeah. What about it?"

"Nothing. I just... never knew his last name, that's all."

Billy laughed. "Guess he wasn't much of a mate, eh?" He shook his head. "You don't have many of them, luv. Not around here. Not right now." He grinned at her, but it wasn't friendly. "Just me, innit? So you'd best be fucking straight with me, before we go in there. Did you know anything about this shit?"

"No. Not before last night. I hadn't seen him in weeks. That's the truth, swear down."

Billy studied her for a moment, then grunted and turned away. Ro relaxed, but only slightly. "Right. Come on then."

The warehouse had been one of the first properties the Kelley firm had bought, when they'd arrived from Northern Ireland. In the decades that followed, the Kelleys had expanded, investing in the East End and in Greater London. They'd sunk their teeth in, and refused to let go. In the bad old days, they'd gone to war with the Krays, the Richardson Gang, and a dozen others.

As far as the firms of the East End were concerned, the Kelleys were old money aristocrats. They'd earned their place at the top of the heap, and only a fool took them on if they didn't have to.

The warehouse was bigger now than it had been. Like its owners, it had expanded. Stacks of plastic crates and cardboard boxes towered over concrete floors marked by old, obsolete drains. The warehouse wasn't used for meat, these days. Instead it was the hub of the Kelleys' black-market commodities ring.

Over the years, the firm had moved on from the old standbys. Now, instead of prostitution, weapons and drugs, they sold food, water, furniture, bootleg electronics – if you could buy it cheap online, the Kelleys could provide it for half that. They left the drugs and the guns to the street dealers, though Ro had heard that the firm was looking into buying surplus from the army and selling it at cost to independent contractors.

Ro had never paid much attention to any of that. She was in collection, not sales. But looking around, the sheer amount of stuff was impressive. Labourers hauled boxes and picked orders, loading trucks for afternoon deliveries. Automated dollies rolled through the stacks, carrying loads. She stopped as one skidded across her path, and Billy gave her a shove. "Keep walking, love. No time to waste."

"Touch me again, Billy, and I'll break your fucking hand."

Billy laughed. "I'd like to see you try, girl. Maybe when all of this is said and done, we'll go a few rounds." Ro shook her head, but kept walking.

The offices were in the back. And so was Mary Kelley.

There were guards of course – hard-faced men and women, standing near the door to the enclosed square of office space erected against the back wall of the warehouse. Ro recognised a few of them, but none of them met her gaze. Her unease grew. She didn't know why she was nervous. She hadn't done anything. Then, that might not matter. She'd seen it before – someone needed to get the blame, and she was handy. Her hands balled into fists as Billy knocked on the door. He glanced at her.

"Relax," he said, softly, as he opened the door. "If she wanted you done over, I'd already be looking for your replacement." He gestured, and Ro stepped past him.

The office was old fashioned. A desk, filing cabinets, a desktop computer. There were pictures on the walls, some black and white, all taken throughout the warehouse's history. The light flickered overhead as Billy shut the door behind them.

Mary Kelley sat on the edge of the desk, waiting for them.

She was an older woman, dressed stylishly in red and black, with short iron grey hair and a sour look on her face. Ro had only ever heard about her second-hand, but she had no trouble identifying the leader of Clan Kelley and the undisputed queen of the East End.

Mary Kelley had earned her crown the hard way. She'd outlived, outfought and out schemed everyone who could have been considered a rival, including members of her own family. She'd brought the firm back from the edge of irrelevance one bloody inch at a time, until they were the preeminent criminal fraternity in London. After the pound had tanked and most of the UK had switched over to cryptocurrencies, Mary had overseen the gang's switch to dark web transactions.

"Do I look upset?" Mary asked by way of greeting, as Ro came to a stop before her.

Ro hesitated. "What?"

"A simple question, sweetheart. Do I look upset to you?"

"Y-yes?" Ro replied, uneasily.

"Too bloody right I'm upset. And do you know why, girl?"

"No. No, Mrs Kelley."

Mary's eyes narrowed. "Could you take a fucking guess?"

Ro swallowed. "I– I don't..."

Mary's gaze flickered to Billy. "Billy. Help her out."

"I can only guess, mum, that your current mood is the result of several intersecting factors, so to speak."

"Don't be clever, Billy, it don't suit you," Mary said, but she smiled. The smile faded as she turned her attentions back to Ro. "Billy tells me that you and Colin were mates, yes?"

"We knew each other," Ro said.

"So you knew he was double-dipping, then," Mary said,

almost gently. "No shame, luv, just tell me up front. Before we go any further."

"No, I didn't know anything…"

Mary picked up a knife off the desk. She touched the tip with a finger. "I have always prided myself on being able to spot a liar." She pointed the knife at Ro. "Would you like to try again?"

Ro glanced at Billy, but there was no help there. The world narrowed to Mary Kelley and the tip of her knife. There were stories about that knife – about what Mary had done with it. It was said that she liked to keep her hand in, when it came to the messy end of things. Ro swallowed and said, "I figured it out. But only, like, ten minutes before he got topped."

Billy grunted.

Ro didn't look at him. "I was going to tell Billy, but–"

"But what?" Mary asked, rising to her feet. "Why the hesitation?"

"I wanted to be sure."

"That's not your job, luv." Mary leaned close and pressed the tip of her blade lightly to Ro's cheek. "That's Billy's job, and he's very good at it, so he is. Your job is to hit who we tell you to hit, and break what we tell you to break."

"I– I know. It's just…"

"Just what?" Mary glanced at Billy. "Was she sweet on this Colin, then?"

"Don't think so, mum. She's just a soft-hearted girl, our Rosemary."

Mary smiled. "People once said that about me." Her smile faded. "They were wrong, of course. My heart is like the proverbial stone of judgement, pressing down on those brought before me. Is your heart soft, Rosemary? Is it light, like a feather? Or is it weighed down by your sins?" She tapped Ro's cheek with the knife. "Don't answer, sweetheart. I can read it in your eyes. Is that why you and him went outside then?"

"He wanted to talk," Rosemary said.

"He wanted to confess all, is that it?" Mary circled her slowly, tapping her shoulders with the flat of the knife. "And what did he say?"

"He – Colin – he was doing some extra runs on the side."

"For whom?"

"He didn't say." Ro paused. "He didn't have a chance."

Mary sat back down on the desk. "So what happened then?"

"Someone shot him."

"Who?"

"I didn't see them."

"How could you not see them?"

"I– I wasn't looking. I mean, I was looking right at him. When he…" She shook her head. "When he got hit. I was looking at him when he died."

"What were you two talking about out there?"

"I'd figured out Colin was the one what Billy was after. Or, I thought he might be the one. So I was trying to find out. For Billy."

Mary's eyes flicked to Billy. "Hark at her now."

"Rosemary is a good girl, mum. Sensible. If she says she was, she was."

"Hear that? Billy is on your side. That means you must be on my side." Mary leaned forward, still playing with the knife. "You are on my side aren't you, luv?"

Ro nodded, watching the knife. Mary sat back. "Good. That makes things easier. Not for you, of course. For me." She pointed the knife at Ro. "I want you to find out what that little gobshite Colin was up to, eh? And then I want you to find out who did for him, and pay them back in kind."

Ro blinked. "What?"

"Are you deaf all of a sudden now? I want you to do what you do, only more so. And if you don't do it, and quickly, I will lose my patience and I will give you what was coming to Colin. Only worse. Now, did you get all that?"

Ro nodded. "Yeah, I got it."

Mary smiled. "That's what I like to hear. Now toddle off and get to it. Billy will see you out. Won't you, Billy?"

"My pleasure, mum." Billy caught Ro by the arm and jerked her towards the door. "Out we go, love. You've wasted enough of everybody's time."

"What am I supposed to do?" she asked, in a low hiss.

"I'd start with Colin's gaff, if I were you," Billy said. "See if he wrote anything down. Check his van too. And I'd be sharpish about it. The Filth will identify our boy soon enough, and then they'll confiscate everything and you'll be shit out of luck."

He left Ro on the street, closing the door behind him. She stared at it for a moment and then turned away with a deep exhale of breath. "Fucking hell."

9: GEARING UP

"Your boss in, my dear?"

Hannah looked up. A man stood in the doorway of her office. Older, heavyset, but dressed well. He stepped inside without waiting for an invitation. "Only I need to see her. It's about yesterday."

"Are you with the police?" Hannah asked. Her Optik gave a trill, and a slow trickle of data spilled across her display – more slowly than normal, as if the program had a glitch. The facial recognition software coughed up a name: *George Holden.*

"No need to look nervous, sweetheart. I'm with Albion, not the plods."

Hannah didn't smile. "If anything, that makes me more nervous – not less. But what can I do for you, Mr Holden?" She let a bit of annoyance creep into her voice. She was busy. The life of a political PA was on of paperwork, emails and scheduling apps. She had half a dozen tasks to complete before Sarah got back from her lunch with Winston Natha.

"Like I said, I need to see your boss." He sat down in one the chairs in front of her desk. "She's not in her office. Thought I'd check with you."

"Do I look like a secretary?" Hannah asked.

"A bit." Holden was trying for charming – and failing.

"Do you have an appointment?"

"Not as such."

"Would you like to make one?"

"I'd like to see her, is what I'd like." He wasn't smiling now. "Where is she?"

Hannah pulled out her Optik. "I can book you in for fifteen minutes tomorrow – say eleven? If you need longer than that, it'll have to be later in the week."

Holden's eyes narrowed. "I want to speak to her about the incident yesterday. Later this week might be too late."

"She's already spoken to the police."

"And I'm not the police." Holden stood and leaned over her desk, close enough that she could smell his cheap aftershave. "Your boss is on thin ice already, dear. Nigel Cass isn't one to let a politician stand in his way. So it might be better for her – and you – if you'd show some willingness to cooperate."

Hannah took a shallow breath. "As far as I am aware, Albion has no investigative remit in Tower Hamlets, or anywhere, in fact. If you would like to make an appointment, or leave a message with me, I will see that she gets it."

Holden stared at her for several moments. He no longer seemed angry. Rather he seemed worried. As if things weren't going according to plan. "Maybe I can help you," she began. He shoved himself away from the desk.

"No. I'll be back." Holden turned away and stormed out, not

quite slamming the door behind him. Hannah felt a sudden spike of anxiety. The way Holden had looked at her – it was as if he'd known something. Maybe about her. Maybe about the information she'd passed on to DedSec. Either way, she didn't like it.

She closed her eyes, and fought to control her breathing. Whatever he'd wanted, he'd gone away empty handed. That was the important thing. That was – wait. Her eyes fluttered open, as a sudden suspicion bloomed. She pulled out her Optik and scrolled through her apps. There were a handful of illicit programs installed on the device – mostly of the data gathering variety. But one or two had more practical applications, including the detection of RF signals. Activating the app, she stood and circled her desk.

Her display was filled with duelling signals. Benign frequencies were white, invasive were yellow and dangerous, red. Invasive frequencies were fairly common these days – every Optik was a passive data-harvester, transmitting information to a central network. But red frequencies were something else again – active, rather than passive.

She found the bug under the lip of the desk. It was impossibly small, barely the thickness of a thumbnail. A sliver of hardware, inserted into the grain of the wood. If she hadn't suspected, she wouldn't have even known it was there. She activated a frequency scrambler app, and stepped back. "Bagley," she murmured.

Hello Hannah Shah. Long time no speak.

"I have a bug."

Perhaps you should call your GP. Or an exterminator.

"Not that sort of bug," Hannah said. She took a picture of

the bug with her Optik. "What can you tell me about it?"

Oh my. That is a clever little thing. Very intricate.

"An Albion representative – or someone claiming to be one – planted it."

Interesting. The signal is encrypted. Downloading to a private server.

"Meaning?"

Whoever is listening, it isn't Albion. At least not officially.

"He was asking about the shooting yesterday." Hannah's mind raced. "He seemed… worried. Upset. He wanted to see Sarah."

Curious. There's a good deal of chatter on the subject of yesterday's shootings.

"Shoot*ings*? As in plural?" Hannah interjected. "Who else got shot?"

An unlucky fellow in an alley behind a pub. Similar modus operandi.

Hannah shook her head. "What's going on here?"

That is what we are trying to determine.

Hannah paused. "What do you need me to do?"

You know what they say about volunteering, Hannah.

"I was a community organizer before I was a PA, Bagley. I've always been a volunteer. Now what do you need?"

Access to Bethnal Green police station. Albion is planning a surprise visit this afternoon, during the shift change. We need to get in there first.

Hannah hesitated. "I think we can do that. I'll need to talk to Sar–"

"Talk to me about what?"

Hannah stiffened, and turned. Sarah Lincoln stood in the

doorway, looking at her curiously. "Is something wrong, Hannah? You look like you've seen a ghost."

"Worse." Hannah faced her boss. "Albion paid us a visit."

"Did they? When? Just now?"

"Yes. And they left us a present." Hannah indicated the bug. Puzzled, Sarah stooped. "What is that?"

"A listening device."

Sarah looked up at her. "And you know this how?"

"You pay me to know about these things," Hannah said, simply. To her relief, Sarah seemed to accept this without question. She grunted softly and rose to her full height.

"Nigel Cass was at lunch. Winston invited him."

Hannah frowned. "Holden didn't mention that."

"Holden? George Holden?"

"Yes, why?"

Sarah picked up Hannah's letter opener and pried the bug out of her desk. She dropped it and stepped on it. Hannah winced, slightly regretting mentioning its existence. The bug might have been of use. Now it was trashed.

"Holden's not an investigator. He's one of the men in charge of the drone base in Limehouse." Sarah looked at her. "Cass mentioned him. Did he say why he was here?"

"He said he was investigating the shooting." Hannah shook his head. "I knew his story didn't sound right. But if he's not an investigator, why would he come?" She glanced at the crushed remnants of the bug. "And why would he bother to bug the office?"

Sarah frowned. "That is a really good question. One I intend to put to him myself."

•••

"You're having a laugh, ain't ya?" Olly said. He trailed after Liz, heading for the armoury. It sat at the back of the cellar, away from anything valuable. "Us? Walking into a police station? Pull the other one." He was honest enough with himself to know he was about three minutes from a full-blown panic attack. Every experience he'd ever had with the plods told him this was a bad idea. Especially when you factored in the presence of Albion.

The thought made him queasy. Bagley had broken the news earlier – Albion was planning to pull a raid of their own, though they had official backing for theirs. They were taking over the investigation into Dempsey's death for reasons no one seemed really clear on. The Met was pissed, the local politicians were up in arms, and Albion was gloating.

"I'm dead serious," Liz said, not looking at him. "We need to get our hands on that Optik before Albion or anyone else. Don't worry. We won't be going in unarmed."

"A lack of shooters is not my main concern with this plan," Olly said, his voice rising. "In fact, I would prefer there not be any guns involved at all, yeah? All I need is in here." He shook his messenger bag as if it were a shield, rather than stitched canvas.

"Well, that's not an option."

"I think it should be," Olly insisted. "Let's put that back on the table."

Liz ignored him. Olly didn't let it go. Couldn't. "How are we even getting in there?" he continued. "What if they recognize us?"

"And how would they do that?"

"E-fits and shit."

Liz laughed. "Worried they've got you in a file somewhere? We've got ways around that, you know. Besides, we're not just strolling in. We'll have cover."

"What sort of cover?"

"The best kind – loud and distracting."

Olly threw up his hands. "Oh well, that's all right then."

"Glad you've come around. Maybe you'll stop whinging now." When they reached the entrance to the armoury, Liz placed her hand on a biometric scanner. It was an older model than the other one Olly had seen. Off the rack, probably hacked.

The door opened with a cheery ping and swung inwards at a touch from Liz's hand. The armoury was cramped, but well-lit. 3D printers and assembly benches on one side and racks on the other. The printers were all makes and models, whatever could be bought or scavenged, and some took up a lot more space than others.

"I really don't like guns," Olly said, looking over the rows of weapons. No two were alike, though there were similarities between them. Guns weren't the only things the printers were used for, of course. The pieces for custom-made drones and spiderbots sat awaiting assembly. There were even casings for explosive devices, like propaganda bombs. Olly picked one up. It was a simple thing, like a Christmas cracker, but louder and full of DedSec propaganda instead of sweets and a paper hat.

"Active resistance sometimes calls for more than chucking rocks or torching parked cars." Liz lifted a weapon and checked the power pack. She set it back down on the rack. "Besides, most of these are non-lethal."

"You carry a real one," Olly said.

"Pensioner's privilege. And if it shoots, it's real." Liz lightly slapped him on the cheek, and then pointed at him for emphasis. "Remember that too."

"I'll remember."

"Because I don't want you shooting me in the back by accident."

"I'll remember!"

"Good. You ever used a firearm?"

"Yeah, 'course."

"A real one. I mean. Not in a game."

Olly hesitated. Liz sighed. "Maybe we should hold off on this."

Olly thought about arguing, but didn't. He had an image in his head of stuffing a piece down his waistband and it getting tangled as he tried to pull it. "Yeah, maybe so."

"How about a stun gun?" She picked up a black unit and gave it a flick. A spark of blue leapt between the prongs, and Olly grinned.

"That's more my speed."

"Good enough." She tossed it and he caught it awkwardly. "Only use it when you have to. We're not going in hot, if we can help it." Olly tentatively activated the stun gun and then stuffed it into his messenger bag.

"So how are we breaking in anyway?"

"We're not breaking in, we're walking in."

"Say again?" Olly looked at her. "They're not going to let us do that."

"They will if they think we're press," Liz said.

"Why would they think that?"

"Because someone's going to meet us with press badges at Victoria Park. Hannah Shah. You've met before, I think."

"She's Krish's government contact, isn't she," Olly said, as he recalled the meeting on Brick Lane. "She's one of us, then. Not like Dempsey."

Liz paused. "No," she said, after a moment. "Not like Dempsey." She looked at him. "Sarah Lincoln, the MP for Tower Hamlets South, is planning on crashing Albion's arrival. There'll be a lot of press, a lot of confusion – that'll give us the distraction we need to get in and out, right under Albion's nose."

"But even with badges, they're not going to just let us wander around..."

"They will if they can't see us."

"You what?"

Liz grinned. "Has Krish not explained that to you yet?"

"Explained what?" Olly demanded, getting impatient.

"You know how your implant works, yeah?" she asked, tapping the implant just in front of his ear. Everyone who had an Optik had one. The Optik's main processor was contained in a miniscule device which was attached to the implant by way of a neodymium magnet. The implantation procedure was non-invasive – about like getting a piercing.

"Yeah, course, it sends data directly to the optical nerve or something, right?"

"Right. So, that means if we hack this–" She tapped her own implant. "–then we hack these too." She indicated her eyes. "Following me?"

Olly frowned. "Yeah, like my camouflage app, only... bigger. You can do this?"

"We can do this. DedSec."

"Why didn't I know about it?"

Because you didn't need to, Olly, Bagley broke in. Less weight to break the thin ice, so to speak. Can't go sharing all our secrets with every Tom, Dick and Harry...

"Shut up," Liz said. "Tell me something useful. How many Optiks in the station?"

Which is it? Shut up, or something useful?

"Bagley..." Liz began, in warning.

Fifteen.

"And how many people?"

The same.

She looked at Olly. "There we go. Everyone in there has an Optik, running on the same software. We'll be the next best thing to invisible. Just keep your hands to yourself, don't bump into anyone and don't attract any undue attention and we'll be fine."

"So if we can do this, why do we need press badges?"

"First rule of DedSec – always have a backup plan. The passes are ours. If we get caught, we have an explanation that most plods will buy without thinking about it too hard. Just another pair of nosy journalists." She poked him in the chest. "But we're not going to get caught, are we?"

"Wasn't on my schedule," Olly said.

"Good to know." Liz paused again. She looked at him. "You haven't asked why yet."

"Why what?"

"Why I volunteered you to help me."

Olly shrugged. "I assumed it was just some arbitrary bullshit, you know?"

"A bit, but mostly I'm trying to educate you." She poked him in the side of the head. "You have a lot of potential, Olly. I'd hate to see you waste it on being stupid."

Olly stepped back, annoyed. "I'm not stupid. What I am, is worried. What if we get caught? What then?"

"We won't."

"But what if? Do we have a backup plan for our backup plan?"

Liz smiled. "Yes. That's rule number two."

"Which is?"

"We improvise like fuck and hope for the best."

10: COYLE

Art Coyle sat facing the window, looking out over London. It was beautiful in the afternoon light. Jagged mountains of steel and glass, overlooking canyons of brick and rivers of pavement. The city was a country unto itself. Looking at it from this height, it almost made him proud to be British. Then, inevitably, he would remember where he was and the pride would fade, replaced by amused melancholy.

He occupied the uppermost floor of the Pinnacle, one of the tallest and most recognisable buildings in London, known popularly as the most civilised skyscraper in the capital. The structure was well known, mostly for its curious shape. Though that shape had made it a recognisable landmark, it had not saved it from the financial crash.

Once, the structure had housed numerous businesses: offices, restaurants, investment and trading firms, even a television studio. Now it housed only a few diehard tenants, including a newsagents and a high end patisserie, which was closed four days out of the week. The previous owner of the building had sold it not long after the Redundancy Riots, and the current owner was a private equity firm.

Coyle had rented the uppermost floor through one of several shell corporations in which he was the majority – and only – stakeholder, claiming the need for offices closer to the financial heart of London. The circular space was largely empty, save for a few dozen barren cubicles, a conference room, a working gender-neutral lavatory and windows that provided a stunning panoramic view.

All in all, well worth a not insignificant amount of money. Someone else's money, at least. For Coyle, it was perfect. He preferred to be high up, when possible. People rarely thought to look up. Especially these days, when the air was full of drones, whizzing and whirring in all directions.

His nest, as he thought of it, was adequate for his needs. It was rather like camping out, and there was enough abandoned furniture on this floor to give him some semblance of comfort. So long as no one stumbled onto his hideaway by accident, there would be no sign that he had ever been there at all.

His operational centre was situated in front of one of the windows, with three walls of a cubicle repurposed in a sort of hunter's blind, blocking off sight of him from the stairwell entrance and the lifts. More cubical walls had been situated to form an improvised kill-box, stretching from the lifts to where he currently sat. Loose cans, plastic bags, bubble wrap and papers had been scattered across the floor, to act as an early warning system. He'd also planted motion sensors and cameras in both lift shafts and the stairwell.

Some might call such contingencies paranoid. For Coyle, it was simply business as usual. The key to success was preparation and patience. The old adage of *hurry up and wait* had served him well in his career to date.

Coyle had been a killer for more than thirty years. He did not care for the term assassin, finding it somewhat too political for his tastes, and detested the Hollywood parlance of "mechanic" and "operator" for similar reasons. He thought such self-aggrandizing terminology lent an undeserved glamour to what was, in the end, a mucky business, often conducted by weathered men in grimy macs and threadbare trainers.

Coyle was simply a killer, a murderer for hire, and content in the simplicity of that description. He killed for money. Ergo, a killer. He was not ashamed of this, though he claimed to be an independent claims adjuster for tax and legal purposes. Given how many of his victims – and they were victims, no bones there – died because someone wanted to claim on their insurance, he thought it appropriate, if perhaps a touch morbid.

After a final look out the window, he sat back and brought up his Optik display. "How are you feeling today, my friend?" he murmured, glancing over to where his partner sat, recharging after last night's successful outing.

The drone resembled nothing so much a rather small stealth aircraft. It was powered by a trio of extremely powerful micro-motors and possessed an astonishing array of anti-tilt and airflow sensors like all counterterror – or CT – units.

Its heavy-duty chassis was armoured, and equipped with a modified M107 semi-automatic sniper system. The .50 calibre anti-material weapon was out of date by a few years, but still eminently useful, nor was it the only one the drone possessed.

Besides its panoply of sensors and its weaponry, it could interface with most operating systems, allowing the operator a variety of tactical and strategic options.

The drone had been upgraded for use in clandestine combat operations, or so the seller had claimed. It was a prototype – the only one of its kind so far. Coyle hoped it would remain so. In his opinion, it was far too lethal a device to allow in the hands of private military contractor like Albion – God alone knew what a prat like Nigel Cass would do with such a weapon. But it was perfect for Coyle's needs.

The man who'd sold it to him hadn't been aware of why he needed it, thinking him just another private collector. He'd been more concerned about the money Coyle was paying him. Given his debts, that wasn't surprising.

After a quick systems check, Coyle dismissed the drone's display. Everything was functioning well within established operational parameters. Given how much he'd paid for it, he was somewhat relieved. Money well spent, and at his age, anything that made his job easier was to be embraced. His knees weren't what they used to be.

Never one to remain idle, he turned his attentions to a partially disassembled spiderbot that lay on a tray on the floor. He set the tray on the low table before him with a grunt. The spiderbot was listed as a Blume brand product, but Coyle knew that it had been developed by an American corporation, Tidis. Tidis hardware married to a Blume operating system.

The unit – with its six segmented limbs and armature array – was designed for small tasks in harsh environments. He'd purchased several dozen of the devices, using one of his aliases and a shell company – an industrial cleaning firm, based in Sheffield. Spiderbots were durable, replaceable and easily hackable. Perfect for his needs. They had autonomous operating systems, using a standard cTOS template. They could interface with anything using the operating system, and required little maintenance.

He'd cracked this one open, and was in the process of testing a new – and highly illicit – upgrade. An improvised firearm – a zip gun, as Americans called them. Though, he hoped, not so crude as all that. Consisting of a 3D printed barrel, breechblock and firing mechanism, it needed to rest easily inside the spiderbot chassis while remaining concealed.

He'd tested several prototypes, making adjustments as he went. Initially, he'd considered just giving the spiderbot a stripped down .22, and seeing how things went. But that struck Coyle as sloppy and one thing he was not, was sloppy.

A person in his line of work couldn't afford sloppiness. Sloppiness led to mistakes and mistakes led to death or worse – incarceration, interrogation and eventually a shiv in your guts in the exercise yard. None of which Coyle found appealing. He liked his freedom. He liked his music and his books and his one glass of wine a day, after dinner.

He paused, frowning now. There was always an element of random chance at play with any hit. You couldn't control for every variable, no matter how meticulous your preparations. You had to learn how to adapt to an evolving situation and roll with the punches. The death of the wrong man at Lister House had been one of these unforeseen variables – not a mistake, as such, but a complication nonetheless. One that would need to be remedied. He checked the GPS signal for the target's Optik, but it was still deactivated.

It was likely in police custody. Another complication, but not insurmountable. He intended to wait until he heard from his employer, however, before he made any attempt to recover it himself. Killing police officers was something he tried to avoid, when possible. Not out of any respect for the authorities, but out of simple pragmatism. Dead policemen tended to complicate matters.

His Optik chimed. A call. He looked at the ID and smiled. His daughter. Answering, he said, "Hello, sweetheart. How was practice?" The conversation that followed was enthusiastic and welcome – a bright spot in an otherwise grey day. A bit of joy before the bollocking sure to come when he talked to his employer.

He chatted to his wife for a few minutes as well, trading affectionate inanities and inquiring as to how things were at home. His family thought he was out on a job – which he was, though not the job they imagined. He missed them terribly, of course. Every moment away was a precious moment missed, as his mother had often remarked.

Still, he had a job to do – and it wasn't finished yet. And might not be, for several days, despite the narrow timetable his employer had given him. They would not be happy about this. His display pinged with an alert, even as his wife hung up.

"Speak of the Devil," he murmured. Time to make the call. He did so at the same time every forty-eight hours, as per the standard contract. He moved the spiderbot aside and reached down for another tray. This one held an assemblage of Optik external devices, mostly stolen, some purchased. Each was linked to the others by a network of cables and wiring.

He was still coming to grips with the new tech. He felt like a man out of time, in more ways than one. But he was learning. Even in privacy mode Optiks collected baseline metadata, recording everything including your location. They were flares, lighting up the darkness of the information superhighway. If your Optik was on, if your implant was in place and functional, it was transmitting information. But there were ways around that, if you had the wherewithal.

The first was to have a black market implant, rather than the standard model. Something not registered in any database – or registered to someone else. Coyle's implant had been taken from a dead man. It transmitted ghost-data, created by a sophisticated bot-program, thus forming a false profile. What he ate, where he went, his favourite films, all of it a smokescreen. Randomised, but pattern consistent.

The second method was to create a crude refractive array. You couldn't cut the flow of data, not without alerting someone, but you could control it – dilute it. It was like diverting a river. Optiks were programmed to synch with every other Optik in range. With the right program, you could send out a flood of misinformation, drowning the signal. And the more Optiks that were synched, the faster it worked.

Each Optik was comprised of two parts – the implant and the external device. On their own, the external devices were basically fancy paperweights. But if you managed to steal one, you could skim-clone the user's browsing data – including any saved passwords and the like. You could also use them to create falsified online identities. The identities wouldn't stand up to human scrutiny, but they could easily pass most bot-detection algorithms.

Using the external devices, the falsified identities and a

signal-splitter app he'd procured on the dark web, he could create a primitive overlay network, allowing him to feed false data from every direction, obscuring his location in a flood of fake news, flame wars and denial-of-service blitz-attacks. In this age of constant noise, he'd found that the best place to hide was amidst the cacophony.

It had all been so simple once upon a time. Burner phones had been cheap and plentiful. But these days, having a phone would be considered suspicious. He set his Optik down near the array, and let it synch to the others, as it was programmed to do.

As it did so, his display broke into multiple windows. It had taken some time to get used to using multiple displays. Thankfully, the flow of information was minimal – mostly GPS data. It still gave him a migraine if he used it for longer than a few minutes.

Once the synching was complete, he lifted the Optik on the far end of the array and made the call. There was only one number programmed into it – encrypted, of course. He never used his own Optik, if he could help it. The GPS for the other external units was programmed to transmit random locations, scattered throughout the city. The call was answered immediately.

"Yes." The voice was not that of a person – or rather it was like that of several persons, each digitally layered over the next, as if it were an unsettling choir speaking, rather than an individual. Coyle was not impressed. There were apps for everything nowadays.

The image on his display was slightly more impressive than the voice. It was... nothing. A face that was as much an *absence* as anything. A crackling, distorted hole in the digital world. If Coyle had been anyone else, he might have found it disturbing.

They called themselves "Zero Day". There was some meaning to the alias, but they had not deigned to share it, and Coyle was not inclined to inquire about such matters, regarding it as outside his purview. What they called themselves made little difference to him, so long as they paid him in full, and in a timely fashion.

"It's me," he said. Something that might have been a smile crossed the void.

"We know. No one else has this number." As ever, he thought he detected the slightest hint of a sneer in his employer's attitude. He was used to that. It took a certain egotism to contract a killer. Often, his employers thought themselves his superiors – as if he were nothing more than a plumber.

"The secondary target has been taken care of."

"And the primary?"

A loaded question. Coyle grunted. "You saw the news?"

"Yes. You failed."

"Failure is a matter of perspective," Coyle said, calmly. Getting angry at the client rarely helped. "I prefer to say that I have not yet succeeded."

"We were under the impression you only needed one shot."

Coyle allowed himself a laugh. "Hyperbole. I need as many shots as are required. One is the preferred number, obviously, but sometimes people don't die when you want them to. So you have to keep trying until it gets done."

Zero Day was silent, save for the crackle of the frequency. Then, "We needed this accomplished yesterday. The schedule–"

"Schedules change," Coyle said. He still hadn't been able to trace their true identity, or identities, if that was what the story was. He wasn't certain as to anything about them: gender, race, creed – all mysteries. Coyle normally made it a point to know absolutely every last thing there was to know about an employer. All such information went into safety deposit boxes, scattered across a variety of banks in several countries. Though he wasn't actually a claims adjuster, he still believed in having insurance.

Another pause. Coyle wondered how many people were actually on the other end of this conversation. Were they using the royal we, or was it a consortium? He had been hired by groups before, though he preferred working for individuals. The more people who were involved, the more risk there was for him.

"Not if they are followed correctly."

Coyle sighed. "I could not account for a pickpocket. By the time a target lock had been acquired, this man Dempsey was already in possession of the Optik. One cannot recall a bullet, once the trigger has been pulled."

"Dempsey is irrelevant. Marcus Tell is not. He must be eliminated." Tell was the primary target. The one he'd been trying to kill that afternoon. He didn't know why a pensioner living in East London needed to die, but neither did he plan on asking. The whys and wherefores were extraneous to his operational paradigm.

"He will be," he said.

"And how will you find him?"

"That is my concern," Coyle said, bristling slightly. "Yours should be the Optik. Until Tell is dead, that device may well reveal whatever it is you don't want people to know. If I were you, I might be inclined to retrieve it from the police." He paused. "Unless... you wish me to do it?"

Silence. Then, a soft, static-edged laugh. "And how much will it cost?"

Coyle said a number. No laugh this time. Zero Day did not find the subject of money amusing – another odd fact to add to the pile. "You ask a lot," they said, finally. "Given that it was your error that allowed the Optik to fall into police hands in the first place."

"Again, not an error. An unforeseen eventuality, easily rectified."

"Tell me your plan."

"For the device, or for Tell?"

"Both."

Coyle considered refusing. The conversation had already gone on far too long for his liking. But he was annoyed. Whoever was under that digital mask was, as his daughter might say, a right twat. "The device will eventually be reactivated. Once the signal returns, my little friend will track it down as before and – pop goes the weasel. The device and whoever is holding it will no longer be an issue."

"What if it is reactivated inside the police station?"

"Then I will use other methods. But I have no doubt they will bring it out – they'll want to find the owner, after all, and that will require activating the external unit and using a reverse GPS search. The moment that happens... well. No more problem."

"And Tell?"

"Locating Tell will be a matter of extrapolation. The

metadata you've provided will enable me to pinpoint him the old fashioned way – the only tools I require for that will be a map and a pencil. If Tell acquires a new external unit, we'll go for a redo. If he doesn't, I'll find out where he resides and make a special delivery." He patted the spiderbot fondly. "Again, it will be no problem."

Zero Day made a sound that might have been a sigh, or a laugh. "Very well. But the schedule stands. You have just over seventy-two hours remaining, Mr Coyle."

He froze. "What did you say?"

"We're sorry. Isn't that your current identity? Arthur Edward Coyle, Art to his friends. Husband of Amelia Coyle, father of Frances Emily Coyle. Resident of–"

"Enough," Coyle said, sharply.

"You tried your best, Art – may we call you Art?" Without waiting for a reply, Zero Day went on, "But you're like a Neanderthal compared to us. Your little tricks were an amusing diversion, nothing more. But now you know, we can get to you – or those you care about –any time we choose."

Coyle was silent for a moment, mind racing. Rolling with the punch. "If your reach is so great, why even involve me?"

"That is our concern. Yours is to complete your assignment. Seventy-two hours, Art. You don't want to know what happens after that."

One by one, his slaved Optiks started to smoulder and smoke. Fat sparks danced along their screens, and he flinched as the connected displays winked out one after the next. He stood, knocking his chair over, went to open an air vent to clear the smoke.

Seventy-two hours? He thought about calling his wife and

daughter again. Decided against it. He looked back the Optik externals. Some of them were salvageable. And there were other apps he possessed. Ones that could be used to trace signals of all sorts, including encrypted ones.

"Seventy-two hours." He glanced at the drone and smiled at last. "Plenty of time."

DAY THREE

TUESDAY

Bagley-bytes 13667-0: Lots of chatter around Bethnal Green Police Station today. By the way, that's probably the first time anyone has used those words in that order in this century. The station will be playing host to all sorts this AM, including our favourite MP, Sarah Lincoln, and our least favourite jackbooted stormtrooper, Sergeant Richard Faulkner, Albion's man in East London. Needless to say, everyone should be on alert — or our beloved Redqueen will have your guts for garters.

+++

We're monitoring more than 250,000 CCTV public surveillance cameras in London and spotting a fair few familiar faces, to which I say — shame on you. Especially you, Terry. Every camera in the city feeds through a cTOS facial scan platform, giving the authorities, the corporations and certain others the ability to trach your every move. So remember your masks, please.

+++

Speaking of cTOS, preparations for the TOAN Conference are underway near Blackfriars Bridge. DedSec needs eyes on the ground. If you're in the area, talk to Wendell.

+++

RE: vlogs and written manifestos. Sabine requests that you please stop posting your fanfiction on operational chat-apps. Except yours, Linda la Potter. We're all dying to know what happens next.

+++

Finally, Albion operatives have been spotted sniffing around the Leake Street field base, creeping out the local street artists. They're likely trying out some new facial recognition software. As I said — remember your masks.

11: BETHNAL GREEN

On a bench in Bethnal Green Garden, Hannah nervously tapped at her Optik as she waited. Bagley had given her a location and a time, but nothing else. Sarah was due at the police station at any moment. She wanted to make her entrance before Faulkner and his bully-boys arrived, no doubt followed by every news drone in the borough. Winston Natha was due to visit later, in a show of solidarity, but it wasn't his constituency. Arranging it all took time and patience, things Hannah had little of at the moment.

She felt somewhat guilty about the whole thing. When she'd made the suggestion to visit the station, Sarah had jumped at it without needing to be convinced. Hannah knew she was still smarting from her meeting with Nigel Cass, and angry about Holden's attempt to bug the office. It wasn't manipulation, exactly – Sarah was too smart for that – but it still made her uneasy. It could all blow up in their faces if they weren't careful. Not just hers and Sarah's, but DedSec's as well.

Then, maybe it was only a matter of time. DedSec

was changing and Hannah wasn't sure she liked what it was becoming. Pacifist activism, like propaganda bombs and jamming television signals was giving way to a more revolutionary philosophy. The Resistance wasn't just a catchy name anymore. It was a mantra. An ethos.

She looked up, and saw news drones gathering – GBB, ITV, EBN, the whole alphabet. Ready to zip down and follow the drama as it unfolded, delivering it in state-approved bite-sized chunks to the people at home, sitting placidly in front of their telly.

Maybe that was why DedSec was changing. As things got worse, the populace became resigned, and resignation soon turned to complacency. How do you fight a system that controls every aspect of your life? The short answer was – you didn't. Not unless you could imagine a different sort of life. A better life. Most people couldn't afford to let themselves think past the next pay-slip.

There was no easy answer. Hannah knew that all too well. Her own life had been one hard decision after the next. Agreeing to work for Sarah had been one such. The only way to change the machine was from inside. Sarah claimed to believe the same herself. And maybe she did … in her own way.

Her thoughts turned to Albion, and Holden's visit. She hadn't been able to dig up much on him that they didn't already know. He was middle management – a technician by training, with an interest in drone technology. By rights, he should have been in a lab somewhere, and not roaming around threatening people.

With Bagley's assistance, she'd managed to turn up a few older CCTV images of him going in and out of pubs and betting shops. More so the latter than former. Holden seemed to have a gambling problem, which was interesting. She wasn't sure what it meant, but it was interesting.

Her Optik chimed, and she pushed the thought aside for later. It was synching with two others, as their owners approached. Another DedSec outlaw app, allowing members of the Resistance to identify each other. She turned. One was Soames, the courier from the previous day. The other—

"Where's Krish?" she asked, as Soames and the woman approached. On her display, the woman's face was scrambled, off-centre, as if there was a glitch in the program, centred right on her features. It was only as she dismissed the display that she could see her clearly. She didn't recognize her, and her facial recognition app wasn't bringing anything up. Whoever she was, she was a blank slate. "And who are you?"

"Call me Liz," the older woman said.

Hannah studied her for a moment, and then nodded. In a way, she was glad. She'd known Krish a long time, before DedSec even, and she doubted he could manage something like this. Krish wasn't criminally inclined. Her eyes flicked to Soames. Olly, she recalled. Liz and Olly. "I don't want to know why you need to get inside. I just want your promise it's not going to come back on us."

"Worried about your career?" Liz asked.

"My life. Albion is sniffing around Sarah, and me."

Liz raised an eyebrow. "You think they know about your connection to us?"

Hannah looked away. "I don't know what to think. I know I don't like it. Something is going on, something big."

"The sooner we find out what, the better for everyone," Liz

said. "Especially you and your boss. Speaking of which, where is she?"

"Waiting for the right moment." Hannah reached into her pocket and produced a set of plastic badges. "We've alerted the major media outlets, as well a number of local news-sites – a few bloggers, one or two podcasters. That should make for plenty of signal noise. These are press passes. Keep them close, ditch them when you're done." She handed them over. "I've told Sarah you're from one of the digital dailies, looking to write a piece on Albion's prospects in Tower Hamlets. She agreed to let you follow us, so you're covered as far as getting in. After that, it's up to you."

"No worries," Liz said. "Thank you."

"Thank me by not getting caught." Hannah looked at Olly. "Or getting me shot."

"That wasn't my fault," Olly protested. Liz silenced him with a look.

"We'll do our best," she said.

Hannah sighed. "Come on. The police station is just the other side of the garden."

Sarah was directing traffic when Hannah finally arrived, two journalists in tow. Sarah gave them a cursory glance. "A bit scruffy," she murmured to her PA. Drones hovered around the area, and flesh and blood press as well. Stage managing it all took a bit of doing – she wanted them to get shots of her entering the station ahead of Albion, and mingling with the hardworking constables like a true woman of the people.

"Independent journalists," Hannah said, not looking at her. "I think they're cultivating a look. Makes them more trustworthy, in the eyes of the public."

"Well, no one ever accused the public of being smart." Sarah looked them over again. The young man looked vaguely familiar, though she couldn't place him off hand. Maybe he'd covered one of her speeches. The woman was older, and had a look that Sarah had previously associated with embedded war correspondents. Satisfied with what she saw, she dismissed them into the background. "We'll do it inside. The drones won't be able to come in, but the reporters will."

Hannah hesitated, but only for a moment. "Are you certain you want to do it this way?" she asked, softly. "We *could* arrange a more regular press conference…"

"The best defence is a good offence," Sarah said, smiling at the drones. "Albion wants a spectacle? Well, I'll give them one. And I'll keep doing it until Cass swallows his pride and gives me what I want – a tour of their facilities in Limehouse."

"And after that?"

"It depends on what we find." Sarah paused. "Anything more on our visitor, Holden?"

Hannah consulted her Optik. "Not much. He's one of the lead techs for the Limehouse facility. Research and development, whatever that means."

"I already knew that." Sarah had done her own research on the Limehouse Basin drone facility. It had been pitched as an economic net gain for the borough, but so far the predicted funds hadn't appeared. The facility was almost entirely automated, save for a skeleton staff. One of whom was Holden. "What I want to know is why he tried to plant a bug in my office." She looked at Hannah. "Find that out, and I'll give you a raise."

"Working on it."

Something in her voice made Sarah pause. After a moment, she said, "Are you certain you're alright? I know these past two days have been… eventful. If you want to take the rest of the afternoon off…"

"No. I'm fine. Thank you."

Sarah looked at her for a moment longer, then nodded. "Good." She turned, smiling, so that a drone could get a shot of her standing beneath the station's blue lamp. "Then let's not beat about the bush. Faulkner will be here any minute."

Inside, it was clear the station house had seen better days. Like much of Tower Hamlets, it was undergoing refurbishment and had been for several years. Clear plastic dust covers hung from abandoned scaffolding or stretched across doorways. Everything smelled of dust, bleach and damp. Sarah chose to make her stand near the front desk, where everyone would have a good view of the confrontation.

PC Moira Jenks was on hand to greet her, one of a handful of uniformed officers in the building. Sarah smiled. "I take it the Chief Inspector is out to lunch?"

"The Guv was unavoidably detained, ma'am," Jenks said. "She sends her apologies."

"And Detective Sergeant Miller?"

"Out sick," Jenks said, briskly. "Stomach bug. Got most of the CID unit too. Strangest thing."

Sarah noticed several of the nearby constables trading meaningful looks as Jenks spoke. She shook her head, disappointed, but not surprised. "Left you holding the bag, eh?"

"It'll be a privilege, ma'am."

Sarah laughed. "You say that now." She paused. "I saw that you had a bit of confrontation with our friend Faulkner yourself. Are you sure you want to bring yourself to his attention again?"

"I doubt he'll remember me," Jenks said, with a shrug.

"I wouldn't put money on it. Faulkner is quite the one for holding grudges." Sarah took a breath, looked at Jenks consideringly, and said, "You know this is a publicity stunt, right? One way or another, he will leave here with that evidence. I have no way of stopping him. He can't get at me, but if Albion's contract is extended, it's very likely you'll be reporting to him in the future."

Jenks paled slightly, but shook her head. "I doubt I'll stay on if that happens, ma'am." She looked at Sarah. "Is their contract really going to be extended?"

"Not if I can help it," Sarah said, smoothly. Hannah gave her a sharp look, but thankfully kept her mouth shut. It wasn't a lie, as such. Currently, she had no intention of letting Albion cement their foothold in the city. But things changed. As Darwin had discovered, adaption was the key to survival, and Sarah intended to survive whatever politics threw at her.

She looked at Jenks. "I don't suppose I could get a cuppa while we wait?"

Jenks smiled. "I think that can be arranged."

But before she could go anywhere, the sounded of booted feet tramping on lino reached their ears. "On second thought, cancel the cuppa," Sarah said, putting on her best smile. "The guests of honour have arrived."

Faulkner entered with all the bellicose militancy she'd come to expect. He slammed the doors wide, a smile on his face.

He wasn't wearing a helmet, but was ready for war otherwise. His men were similarly kitted out. As if they'd expected a fight – or were hoping for one. "Hello officers, we're here to pick up some evidence," Faulkner said, loudly. "I hope you have it ready for us..." He trailed off as he caught sight of Sarah and the coterie of reporters and police constables. "Ah."

"Hello again," Sarah said.

"And why are you here, minister?" Faulkner asked, bluntly. "I don't see how this involves you at all." He glanced at the reporters, but his expression didn't change. He'd obviously expected there to be a few hanging about.

Sarah smiled with as much geniality as she could muster. "I am here to look after the best interests of my borough, Mr Faulkner."

"Sergeant," Faulkner corrected icily.

"Of course, forgive me. I have a hard time remembering such things. Sergeant Faulkner – I'm told there was a bit of a set-to yesterday. Care to explain?"

"To you? No. I answer to my superiors, not civilian authority."

Sarah's smile didn't waver. "I suppose I'll just have to ask Nigel Cass next time I see him. I think we're becoming great friends, he and I."

Faulkner hesitated, weighing the implications. "We're here to collect evidence in an ongoing investigation," he said, finally. Before she could interject, he added, "An internal investigation, I should say. One we are conducting in the interests of continuing our working relationship with the UK government."

"And what does that have to do with a shooting in Whitechapel?"

"I'm not at liberty to say." He turned to Jenks. "The evidence?"

"Still in the property room," Jenks said, not quite politely.

Faulkner tilted his head. "I was assured by your Chief Inspector that you'd be providing us with all due assistance, PC Jenks."

"He hasn't been in today," Jenks said.

Faulkner snorted. "Of course not." He looked at Sarah. "Politicians all. That's why you need us, you know – the Met is full of politicians, more worried about budgets than policing. That's why this borough, why this city, is in the shape it's in now... wouldn't you agree?" He'd pitched his voice so that it could be heard by everyone.

Sarah frowned – a calculated look of disapproval. "I wouldn't, actually. In fact, I think the last thing Tower Hamlets needs is a paramilitary force with zero accountability roaming the streets. And I intend to say as much."

Faulkner nodded. "Say what you like. I just follow orders. Speaking of which... Tyerman, McCoy, go to the property room." He glanced at Jenks. "No need to show them where it's at."

"They'll need a code," Jenks began.

"Got it already," Faulkner said, an unpleasant smile on his face. Sarah wasn't surprised, but she was somewhat offended on the Met's behalf.

Faulkner looked around. "We might keep this place on, afterwards. Have to give it a good cleaning first."

"Counting your chickens a little early, aren't you?" Sarah said.

Faulkner laughed. "I like to plan ahead." He fixed her with a steady look. "You can leave now, if you like. I'm sure you have other places to be."

"I intend to stand here until you leave, Sergeant. Just to make sure you don't accidentally overstep the limits of your authority, as you did yesterday."

Faulkner grimaced, but didn't reply. Instead he turned away, obviously intent on ignoring her. Sarah gave him a few moments and then sidled over. She leaned close, so that they wouldn't be overheard. "A man named Holden came to my offices today. You wouldn't know anything about that, would you?"

Faulkner hesitated. Just for an instant. If she hadn't been looking at him, she might not have even noticed. "No. Did he say what he wanted?"

"To talk to me. Claimed he was investigating the shooting." She watched Faulkner's face, but could read nothing in his expression. "Which is odd, because the only Holden I know who works for Albion is in your R&D division. Specifically, he works in the drone factory in Limehouse. The one I've made numerous requests to visit." Faulkner blinked. Sarah nodded. "You're not the only one who knows things, Sergeant."

"Duly noted," Faulkner murmured. "I don't know anything about that. But I'll find out for you, if you like."

"And what would you expect in return?"

"We can discuss that later. Perhaps over lunch? Albion's treat, of course."

"Why don't we discuss it during a tour of the factory?"

Faulkner glanced at her. "You don't give up, do you?"

"Not until I get what I want, Sergeant." Sarah smiled. "And I want answers."

12: THE PROPERTY ROOM

Olly watched as Lincoln and Faulkner faced off. The tension in the air was palpable, and both the plods and the Albion goons looked nervous. The reporters just looked excited. Liz tugged on his sleeve. "Come on," she murmured. "Now's our chance."

As she spoke, Olly's display flickered. He realized that she'd activated her camouflage program, and he hastily followed her example. When he was done, he looked down at himself, but things didn't seem different. Not that they would've.

How did the Invisible Man see himself? A question for the ages.

"Ta, Bagley," Olly muttered. "Anything useful to contribute?"

Yes. You are only invisible to someone looking at you through a display. If they use their eyes, infrared or anything else, they will spot you right off. I would move quickly, if I were you. Bagley sounded almost amused.

Olly shook his head and glanced back towards the confrontation. Lincoln and Faulkner were trading words – not especially heated ones, but certainly not friendly. "I almost want to stay and see which of them wins," he said as he hurried after Liz.

"Any other time I'd say feel free, but we've got more important things to do."

"Are you sure you know where you're going?"

"Bagley scrounged up the floor plans for this place. Unless they changed something in the last six months, we're fine." She led him quickly through the police station, away from the office spaces and into the back.

Olly felt his nerves twist and tighten the further they went. He'd enjoyed the Met's hospitality more than once, usually after a night on the tiles. Being here brought back memories and anxieties he'd done his best to move past in the months since he'd joined DedSec. "What if we can't find it?"

Liz didn't reply. Olly fell silent. The station house looked larger from the outside than it was. They moved past the interview rooms, the custody suite and finally down the stairs and along a corridor. They stopped in front of a heavy door, with a mesh viewing slot and a touchpad digital lock.

"Can you get it open?" Olly asked. Liz looked at him.

"Sure. The question is – can you?"

"What?"

Liz stepped back. "Consider this a surprise test, Olly. Get the door open, and without setting off the alarm. I'll keep watch. You've got two minutes."

Olly stared at her. "You can't be serious…"

"One minute, fifty-seven seconds," Liz said, not looking at him. Olly swallowed and turned back to the door. He took out his Optik, and activated a subroutine on his display. A moment later, a disguised toolkit unrolled across his display – apps for every occasion. The lock was an older model, requiring a digital PIN code to unlock. There might be just one, or several. No way to tell. Input the wrong one too many times, and it would perma-lock the mechanism until someone input the master reset code. Or worse, it would activate an alarm.

He activated a schematic app, trying to find the right one in his saved files. If he had it. If it wasn't too old. "How's it coming?" Liz asked.

"Got a knife?"

"Will a multi-tool do?"

"Long as there's a blade." Olly took it and slipped the knife out. Carefully, he extracted the touchscreen module, exposing the connector. He took a capture of it, and compared it to the schematics. He handed her back the multi-tool. "Right, I've got to brute force it. That means I need to–"

"I know what it means, Olly. Can you do it?"

"I need more time."

"Minute ten," Liz said.

"It's not going to be enough," Olly hissed.

Liz sighed. "I could bust this lock in ten seconds with a bricked 5G handset and a bit of a sing-song if I wanted. If you can't do the same, what good are you?"

Olly wanted to glare at her, but refrained. He focused on the lock. Once upon a time, a hacker would have needed something to attach to the connector, which didn't care what it was attached to. These days, you could just connect the lock to an Optik, via a modified power adaptor. Luckily, he had one on him.

With a home-made predictor app, Olly could check

around five hundred possible code combinations per minute. Another app sent a signal to the lock every fifteen seconds, resetting the failed attempt counter. A third redirected the alarm to his own display. Even so, he was still running out of time.

"Under a minute left," Liz said. "Better hurry."

"You're not helping," Olly snarled.

Liz chuckled softly. Olly bit back a curse. A moment later, his Optik gave a flash and there was an audible click as the door opened. Olly scrambled to his feet in relief. "Done."

"Two minutes, ten seconds. Not bad."

Olly detached his Optik, and replaced the module. "You know, normally it takes around ten minutes to pick a lock." He pulled the door open. "A bit better than not bad."

"Used to take thirty," Liz said, stepping past him into the property room. "We had to take pictures, go away and build our own circuit board and counter, and then figure out a way to reboot the system so the alarm didn't go off. Even then, it might still take an hour, depending on how fast you could crunch the possible code combinations."

"If you knew that why did you give me two minutes?" Olly demanded.

"Like I said, it was a test. You passed. Good on you, mate. Now get in here and close the door before somebody sees you."

Olly closed the door as quietly as possible. He froze when he spotted the security cameras. Liz noticed him tense and said, "Relax. Those are Blume cameras. Remember, anything on cTOS can't see us – that includes those."

He let out a slow breath. As he looked around, a thought

occurred to him. "Used to take thirty, you said…"

"What about it?" Liz said, as she looked through the boxes on the shelves. Each was marked with a number sequence: date, case, assigned officer.

"You've done this sort of thing before?"

"I've done a lot of things. I was a black hat cracker when you were just a script kiddie. I put myself through university by busting open digital piggy banks and taking what I needed. Here – here it is." She pulled a box off the shelf and pulled out a plastic evidence bag. It had clothes in it, wallet, keys – the detritus of Alex Dempsey's life. She stared at it for a moment, and then shoved it against Olly's chest. "The Optik's in there. Get it out."

Olly carefully opened the bag and fished the external unit out. It was an older model. He tossed the bag back into the box. "We need to get out of here. Get somewhere quiet, maybe get a cuppa while I figure out how to bust the encryption."

"Easily done. We just walk out the same door we–"

The door opened. Two Albion operatives stood in the doorway. Neither was wearing a helmet, but both were armed. Their weapons were slung, not in their hands.

"Bugger," Liz said.

"Who the fuck–" one of the newcomers began, his eyes widening.

Olly lifted his badge. "Press?"

Liz came at them from the side. Watching her, Olly wondered what they saw, if anything. Her elbow flashed up and out, connecting with one's nose and sending him reeling back into the corridor. The second was turning even as she dropped into a crouch and scythed his legs out from under him with a kick. She looked at Olly. "Move it!"

Olly's paralysis broke. He leapt over the fallen men and out the door, rebounding off the opposite wall of the corridor before righting himself and sprinting for the exit. Liz followed. Someone shouted behind them. Liz caught Olly by the back of his shirt and propelled him through the doors at the end of the corridor as the Albion goons gave chase.

"I thought you said they couldn't see us," he yelped.

"I know what I said," she snarled, pushing him along. "Now run!"

We have a problem, Bagley whispered into Hannah's ear.

Hannah was careful to control her expression. "What sort of problem?" she murmured. Before Bagley could answer, she heard shouts and then a crackle from the Albion radios. Faulkner grabbed his and spoke into it quickly. His expression turned thunderous. "What the fuck is going on in here?" he snarled, his gaze fixed accusingly on Jenks. "Someone's attacked my men! What's the meaning of this?"

They're making for one of the other exits, Bagley said. But we need a distraction.

Hannah frowned and pushed towards Sarah. A babble rose up as the reporters shouted questions, police hurried towards the property room, and Faulkner barked orders. "We should go," Hannah muttered, tugging on Sarah's sleeve. She said it loud enough for Faulkner to hear and he rounded on them, face flushed with anger.

"What do you know, lady?" he growled, pointing at Sarah. "If I find out that this some sort of publicity stunt, I'll–"

"You'll *what*?" Sarah growled back. "And get your finger

out of my face, or I'll bite the bloody thing off."

Hannah winced. It was almost guaranteed that a few news drones had caught that. There was no telling how it would play. She tugged on Sarah's sleeve. "Let's go. I'll call the car around." Again, she made sure Faulkner heard her. She needed to keep his attentions focused here, rather than on directing his men, and buy the others time.

Faulkner's gaze slid towards her. "You're not going anywhere." He turned to his men. "Lock this place down! No one in or out, except with my express permission."

"Hang on now, you can't do that," Jenks said, getting in Faulkner's face, alongside Sarah. To his credit, Faulkner didn't retreat in the face of the combined assault. At Jenks' words, the other constables started pushing forward. Faulkner's men were outnumbered, but better armed. They reacted like soldiers under fire, hunching up, waiting for orders.

Sarah bared her teeth at Faulkner. "In a few moments, things are going to get very messy, Sergeant. Unless you do the smart thing and back off."

Faulkner rounded on her. "Is this what you wanted, woman?" Beyond him, Hannah could see that trouble was brewing. It wouldn't be long before someone threw a punch, or got shot. Even as she shrank back, she hoped Bagley appreciated it.

"What I wanted was a photo opportunity. And that's what I'm getting, though perhaps not the one I expected. Call off your dogs, and we'll see what we can do to fix things before they get out of hand."

Faulkner licked his lips. Hannah could read the violence in his eyes. She'd looked up Faulkner's record, what there was of it, and knew he wasn't the sort of man to back off from a challenge to his authority – not when he had the advantage. She could read the calculation in his expression. He was wondering if he could get away with an incident, perhaps blame it on the Met's lack of training, or–

"DedSec," he said, abruptly.

Sarah frowned. "What?"

"It's DedSec. Trying to hide their involvement…"

"In the shooting?"

"Yes," Faulkner said, quickly. He didn't really believe it, Hannah knew – or at least, he wasn't certain. But he was looking for an excuse to back off. He'd realised that whatever happened, it wouldn't help Albion's mission in East London if he got into a firefight in a police station. "Got to be. There's a cell of the insurgent bastards in Tower Hamlets, Ms Lincoln. Acting right under the noses of the Metropolitan Police," he added, glancing at Jenks. The constable flushed and took a step towards him, but Sarah got there first.

"Be that as it may, they're not here now," she began.

"Do we know that?" he said, smiling nastily. "I don't. DedSec aren't all hooligans and spotty-faced shut-ins. Some of them are right hard bastards, pretending to be upstanding citizens. Maybe even officers of the Met."

"What the hell are you implying?" Jenks demanded.

"You know damn well what I'm saying, Constable," Faulkner spat. "Someone must have let them in. Why not you?" He looked past her, at the press. "Or them?"

At his words, Sarah glanced at Hannah, and Hannah fought to give no sign she'd noticed. Silently, she cursed Liz and Olly, and Bagley too, for good measure. But Sarah said nothing to her. Instead she focused her attentions on Faulkner.

"We can address potential leaks later. Right now, we need to ensure that no one gets shot. That includes whoever your men are chasing right now."

"Are you giving me orders, then?" Faulkner said.

"That depends – are you planning to follow them?"

Faulkner stared at her a moment longer, and then turned to bark orders. His men retreated, putting space between themselves and the constables. Sarah turned to Jenks. "That goes for you lot as well. Calm them down, or I'll have them on report."

Jenks frowned, but nodded and turned to do as Sarah had demanded. Hannah let out a breath she hadn't realised she'd been holding. "That went well."

Sarah reached for a nearby chair, and sat down heavily. "Did it?" she said, in a shaky voice. "That's good." Hannah realised she was trembling.

"Sarah, are you – are you alright?"

"Scared out of my wits, actually. Things got very close to going very badly there. Faulkner came here looking for an excuse to shut this place down and someone has given him one." She looked at Hannah. "Those two reporters… where are they?"

"I– I don't know. They might be outside."

Sarah frowned. After several moments silence, she said, "You'd better hope Faulkner doesn't find them, for their sakes if nothing else." She closed her eyes and rubbed her brow. "Remind me again why I did this?"

"Photo opportunity," Hannah said, quickly.

"Oh right, yes." Sarah opened her eyes. "I do hope they got

some good ones." She took a deep breath and stood. "If this is a sign of things to come, it does not fill me with confidence, I must say."

"Rethinking your potential support of Albion?"

Sarah looked at her, a slight smile on her face.

"Let's just say, their sales pitch needs work."

13: ESCAPE

Liz moved quickly down the hall, the blueprints for the police station overlaying her vision. There were two fire-doors between them and the secondary exit. The doors were new, but wired into the building's security grid. Thankfully, that had been updated with all the rest of the Met's network and now ran on cTOS programming. Her thumb moved automatically across the screen of her Optik, and the doors swung open ahead of them.

Olly was panting in her wake, more from fear than effort. "What are we going to do? What are we going to do? They're right behind us!"

"Yes, Olly, that is what these sorts tend to do when someone runs away from them." Liz tapped the Optik again, and the fire-doors slammed in their wake. The sound gave her an idea. Another tap, and the fire alarms started going off as she activated the building's A-TACS – the automatic test and control system. Sprinklers spewed water as the fire-doors automatically locked.

She paused, breathing heavy. She was in good shape, thankfully, but she was still pushing the limits of a no-longer youthful endurance. Gulping air, Olly said, "Maybe we should show them our badges again…?"

Liz waved him to silence. "Shut up. Bagley, how far…?"

Another few metres, and then you'll have street access. It's getting crowded out there however. And while I'm scrambling their communications, I can't do it forever.

"Understood." She looked at Olly. "Ideas?"

Olly looked at her. "We're near the motor pool – if we can get to a car–"

He was interrupted by a sudden banging behind them. The Albion goons would be through the fire-doors in a few minutes, if they gave it some welly. That didn't give them much time. Liz glanced at him. "No time to get to the garage. We're heading for the street." If they could make it into the open, their camouflage system might allow them to slip away.

"What if they call in drones?" Olly asked.

"Drones can't see us, if we've got our camo up and running. The problem is, once they triangulate on us, it won't matter if they can see us or not. They'll just hose the area down indiscriminately. Being invisible doesn't mean we're invulnerable." Liz picked up the pace. "I'm more worried about Albion's flesh and blood goon squad. If they figure out what we're up to, they'll turn off their displays and that'll be the end of it – unless we can put some distance between us and them."

"Be easier to do that in a motor."

Liz ignored him. The door was just ahead. She hit it at a run and vaulted over the rail outside. She landed in a crouch and looked around. A car park, all but empty. The entrance to the garage was to her right, and she could hear the rattle-clank of its security gate opening. They were out of time. Olly hurried down the ramp, behind her. "Should we nick one?" he asked, indicating a car.

"No. Better idea." Every car in London was required to include a self-driving mode, networked to the new Smart City traffic grid. Government sponsored retrofit initiatives and buy-back schemes had ensured that almost every vehicle in the city now used cTOS programming. Which meant almost every vehicle could be hacked, if you had the right backdoor app installed.

Liz flicked her Optik, and engines turned over. Olly looked at her. "What's the plan?"

"Confusion and chaos." Another flick, and the cars started reversing out of their parking spaces. The only real issue with the autonomous car initiative was that vehicles lacked sensors and on-board programming. They weren't smart cars – just puppets on digital tethers. If you bypassed the central traffic control AI, you had a multi-ton battering ram that went wherever you aimed it.

Liz aimed them all in different directions, and let them go. Except for one – that one she aimed at the garage gate. It struck with a crash of abused metal, and she looked at Olly in satisfaction. "Now we go. Come on."

They raced across the lot, heading for the gates. Behind them, the doors busted open, and an Albion trooper stepped out – and stopped, confused by the vehicles racing in all directions, crashing into one another and the walls that surrounded the car park.

With the cars running interference, Liz and Olly made it to the other side of the lot. They went over the brick wall with a modicum of difficulty, and into a second lot, this one belonging to the building next to the police station. Olly slumped, panting. "Do we keep going, or...?"

"There's a street entrance. We'll hit that and make for the park. Think you can keep up?" She swatted him on the chest with the back of her hand. "On your feet. Bagley – give me a sit-rep!"

Patching you in to the garage's CCTV system now.

A moment later, the lot spread out across her display as if she were looking down on it from above. She experienced a brief moment of vertigo, but quickly recovered. She could see three Albion operatives moving carefully across the tarmac, avoiding the weaving cars.

"Three of them. Fuck." Liz checked her pistol. She wasn't a bad shot, but Albion employed hardened killers. She didn't rate their odds in a straight up fight. Olly pulled out his stun gun and she looked at him. "No. Put it back."

"But–"

"No. Ideas?"

Olly stuffed the stun gun back into his hoodie. Brow furrowed, he looked around. "We won't make it. Not unless we can... fly..." He looked up. "That's it. That's our way out!"

"What?"

"Drone," he said. He tapped his Optik, activating a cracker app and aiming the signal upwards. A large Parcel Fox cargo drone wavered and then descended with a whirr of its fans. Olly forced it to release its cargo, to lighten its load.

"It can't carry both of us," Liz protested. She could hear

shouts. The approaching operatives had seen the drone and were hurrying towards the wall.

"It can, just not far." Olly said. "Hurry!"

As they sprinted for the drone, two Albion goons climbed over the wall. Their rifles came up even as they dropped into the lot. Shots puckered the pavement and brickwork as Olly and Liz clambered onto the drone, and it rose on straining motors. "Jesus! They're actually bloody shooting at us!"

"What do you think they carry those guns for? Decoration?" Liz twisted around and returned fire. It was awkward, but effective – both men went flat, seeking cover instinctively. By the time they'd recovered, the drone was on the move. "Fuckers were just waiting until we were clear of the station. Wouldn't want to damage relations with the plods, after all."

Olly tried to keep the drone steady without much success. Taking control of it meant he had to override most of its autonomous controls, including its stabilisers. "Maybe we should have pinched a car instead," he muttered, flinching as a shot came too close for comfort. Via the CCTV, Liz saw that the pair of Albion goons were hurrying across the second car park in pursuit. One was still in the first, speaking into his radio.

"Head for Victoria Park," Liz said. "We'll lose them there."

They zipped along over the streets of Bethnal Green, and cut along Old Ford Road, heading towards Regent's Canal. Traffic was light, but they bounced off a few car roofs and Olly could hear the motors straining. Drones were sturdy, but there were limits.

"We're too heavy, we need to put down somewhere," he

began, but was interrupted by the thunderous growl of an engine. On his display a flashing threat marker appeared. "Bagley, what the hell is that?"

Tidis brand APVs – armoured pursuit vehicles. Like a cross between a tank and a four-by-four. Albion aren't supposed to deploy them in the city. Oh well...

"I thought you were scrambling communications," Liz snapped.

I was. Unfortunately, they unscrambled them.

Olly's display pinged. Someone was trying to get a GPS lock on the drone. "Shit, shit, shit – they're triangulating on us, innit?" He urged the drone to greater speed, and it began to veer wildly as it skidded over the trees. Liz leaned towards him.

"Slow down," she shouted.

"Are you mental? They're right on our arse!" The thought of being shot wasn't one he'd ever seriously considered before today. Right now it was all he could think about.

"Just do it," she snarled. He glanced back, and saw that she had her Optik out.

"What are you doing?"

"Getting a cab. What does it look like?" A proximity alert flashed, seconded from the drone's sensors. He spied a second drone closing in, and he realised what Liz was planning.

"Are you sure about this?" he asked, as he tried to hold their ride steady.

"I'm improvising. You remember the rally point?"

Olly nodded convulsively. They'd arranged a rally point before coming out – a place to meet up if the worst happened and they got separated. Liz caught his shoulder and squeezed.

"Good. Lead them around a bit and head straight there when you lose them, understand? No dilly-dallying, Olly. And whatever you do, don't lose that damn Optik."

"I won't," he said, but she was already jumping onto the newly arrived drone. Liz peeled away from him as the first of their pursuers burst through the treeline, scattering civilians. The vehicle was boxy, built to withstand the rigours of terrain and roadside explosives alike. It gunned towards them, and Olly swooped away. The drone was faster now, with some of the weight off – but was it fast enough?

He hurtled over the park, arrowing past the boating lake. The air lashed him as he crouched low atop the drone, trying to keep his balance. "Bagley, I need a route out of here," he said, hoping the AI would have good news for him. A moment later, an overlay map of the park appeared on his display, with a flashing yellow line stretching ahead of him.

Ask and ye shall receive, but I warn you – it's going to be bumpy...

"Whatever, so long as it gets me out of here quick." Head down, he guided the drone along the yellow line, towards the eastern end of the park. Groups of people scattered, yelling, snapping pics – he could almost feel the CCTV breathing down his neck, even as his app made to erase him from the cloud. The APV gunned its engines, and stayed on his tail.

Bagley's trail sent him out over the East Lake and he skidded across the surface, leaving waves in his wake, and a number of cursing fishermen. The APV was angling on a parallel course, keeping him in sight as it tore up a walking trail with its wheels, lights flashing.

An alert flashed – someone was trying to break his hold

on the drone. Forced to split his attentions, he almost fell off when he sped past the Hub Building, but managed to right himself at the last moment.

"Two can play at that game," he said, aiming his Optik at the APV. He tapped the screen and was rewarded by the APV suddenly slewing to the side as its wheels locked up and its engine went dead. Momentum carried the heavy vehicle down a shallow incline and into the model boating lake with a loud splash. Olly gave a shout of glee and punched the air.

I wouldn't celebrate just yet, Oliver. Bogies on your six, as they say.

Olly risked a glance. Three drones with yellow chasses and widely spaced motors. They were moving on an intercept course, and fast.

Tidis AV-50 Pursuit Drones. Designed to fly at high speed, on autonomous pursuit courses. Capable of disabling networked machinery – including other drones, I might add – via short-range override transmitter.

"Wonderful. Suggestions?"

Try to land somewhere soft, when they catch you.

"That's not helpful, Bagley!"

Oh very well – calculating a new route for optimum evasion...

The yellow route marker vanished, replaced by a red one. Olly veered after it. Very quickly, he realised it was guiding him towards the street. "Bagley, you sure about this?"

Feel free to disregard, Oliver. After all, I am only a highly advanced AI, designed for rapid calculation and computation. I'm sure your meat brain will get you out of this sticky wicket in one piece, if you ask it nicely.

"Point taken," Olly said, through gritted teeth. The pursuit drones were closing the distance now. They were coming in on all sides, trying to hem him in – or maybe herd him back into the park. Whatever they were trying, it didn't work. He burst out of the park and banked out over the traffic, heading towards Hackney.

But even as he did so, a new alert flashed. A fourth pursuit drone swung towards him, as if out of nowhere. Something sparked, and he felt his ride shudder as its systems locked up. The drone fell, a dead weight – the world spun – his vision filled with red and streaks of neon colour – there was a burst heat and light as the dead drone impacted with something and went to pieces – and then he was down and the world was shaking.

Olly cried out as he rolled across the roof of a New Routemaster, his body aching with the sudden impact. The bus kept going, despite the crashed drone. The pursuit drones closed, swooping towards him like giant wasps.

On your feet, Oliver, now's not the time to be laying down on the job!

Olly shoved himself to his feet and ran along the top of the moving bus, his brain still rattling in his skull. He had no idea where he was going, only that he needed to get there quick. Bits of burning drone littered the front of the bus and he skidded through them as the vehicle picked up speed.

Best hang on, Oliver. They're about to–

The bus shuddered as the pursuit drones shorted its systems. Olly sank into a crouch and tensed, ready for what he knew was coming. There were startled shouts from the passengers as the vehicle locked and careened across a corner, glancing off a traffic light post in a spray of sparks and a yelp of abused metal, before plunging into oncoming traffic.

Horns blared, brakes squealed and glass shattered as a ripple of collisions expanded outwards from the Routemaster. Olly found himself skidding across the top of the bus and then off the side. He got a flash of the shocked face of a tourist peering out at him. His fingers scrabbled vainly at the metal surface for a few moments – and then he was falling backwards. He struck the roof of a car, rolled down its bonnet and onto the street, hard enough to steal the breath from his lungs.

Gasping, aching, he hauled himself to his knees. The pursuit drones were circling, as if confused. Despite the pain of his landing, he smiled. Not as if – they were. They were running cTOS facial recognition software, trying to ID him, and failing. Hand on the front of the car, he pushed himself to his feet. His Optik was cracked, but thankfully still working.

The drones descended, still circling. He could hear the growl of high-powered engines. Albion was closing in. People were out of their cars now, shouting questions. Olly waited until one of the drones got close enough – and struck.

The pursuit drone had a more sophisticated firewall than a courier, but not sophisticated enough. Olly had control three seconds later. The drone spun on its rotors and disabled the nearest of its fellows. It fell to the street a moment later, disabled by the third. And while that one was distracted, Olly struck again.

Hobbling towards the pavement, Olly gave the remaining pursuit drone a new target – the Albion APV that had just turned the corner at the other end of the street. He didn't stay to watch what happened next. Activating the camouflage app, he wove through the growing crowd. "Bagley, give me the straightest route to the rally point."

Say the magic word.

"Now."

Close enough. Well done, by the way.

Olly didn't reply. He was too busy running.

14: SIBLING RIVALRY

Ro looked down the corridor first one way, and then the other. No one in sight, though she could hear the shouts of the corner boys outside. Colin's flat was on the third floor, and at the end of the corridor near the stairs. She'd visited once, and remembered the smell of takeaways and body odour. Colin was a confirmed bachelor.

She eyed the lock, stepped back and gave the door a precisely placed kick, then another. On the third, the lock popped and the door swung in. She paused, waiting to see if anyone had heard or was otherwise coming to investigate. When no one showed up, she went in and pushed the door closed behind her.

She'd spent most of the day trying to get a lead on Colin's mates, hoping one of them might be able to help her. But they'd proven elusive, so she'd decided to hit the flat, like Billy had suggested.

It was as messy as she remembered. Clothes everywhere, magazines and games piled sloppily around a ratty couch. A big flat screen television occupied the opposite wall. Besides the television and the couch, there wasn't much in the way of furniture. A smallish balcony looked out over a shared green space that was mostly dirt and crisp bags.

She made her way to the back of the flat, investigating the kitchen and the bedroom. She left Colin's bathroom for last. The kitchen was the cleanest room in the flat, mostly because it looked as if it hadn't been used. Stacks of takeaway menus sat on the table, and the bin was full of Styrofoam containers and plastic cutlery. She could still smell Colin's last meal, and wrinkled her nose in disgust.

The bedroom was as much a tip as the sitting room. She didn't find anything under his bed other than a dizzying assortment of pornography. The closet had nothing of interest, nor was there anything under the mattress. Her annoyance grew. Colin wasn't her responsibility, but she was taking the blame for his mistakes. It wasn't fair.

She pushed her brimming frustration down. She'd gotten good at that, over the years. She knew better than most that life wasn't fair. It wasn't a question of getting hit – it was only a question of what you did afterwards. You could lie around and feel sorry for yourself, or you could get up and maybe throw a few punches of your own.

Ro leaned against the bedroom door, thinking again about the moment Colin had gone down. The way he'd folded up as the life went out of him. She didn't feel sick, thinking about it now. Instead, she felt angry. Billy was right, she and Colin hadn't been friends, but she was angry nonetheless. He'd been a mate, if nothing else. She wanted to find whoever'd done for him, and teach them the error of their ways. She punched the wall in frustration, putting a hole in the plaster. She drew her fist back and looked at it. She flexed her fingers, cursing herself for an idiot. If she'd connected with a joist, she'd have broken her hand.

Even so, she felt a bit better. Hitting things always helped her clear her head. It always had, even when she was a kid. Though Danny probably didn't look back on those days with any fondness. She smiled, but only for a moment. She couldn't find it in herself to be overly concerned with what Danny thought, these days.

Being in the military had been bad enough, but joining Albion…? She rubbed the back of her neck, feeling worn out. Danny might as well have put a target on her back. Mary Kelley hadn't mentioned anything about it, but Ro knew it'd come up sooner or later. Especially if Albion managed to take over for the plods. They'd use her – or mum – to get to Danny. And Danny, tight-arse that he was, wasn't likely to play nice. No telling what would happen then. Whatever it was, it wouldn't be good.

For a moment, she considered punching the wall again. But she resisted the urge and made her way down the hall to the bathroom. It smelled of mould and cheap deodorant. It hadn't been cleaned in some time – maybe never. Her eyes strayed to the cistern of the toilet. She frowned, and removed the top. As she had suspected, a trio of waterproof baggies sat at the bottom of the tank, tucked beneath the flush valve.

Grimacing, she fished them out one at a time and tossed them into the sink. Two of them contained rolls of bank notes and several cheap flash drives. No telling what was on those. She pocketed the cash without thinking about it. Few people used it these days, but money was money and Colin didn't need it anymore, poor sod.

The third baggie was more interesting. It contained an Optik external unit as well as an old fashioned flip phone. She knew a burner when she saw one. Everyone'd had one, back in the day. These days not so much. It had a list of pre-programmed numbers, but no names or references. The Optik was more interesting.

Colin's Optik had been broken when it hit the ground, and what was left was now at the bottom of the Thames. Ro wasn't much for technology – she had an Optik of her own, everyone did – but she knew enough to get by. External units would synch up automatically with the nearest base unit. Granted, everything on it would be encrypted, but Colin wasn't the sort to trust weird hacker bullshit. Colin was a straight out of the box, default password sort of guy.

But that didn't explain why he had two Optiks. She turned the device on, waited impatiently for it to synch up, and then started trying passwords. She got it on the second try – Colin had used his birthday, like a proper numpty.

Files skittered across her display. She zeroed in on a scheduling app and was rewarded by several dozen entries. Some she recognised as legitimate – well, mostly – deliveries, but some of the others were at unusual times.

One stood out. An address in Hackney, a contact number and a name – Holden. The name wasn't familiar, but something about the address was, though she couldn't say what. She'd have to go see it for herself, maybe talk to this Holden, whoever they were. She pocketed the Optik, turned – and stopped. She'd heard something. Voices.

The walls in the flat were thin and she could hear someone, or several someones out in the corridor. The police? Either way, she didn't want to be caught in the flat, if they were coming in. She needed an exit.

The balcony. She moved quickly, out the doors and paused, looking down. Not a long drop to the next balcony, but far enough to make her hesitate.

Behind her, someone eased open the door. No more time.

Ro went over the side.

When Danny spotted the broken lock, he signalled Hattersley. The other man nodded. Danny drew his pistol and eased the door open. They'd spent most of the previous day going back and forth over Colin Wilson's trail. They'd located his van parked along Regent's Canal – someone had set it on fire, helpfully. Probably the Kelleys.

He and Hattersley were in their civvies. They were both wearing their body armour under their coats, with the Albion insignia emblazoned on the chest, but no helmets to hide their faces, and no combat rig other than a concealed P9 pistol. Danny had made the call. Given the Kelley's involvement, he thought they should be prepared, just in case, but didn't want to spook the locals unnecessarily. Hattersley hadn't argued.

"How do you want to do this?" Hattersley murmured.

"By the book," Danny said, studying the door. Someone had clearly kicked it in.

"Think it's Bloody Mary?" Hattersley said, referring to the Clan Kelley matriarch. Every Albion operative in East London knew Mary Kelley's reputation.

"You can relax, I don't think she's in there," Danny muttered.

"Ha-ha. I meant you think it's her goons?"

"Only one way to find out." Danny waved him back and reached for the door. He eased it open, pistol at the ready. When no shots came, he stepped inside. As he did so, he saw a flash of movement near the balcony. He opened his mouth to shout, but whoever it was, was already gone. "Clear the flat. One of them is going out the window. I've got them." He shoved past Hattersley and pounded towards the stairs.

He took the steps two at a time and hit the doors at a run. He saw a figure drop from a second storey balcony to the grassy courtyard, roll to their feet and start running. He paused, falling instinctively into a shooter's stance. "Halt – I said halt!"

The figure stumbled – stopped – turned. Danny froze. "Ro?"

His sister stared at him, her eyes wide. Danny took a half-step towards her. "Ro… what are you doing here?"

She stepped back, retreating as he advanced. She shook her head. Danny stopped. "Don't run," he said, under his breath. "Don't do it. Please don't do it. Ro, please…"

Ro turned and sprinted away, between the buildings. Danny took off in pursuit, cursing the entire way. If only his parents had stopped with one kid, this wouldn't be happening. She vaulted a low brick wall, vanishing around a corner. Danny skidded after her, remembering too late what happened every time he'd chased her as a kid –

Danny ducked. Ro's punch caught him in the cheek rather than the side of the head, and he stumbled. He swung his gun up, and she brushed it aside, out of his grip, and hit him again. She yelped as her fist connected with the plates of his body armour, and he shoved her back. He raised his fists, searching for his weapon. Ro circled him, ready to fight.

"Why the fuck you chasing me for?"

"Why the fuck you in that flat, sis?" Danny snarled back. She lunged, and he caught the blow on his forearm. Before he could recover, she hit him in the side, just below the edge of his armour. He threw his own punch in response, and she jerked aside.

"Well weak, bruv," she said.

"Why are you here?"

"Free country, innit?"

Danny grimaced. He didn't want to trade punches with Ro, no matter how much she might deserve it. "You shouldn't be here."

"I was trying to leave, but you had to chase me, didn't you?" She feinted right, and he flinched back, forearms raised to absorb the blow. She looped a blow towards his head and he fell back against the wall, narrowly avoiding it.

"Are you here working for the Kelleys?" he demanded. Over her shoulder, he spotted Hattersley, running towards them. "Shit. Trip me."

She frowned and lowered her guard. "What?"

"Trip me, idiot." He lunged, and she dropped, sweeping his legs out from under him. He fit the ground, catching himself on his palms. She leapt over him and was gone, running full pelt. Hattersley shouted something, but she didn't stop this time. Danny partner reached him a moment later, puffing slightly. "Holy shit, she was fast."

"Yeah," Danny said, pushing himself to his knees.

"What happened?" Hattersley asked, looking around. "You okay?"

"Yeah. Yeah, just... surprised me."

"Looks like they kicked your arse." Hattersley reached out a hand, and Danny took it. The other man hauled him to his feet. "Should we go after them?"

"Nah… no. Leave it. Anything in the flat?"

"Not that I saw." Hattersley leaned over and spit. "It's a shithole."

"Worse than yours?"

"Hey, I resemble that remark." Hattersley looked up. "Lot of drones. Bet one of them got a look at the intruder. We might be able to pull an image."

Danny froze, just for a moment. Thankfully, Hattersley didn't notice. "Yeah. Good idea. I'll handle it when we get back to base."

"You sure? It'll take some time."

"Don't you have a date?"

"I probably do, and thank you for your sacrifice." Hattersley grinned and slapped him on the back. "You're a true brother in arms, Hayes."

Danny snorted. "You're welcome." His gaze strayed in the direction Ro had gone. He turned and clapped Hattersley on the shoulder. "Right. Let's get back in there and take a look. That way we can tell Faulkner we did it."

"If we don't find anything, he ain't going to be happy," Hattersley said, doubtfully.

"When is he ever happy?"

"He smiles a lot."

"So do fucking hyenas. Don't mean they won't eat you." Danny shook his head. "Come on, move. Before the local dope heads clean the place out."

14: SIGNAL

It was getting dark by the time Olly arrived at the rally point, dishevelled and out of breath. Liz watched him through the window. The glass had been soaped, but she could just about see through it. "He looks like he's been run over."

He almost was. But he managed to scrape a win, in the end.

"You sound almost proud, Bagley."

If I could feel such a thing, now would be a moment for it.

Liz sat back in her booth with a snort. Her own journey had been no easy thing. She'd ditched the drone in the park and made for the Chisenhale Gallery. There was a showing and crowd. She'd blended in, and left Albion looking lost. As far as she knew, they were still chasing her ride. She'd sent the drone towards Clapton with a false GPS ping attached.

She looked around. The café was a pop-up, nesting in the refurbished remnants of a Staroger coffee shop across from the park. All the bland company branding had been gutted and loose wiring, decorated with fairy lights, hung through the ceiling tiles. The floor had been stripped of lino, but someone had taken the time to put down carpet squares under the seating section.

It was cramped, the lavatories were out of order and the menu was miniscule, but it was safe enough and she like the place's counter-corporate vibe. Olly spotted her, and sidled towards the booth, looking around nervously. As he sat, she said, "Have fun?"

"No," he said flatly. "I never want to do that again."

"I've got some bad news for you, then. That was just another day at the office for us." She paused. "Do you still have it?"

"Safe as houses," he said. He patted his bag. "I thought at first I'd broken it when I fell off the bus, but it's still in one piece."

"You fell off a bus?" Liz asked, in some surprise.

"Yeah, after the drone crashed."

She shook her head. A waitress came by to take Olly's order. When she'd gone, he said, "Maybe we should keep moving. They'll be looking for us..."

"Which is why we sit tight, until it gets dark. Then we take the underground and head back to the cellar." She closed her eyes for a moment. "I wonder why they want it."

"That's what we want to find out, right?" Olly pulled out the Optik and studied it. "It doesn't look special." He frowned at it for a moment, and then turned it on. "I can maybe brute-force a synchronization with my Optik, but that'll require a hard reboot..."

"Which might erase whatever data we're looking for," Liz said. She reached out and put her hand over the device. "Leave it for now. We'll clone it first before we do anything."

Olly nodded and put the device away. "That was too close for comfort back there. The way you went after them... I just froze." He fell silent as their coffees arrived. "I'm sorry," he said, after a moment. "Didn't even think to use the bloody stun gun."

"Probably wouldn't have worked anyway, unless you hit them in the right spot. Albion uniforms are insulated." Liz smiled at him. "Don't worry about it. You did good, for your first time out."

Olly shook his head. "Doesn't feel like it."

"It takes some getting used to. Trust me. Next time, you won't freeze."

"Next time?"

"There's always a next time, Olly. That's the way this works now." Liz stretched, and could hear her own joints popping. Riding on drones and getting in punch ups was hard on a girl's body. She grunted and rotated her shoulders. "I might be getting too old for it, though."

"How old are you anyway?"

She gave him a sideways look. "What sort of question is that to ask a lady?"

"I'm not asking a lady, am I?"

Liz snorted. "Cheeky git." She tipped her head back, looking at the ceiling.

Olly cleared his throat. She could tell that something was on his mind. "Earlier, when you said you were a black hat cracker…" he began, hesitantly.

Liz lifted her cup. "What about it?"

"Were you being serious? You weren't just taking the piss?"

She paused, then took a drink. "No, I wasn't taking the piss."

"And now you're … a freedom fighter? Bad guy to good guy, just like that?"

Liz looked out the window, watching the street. "I don't think I was a bad guy, per se..." she began, slowly.

"But you stole money."

"And you stole food."

"Yeah, but for other people," Olly said. "Who'd you give the money to?"

Liz smiled. "Fair play."

"So why'd you join DedSec, then?"

Liz was silent. Then, "What does London mean to you, Olly?"

Olly frowned. "You what?"

"Simple question. Is it your home? Are you just passing through? What?" Liz looked at him. "What does this city mean to you? What are you willing to do, to save it?"

Olly shook his head. "I don't – I've never thought about it. I'm doing what I'm doing, yeah?" It was the answer she'd been expecting, but it still disappointed her. She sighed and looked away.

"That's what I thought."

Annoyed now, Olly said, "Well what does it mean to you, then?"

"Everything," Liz said flatly. "I was born here. I grew up here."

"You don't sound like you grew up in East London..."

"There's more to city than East London, Olly." She sighed. "I was born in Catford. My parents were antifascists. They met while beating the piss out of National Front members in '77. They served in the emergency government of the People's Republic of Lewisham Clock-Tower."

Olly frowned. "I have no idea what that is."

"Most people don't." Liz smiled. "My parents loved London, Olly. Loved it enough to fight for it, with bricks and boots. And they taught me to love it too. But you can't win a fight with bricks and boots these days." She looked around the café. "All that stuff back in the cellar? I helped build that, you know. Back in the day, I was the one crunching numbers and cracking encryption programs. I was the one setting up bots to farm gold in MMORPGs, and more bots to turn that gold into cryptocurrency – money we used to set up everything. Because I knew all of this was coming."

"All what was coming?"

"Blume. Albion. All of it." Liz looked at him. "We're paying for the sins of previous generations – for their decisions, for their lack of forethought – and for our own mistakes too. It's all compounded into one big cancerous mess, resting right in society's gut. The longer it goes on, the sicker we all get."

"Maybe you should have warned some people."

Liz leaned back. "I did. I was on every forum, message board and chat app. I sounded the alarm around the clock and nobody listened – not until it was too late." She paused. "No, some people listened. Some saw what I saw, and we found each other. Just like my parents and their friends did, back in the day."

"DedSec," Olly said, softly.

"DedSec," Liz agreed. She paused. "Look around."

Olly did. Liz did as well. Information rippled across her display as the facial recognition software went to work. There weren't many patrons in the café, but there were enough to make interesting reading. She fixed on one. "The geezer in the corner," Liz murmured. "Tell me about him."

Olly turned. Liz knew what he saw. The old man was worn down, frayed looking, with thin hairs clinging to his spotted pate. His suit had been fashionable once, maybe. Now it looked a bit silly on his shrunken frame. But his hands were big. She watched Olly scroll through the data. "Ian Parker. Just got out of Maidstone. A thirty-year stretch. Category C. Firearm offences, wounding with intent, conspiracy... Bloody hell, he's a proper old school gangster."

"Good. What else?"

"Uhm..." Olly continued to scroll. "Got a granddaughter in Hackney. She – huh."

"What?"

"She works for Blume. In their research and development division."

"What's their relationship like?"

"How would I know?"

"Study the data," Liz said, softly. "What does it tell you?"

She watched as Olly combed through social media feeds, posts to Invite, online journals, calendar apps – nothing was hidden from DedSec. If it was online, they could see it. "She visited him regularly while he was inside. He's going to be staying with her temporarily, if her social media is anything to go by."

Liz nodded. "Interesting, isn't it?"

"What do you mean?"

"What do you think she tells him?" Liz looked at him. "Think about it. He's a link in a chain – just like you, just like me. If we needed to get into Blume, he's a way in. Especially if you dig a bit deeper and... ah." She smiled. "He's got a major grudge against the Kelleys."

Olly tensed. The Kelleys scared the crap out of him. "So?"

"So if we helped him, what might he do for us in return?"

Olly sat back. "You mean… he'd join DedSec?"

"In a certain sense, he already has. Look who he's with." Liz twitched her chin towards the corner, where an older woman had taken a seat opposite the old man. Alarms and alerts flashed on her display, as they no doubt did on Olly's. Old photos, video-streams, news conferences…

"A copper?"

"Retired copper." Liz waved surreptitiously. The woman noticed, and gave a terse nod, before turning back to the old man. Olly looked on in puzzlement.

"You know her?"

"In a sense. DedSec did her a favour, once. Now she owes us a favour. Which is why she's here. Digging up information on the Kelleys – they're just as much a part of the problem as Albion, Olly. All part of the same cancer." She knocked on the table. "DedSec is people. People talking to people, people helping people. We're all part of the resistance, in our own way. Remember that."

As she spoke, the door to café slammed open, causing the bell to jangle. An armed Albion trooper stepped in, gaze sweeping over the patrons. He paused a moment, then ambled to the counter and ordered a coffee. Through the window, Liz could see two others standing on the street. Olly looked her, and she gestured for him to remain where he was.

She couldn't tell if they were the ones who'd pursued them from the station, but it didn't really matter. The one at the counter scanned the patrons faces as he waited, using his Optik's facial recognition software. Liz tensed as he turned towards their table – and then passed on. Olly glanced at Liz and she smiled thinly.

When the trooper had ambled out, coffees in hand, Liz said, "Don't worry. They won't get any matches."

"You sure about that?" Olly asked as he slumped back in his seat. Outside, orange light cast long shadows. "I know I'm not in the system, but you ..."

"I should have said, they'll get matches, but the identities are false. Innocuous. During the early days of the cTOS upgrades, we built a few hundred fake identities. When they use the facial recognition software on a member of DedSec, it attaches our picture to a randomised identity. It wouldn't hold up against a second look, but it's usually enough to satisfy the grunts on the street."

Olly shook his head, visibly impressed. "When was anybody going to tell me about all of this?" he asked, somewhat plaintively.

"When you needed to know," Liz said. She smiled. "Welcome to the Resistance."

Coyle looked up as his external Optik chimed. He brought up his display, and saw that Tell's device had been activated. "Finally."

With a grim smile, he rose to his feet. He retrieved his Optik and brought up the control app for the drone across the room. With a tap of his screen, the drone's motors whirred to life. It was quieter than one might think. Another improvement over the standard model. He opened a window, and the drone passed out into the late afternoon light. As it left the building, he activated its secondary systems.

The sleek lines and rigid angles wavered, seemingly changing before his eyes. A moment was all it took. The drone no longer resembled a combat model, but instead looked like a common Parcel Fox courier drone. And as far as any electronic recording devices were concerned, that was exactly what it was.

Coyle activated the remote HUD connected to the drone's sensory suite. It was strange to see the city this way, and he doubted he would ever grow used to it. The drone could perceive things invisible to the human eye. A constant drip of data scrolled down either side of the display. The drone's AI was responsible for most of its everyday functions – leaving only the execution of the kill-shot to Coyle.

The drone soon locked onto the Optik's signal, and headed out over the city, heading towards Victoria Park. That made sense, given how close it was to the police station. He wondered who was in possession of it – a police officer? An Albion operative? Either way, their fate was sealed. He felt a flicker of regret, but quickly pushed it aside. It was a vice he could not afford. Especially now.

There was still Tell to find, after all. The enigmatic Marcus Tell. The other half of Zero Day's equation. Coyle had done his research there as well, digging in to his primary target. Tell did not exist, save on paper, much like Coyle himself. Oh there had been a man named Marcus Tell, once. But the man who bore that name now had not been given it at birth. Coyle had not yet found out the man's true name, and only had bits and pieces of his bloody history.

According to Zero Day, Tell was a bomb maker by trade. An expert in improvised explosive devices, with connections to several now-defunct terrorist organisations. And it was in that capacity that he had been employed by Zero Day. But now his employment was at an end, and Zero Day wanted the loose end tied up.

Coyle had performed similar clean-up operations before. Tell was a clear and present danger to Zero Day in some fashion. Perhaps he had threatened to go to the authorities. Or maybe he had reneged on the deal somehow. Coyle had considered that Zero Day might do the same to him – they wouldn't have been the first – but he wasn't unduly concerned about it. Professional killers did not last long if they did not instinctively consider such things.

Once he was certain the drone was safely underway, he minimised the HUD. It would alert him if and when it located its target. He turned his attentions to a different app suite – an encrypted bloodhound program, designed to analyse and develop projections based on specific data trawled from a target's phone data, social media, site profiles and shopping habits. The suite came in handy during the planning stages of his operations.

He'd programmed in every scrap of information he'd collected, every recording he'd made, of his employers. Now it was searching the net for similar turns of phrase and the like. So far, the program had come up with nothing. But soon enough, something – some phrase, some reference – would strike a hit, and he'd have their scent. Then, it would only be a matter of time until he tracked them down.

Coyle intended to complete the job he'd been hired for. He was a professional, after all. But afterwards, there'd be a reckoning with Zero Day – whoever they were. He allowed himself a small smile of satisfaction. It was quickly wiped away by an alert – an incoming call, for one of his aliases. He recognised the number and cursed. He activated an encryption app before he answered. "Holden. I thought I told you not to call me."

"Was that you?"

Holden's voice sounded scratchy, electronically distorted. He was using a scrambler. "Was what me?" he asked, already knowing the answer.

"The shootings on Sunday – it was you, wasn't it?"

"I don't know what you're talking about."

"I think you do. And if you're smart, you'll drop the act. I don't have much time."

"Then by all means, get to the point." Coyle considered trying to trace the call, but Holden was surely too smart for that sort of thing.

"I need money. And I need it now."

"I believe I already paid you, and quite fairly."

"I know who you are."

Coyle hesitated. "Do you? Please enlighten me, Mr Holden."

"Your name is Coyle…"

"I get the picture. Fine. What do you want?"

"I need money. Enough to get out of the city – the country…"

Coyle's eyes narrowed. "What have you done, Mr Holden?"

Silence. Coyle sighed. That was answer enough. "Where are you?"

He could sense Holden's sudden hesitation. Greed and fear had made the other man incautious. But now he was beginning to realise that he'd just tried to extort a man in possession of a combat capable drone. Coyle chuckled. "Come now, Mr

Holden. No sense acting shy now. Where are you?"

"I– I want to arrange a drop. Somewhere indoors. Whitechapel Terminus."

"By drop, I assume you mean that I'm to leave you a certain amount of money in return for… what? Your silence?"

"Something like that."

Coyle laughed. "No, I don't think so. In fact, I think you leave me with little choice but to ensure your silence by any means necessary. Do have a nice day, Mr Holden."

He ended the call before Holden could reply and shook his head. Holden was a loose end he'd intended to leave until after everything was settled. He'd clearly underestimated the man, however. Holden had put two and two together with remarkable alacrity.

Still, if he was as smart as all that, he would leave the city as soon as possible. Whatever had prompted this unwise attempt at blackmail would no doubt keep him occupied until Coyle could catch up with him at a time and place of his choosing. Satisfied, he sat back down and returned his attentions to the spiderbot.

Over London, the drone continued the hunt.

16: HUNTED

George Holden sat on a camp bed in his lock-up garage in Hackney, and stared at the burner in his hand. He'd made a mistake, contacting Coyle. He'd known that as soon as Coyle had picked up the phone. Not his first mistake, but possibly his last.

His heart was beating too fast, making him feel sick. He'd known there was something wrong with Coyle the first time they'd met. A sort of cold calculation. You saw it sometimes in the men and women Albion employed – like they'd been too long in the sandbox, and seen too much to ever slip back into civilised society. Coyle reminded him of Faulkner, Albion's man in East London, a little bit. There was that same animal viciousness there, hidden beneath a veneer of faux-affability.

And now that viciousness was aimed at him.

He'd been desperate, hoping for a quick pay-out to get him free and clear. Not for the first time, he'd let his greed outweigh his common sense. But now there was probably a killer drone prowling the skies, looking for him. He peered about him, at the racks of Albion surplus and equipment. He'd been selling corporate kit for months, trying to cover his debts.

Nobody had noticed, until, suddenly, somebody had. They called themselves Zero Day, though whether that was the name of a person or a group, Holden couldn't say. They'd contacted him out of the blue, using an encrypted program that he had yet to crack. They'd wanted supplies – made to order. They'd promised a good deal of money in exchange, and Holden had jumped at the deal. He'd forgotten that a sure thing rarely was, no matter what some insisted. He lay back on the bed, massaging his temples.

Things had quickly become far too complicated. Zero Day, whoever they were, had provided Holden with a number to call. He'd done so, and received a list of materials to be provided for pick up by a courier. Some weeks later, a second number had been provided – a man looking to buy a drone.

That was where things had started to go wrong. The UCAV drone was a prototype from Project LIBRA, one of Albion's black book initiatives. He never should have taken the chance, but the money had been too good and he had bad people knocking at his door all hours, wanting what he owed. And Albion had all but mothballed the damn thing anyway. It was too expensive to maintain.

Only now, it had been used in two murders. One of them, the poor bastard who'd acted as a go-between. That had scared him. He'd already been worried. Not long after he'd sold the drone, he'd started to wonder. Too little, too late, as it turned out.

Going to Lincoln's office had been a mistake as well. Initially, he'd hoped she'd be able to tell him something about the investigation, to give him some idea how close the police were to figuring out that the shooter wasn't flesh-and-blood at all. Because once they figured that out, Albion would know what had happened. Then they'd come for him.

That was why he'd left his flat and moved to the lockup. It wasn't set up for comfort, but he told himself it was like camping out. And more importantly, Albion didn't know about it. Nobody did. Except the courier, who was now dead.

Holden swallowed a sudden rush of bile. He hadn't meant for that to happen. He hadn't meant for any of it to happen, but it had and he was as responsible as the man pulling the trigger. He needed protection. Failing that, he had to get out of the city. Out of the country. Somewhere neither Coyle nor Albion could find him.

He laughed. There weren't many places that fit that definition.

"Protection," he muttered. He sat up. Albion was still feeling out the territory. The government hadn't yet delivered that blank cheque that Cass wanted. There was still resistance to their presence in London. He could use that. He knew plenty about all the dirty tricks the company had got up to over the years – and what he didn't know, he could fabricate. What he knew about the drone program alone might be enough to sink Albion's prospects in London. The question was, who to sell it to?

A news alert popped up on his display. He expanded it, and saw that it was a GBB report from the Bethnal Green Police Station. He watched as Sarah Lincoln went nose-to-nose with Faulkner.

A slow smile spread across his face.

•••

The man who called himself Marcus Tell sat in his tiny council flat, watching the sun set over the city through the kitchenette window. He'd done so almost every evening for ten years, from the same spot.

A cup of red bush tea sat cooling on the table before him, with only a few sips taken from it. He'd grown to tolerate the flavour. His GP had cautioned him against overindulgence in caffeine – bad for his blood pressure. Or was it his kidneys? It was hard to remember. These days, his body was nothing but a tangle of problems, held together by sinew and stubbornness.

He wasn't long for the world. Death had always stood at his side, but now he could feel a bony hand on his shoulder. Time was running out. If his own body didn't kill him, someone else would. He took a sip of the tea, grimaced, took another sip.

According to the news, there'd been another shooting. He'd known the victim's identity before it had been announced. Colin Wilson had been a petty criminal, and lacking in respect for his betters, but he had not deserved such a death.

Tell – he thought of himself as Tell, now, though the real Marcus Tell was buried somewhere in Epping Forest – knew he would have to leave soon. The flat wasn't safe. He would need a new Optik external as well, but that was easy enough to acquire. He tapped the implant, wondering if he ought to replace it. Better safe than sorry. But that would take time to arrange – and time was something he didn't have a lot of.

He looked up at a picture on the wall – himself, in better days, and Peter. Dear, sweet Peter. Middle-aged, comfortable, content. Life had not been perfect, but good enough.

For a time, at least.

Peter was dead now. Cancer. A bad way to go. Painful and

debilitating. He abandoned that train of thought as quickly as he'd boarded it. Peter was gone. The dead could feel no pain, and their ghosts did not haunt the living. That was what Tell told himself. He took another sip of tea, savouring the bitterness. If he was wrong, if the dead did not pass on, but instead stayed… there would be a crowd waiting for him when he passed.

He did not know how many people died due to his actions over the years. More than a few, less than a crowd. More had been hurt, crippled, traumatised. The man he had been had left behind a trail of human wreckage, stretching across continents. The reasons why no longer mattered, if they ever had to begin with. Looking back, he could not recall what had prompted him onto his path. It had seemed important at the time, he was sure.

Tell shivered and looked around. The flat was small, but full of memories, most of them Peter's. Tell was not sentimental. He could not afford to be. But even so, the thought of leaving it was painful. He finished the tea and put the mug in the sink. Out the window, the sky was full of hornet-shapes – drones, whisking to and fro. The future was automated. Maybe the machines would make a better go of it than mankind.

He leaned over the sink, looking at nothing. He closed his eyes. Thinking now. The old instincts were starting to kick in finally, after the paralysis of the last twenty-four hours. He had three safe houses in the city, all registered under different names. He didn't need to activate his Optik to see them in his head. He was old enough that he could find his way around London without a GPS.

Each contained the bare necessities – fake passports,

falsified identification papers, the passwords for half a dozen different cryptocurrency accounts as well as packs of hard cash, some of it counterfeit, but not all. Weapons as well, though not many. Handguns, mostly. And the tools of his trade.

His hands knotted into fists on the edge of the sink. He still wasn't sure how they'd found him. His blackmailer – or blackmailers. He wasn't sure whether they were one person, or many. A ghost in the frequency, reminding him of who he'd been – threatening him. Threatening to reveal who he was, beneath the mask of Marcus Tell.

He'd thought fear had been burned out of him long ago. But he'd been wrong. He feared losing his little flat, his memories. That was why he'd done it, in the end. To hold onto what he had, just for a little longer, just until… well.

So he'd picked up his old tools, and added some new tricks to his repertoire. He'd kept abreast of modern advances and techniques. The old stuff wouldn't have done the job. Not the way his blackmailers wanted it done, whoever they were.

"Impatient bastards," he murmured. He turned away from the sink, eyes straying again to the window. They'd wanted bombs and they'd wanted them fast. He'd done his best. Most of his old contacts were out of business or had been replaced by younger models with no respect for an old man. Not to mention trying to get the necessary materials without alerting the wrong people was harder than it had been. That his blackmailers had left it to him implied that it was his expertise they needed as much as his skills at constructing improvised explosive devices.

In his younger days, he might've tried to do something

with that information. Maybe even find them, and teach them a lesson in respect. They were arrogant – overconfident. They had made no great secret as to their intentions towards him, once he'd completed his part in the affair. Perhaps they thought him too stupid to see what was coming, as Colin had been. Or maybe they simply didn't care. What could one old man do, after all?

That he'd survived this long was more due to chance than any skill on his part. It had been sheerest luck that he'd spotted the pickpocket working the crowd on Sunday. He'd known he was being tracked, though he hadn't yet realised why. It had been a simple matter to flash his Optik and then put it in his pocket in a position so as to invite theft.

The thief had been skilled. Tell had barely felt it when his Optik had been purloined. He'd thought to buy himself some time. When he heard the shot, he'd known there was no time left. They wanted him dead, and it was only a matter of time until they came looking. He'd expected someone to bust down his door before now, but so far – nothing.

But he couldn't remain in hiding here. Eventually, he would have to leave, if only for his own sanity. They would find him sooner or later.

For him to survive, Marcus Tell would have to die. He would need a new name, a new life. He would have to start over again. He sighed. It seemed pointless, and a part of him wondered if it might be better to simply… wait. Make them work for it, but not too hard. Just enough to teach them some respect.

The thought of dying made his heart speed up. He looked at his hands – lined and spotted, but steady. You had to have steady hands, when you handled explosives. One wrong twitch and that was it.

Tell let out a slow breath, calming himself. He didn't want to die. If he did, he wouldn't have bothered becoming Marcus Tell. He would never have met Peter. He wouldn't have had ten good years to overlay all the bad ones before.

He didn't want to die. That meant he had to hide. He had to move and keep moving, until what was going to happen, happened, and his status became irrelevant. They would forget about him then, maybe. A small chance, but a chance nonetheless. A chance for another ten years. That was worth the effort.

Tell pushed away from the sink. Moving quickly now, decisively. He checked his wristwatch – an old fashioned habit. No one had watches, these days. He paused. Peter had given it to him. An anniversary gift, he thought.

He noted the time, took the watch off, and tossed it into the cutlery drawer. He couldn't afford to take anything with him, just in case. That was for the best. He would make do with what he had on him until he reached the first of his lockups.

He looked around one last time, fixing the place in his mind and headed for the door.

DAY TWO

WEDNESDAY

Bagley-bytes 13675-8: Attention, DedSec Wandsworth – this means you, Terry – members of a certain prominent criminal firm have been seen wandering about the Solar Garden at night. Maybe have a sneaky peek and get back to us. By which we mean you, Terry. Go. Or I'll send a copy of your search history to Albion – or worse, your mother.

+++

On the subject of Albion, our recent POI, Richard Malik, has been seen trundling about in the company of its very own Mr Nigel Cass, as well as representatives from Blume. Dalton, if you're still in contact with your MI5 chums, you might want to ask what all that's about.

+++

Over to Islington. There's a work-site in Finsbury that seems to be playing host to our old friends in Clan Kelley, including a gentleman by the name of Billy Bricks. Lot of bulky merchandise going into vans. Rasheed, see what you can dig up – but be careful. Things are in the wind.

+++

RE: Zero Day. No, I have no information on that phrase currently. Sorry, Dalton.

+++

Something's afoot at the drone facility in Limehouse. An internal problem? Time will tell. But we'd like to know sooner, rather than later. Anyone in the area, keep an eye out and an ear to the ground, if you would – especially if anyone mentions the names Holden or LIBRA.

+++

Protests are scheduled for the day of the TOAN Conference. Anyone with any interest in setting off some propaganda bombs or defacing public property or, say, crashing the conference, should check in with Sabine first.

17: ARRANGEMENTS

"You look like death warmed up," Winston Natha said cheerily, as he lowered himself down opposite Sarah's desk. He set a recyclable coffee cup down on the desk, and nudged it towards her. She took off the plastic top and gave it a sniff.

"Hazelnut?"

"Something godawful like that, yes." Winston leaned back in the chair, legs crossed. "How long did Faulkner hold everyone, then? We got turned back at the cordon."

She rubbed her eyes. They felt gritty, despite the drops. She hadn't gotten much sleep. She'd fielded dozens of calls after the news had gone out. She'd finally collapsed on the couch in her office for a nap at three AM. "About two hours longer than strictly necessary."

"I hope you spent the time productively."

"I had a lot to do. They started bloody shooting the place up." She felt a spurt of anger. "Which they do not have authorisation for. Or so I thought." And hadn't that been a fun phone call, with Faulkner grinning at her the entire time? It turned out that authorization had come down from on high in the aftermath, after Faulkner reported that his men had been attacked. Cass's influence, she thought.

"I told you, things are changing."

"Yes. For the worse. Still, I made some new friends among the press and the police. Shared hardships and such." She took a sip of the coffee. "Faulkner thinks it was DedSec."

"And what do you think?"

"I think it doesn't matter what I think. Whoever they were, they got away."

"And made Faulkner look quite a prat in the process." Winston scratched his nose. "That's twice in two days you've tweaked his nose. I'm surprised he hasn't bundled you off to one of those illicit black sites the media like to bloviate about."

"I suspect he needs to warm up to it." She didn't smile. There was enough evidence as to the very real existence of those sites that she didn't find it as funny as Winston did. Most of what Albion did wasn't funny. "Has Cass been in touch yet?"

"That's what I wanted to talk to you about. It seems the Limehouse facility is undergoing necessary renovations and will unavailable for public tours for the foreseeable future." Winston shook his head. "Albion is closing ranks."

"Something is up with them. And it has to do with the shootings."

"A word of advice, Sarah – leave it to CID. Let the Met handle this mess. That's what they're paid to do. We're paid to make speeches and shake hands." He leaned forward. "Speaking of which – the TOAN protests..."

Sarah grunted. "Yes, I saw that." The media were having a field day. They'd taken to referring to the conference as "TOAN Deaf", mostly because of it its wildly inappropriate marketing efforts. Efforts which were having quite an effect, though possibly not the one the conference's backers – not to mention the government – had hoped for.

The rapid automation of the British industrial sector was a sore point with most, if not all, of the country's trade unions. Joblessness was on the rise thanks to new technological innovations, and here was a celebration of the same. TOAN Deaf, indeed.

Protests were inevitable. The Met was underfunded and lacked the manpower to tackle what was coming. "I'm sure our friend Nigel Cass has already offered the services of Albion to alleviate some of the pressure on the Met."

"He claims some experience with crowd control," Winston said. His smile was grim. "All it will take is some fool throwing a Molotov or a brick, and there'll be blood on the streets. Worse than the Redundancy Riots." There was an understandable edge to his voice when he mentioned the riots.

The Riots had consumed the city for several, and nowhere had been hit harder than East London. Too many people already on the edge, and the first wave of automation had pushed them over, and onto the dole. Sarah herself had ridden into office on a wave of dissent. She'd promised to get people back to work. As yet, she had not been able to keep those promises. Initially, she'd hoped Albion would provide the answer.

"I'm sure that's exactly what Albion is hoping for." Sarah sighed. "There might be an opportunity there, though. Not just a photo op this time, either. Something substantial. Have you talked to anyone else?"

Winston shrugged. "Most of them are keeping their heads down. The Labour Party is officially noncommittal, and unofficially has its head thrust squarely up its–"

"I get the picture, thank you." Sarah massaged her temples. She'd had a persistent headache since last night. Faulkner had questioned everyone present in the station at least twice, while his men had scoured the surrounding streets, looking for any signs of whoever had stolen the evidence. If they'd stolen anything at all.

A part of her suspected that it was all a ruse on Faulkner's part. An attempt to make himself look the hero for his bosses and the media. The man taking charge of an impossible situation. Only the situation was largely of his making. At least that was how it seemed to her. She recalled how he'd reacted when she'd mentioned the mysterious Mr Holden.

Winston cleared his throat, startling her from her momentary reverie. "Do you have a strategy in mind? Besides decamping for Bruges, I mean."

Sarah raised an eyebrow. "You make it sound like we're facing an invading army."

"What would you call them? They can now freely use those weapons they like to brandish…"

"Not freely," she corrected. "Only when attacked."

"Yes, but who gets to define what is an attack, and what isn't?" He made an exasperated gesture. "My office has been dealing with reports of overstep by Cass's thugs all day. I assume yours has been the same."

Sarah fell silent. She glanced towards the door of her office.

Hannah had been answering calls all morning. She'd assumed most of them were from the press. She resolved to seriously consider giving the young woman a raise at some point.

"It's getting bad out there," Winston said, softly. Sarah didn't reply. He cleared his throat. "And not just out there. You can feel it, in Parliament. A sort of miasma. Don't you think?" He looked at her expectantly.

"I think this has gone beyond surgeries and press conferences," she said. "How many of us are there?"

"Us?"

"The loyal opposition."

Winston sat back. "By which I assume you mean those opposed to the current direction of the government."

A sudden suspicion came to her. "You aren't recording this, are you Winston? Trying to get me to say something I shouldn't?"

Winston stared at her. "What possible reason could I have to do that?"

Sarah met his glare with one of her own. Then, she sagged back into her chair and gave a weak smile. "I'm sorry, Winston. The events of the past few days have me… on edge. I'm jumping at shadows."

"I understand. For what it's worth, I think you're right. A headcount is in order. We need to know how much opposition we can muster in the event it comes to a vote. I'll start working on my end." Winston stood. "I know we've had a somewhat contentious relationship, Sarah, but… we are on the same side. We both want what's best for Tower Hamlets and the people here. And if that means we have to give Albion a kick up the rear, then we'll make it a damn good one."

"Inspiring, Winston. Make sure to put that in your speech."

"Already have, my dear. Ta."

Sarah watched him leave, an amused smile on her face. It faded quickly, however. She swivelled her chair and looked out the window, watching the drones and wondering what she was missing. She felt as if she were at sea, being buffeted by unseen leviathans.

"I suppose the only thing to do is to swim," she murmured. She pulled out a pad and a pencil. After a moment, she began to make a list of names. When she'd finished, she called Hannah into her office.

Hannah ducked her head in, a pensive look on her face. "Yes?"

Sarah considered the list for a moment longer, and then passed it across her desk. "We're going to have a dinner party. Won't that be fun?"

"A ... party?" Hannah replied. "Are you sure that's wise?"

"Take a look at the guest list before you judge."

Hannah read the list, eyes flicking back and forth. She frowned. "If I didn't know you better, I'd say you were planning a revolt – or a coup."

"Nothing as revolutionary as that," Sarah said, turning to face the window.

"And when is this soirée to be held?"

"The day of the TOAN conference." She leaned back in her seat. "There's a certain symbolism there, I think. While they pretend to fix the world's problems, we'll do the actual work. It'll make good copy for the press, if nothing else."

"And what if no one RSVPs? Some of these people definitely wouldn't want to be seen with you – or in East London, for that matter."

Sarah smiled lazily. "They will. There's plenty of dissent in the Commons. Even the Tories aren't a hundred per cent on board with the Prime Minister's current vision for the country. But any resistance is doomed to fail – unless someone takes charge."

"Welcome to the Resistance," Hannah said.

"Exactly." Sarah looked at her assistant. "They never located those two reporters, you know. I described them, but Faulkner found neither hide nor hair of them. Curious that, don't you think?"

"Maybe he's lying," Hannah said, after a moment.

"Maybe." Sarah studied the other woman. Hannah had seemed… off, of late. Bothered about something. Maybe it was the stress of the job getting to her. Or maybe the shooting had affected her more than she was letting on.

"If there's nothing else…?" Hannah began.

"No, no. Thank you," Sarah said. She turned back to the window, fully awake for the first time since yesterday. There was a plan now. A way forward.

But would it lead to victory… or something less pleasant?

Hannah sat at her desk, considering the list. The names were those of people of similar dispositions and goals – and people with no interest in allowing Albion a foothold in London, if it could possibly be helped. If one were planning to organise political resistance to the government's current plan, the names on the list would be a necessary foundation.

She found herself admiring the ruthless pragmatism of it. In one motion, Sarah would find out who could be trusted, and irrevocably bind them together. Anyone who went to this party would soon be outed – and those who chose not to go, as well.

Once, she might have leaked the guest list to the press, and to DedSec. If Sarah had decided to come down on the side of Albion. But so long as Sarah was aimed in the right direction, there was no need to sabotage things.

Instead, she would put her efforts into making sure it all ran smoothly. The biggest issue with planning such an engagement was the optics. Anyone who looked at the guest list would immediately know what was up. Ordinarily, that wouldn't be an issue, but these days it would be inadvisable, perhaps even dangerous. Perhaps that was why Sarah had written the guest list on paper. Analog materials were more secure.

Hannah chose to follow her example, and laboriously scribbled plans and phone numbers as she made the preparations. It gave her something to occupy her mind, at least. To keep her from thinking about the previous day. About the way Faulkner had looked at her.

She'd heard nothing more from Bagley or Krish. From the police reports, it seemed Liz and Ollie had gotten away, but Albion had mobilised throughout Tower Hamlets. They were on every street corner as of last night, questioning potential witnesses, i.e. anyone who caught their eye.

While they couldn't arrest anyone, that hadn't stopped them from bundling suspects into armoured transports for enhanced interrogation at undisclosed locations. Faulkner had called twice, demanding to speak to Sarah. So far, Hannah had managed to put him off, but she couldn't do so forever. Eventually, he was just going to show up. She was certain he suspected that Sarah had something to do with the theft.

In some ways, that was good. The longer Sarah and Faulkner

were focused on one another, the more it pushed Sarah to kick against Albion. While most of her peers in DedSec were more concerned with graffiti and digital redistribution, Hannah had long thought the key to the Resistance was in the halls of power.

It wasn't the man on the street you needed to convince – it was the man in Parliament. The one with their hand on the lever of government. Get them thinking the right way, and you could do anything. Or so she hoped.

Not everyone believed the way she did. Some thought the only way to make things right was to start over – crash the system and reboot. Rebuild society from the ground up. But Hannah wasn't willing to pay the inevitable cost for such an extreme solution. How many would die, not in riots or upheaval, but from simple starvation or sickness?

She shook her head. No, the only way was to work within the existing system. To change it one part at a time, until it was running the way it was meant to run.

She shook her head. Time to worry about that sort of thing later. She pulled out her Optik. "Bagley," she murmured.

Greetings, Hannah Shah. I trust you are well today?

"I would be better if I knew whether Albion were going to be kicking in my door today. I don't suppose you can shed any light on that?"

Have no fear. Nothing I have heard implicates you or your employer. Though she is making quite a few enemies…

"The right ones, I hope. Liz and Olly?"

Safe as houses. You played your part well.

"Happy to be of service. Now you can help me. Have you found him yet?"

The mysterious Mr Holden, you mean?

"That would be him, yes. Stop prevaricating, Bagley. Has anyone found him?"

Not as yet. Though we have noticed an increased amount of chatter surrounding the subject of Holden on Albion's internal communications network. He seems to have been a very bad boy indeed.

"What do you mean?"

Whatever Holden is up to Albion hasn't sanctioned it. And they aren't happy about it.

Hannah sat back, thinking about it. "It must have something to do with the shootings. He knows something. Or thinks he does." She paused. "I think it might be in our best interests to find him, if we can. And not just to satisfy my curiosity."

That was the thinking in the DedSec canteen as well.

Hannah stifled a laugh. "I'm sure."

We are – ah. Hang on. You've got an incoming call. I think you should take it.

Hannah frowned. Before she could speak, a call alert flashed on her display. She answered. "Hello?"

"Is this the woman I spoke to before?"

She recognised the voice instantly. "Mr. Holden... I didn't expect to hear from you again. Especially after I found your bug."

A moment of silence. Then a rueful chuckle. *"Is that what happened to it?"*

"Technically, my employer happened to it. She does not look kindly on would-be spies, Mr Holden. I would suggest you remember that. What can I do for you today?"

"It's your employer I need to speak to. Today."

"I'm sorry, but today–"

"Today," he repeated. "It's a matter of life and death."

Hannah paused. "Is it about Albion?" she asked, softly. She heard an intake of breath.

"Yeah, you might say that."

"Then it might be in our best interests not to meet with you." She heard a knock on her door and looked up. Sarah stood in the doorway. She mouthed a question and Hannah pointed to her Optik, and scrawled Holden's name on her pad. Sarah's eyes widened and gestured furiously. Hannah put the call on speaker.

"That'd be a mistake," he said. "Your boss wants dirt on Albion, doesn't she? I can give it to her."

"In return for what?"

"Protection."

"From Albion?" She looked up as Sarah snapped her fingers. She gestured, but Hannah motioned for her to be patient.

There was a noticeable hesitation before he answered. "Yes."

"Done," Sarah said, before Hannah could speak. "I'll clear my schedule. Where do you wish to meet?"

18: MASKS

Liz leaned forward, watching the TV screens. The screens were tuned to different stations, one of which was a pirate broadcast out of Charlton. All of them were talking about the same thing – Albion. On the streets, in businesses and homes. No official word had come down regarding an increase in Albion's remit, but most of the talking heads were taking the government's silence as tacit approval.

On one screen, Nigel Cass was talking breezily about the need for an Albion presence at the TOAN conference. On another, MP Sarah Lincoln was making the most out of Albion patchy record regarding human rights. Three stations, including GBB, were still on what was being officially called "The Bethnal Green Incident", and how it might be the work of DedSec, which GBB at least were calling a terrorist cell.

"Not good," Krish murmured, from where he sat nearby. He wasn't the only one. At least a dozen people sat or stood in the cellar's central room, watching the news reports. "Really not good."

"We've been called worse," Liz said, without looking at him. Someone laughed. Krish didn't. He'd started to pace.

"They're already cracking down. Drones in the air, APVs on the streets. What are we going to do?"

"Well, not panicking is a start." Liz stood and stretched. She'd slept on a camp bed the night before, and was paying for it now. She had a flat in Whitechapel, but rarely spent any time there. It was rented under another name, obviously and was sparsely furnished. Barely better than the cellar for comfort. She wondered if she out to simply move out and stop pretending. "Next, we'll crack open that Optik and see what secrets it holds."

"Olly's been working on it all night," Krish said, somewhat accusingly.

"He's a good lad," she said. "Is there any coffee left? I need a caffeine hit." She collected coffees for herself and Olly and went downstairs. Olly was right where she'd left him, feet up on the table, leaning back in his chair, dozing. What was left of the Optik lay on a towel on the table, its internal workings exposed, its wiring connected to circuit boards and tiny components.

She considered pulling the chair out from under him, and then decided to be merciful. She put the coffees down and cleared her throat. "Wakey-wakey."

Olly jolted awake, nearly falling backwards. "What? I'm up!"

"Coffee." Liz indicated a cup. Olly reached for it and she snatched it out of reach. "First tell me what you found."

He sat back. "Does the name Marcus Tell mean anything to you?"

"No. Should it?"

"Dunno. Why I asked, yeah?" Olly frowned and sat back, staring at the gutted remains of the Optik, as if it had offended him. "He's the owner, which means he's likely the bloke Dempsey stole it from. Which means…"

"He's the one the shot was intended for. Any reason why?"

"Not that I can see. But there's something… something off about him."

Liz stood and came around the table so that she could look over his shoulder. "Show me," she said. Olly brought up a batch of profiles, forms and data, transmitting them to the overhead display.

"Right, so, on a surface skim it's all good. But you spend as much time as I have building ghost profiles, and you start to get a feeling for when something's artificial-like. Like, too perfect, in that imperfect sort of way. Does that make sense?"

Liz nodded. "Say it does. You're saying the profile is dodgy?"

"I'm saying it's all dodgy. Census data, GP records, birth certificate – every bleeding bit of it is artificial. Oh it's a lovely fake, but it's still a fake. I doubt anyone would've spotted it a few years ago, but these days you can see the cracks, if you know what to look for." Olly gnawed on a knuckle as he glared at the data. "Whoever he is, he's put a lot of effort into this. He's made himself a whole life, and he's wearing it like a mask."

"You only wear a mask if you have something to hide."

"Like us," Olly said, not looking at her.

Liz paused. Olly was proving to be perceptive. "Yeah," she said. "And maybe he's hiding for the same reasons we do. But we need to find out who he is, regardless. Two people have been killed so far. Whoever is hunting him, it doesn't look they're planning to stop until they get him."

"So we need to find him first," Olly said, hunching over the Optik. "I can do that. I can get into the cloud, dig around in the GPS data, and see where he might be."

"Good thinking." Liz hesitated, and then squeezed his shoulder. Olly glanced at her and then away. Liz sat down, thinking. Trying to assemble the pieces.

"What I can't figure," Olly said, "Is how the other poor sod fits in. You remember, the one shot behind *The Wolfe Tone*?"

"Wilson," Liz said, dredging up the name. "Colin Wilson."

"Right. So, same MO, innit?"

"Yes."

"So we know what Dempsey did. But what did that poor fucker do?"

Liz looked at him. "That, Olly, is a very good question." Tapping at her Optik, she brought up Bagley's model of the first shooting. And then added the one the AI had constructed for the second.

She watched the reconstructions play through several times. The angle of the two shots was different, but each had come from above. Not the rooftops, but higher. A high calibre weapon in each case. The same weapon.

"A drone," she murmured.

"What?" Olly was looking at her.

"It's a drone."

"What is?"

"The killer. It's a drone."

Olly nodded slowly. "That'd explain the height, and the

whole triangulation thing. The Albion pursuit drones do the
same thing – they track you by your GPS signal. If someone's
got an armed drone…" He trailed off. "Bloody Hell. That is
some serious shit. What's going on here?"

"I don't know." Liz sat back and swung her feet up onto the
table. "Every answer we find leads to a new question." She
pinched the bridge of her nose. "I fucking hate mysteries."

"Me mum loved them," Olly said. "Watched *Miss Marple* on
the telly all the time."

Liz looked at him. "Do I look like your bleeding mum,
Olly?"

"I mean, it's just – you're both of a certain age…" he trailed
off as her expression registered. "Never mind," he added,
quickly.

Liz stared at him for a moment longer, letting him sweat,
before closing her eyes again. Something occurred to her.
"Past tense," she said, softly.

"What?"

"She loved them. Used to watch them. Past tense."

Olly was silent. Liz had read what Krish had compiled on
Oliver Soames. There wasn't much that wasn't immediately
obvious. But sometimes not everything got shared online,
or included in super-secret resistance movement dossiers for
that matter.

Finally, he said, "She died, didn't she?" He cleared his throat.
"Got sick. With a virus. Funny, 'cause she was a nurse an' all."
He fell silent again.

"It doesn't sound funny at all." She peered at him, trying
to read his expression. "Were you young when it happened,
then?"

"Young enough." He rubbed at his eyes with the heels of his palms. "Is what it is, innit?" He turned his attentions back to the Optik.

She felt a moment's sympathy, watching him. Olly was young, inexperienced. Not exactly a hardened criminal or a revolutionary. He was just a kid who'd pulled some clever clogs shit and gotten drafted into a fight he didn't really understand. So few of them did. The thought made her feel old, so she pushed it aside.

She paused. "Hell."

"What?"

"Holden."

"Who?" Olly was staring at her now. Liz ignored him.

"Bagley, who's the bloke Hannah is looking for? Holden something?"

George Holden. A managing technician at the drone facility in Limehouse. He's gone walkabout apparently. Why – oh. Ah. I see.

"I bloody don't," Olly said.

"Holden was looking into the shooting as well. And being sneaky about it. That's not a coincidence."

"You think he has something to do with it?"

Liz leaned back. "Maybe. Maybe it's just coincidence. But I don't think so. Either way, I need to inform the others. If there is a killer drone flying around, all of DedSec London need to keep their eyes and apps peeled for it."

"I'll get back to it then," Olly said, turning back to his work. Liz watched him for a moment, then made the call.

"Yes?" a voice answered. "Sabine," Liz said, softly. She moved away from the table, activating a scrambler app as she did so. Not that Olly was paying attention, but better safe than sorry. Like a genie springing from a bottle, Sabine Brandt's ovoid icon appeared on her display.

"Liz. Anything new?"

"Some. None of it good. We have the Optik. It belonged to a Marcus Tell. That name seem familiar to you?"

"No, sadly."

"What about Colin Wilson?"

"Again, no. Though I might be able to find something out."

"I'll work on it from this end as well. There's more. Bagley got us the scene-of-crime analysis reports for both shootings. The shots were made by a high powered semi-automatic rifle. And the trajectory – they could only have come from above."

"The rooftops?"

"Higher."

Sabine was silent. Then, "*That* is an interesting wrinkle."

"I thought so. I think someone is using a drone. We know Albion have combat operational models, but someone would have seen something. Unless…"

"It was camouflaged somehow."

"Exactly." Liz frowned. She could hear the doubt in Sabine's voice. "Whoever Marcus Tell is, someone wanted him dead. I intend to find out why."

"You sound angry, Liz. Maybe you should leave it to someone else." Sabine paused. "I know Alex's death must have hit you hard, but…"

"But what?" Liz snapped. She shook her head. "I'm sorry, but no. No, I'm not handing this off. We need to know what happened. If there's some lunatic out there using a drone to snipe targets, we need to stop them."

"We're not the police, Liz," Sabine said. "DedSec has a

mission. *We* have a mission. Leave this one to them, or Albion, or whoever. There are more important matters to hand. This city is a powder keg, and someone somewhere has lit a fuse."

Liz recognised that tone. "Dalton found something."

"Of course he did. He always does." There was a trace of bitterness there. Liz had often wondered if Dalton Wolfe and Sabine Brandt had had something together in the past. The former MI5 operative and the outlaw hacker – it was a Hollywood screenplay waiting to be written. The way they'd acted around one another the few times she'd seen them in the flesh… but she'd never dared broach the subject. It wasn't her business.

"Well it's no surprise he's good at his bloody job, is it?" Liz murmured.

"He suspects someone is planning an attack. No idea who, but there's been mutterings around the TOAN conference…"

Liz glanced back at Olly. "Do you think it's connected?"

"Not this time," Sabine said, firmly. "Not everything is part of some grand conspiracy, Liz, no matter what your parents taught you."

"That was low," Liz said. "But point taken. So what is it?"

"I don't know yet. When I figure it out, I'll let you know." Sabine paused. "I think things are going to get worse before they get better. Be safe, Liz."

"You too, mate." Liz cut the connection.

Not for the first time, Olly found himself wondering what he was doing with his life. Why was he still in London? Anyone else with any sense and the ability to falsify travel documents would be on a plane to Ibiza. Instead, he was in a subbasement, dissecting proprietary technology and breaking dozens of laws.

Yesterday had been close. Exciting, but it could have ended badly. Might still end badly, unless he was careful. He thought about what Liz had said, about London. Did he feel the same? He'd never really thought about it. Not like that. London was just… London. It was the place where he was. He'd never thought about being anywhere else.

East London was home.

He paused, looking at the Optik. It was home, and you defended your ends when some fucker came looking to mess things up, right? It sounded simple, but it wasn't really. This wasn't the sort of thing that could be solved with punches or hacking a program.

A string of scrambled texts appeared on his display, dredged from the memory of Tell's Optik. The scrambling was due to an encryption app. You had to have the right cipher to decode it. Luckily, he had a universal decryption program – it was useful for password prediction. The texts were lists – materials, he thought, though for what he couldn't say.

They'd been sent to a number that he knew right off was for a burner phone. Old fashioned, but not unexpected. He made a note of the materials. Whatever project Tell had needed them for, he'd probably already completed it.

"Bagley?" he asked.

Oliver.

"What do you make of this list?"

Ah. Oh. Oh my. That is naughty indeed.

"Meaning?"

These materials have a multiplicity of uses, but their

accumulation on a single list implies they are being combined into an improvised explosive device. And not just one.

Olly felt a chill. "How many?"

Ten, at least. It depends on the payload.

"Jesus," he blurted.

"What?" Liz asked, from behind him. She'd finished her call, and he flushed slightly as he realized she'd been listening. He turned.

"Tell was making bombs. Or helping someone make bombs."

"Bombs?" Liz joined him. She looked at the list, and whistled softly. "Oh that is not good. Not good at all." She frowned. "Wilson – the second victim – was a van driver, wasn't he?"

Indeed, though not what you'd call a successful one.

Liz waved Bagley's observation aside. "So what was he delivering?"

"Maybe we should ask Tell," Olly said. "I got an address." He brought up a map of Whitechapel on his display, with the GPS pings arranged on it. "Right, so, the majority of the Optik's pings are here. Now, given the data, I figure he's an old geezer, which means on an average day he doesn't go very far, right?"

"Depends on the geezer."

"Well, the data tells the story," Olly insisted. "And I figure he's got to be local to Whitechapel, probably Lister or Treves House, if he was at that rally, right?"

"So far so good," Liz said.

"I narrowed it down further, cross referenced the name with Council records, and what do we find but – voila!" He gestured, and an indicator arrow flashed over Lister House.

"Marcus Tell, resident for a decade."

Liz nodded again. "Very good. What else?"

"He's got a debit card, a credit card, but neither have been used in a week. Not much money in his account, but there's a lot of activity nonetheless. He keeps a minimum in the account, but he's got more somewhere else. I haven't found it yet."

"Cryptocurrency?"

"Yeah, but it's the same. Bare minimum. Like, exactly the amount you'd expect a guy like that to have. And no movement on it either. I bet he's got another account, maybe two or three. A bit more time, and I might be able to narrow them down."

"No. I think this is enough." Liz studied the map. "Whoever killed Alex has probably figured out by now that they got the wrong person. Tell must have suspected that as well, which is why he's in the wind now."

"So, I might be able to clone his Optik data and figure out where he is now, especially if he got a new external unit. But he doesn't have any social media which is just bizarre. Even my nan had instant messaging."

"Not bizarre if he's trying to hide. Social media is just handing over data that can be used to find and identify you. If he's really in hiding, he won't have anything like that, or if he does, it'll be faked."

"This bloke was somebody bad, wasn't he?" Olly asked, hesitantly. "I mean, a bomb maker? Those don't grow on trees." He looked at her. "So what do you want to do?"

"We go."

"Where?"

"Where do you think?"

"He's probably not there anymore. I know I wouldn't be."

"No, but we should check it out anyway. There might be something we can use to find out where he went – or what he was doing that got him marked for death."

"Yeah, but... Albion will be looking for us. They're all over the streets."

"What's life without risk, Olly?"

"Safe?"

"Boring," Liz corrected. "Up. You can drink your coffee on the way."

19: PROTECTION

Sarah sat in an espresso bar on Whitechapel High Street, near Aldgate East Station. It was located inside the eight storey White Chapel Building, and was far too spacious and clean for her liking. Sarah preferred her coffee shops small, cramped and full of homey tat. Maybe some godawful indie music playing in the background.

Artfully exposed conduits and pipework lent a glamorized industrial air, and the tastefully mismatched colour palate reminded her of a university common room. Her mocha was excellent, if lacking in personality. Hannah sat nearby, and PC Jenks as well, dressed in her civvies and nursing an English Breakfast Tea.

When Hannah had put the request in, the young constable had volunteered for bodyguard duties. Jenks was somewhat on the outs with her superiors. They weren't quite blaming her for the theft of evidence, but Albion wanted someone's head and it looked like the Met was going to give them hers. For that reason, among others, Sarah had been happy to accept. She liked Jenks. The constable had a bulldog tenacity she appreciated, as well as a refreshing lack of curiosity.

"Are you certain this is the place he suggested?" Sarah said, as she idly scrolled through her Optik feed. The news seemed focused on preparations for the TOAN conference, in three days' time. Not a word about Sunday's shooting. Someone had a vested interest in distracting the public. She hadn't yet decided whether that was to her benefit.

Hannah, sitting behind her, said, "Yes. He wanted a public place."

"That leads me to more questions," Sarah replied.

"Perhaps I can give you answers," Holden said, as he abruptly sat down opposite her. Sarah recognised him from Hannah's description, and the information in the dossier they'd gathered on Albion.

"Mr Holden, I presume."

"I wasn't sure you'd meet me." He was unshaven, wearing a rumpled suit and too much cologne, likely to hide the fact he hadn't taken a shower. He sat down heavily, causing the chair to creak.

Sarah sipped her mocha without pleasure. "I was curious. I assume this is in reference to my request to visit the drone facilities?"

Holden smirked. "Not quite."

"You bugged my assistant's office," Sarah said, mildly. "Why?"

"Right to it, then?" Holden said, after a moment's hesitation. He ran a hand over his unshaven cheek. "Fine. I needed to know what you knew. Turns out you know sod all."

"Oh, I know more than that – I know you're in trouble."

Sarah sat back in her chair. "So why don't you tell me about it?"

Holden stared at her, considering. She could practically hear the wheels in his head grinding away. Finally, he said, "I'll need protection."

"From whom?"

"Everyone."

Sarah raised an eyebrow. "Narrow it down for me."

"Can you get me protection?" Holden insisted. "I'm not talking without some guarantee…" He looked around nervously. Spotted Jenks. Tensed.

"She's with me," Sarah said, softly.

Holden gave a crooked smile. "Worried about my intentions?"

"It seemed prudent, given how you threatened my assistant."

"I didn't threaten her," Holden growled.

Sarah made a dismissive gesture. "What matters is why you are here now. I assume it has something to do with the shooting, given your questions."

"Shootings," he said. "Plural."

"Another one?"

"Night before last." Holden ran his hand through his hair and leaned forward. "You didn't answer my question. I need protection. MI5, the police, someone. Everyone. What I know – it's big. Albion won't want it to get out."

Sarah frowned. "Is that who you're worried about then? Albion?"

"Among others." Holden gave a sickly grin. "It's not them. Not really. But when they find out, they'll be looking to shut me up." His grin faded. "Or worse."

Sarah paused. "What is this about, Mr Holden? I need something other than vague statements if I am to do anything."

Holden licked his lips. "A conspiracy. I don't know what its purpose is, but I know some of the players, and they're making their moves even as we speak."

"Albion, you mean…"

"You're not listening," Holden blurted. "Albion are tangential. Or maybe not. But they're not the ones pulling the trigger." He pulled out his Optik in sudden, convulsive motion. Out of the corner of her eye, Sarah saw Jenks start to rise, and waved her back. She didn't want to startle Holden. Not when he was finally getting to the point.

"Look, look here – these are pictures, he didn't realise I'd taken them," he began, then hesitated. "Or maybe he didn't care. Either way, I have them." He brought up an image, a hasty snapshot of an average looking man, dressed in the subdued browns and greys she'd come to associate with a certain sort of middle class undecided voter.

"And who is this?"

"The one pulling the trigger." Holden frowned. "At least I think so."

"And why do you think this?"

Another pause. Longer this time. She could smell his sweat, seeping out from under the shroud of cologne. "Because I sold him the gun." He laughed harshly. "I needed the money. I didn't think… and now…" He sat back, a hollow look on his face. "But it's bigger than him. I've been putting the pieces together. Little bits here and there. Things he said. Things the others said…"

"Others?"

"He's not the only one." Holden caught her wrist in a tight grip. "I need a guarantee of protection before I say anything else."

Sarah waved Jenks back again, not taking her eyes from Holden. No one had noticed his increasing anxiety yet, but eventually someone would. She needed to keep him calm. "Why come to me, Mr Holden?"

He released her and sat back. "Who better? Everyone knows you've got a grudge against Albion. That's why you wanted to see the drone facilities, isn't it? You're trying to dig up dirt on them, on Cass. Well, what I can tell you will make that easier."

Sarah said nothing. She rubbed her wrist where Holden had caught her. He was frightened and desperate, and that in turn made her uneasy. It was as if she had gone fishing and caught a shark by accident. What was she supposed to do now? Reel it in and hope for the best – or cut the line, like a sensible person?

Her choice was made for her when Holden's Optik gave a shrill ping. He looked at it, eyes widening, and then at her. "You told them we were meeting," he said, accusingly.

"What? Who are you talking about?"

"Albion! They'll be here any second. I knew I shouldn't have trusted you." Holden shot to his feet, knocking his chair over backwards. He was wild-eyed as he looked around. "This is a trap!"

"It's no trap, Holden," Sarah began, half-rising to her feet. "I didn't tell anyone. I – oh shit shit." She hesitated. "Faulkner. I mentioned you'd come to see me ..."

"Faulkner? You fucking told Faulkner?" He was shouting now, and as he backed away from the table she caught a flash of a pistol holstered beneath his coat. Jenks was on her feet as well, moving towards him.

"Moira, no – he's armed," Sarah said. Jenks froze, just for an instant, and then dove towards Holden, clearly intending to rugby-tackle him to the floor. Holden cursed and fell back, and the two of them went down in a tangle. Sarah hesitated, unsure of what to do. It wasn't a feeling she liked. Hannah caught her wrist and pulled her back. The café was in an uproar now as the struggle upended tables and knocked over chairs.

Despite the differences in their weight, Jenks had the better of Holden from the outset. She hit him quickly, in the sides, and then across the jaw. It was only thanks to his desperation that he managed to throw her off, and her bad luck that she went face-first into a table. As Jenks rolled away, Holden scrambled to his feet. Through the big windows at the front of the café, Sarah saw three Albion drones drop down. Computerized voices bellowed commands as Holden lifted his Optik.

He did something, and all three drones fell out of the air. A moment later, Albion APVs skidded into view along the street, disgorging men and women in fatigues and body armour. Holden backed away from the entrance, eyes wide. He drew his weapon, and for a moment, Sarah thought he was going to make a fight of it.

Holden turned and ran for the kitchen. Sarah almost followed, but common sense kept her in place as Albion burst into the café and spread out with military precision. Every patron who hadn't already fled was held at gunpoint, as were the staff. Shouted commands dropped people back into their seats. On the other side of the café, a child started to cry.

Sarah ignored the guns, and the shouts, and went to help

Jenks to her feet. Her nose was busted, and Sarah grabbed a handful of napkins. She sat Jenks down. "Doesn't look broken," she said, passing the napkins to her bodyguard.

"Adding field medicine to your resume?" a familiar voice growled, behind her.

Sarah turned and put on an icy demeanour. "Sergeant Faulkner. Is there a reason you're waving a gun in my face? I trust I haven't done anything to make you fear for your life?" She looked around. "I would put them away, before I'm forced to take this up with your superiors."

"Sit down," Faulkner said, gesturing to a nearby table.

Sarah sat, smoothing her dress as she did so. "He went out through the kitchens. If you hurry, you might be able to catch him." She looked around. "As it stands, this isn't looking good for your reputation."

Faulkner grabbed a chair and sat down opposite her. "Why were you having coffee with a wanted terrorist?"

Sarah paused. "I wasn't aware he was such. As far as I knew, he was a potential whistle-blower."

"And you wanted to hear him out, did you?"

"Obviously."

Faulkner frowned. "You should take this more seriously, Ms Lincoln. Holden is a wanted man, and we could hold you as an accomplice."

"Unless something has changed in the last twenty-four hours, you can't hold anyone for anything." Sarah considered her next words carefully. "But, you know – let's go."

"Go where?"

"Your holding facility, obviously. Take me to wherever you're keeping the people you've been snatching off the streets the past day or so. Take me right now, Faulkner. Right here, in front of all those news drones that followed you here, in front of all the recording devices even now fixed on us." She set her hands on the table. "Slap the cuffs on me, officer. It's a fair cop."

Faulkner stared at her for a moment, and then snorted and looked away. "I wish I bloody could. I really do." He paused. "And maybe one day I will."

"I'm sure you're looking forward to it."

He laughed and looked at her. "Your parents were immigrants, weren't they?"

It was Sarah's turn to frown. "I don't see what that has to do with anything. But yes. My parents were indeed immigrants. Law abiding, productive members of society who were nonetheless often treated like second class citizens. One of the reasons I got into politics was to ensure that–"

"Save it," Faulkner said, flatly. He studied her. "If I thought for one moment you were serious about all that, I might respect you. But I know your type. I saw plenty of your sort overseas…"

"I'm sure you did. And I'm sure you shot a good many of them." Sarah knew she was pushing too hard. She also knew that she had stay on top of him. To keep him angry, rather than thinking. From the look on his face, it was working.

"Why were you meeting Holden?" he growled.

"He said he had something to tell me."

"What?"

"I don't know. You came in guns blazing before he had a chance to say anything." She made a show of looking around, at his men standing on guard. "Well done, by the way. You've pacified an upscale expresso bar. Nigel Cass would be so proud."

Faulkner's eyes narrowed. "You don't know when to quit, do you?"

"Like the Americans say, the best defence is a good offence."

He looked away. "Holden is no longer employed by Albion. He is a rogue element. A terrorist, as I said."

"Like DedSec?"

His eyes strayed back. "Maybe. My orders are to apprehend him."

"And turn him over to the proper authorities," Sarah said.

He smiled. "We are the authorities."

"Not yet. Not ever, if I get my way."

His smile widened and he stood. He looked around, his eyes passing over Jenks and settling on Hannah. She shrank back and he turned back to Sarah. "I would reconsider involving yourself in our affairs in the future. And if you happen to see Holden again, it'd be in your best interests to report it to us."

"And if I don't?"

He leaned over the table towards her, no longer smiling. "Then our next conversation will end poorly for you, Ms Lincoln. MP or no MP." He straightened and turned, signalling his men to withdraw. "Let's move."

Sarah let out a slow breath as they departed. She turned to the others. "Is everyone all right? PC Jenks – Moira?"

Jenks nodded, dabbing at her nose with a handful of napkins. "I'm alright, ma'am. Been knocked about worse by bigger."

"I'm sure. Hannah?"

Hannah nodded, her eyes wide. "Sarah, I–"

"Later." Sarah took a deep breath, composing herself. The remaining patrons had their Optiks out now, and were recording. She put on a confident smile. "Right now, I have to speak to my constituency about the gross abuse of power they just witnessed."

20: LOCK-UP

It only took one phone call for Danny to find out where Ro was living these days. His mum was only too happy to share. Danny thought she was hoping this was the first step to her children's reconciliation. She was probably going to be disappointed in that regard.

He and Ro had never gotten along, and there was too much time and bad feelings between them to change that. He still wasn't sure what he'd done, or not done, to piss her off. Sometimes he wondered if Ro herself even knew. Maybe she just liked hating him.

But this, whatever it was, was bigger than them. Danny had been a soldier long enough to know when something was up. There was a feeling in the air, like when you were riding down a stretch of mountain road and knew – you *knew* – that there was something bad waiting for you up ahead. But there was no way to tell what it was until you ran up on it.

Faulkner was up in arms about something. Some drone technician named Holden was on the run. Danny figured he was carrying a load of proprietary information, the way Faulkner was acting. Or maybe it was something else – something related to the shootings. He couldn't see how, but that didn't mean that the connections weren't there.

Danny was torn between his desire to investigate, and his desire to keep his head way down. Curiosity got men killed. Danny had seen it more than once. He didn't intend to suffer the same fate. All he wanted was to do his job, get paid and maybe visit his mum more than once in a blue moon. But if Ro was involved – if the Kelleys had her doing some shady shit related to what he was looking into – keeping his head down wasn't going to be an option. That was why he'd come all the way out here without telling anyone. There would be no record of this visit, and nothing to tie Ro to the scene. He'd made sure of that.

Ro's flat wasn't far from his mum's. It was on the second storey of a new build council estate, set atop the bones of old row houses and corner shops. Wide boys lurked in the corners, watching him with hooded gazes. He was thankful he hadn't come in uniform, and equally thankful he had his sidearm holstered under his coat.

He stopped. The door to Ro's place was in front of him. All he had to do was knock. Maybe she wasn't in. Maybe she'd just kept running. That's what a smart person would have done. Ro was smart, but not that smart.

He knocked on the door and waited. A moment later, the door cracked open. Ro peered out, jaw set, eyes narrowed. "What do you want?"

"Are you going to let me in?" he said.

"Are you alone?"

"Of course."

The door shut. He heard the jangle of a chain, and then it swung open in invitation. Ro gestured impatiently. "Well?" she said. "In or not?"

"In," Danny said. She closed the door behind him, after a quick look down the corridor. "I told you I was alone."

"Yeah, forgive me for not trusting you." Ro fell back onto an overstuffed couch that had seen better decades. She indicated a wicker chair nearby. "Sit, if you want."

Danny sat. They stared at each other in silence for several moments. Danny tried to think of how best to begin, but the longer it took, the more pugnacious Ro's expression became. He cleared his throat. "Nice place."

"Cheers."

"The Kelleys own the building, don't they?"

Ro looked at the ceiling. "What does that matter?"

"You're paying your bosses for a place to live."

"And you stay in barracks."

"I get paid to stay in barracks." He raised a hand, interrupting her retort. "Never mind. Colin Wilson's flat," he said, finally.

"What about it?"

"Don't fuck with me, Rosemary."

"Ro," she corrected. Danny met her glare and held it.

"What were you doing there?"

"I could ask you the same thing."

"I was conducting an investigation."

She laughed. "You a plod now?"

Danny looked around, taking in the lack of furnishings, the peeling paint, the stains. "Why were you there?"

"Wasn't."

"You literally punched me."

"Didn't."

Danny sank back into his chair. "You think this is funny?"

"I'm amused," Ro said.

"Five different CCTV feeds caught you running away. Three caught you entering the building. Six drones spotted you making your way down the street. Do I need to go on?"

Ro wasn't smiling anymore. He could tell she was rattled. She hadn't thought about it. She never really did. "Are you here to arrest me then? Mum will be cross."

"I'm not here to arrest you."

"Then why you here, bruv? You ain't missed me."

"Maybe I did," Danny said. "Maybe I'm worried about you. Maybe I don't want some trigger-happy operative to put a bullet in you, because you're standing next to one of the Kelleys at the wrong time."

Ro looked away. "That won't happen."

"You don't know that." Danny leaned forward. "You don't know anything. Otherwise you wouldn't be messing with this shit, yeah?" He paused, forcing himself to stay calm. "Why were you there?"

Ro was silent. Then, "Had to be, innit?"

"The Kelleys sent you?"

"Yeah." She ran a hand through her hair. "Bloody Mary wants to know what Colin was up to. And since I knew him…" She met his eyes challengingly, but he didn't speak. She went on. "Since I knew him, I got the job."

"You saw him get killed," Danny said, softly. He'd seen the CCTV footage from the pub – what there was of it. Ro had been talking to the victim when he'd been shot. She nodded.

"Was he a friend?"

"No, I just knew him, like."

Danny could hear the tremor in her voice, but didn't press her. "What did you find?"

"What makes you think I found anything?"

"Because you were running like you did."

"Maybe I just didn't want to get caught." Ro looked at him. "If you're not here to arrest me, or take me into custody or for questioning or whatever bullshit you call it – why are you here?"

"Maybe I wanted to check on you."

"I wasn't the one who got my arse kicked."

Danny bit back a retort. "But you were the one on the cameras. Or you would be, if I hadn't dealt with the footage."

Ro stared at him. "You what?"

"I'm the only one who knows. I haven't told anybody, and as soon as I can figure out how to erase it, or copy over it or whatever, I will." He paused. "I'm risking my job, maybe more than that, for you. The least you could do is tell me what you found."

"I didn't ask you to do that."

"You didn't have to," he snapped, raising his voice. "You're my sister, remember? What am I supposed to do? Just leave you to it?"

"It's what you've always done before," Ro snarled back.

Danny opened his mouth. Closed it. Looked away. Arguments with Ro were circular things, always going back around to old hurts. She couldn't let go of the past, couldn't see that he wanted what was best for her. Finally, he said, "I'm not dad."

Ro jerked as if he'd slapped her. She fell silent. Danny looked at her. "You're mad because I went away? Fine. I went away. But I went for you and mum. We needed money and I got some. And I never expected a word of thanks..."

"And you won't be getting one," she said. "We didn't need money, we needed you. And you ran away. You went halfway across the bloody world – for what? Not for us."

The words stung because there was some truth to them, however much he wanted to deny it. It had all been too much for him. Everything had been on him, or at least it had felt that way. Mum had been working all hours, Ro acting out, and school... well. Danny had never been the best student. Under different circumstances, he might've ended up with the Kelleys as well. Joining the army had almost been a relief. But he didn't say that.

"I don't have to justify myself to you," he said.

"Same," she said, arms crossed.

They stared at one another in silence for several long minutes. Danny sighed. He'd messed up. He'd come for information, and gotten nothing in return except hostility. And now Ro knew Albion was on the same trail. If she told the Kelleys, who knew what would happen? "You need to stay out of this, Ro," he said, as he pushed himself to his feet. "Tell the Kelleys you didn't find anything. Tell them whatever, just stay out of it."

"Stay out of what, exactly, Danny?" She rose as well, fists tight. "What do you know that you're not saying?"

"Nothing, except it's probably way beyond either of us. So use your head and stay out of it. For mum's sake, if nothing else."

"Dirty fighter," Ro said, frowning.

"Like brother, like sister." He went to the door. "Don't get up. I'll show myself out."

He managed not to slam the door – just. He stood in the corridor, still angry, but no way to release it. He glanced back, wanting to go back in, to shout some or maybe apologise, or both. Instead, he shoved his hands in his pockets and walked away.

Ro waited until she was sure Danny had left before she went out. She was sure he'd been telling the truth. Her brother only got that upset when he was being honest. And, too, he'd mentioned their father, something he didn't often do.

She could tell he was scared, not just for his job. But if she screwed things up now, Bloody Mary would kill her, and maybe her mum too, and Danny as well. That was the way the Kelleys worked. They took you and everyone you knew, and made you all a lesson to everyone else. That fear was what was driving her now. Danny wanted to protect her – and Ro wanted to protect him. Even if she didn't like him much, he was still her brother.

The address she'd found at Colin's flat proved to be a council estate in Hackney. It didn't take her long to get there. It was an unprepossessing sort of place, made of grey-brown residential squares surrounding a stretch of dirt and some benches.

There was a greasy spoon café across the street, and she went in. It was nearly empty, and air smelled of stale coffee grounds and steamed milk. She ordered a builder's tea and took a seat near a window. She took out the burner phone and turned it on. A few taps later, and she spotted the number listed in the Optik. She hesitated. This wasn't her sort of thing, really. She didn't usually have to find the people she needed to hit, or if she did, they weren't difficult to track down. But this was different. She didn't even know who this guy was, or how he was involved. If he was involved.

"Only one way to find out," she murmured. She tapped the call button. After a few moments, someone answered, but said nothing. She could hear them breathing, though. "You don't know who this is, but I know who you are. And we need to talk. I'm in the café around the corner. You know which one. I'll be here for an hour. After that, I'll have to find you. And you won't like that." She ended the call and set the phone down. Waited.

It buzzed and she picked it up. "Yeah?"

"This is Holden. I'll be there in twenty." His voice sounded rusty, haggard. Like he was having a bad day. She smiled, pleased at the thought.

"I'll be here." She closed the phone and sat back to wait. It didn't take twenty minutes. Whatever else, he was punctual. He sidled in, wearing a suit that looked like it had been slept in, and stinking of nervousness. He was tapping at his Optik even as he sat down.

"Did I interrupt you?" she said.

"Shh," he muttered. "Too many cameras." He made a final tap and set the Optik down. "There. They won't see us now."

"Who?"

"Whoever decides to come looking." He stared at her for a moment. There were cuts on his chin and cheek – not shaving cuts, either. And stains on his trousers and jacket. Like he'd been running. "How did you get that phone?"

"I found it. In Colin's flat."

"You knew Colin?"

Ro nodded. "Did you?"

"He made a few deliveries for me."

"Like what?"

Holden sat back. "Who do you work for?"

"The same people Colin did." Ro leaned forward. "They ain't happy."

"Neither am I."

"You're going to feel a lot worse if you don't tell me what I want to know."

Holden flinched. He looked around, and sighed. "Finish your tea. I'll show you."

Ro knocked back her tea and stood. "Lead on."

He led her out of the café, and across the street. She wondered if he lived here. Surely Albion paid better than that. "You work for the Kelleys, then?" he said, not looking at her.

"What about it?"

"Nothing, nothing. I knew Colin was one of theirs. I assumed you were too." He glanced at her. "The Kelleys want to know who killed him, then? Surprised old Ma Kelley doesn't know all about it already."

Ro nodded. "Do you know?"

"I could give it a good guess." He paused. "Is there a… reward, so to speak?"

"Maybe." Ro wasn't so sure about that, but saw no reason not to play along.

Holden nodded. "Well, discussion is the key to any negotiation." He stopped in front of a lock-up garage, set off side and around the corner from the flats. "Here we are. My little home away from home."

"You're staying here?"

He gave a sickly smile as he swung the door up. "Everyone needs some place to stay. And my gaff, nice as it was, is no longer hospitable."

"Why?" Ro asked, as she followed him in. "Someone after you?"

"You might say that." Holden closed the lock-up. Automatic lights flickered on, illuminating racks of equipment crammed into a too-small space. Military grade hardware, disassembled drones, communications equipment.

Ro stared at it all in incomprehension. "Holy shit."

Holden shrugged. "Albion's got more kit than it knows what to do with. Half of it goes into storage or gets sold off to their partners. I just decided to cut out the middleman."

"You mean you nicked it."

He grimaced. "Yes, fine. I nicked it. What's it to you?"

"You work for Albion."

"I did. I doubt I do anymore."

"Was this shit what Colin was moving?"

He looked at her. "Some of it."

She held up the phone. "There's two other numbers on here. Who do they belong to?"

He sank back against a bench and ran his hands through his hair. "I don't know."

Ro took a breath. Then, she hit him. Just a quick jab, under the ribs. He gave a strangled yelp and fell off the bench. She kicked him in the belly before he could get up, and dropped her knee onto his chest when he rolled over. Using her weight, she pinned him to the floor, extracted the pistol from his shoulder holster, ejected the clip and tossed the weapon into a nearby cardboard box.

She grabbed a handful of his hair, and made him look at her. "Who do they belong to?" she asked again, calmly. One of the first lessons Billy had taught her was to stay calm when you were giving someone a thump. If you lost your head, you might permanently injure or even kill them. Or they might stick a shank in, while you were distracted.

Holden clawed at her wrist. He was a big man, but he was in bad shape, and she was on top and ready. She popped him in the nose, and something crunched. He yelped and fell back, clutching at his face. She batted his hands away and jerked his head back up. "Stop whining. It's not broken – just bent. I will break it if you keep acting like a wasteman. Who do the numbers belong to?"

"I– I don't know their names!"

She let his head fall back with a thump. "But you know who they are?"

"Yes! Yes, goddamn it."

She rose smoothly to her feet, and let Holden scramble to his. He sat on the bench, holding his face. "Who are they?"

"Clients," he said, in a strangled voice. "Colin was a go-between. They bought, he delivered…" He hesitated. There was something else.

"Tell me," she said.

"They might have… sub-contracted him. If you get me."

"To deliver for them."

"One of them, at least, yeah. He mentioned something, and I put it together. Later. After… after what happened."

"After he was murdered, you mean."

Holden swallowed. "Yeah."

Ro looked down at him. "One of them killed him. With something *you* sold him." Even as she said it, she knew it was right. "Which one did it?"

Holden looked away. "I need protection."

Ro paused. "What?"

"Are you deaf? Protection. Help. If I say anything, I'm as good as dead. And not just because of these guys. Albion wants to shut me up as well. They almost caught me earlier today. I've been living out of this box for the last forty-eight hours."

Ro shook her head. "I need more, or you can stay here for all I care."

Holden stared at her. Then, softly, "I know who they're working for."

That got her attention. "Talk."

He shook his head. "Look, I'll tell you, and I'll give all of this to your bosses if they can get me out of the country." He gestured. "I got enough equipment in here to outfit a small army. You're telling me the Kelleys can't use some of it?"

Ro frowned. The Kelleys could always use a few extra shooters. And it might be enough to get her off the hook for Colin's mistakes. "I can't make any promises," she began.

"Then take me to someone who can," he said.

21: THE FLAT

Marcus Tell's flat was empty when Olly and Liz got there. Not totally stripped bare, but empty nonetheless. Olly could feel it. "Done a runner," he said.

Liz nodded. "Yes. But to where?"

"A person with this much to hide – he's probably got a few places hidden in the city. I know I would." Olly looked around, thinking. "Nothing on his Optik, but maybe something written down?"

"Analog. Old school."

"He's in his sixties, according to his – I mean Tell's – current ID." Olly paused. "Though that doesn't mean much. My nan used to love the internet."

"So you've said. Still, it's somewhere to start at least. I'll check the loo."

"I'll check the fridge." Olly opened it, and looked over the contents. Nothing special, nothing curious. The sort of things you might find in any pensioner's larder. But as he closed the fridge, his Optik gave a chime and he pulled it out.

He had a number of passive apps installed, including one used to detect signals from web cameras and the like. In a lot of laptops and tablets, the camera app was always recording in some fashion, even when you thought otherwise. Most of what it recorded it automatically sent to the cloud, but if you were clever you could divert the data into a private server.

Olly activated a signal tracer and followed it around the kitchen, and then across the small sitting room. It faded and strengthened by turns. Where was it coming from? He could hear Liz rooting around in the loo. "Liz…?" he called out.

"What?"

"I think I've got something."

Liz came into the setting room. "What is it?"

"There's a signal. I haven't found the source yet, but I bet it's a camera." He looked at her. "If it was me, and I was going to hide, I might leave a camera behind just to see who came looking."

"Smart." Liz turned, studying the ceiling and the moulding. "If you find it, don't touch it. It might be booby trapped."

"You what?" Olly said, startled. "Like a bomb or some shit?"

"Yeah, something like that. We don't know who Tell is, or why they're after him. We don't even know who's after him."

Olly frowned. "I figured it was Albion."

Liz shook her head. "Maybe. Or maybe someone else entirely." She sat down on the couch. "The possibilities are fair endless at this point."

"This is getting complicated."

"You don't have to tell me. I – hang on." She pulled out her Optik as it buzzed, her eyes narrowed. "What is this… a photo?" Bagley's voice filled the air a moment later.

Courtesy of Hannah Shah, Elizabeth. Lincoln met with a certain Mr Holden, in Whitechapel. It seems that he's tied up in Dempsey's death.

"How?" she demanded.

Unknown at the moment.

"Where is he now?"

Also unknown. Albion arrived. He made a daring escape.

"Shit. Have we got people looking?"

Obviously. As soon as I know anything, you'll know.

Liz looked at Olly. "Looks like Hannah might have found something."

"I heard."

"You sound surprised."

Olly shrugged. "No. I mean, she got us those passes, but she ain't exactly bypassing firewalls, is she?"

"Not everyone is a spy or script-kiddie, Olly. But they can all be useful."

"Like Sarah Lincoln, you mean? Is she one of us too?"

Liz laughed. "God, no. No, she's playing her own game. But Hannah, bless her, thinks she can aim the honourable MP for Tower Hamlets South at the right targets." Liz sat back, arms crossed. "I wasn't keen on the idea, I admit, but it seems to be working. At least for now."

"And what about when it stops?" Olly looked down at her. "She ain't one of us. Not really. Politician, innit? Albion is bad now, but what about when it ain't politically expedient to bust their balls?"

"Expedient?" Liz said, eyebrow raised.

"I know what it means."

"You're like an onion, Olly. Layers and layers."

"Thanks," he said.

"Also, you can be a bit whiffy."

Olly made to retort, when his Optik vibrated in his hands. "Found it," he said. "Right there, in the moulding over the kitchen door."

Liz stood, eyes narrowed. "There's a knothole there. Might be something behind it. Get me a chair." Olly grabbed a chair from the kitchen and she clambered up to the hole, pulling out her multi-tool as she did so. Carefully, she prised away a cork blind to reveal a neatly cut hole, just large enough for a web camera. She pulled it out and studied. "I know this model. Runs off the wifi. Has a battery life of a day or two. People use them as nanny-cams. Here, see if you can trace the signal."

Olly caught it. But as he did so, a second alert chimed. "What the hell … ?"

Liz looked down. "What?"

"I think someone is trying to – shit! Liz!" Olly lunged and tackled her from the chair, even as the first shot sounded. It was like a whip-crack, echoing amid the sound of breaking glass. The shot passed through the air where Liz's head had been and punched into the wall opposite, filling the air with plaster dust. A second shot followed, and a third.

"I think we found the drone," Olly shouted.

"More like it found us – stay down. We got to get to the door." Liz pushed Olly aside and rolled onto her stomach. Follow me, and keep your bloody head down."

"Where are we going?"

"Out of here. Bagley – I need a route, something that won't walk us in front of a bullet," she snarled.

Calculating. You should know that the police have been alerted. That almost certainly means Albion has been as well.

"Wonderful," Olly said. "If the drone doesn't shoot us, they will."

"Not if we move quickly. Come on." Liz crawled towards the front door. Out of the corner of his eye, Olly saw a dark shape pass across the window. He grabbed Liz's ankle.

"Wait! I think he's tracking us."

Liz froze. Olly watched the window. The drone hovered for a moment, and then dropped away. Olly released Liz. "Go, go, go."

They reached the door a moment later, and went through into the corridor. Doors slammed as eavesdroppers retreated. There were no windows in the corridor, but that didn't mean much, especially given the calibre of weapon involved. Olly had watched enough online ballistic tests to know the walls of the building weren't going to be much of an impediment. As if to prove the point, the wall abruptly burst inwards, showering the corridor with chips of brick and splinters of wood. A second shot followed, burying itself in the doors of the lift at the other end of the corridor.

"Stairs," Liz said. "Hurry!"

"How the hell can he see us?" Olly shouted.

Liz grabbed him and yanked the Optik out of his hand. "This. You cloned Tell's Optik, remember?" She smashed it against the wall and flung it back the way they'd come. "Right. Keep moving."

They hurried down the stairs. Olly's back itched the entire way, in expectation of a bullet. But no more shots followed. "He can't have many bullets left," he said, panting slightly.

"Weight requirements alone would throw off the ammunition capacity…"

"All he needs is one," Liz said, over her shoulder. "We have to get somewhere a drone can't follow, right now, or we're dead."

Coyle frowned in concentration as he strafed the side of the council block. Calculations ran through his head as he fired, trying to predict and track the movements of targets he couldn't see. He needed them out in the open, and quickly. It wasn't like the other times – this was a prolonged assault rather than a surgical strike, and that could have consequences.

A certain amount of collateral damage was acceptable, but too much and it attracted the wrong sort of attention. If Albion managed to tag Holden, there was a chance he might have information that could compromise the operation. Then again, maybe not. But whoever these two were, they were a definite danger. They'd raided a police station, and they'd located what he was now certain was Tell's flat, something even he hadn't been able to do – that implied a level of professionalism he found unsettling.

No one had warned him that there would be other specialists in play. That added a layer of complication to an already complex problem. Albion was bad enough, but another group – equally skilled – meant the chances of discovery had gone up.

In all his years as a killer, Coyle had only ever come close to discovery on a few occasions. In every instance, he had pulled out of the operation in question, and made himself scarce. Professional ethics aside, discretion was the better part of valour.

Unfortunately, that option was not available to him here. If he departed, Zero Day would almost certainly seek to punish him – not to mention those he was closest to. Unless he managed to get to them first. His eyes flicked to the tracker program, still sifting through the jungles of data in search of its prey, and his. Until it located Zero Day, there was nothing to be done save press forward and do what he'd been hired to do.

He pulled the drone back, letting them descend. They'd make for a vehicle of some kind. There was a smallish car park not far from the doors. He let the drone circle the building while he considered his options.

The GPS he'd been using to track them was gone. They'd figured out how he was tracking them. Luckily, there were other methods available to him. He brought up the drone's proximity-grid and saw that there were almost a dozen other drones in the area. It was a matter of moments to hijack their sensors and build a picture of the area. He didn't have much time. Already, the police were on their way, Albion too. His window for dealing with this particular problem was rapidly closing.

His Optik trilled. Frowning, he answered the call. "Hello?"

"What *do* you think you are doing?"

Zero Day.

"I am handling a situation, as we discussed."

"As solutions go, that will only lead to more problems."

"If you had located Tell's Optik in time, it wouldn't be an issue. But here we are." Coyle turned his attentions back to the drone's display. "Rest assured, I will keep collateral damage to a minimum."

"Collateral damage is irrelevant. Your actions threaten the

security of our ongoing operation – ironic, given that you were employed to do the opposite."

Coyle smiled. He could hear the anger in Zero Day's voice. "I am merely attempting to hold up my end of the bargain." He paused, and then added, "I was not warned that there were other professionals involved."

"An unforeseen complication."

Coyle's smile faded. Had there been a hesitation there? Grist for the mill. He filed the possibility away for later. "If you have a better solution, I'm all ears." He toggled the drone's control and sent it veering out over the street. As he did so, he saw the side door of the building open, and two figures sprint for the car park. "Targets sighted. Do I take the shot – or not?"

No reply. For a moment, he thought Zero Day had cut the connection. Then, "Do as you think best. That is why you were hired."

Coyle fired.

22: SACRIFICE

The shot sounded like a thunderclap.

Liz felt it burn through the air past her, and into the side of a nearby car, rocking the vehicle on its axle. The shot had narrowly missed her, and only because she'd been helping Olly to his feet when he'd slipped. Too close for comfort.

"Car! Get a car!" Liz shouted, shoving Olly down and out of the line of fire. The drone was moving fast, arrowing towards them. Her display futzed and fizzed as she tried to get a bead on it. Something was wrong. "Bagley – what's going on?"

The drone. It has a more extensive set of tools than we predicted. I would suggest getting out of sight and quickly. The police are coming, and Albion aren't far behind.

"So you said. Olly?"

"Got one," he said. The doors of a nearby Sumitzu swung open. Liz shoved him towards it as the drone approached. She spun, firing. The drone veered off at the last second and she dove into the car. Olly was already in the driver's seat.

"Do you actually know how to drive?"

"Yeah, of course," he said, but didn't sound confident. The car growled to life.

You're welcome. Now get your posteriors in gear.

A shot puckered the pavement, and bits of tarmac punched into the side of the car. Olly reversed, stomping on the accelerator. Liz was flung back into her seat as he spun the wheel and took them onto the street, banging up against a few other cars on the way. "This isn't as easy as games make it out to be," he said, apologetically.

Liz laughed. "No, I expect not. Just keep us moving."

"Where to?"

"Whitechapel Station. There's an entrance on Durward Street, that's closest. Bagley, pull us up a route." She turned, checking for pursuit. Police cars were swarming in the distance, lights flashing. The plods would have the car's registration in a few minutes. They'd have to ditch it as soon as possible. "We'll leave the car and go on foot from there."

"Is that thing still after us?" Olly asked.

She looked up. There were plenty of drones in the sky. No way to tell if the sniper was among them. "I can't see it. Keep driving."

"Maybe he's gone."

"Maybe," she said, but she didn't believe it.

"Do you think – is it Albion? It's got to be, right?"

"I don't know." Liz saw a drone lose altitude as Olly wove through traffic. Horns sounded, tires squealed, but he kept the accelerator down. "Bagley, see if you can get into the traffic grid and get us a clear lane."

Already working on it…

There was a flash of light and a boom of sound. The boot

of the car exploded, the metal lid tearing off its hinges, pinwheeling up over the roof and down off the bonnet. The car bucked on its shocks and Olly struggled to maintain control. Smoke filled the inside of the vehicle, and Liz could smell burning oil. Through stinging eyes, she saw the drone closing in. She crawled into the backseat, ignoring Olly's protests. "Just keep driving," she said.

Liz used the pistol to knock the remaining shards of glass out of the rear window and fired off a rapid series of shots. Her chances of hitting the damn thing were slim to none, but she had to do something. The drone veered and banked. Leaving? She felt a tingle of hope.

He's coming up fast, Elizabeth. Oliver, I would prepare to brake...

"What?" Olly said, even as a car far ahead of them stalled and died. Traffic slowed, but not soon enough. Olly skidded into the car ahead, and there was a crunch and a groan of abused metal. Olly jolted in his seat, his face bouncing off the steering wheel. He fell back, clutching at his nose. Liz was flung into the back of his seat, and for long moments, she couldn't breathe. She could hear sirens.

Olly reached over and grabbed her. "We got to go," he mumbled. "Pursuit drones."

Liz pushed him away. "Go, I'm right behind you." Aching, moving slow, she pushed the seat up and half fell through the open door. Olly was close, a dazed look on his face, turning as if he wasn't sure which way to go. There was glass in his face and in her hair. She could smell the fumes from the engine block. She pushed herself to her feet.

She stumbled towards Olly, and pushed him into motion.

"Bagley – I need a direction!" An illuminated map filled her display. Durward Street was only a few minutes' jog away. She picked up speed, and Olly followed her wake.

"We're sitting ducks out here," he said, looking around wildly. "That thing is probably coming back for another pass."

"We're almost there." Liz kept one eye on the sky. Traffic was locked up and the sky was full of drones whizzing in all directions. But no sign of their pursuer.

When they finally reached Durward Street, she saw why. The drone hovered boldly over the entrance to the station, waiting. She caught Olly by the sleeve and yanked him behind a parked car. The drone gave no sign of having spotted them. Olly ran his hands through his hair. He was breathing fast, maybe on the edge of a panic attack. Liz shook him. "Calm down. Can you do that for me?"

Olly gulped and nodded. "What do we do? The camouflage, maybe?"

"Maybe," she said. "But I don't want to risk it until we know for sure. Bagley, what can you tell me about that thing?"

From what I've been able to glean, it has a large sensory suite than we expected. Your camouflage isn't going to work. Not at such close range, anyway. And there's someone on the other end – a human controller.

Liz leaned back against the car and slid down into a sitting position. "Damn it."

"What?" Olly asked.

"That explains how it got ahead of us." She peered around the edge of the bumper. She could see the red and white sign for the underground. It was a small door, barely there at all. A largely unused entrance, these days. But it was across open ground, and no cover to be seen. They couldn't sit here forever. Eventually it would come looking, or the police would show up. It'd be over for them either way. She closed her eyes. "Fuck."

"What are we going to do?" Olly asked.

Liz opened her eyes, checked her pistol, ejected the magazine, popped it back in. "Olly… think you can make it to the door in good time?"

Olly looked at her, his face white, eyes wide. "It's waiting for us to try that."

"I know. Think you can make it?"

"Yeah. Yeah." He nodded. "We going to make a run for it, then?"

"You are. I'm going to distract our friend."

He frowned. "That's a bad plan."

"It's the only one we've got."

"Maybe I can get into the fucker…" Olly reached for her. "Gimme your Optik."

Liz passed the device to him without looking at him. She could see the drone now – one moment, it was a sleek, black UCAV and in the next, it was a Parcel Fox courier or a cargo drone. "Bagley, I hope you're taking notes on this thing."

Indeed, Elizabeth. But its firewall is difficult to crack. It appears to have been constructed under the assumption that someone might try and take control of it.

"Imagine that," she murmured. At the far end of the street she could see the blue glow of police flashers, and hear sirens. "Now or never, Olly."

"Just a couple more seconds. It's not close enough."

"No more seconds. When I say run, you *run*."

He looked at her. "What about you?"

"I'll be right behind you," she said, and smiled. "Trust me." She peered over the top of the car. The drone was circling, waiting for them to make a run for it. She closed her eyes, took a breath, and stood. "Go!"

Olly darted for the entrance. The drone turned, momentarily exposing itself. Liz fired. Sparks burst on the drone and it dipped, trailing smoke. She could hear its motors straining and she felt a brief moment of elation, wondering if she'd managed to bring it down after all. But it soon righted itself. It was tough, whatever else.

She fired again, emptying the weapon in an attempt to hold its attention. As she pulled the trigger, she saw that Olly had made it to the entrance. She relaxed slight. "Bagley?" she asked, as the drone drifted towards her. The barrel of its weapon swung up. She thought about running, but there was nowhere to go.

Elizabeth?

"Do me a favour and wipe my hard drives, yeah?"

Leave it with me, Elizabeth.

"Thank–" she began.

She never finished the thought.

Olly heard the shot. Turned. Hesitated.

Keep moving, Oliver.

Bagley's voice was sharp. It pricked Olly from his paralysis. "She might still be alive..." he began.

She's not. Keep moving.

Olly turned back to escalator. Went down. Adrenaline bled out of him, and he was left on autopilot. The next thing he knew, he was on the East London Overground to Shadwell.

He sat back, and watched the city pass in greys and browns. He tried to think, but his brain refused to work. All he could think about was the sound of the shot – the same sound. The same sound, and two people dead, in as many days.

He thought about Liz, imagined her face going slack the way Dempsey's had. His stomach heaved, and he wanted to vomit, but there was nothing in him but Haribos and coffee. Instead, he wrapped his arms around his midsection and squeezed.

When the train finally stopped at Shadwell, he stumbled off, head bowed, hands in his pockets. He bumped into several commuters, paying no attention to any of them. It wasn't crowded, but there were still too many people for his tastes. Too many drones. He kept waiting for the UCAV to drop down, to put a round through him as he sat on the train. But he saw nothing. Heard nothing, save the beep of unanswered calls on his display. Bagley or Krish, trying to get in touch. He couldn't muster the energy to answer them.

Part of him wanted to just ride the train to the terminus and back again. To wait and see what happened. Full lucidity didn't return until the DLR train from Shadwell kicked into motion, jolting him on his uncomfortable seat. Olly's eyes instinctively flicked to the cameras that were in every train car these days. He knew his program was still running, even if his external unit was in pieces. But it made him itch nonetheless.

He scrubbed the heels of his palms into his eyes, and forced himself to sit up. He had six minutes until he reached Limehouse. And then what? Liz was the one in charge. She was the one who'd known what to do. Without her – what?

His eyes went to the cameras again. A thought occurred to

him. Six minutes until Limehouse. Six minutes was forever, if you knew what you were doing.

"Bagley?" he murmured.

Oliver. Back with us?

"Yeah. What do I do now?"

That is up to you. I would recommend getting back to the hideout as quickly as possible. Things have been afoot in your absence, and the others are waiting to debrief you.

"Others?"

The great and the good. DedSec London has lost one of its own, and they want answers. That means you, Oliver.

"You tell 'em," he said, pulling out Liz's Optik. An older model, but still functional. "I think I've got something more important to do."

Care to fill me in?

"The camera. The one we found in the flat. I was trying to back-trace the signal when things… started happening. The app was still running when my external unit got smashed. But Liz's will work just fine for what I have in mind."

You intend to track down Tell.

"Got it in one," Olly said.

And what about the drone?

"I'll risk it. Everything we've found is on the cloud. If something happens…"

I'll see that it gets to the right people, Oliver.

"Thank you." He paused. "What about… what about Liz? We're not going to just leave her there, are we?"

Arrangements will be made. DedSec has connections everywhere.

"We're all part of the Resistance in our own way," Olly said.

Exactly. What are you planning, Oliver? Tell has gone to a lot of trouble to obscure his location. I can't imagine he'll be pleased to see you.

"That's his tough luck." The train began to slow. Olly slipped Liz's Optik into his pocket and stood. He knew where to go now. No telling what was waiting for him at the other end. But he'd deal with it when he got there.

And if things turn nasty?

"I'll do what Liz would do," he said, softly. "I'll improvise."

23: BETRAYAL

"Are you sure this is the place?" Holden asked, as he peered up at the warehouse in puzzlement. "Not that I was expecting anything different, mind."

Ro grunted and shoved him towards the door. When she'd made the call, Billy Bricks had answered, and told her to meet them at the same East End warehouse as last time. There was no one on the door, and the place was busy when they went inside. Pallets of product were being moved out to trucks and transit vans, and nothing was coming in to replace it.

Billy met them inside the door. "This him, then?" he asked, looking Holden up and down. "This the fellow with the shooters for sale?"

"All that and more, if you can get me out of the country," Holden said. Ro pushed past him and looked around.

"What's going on?"

Billy smiled. "Moving operations to a new location. Only temporarily of course." He patted her cheek. "Proper job, Rosemary. Not quite what we were looking for, but good all the same."

Ro shoved his hand away. "Am I sorted, then?"

"Depends on what this one has to say for himself, don't it?" Billy turned and crooked a finger. "Follow me."

He led them back through the rapidly emptying warehouse to the office. As before, Mary Kelley was waiting for them. She wasn't alone, this time. The Godfreys were there as well. "Saul. Reggie," Ro said. They nodded back in reply.

Mary was sitting at her desk, playing with her knife. "Well now. This isn't exactly what I asked for, is it now?" she said, when Billy closed the door behind them.

Ro made to speak, but Holden beat her to it. "I know what you want to know, and I can get you guns, bombs, whatever you want, on top of that."

"Information and explosives – two of our favourite things, eh, Billy?"

"Indeed they are, mum," Billy said, leaning against the door. Ro looked at him, and then at the Godfreys. Neither Saul nor Reggie met her gaze. Something was up. Why were they emptying the warehouse today?

She turned her attention back to Mary, and found the other woman watching her, a slight smile on her face. "Right little bloodhound you turned out to be."

Ro swallowed. "Just doing like you told me."

"Hear that, Billy, she was just following orders."

"She's a good girl, mum." Billy sounded like he was trying not to laugh.

"Maybe not that good, eh?" Mary rose to her feet and came around the desk. "Your brother came to see you this morning. What was that about, then?"

Ro paused, startled. "He… he wanted to talk about mum.

She's not been well," she said quickly, trying to cover her hesitation. They'd been watching her – why? Then it hit her. They suspected her of something. That was why the Godfreys were here. Extra muscle, just in case.

"Is she feeling rough then, been in the wars? That's a genuine shame." Mary sat back on the desk and turned her attention to Holden. "Albion are after you."

Holden blanched. "And that's why I'm here."

"You were the one working with our Colin?"

"One of them, yes. And I can tell you all about that, if you promise to get me out of here. I've got names, dates... I know everything." He looked around. "The information I've got, you could use it. Something big is going to happen. The whole city..."

"I don't care about the whole city – just the parts I'm partial to," Mary interjected. "Anyway, I already had a very productive chat with some new associates, who told me everything I needed to know about what that fucking toerag Wilson was doing on my clock in one of my vans. Might even be some decent business to be done there." She shot Ro a humourless grin. "See, Miss Bloodhound: you ain't the only one who knows how to winkle out the properly useful information round here."

Holden glanced at Ro in confusion, then cleared his throat and tried again.

"But there are others who might pay good money to know what I know, especially about what Albion are planning. And I'll sell it to you, at a discount. I just want to get far away from here."

Mary peered at him. "Word is, there's a target on your back. I've been where I am long enough to know when someone is cleaning up after themselves. Your name is on a list somewhere, sunshine, and that means you're in no position to call the odds." She smiled. "So here's how we're going to do this. First, you're going to tell me everything. And then, assuming you actually tell me anything I don't already bleeding know, I'll decide whether it's worth keeping you alive afterwards."

Holden took a step back. "I was promised protection..."

Mary laughed. "Who by? Her? She can't promise shit."

Ro flinched, but said nothing. There was still a chance for her to get out free and clear, and that meant doing her best not to piss off Mary.

Holden nodded. "Fine. What do you want to know first?"

"Oh, I'm not going to ask you. *They* are." She indicated the Godfreys. Saul – or maybe Reggie – stepped forward and cracked his knuckles. "But first..." She pressed the tip of her knife to his throat. "Give me your Optik."

Holden did as she asked, and she tossed it to Billy.

"It's encrypted," Holden said.

"That's what hackers is for," Mary said. She glanced at Ro. "You brought the phone? The one you found in Colin's place?"

"Yeah, but–" Ro began as she fished the phone out. Mary took it from her.

"Shut it. There are numbers on here. We can track them. Which means we can find everybody else Holden here was dealing with."

"Unless they've already gone to ground," Holden said.

Mary smiled. "This is my manor, Mr Holden. No one hides from me here." She put the phone on the desk and gestured. "Saul, you and your brother know what to do. I want everything out of him before we hand him off."

"Hand him off?" Ro asked, looking at Holden. "What do you mean, 'hand him off'?"

"What do you think I mean?" Mary stepped back as the Godfreys moved up to either side of Holden. "We're turning him over to Albion. The only question is whether we're turning him over warm or cold."

Holden made to protest, and one of the Godfreys hit him – hard. Holden folded over and fell onto all fours, wheezing. The Godfreys took turns kicking him for a few moments, and then hauled him back to his feet. Ro started forward, but stopped as Billy put himself between them. "You're in more than enough trouble as it is, love," he said. "Don't make it worse."

"This ain't right," she said.

"Hark at this one," Mary said. "Right and wrong are what I say they are, luv. And this is right, for us. Albion have been breathing down our neck since they set up shop in East London, and this is a quick way of getting them off our back so we can all get on with our business. We turn him over, they leave us be. Good for everyone, good for future relations."

"And what if they don't agree?" Ro said.

Mary shrugged. "That's why I'm wringing him dry first. And it's not like we'll be any worse off for it." She looked at Ro. "But now then, what *do* we do with you?"

Ro's hands tightened into fists. "I did what you asked."

"That you did, that you did. Which is why you ain't floating in the canal." Mary pointed at her with the knife. "How long did you think this was going to last, luv? Your brother's with Albion, and they're looking to put us out of business..."

"I don't even like my brother," Ro protested.

Mary smiled. "Once, I might have given you the chance to

prove that. Put a shooter in your hand, and set it all up nice. But we're doing things differently these days. We're not ready to go to war with them – not just yet." She leaned close. "But before I decide, I want to know whether you're a grass."

"I'm not an informer," Ro said.

"Billy?"

Billy hit Ro with a stiff thump to the ribs. She was ready for it and turned with the blow. Her own fist snapped out and he grunted as it struck home. Mary retreated as the two of them circled one another. "What was you talking about with Danny last night then, Rosemary?" Billy asked, raising his fists.

"I told you, our mum." Ro hunched forward, trying to make herself a smaller target, her own hands ready. Billy came in quick, with complicated salvo. Ro swatted one aside and took the other on her shoulder. She resisted the urge to go after him. That was what he wanted. When he realised she hadn't taken the bait, he pressed in on her.

She retreated, wondering if she could make it to the door. Over Billy's shoulder, she saw Mary watching – smiling. The Godfreys were watching as well, eyes narrowed. She hoped they stayed out of it. "Are you sure?" Billy said, throwing another punch.

Ro avoided it, but only just. "I'm no bloody grass!"

Billy hit her twice in the time it took her to speak. She stumbled but didn't fall. Mad now, she responded in kind, and her fist caught him on the side of the cheek. He staggered, blinking, and she bent and loosed a kick. His hands snapped shut around her ankle, and suddenly she was flying. She hit the desk, the edge digging into her back, and went down. Billy was on her before she could get up.

He was faster than he looked, and stronger. Ro tried to shove him back, but he was having none of it. Blows rained down, and the world started getting blurry. She took it all, and when he gave her an opening, she went for it with every bit of strength left to her. She caught him in the kidney twice. He rolled off her, and she kicked him in the hip. He fell onto his back, laughing, and Ro straddled him in an instant, fists raised.

She froze as something sharp pricked her throat. "That's enough of that," Mary said. She held her knife to Ro's neck. "What do you think, Billy?"

Billy scrambled to his feet, grinning. "She's a bloody terrible liar, but she throws a good punch." He rubbed his hip. "For what's worth, I don't think she's anybody's snout."

Mary chuckled. "Can't trust her, though. Too much at stake." She gestured for Ro to rise and looked at her. "So what *do* we do with you then, luv?"

Danny climbed out of the unmarked car, one hand on his sidearm. He was out of uniform, but wearing his flak vest under his jacket. Faulkner, coming around the front of the car, was dressed the same. The warehouse was a square lump against the dark sky. Floodlights popped on as they got in range of the motion sensors.

Cameras mounted along the walls whirred and pivoted, following them. Danny eyed them warily. "They're watching us, Sarge."

"I'd be disappointed if they weren't," Faulkner said. "Probably recording us, too."

"That doesn't bother you?"

"No. Does it bother you, Danny?"

"A bit, Sarge."

Faulkner paused. "If I were you, Danny, I'd be more worried about things you can control. Now stiffen that lip, and raise the flag. We're heading into enemy territory and I'd prefer you didn't embarrass me."

Danny fell silent. When he'd gotten back to base the day before, Faulkner had been out hunting for someone named Holden – a tech who'd gone rogue, according to Hattersley. At first, there hadn't seemed to be any connection at all to the dead white van man, Wilson. Then Faulkner had called Danny into his office, and now here they were, outside a Kelley-owned warehouse, acting on an anonymous tip. Or so Faulkner claimed.

All Danny knew for sure was that he didn't like any part of this. He felt like he had a target on his back, though he couldn't say why. Something was going on, but he wasn't in a position to ask. As Faulkner often reminded him, his was but to do and die.

The digital lock clicked as they approached the door. Faulkner drew his sidearm and glanced at Danny. Danny nodded and took up a position on the other side of the door. Faulkner tried the door, and it swung open. He gestured, and Danny followed him in, pistol at the ready. As they entered, the warehouse lit up, one overhead fixture at a time.

The warehouse was empty. Stripped down to the concrete floors. Faulkner chuckled. "Taking no chances is she, eh? Come on."

They proceeded slowly, their footsteps loud in the emptiness. When they'd reached the halfway point, there was a crackle from above as a PA system kicked into life. "Right on time, Faulkner. But then, punctuality is a virtue in the military, so I've been told."

A woman's voice. Harsh and pure East End. Faulkner stopped and signalled for Danny to do the same. "Is that you, Bloody Mary?" Faulkner called out.

"I prefer Ms Kelley," she replied. "We are all professionals here, after all."

"Debatable," Faulkner said. "Why don't you come out and we'll discuss it over a cuppa, what say?"

"We're not quite there yet, Sergeant."

"Disappointing, but understandable. I'm told you have information for us?"

"Oh, better than that. A little birdie told me you're looking for a certain gentleman by the name of... Holden? Is that right?"

Faulkner smiled. "You heard right."

"What if I were to tell you that I know where he is – that I could even get him for you? What might that be worth?"

"What do you want?"

"Nothing excessive. A bit of consideration is all."

Faulkner paused. "I'm listening."

"Word is, Albion's remit will be expanding. I want a guarantee you lot won't interfere with Kelley businesses for, oh, let's say... a year from now. How does that sound?"

"A year is a long time."

"But not forever."

Faulkner holstered his sidearm. "Agreed."

"I am recording all of this, by the way. Just in case you get any ideas."

"Trust me when I say that your piddly little crypto-scams

aren't exactly high on our list of priorities, Ms Kelley. But feel free to protect yourself however you see fit. Where's Holden?"

"There's an office at the back of the warehouse. See it? He's in there. Plus something extra, just to sweeten the deal."

"And I assume you're not here at all. Clever." Faulkner started towards the back. Danny trailed after him. There was no response from the PA. Mary Kelley, if that was indeed who it had been, was obviously done with them.

The office was a square along the back wall. The door was open, and Faulkner led the way inside. The room was bare, save for the two figures who sat within, both zip-tied to chairs in the centre of the room. One was a dishevelled man of middle age, the other was –

Danny froze.

The other was Ro. She sagged on her chair, her face bruised and bloody. She looked up as they entered, but the light was behind them and she obviously couldn't make out their faces. Faulkner turned on the lights in the office, and her eyes widened. Thankfully, she said nothing. Faulkner glanced at her, and then turned his attentions to Holden.

"Hello, George. You've looked better."

"Faulkner…" Holden said hoarsely.

"Clever trick with the drones, earlier. Shorting them out like that. Luckily, they're easy to replace." Faulkner circled him. "You went looking to the Kelleys for protection? Not your smartest move."

"I am aware," Holden said. "What now?"

Faulkner stopped in front of him. "Now I debrief you, George." He glanced at Danny. "You know what that means, don't you, Danny?"

"Means we're to question him, Sarge."

"Close. It means to question *vigorously*. Like so." Faulkner swiped Holden with the back of his hand. Holden rocked in his chair, his cheek split and already swelling. Faulkner caught the back of his head, leaned in and gave him a sharp jab to the ribs. Holden wheezed and sagged. Faulkner stepped back.

"Right. Take notes, Danny."

"Sarge, shouldn't we take him – them – back to base first?"

Faulkner didn't look at him. "No need. Now holster your sidearm and take notes."

Danny did as he was ordered. His eyes kept straying to Ro, but she hadn't spoken. She looked dazed. Out of it. He realised she might have a concussion. No time to worry about that now, though. He took out his Optik and began to record.

Faulkner hit Holden again – another quick jab. "Where were you hiding?"

"A lock-up… in Hackney," Holden coughed. He rattled off an address, and Faulkner glanced at Danny to make sure he'd gotten it.

"And what about LIBRA?"

Danny frowned. He'd never heard that name before.

Holden had, though. "S-sold it."

Another jab. Holden grimaced. "To who?" Faulkner asked.

"C-Coyle. Bloke named Coyle."

"Coyle…" Faulkner hesitated. Danny wondered if he recognised the name. "When?"

"Few days ago. Didn't think anyone would notice."

"Until someone did. And then you tried to cover it all up. Wilson was one of the Kelleys' drivers. What were you doing mixed up with him?"

"A– a mutual acquaintance put us in touch."

Faulkner paused – and hit him again, twice. Back to the face this time, but the punches were pulled. Just hard enough to rattle Holden, not enough to stun him.

Watching, Danny could tell Faulkner had done this before. "Sarge, maybe you should lay off him."

Faulkner turned. "Wish I could, Danny. But there's bigger stakes at play here than you can see. Lives in the balance. Old George here, he sold some nasty equipment to some bad people. The sort of kit you probably saw in the sandbox – isn't that right, George?"

"I– I didn't know what it was for," Holden began.

Faulkner slapped him. "IEDs, Danny. Ordnance for amateurs. And LIBRA, let's not forget that." He slapped Holden again, and the other man groaned in pain.

"What's LIBRA, Sarge?"

Faulkner stepped back. "Nothing you need to worry about, lad. Now this *Coyle*, George – where is he?"

"I don't know. I've got a number, that's all."

Faulkner leaned close to him. "And where is this number?"

"On my Optik."

"And where's your Optik?"

"The Kelleys took it."

Faulkner grunted. Then he hit Holden again, nearly knocking him over. "Anything else you'd like to say for yourself?"

"Go screw yourself, Faulkner," Holden mumbled, through bruised lips.

Faulkner laughed. "That's the spirit." He looked at Danny. "What do you think, Danny? Is he telling the truth?"

"I don't know, Sarge."

Faulkner turned back to Holden. "I think he's telling the truth. Of course, that means he's a traitor to Albion. And what do we do with traitors, Danny boy?"

Danny didn't say anything and Faulkner didn't appear to expect an answer. Holden licked his lips and looked up at Faulkner. "I need to warn you – I've taken measures. Everything I know has been uploaded to my private servers. If something happens to me, if I don't check in every four hours, it'll get sent out to certain parties."

"Like Sarah Lincoln, for instance?"

"Among others."

"Good to know. The company thanks you for your service, George." He drew his sidearm and Holden began to speak – maybe to protest, maybe to beg. But he never got a word out because Faulkner painted the concrete with his brains. The chair rocked and settled, Holden sagging in his bonds. Smoke rose from his head. Faulkner turned to Danny. "Right. That's taken care of. Let's go."

"I thought we were taking him back to base," Danny said hoarsely, staring at the body.

"No need. I already know what he did, Danny. And once we get to that lock-up, we'll have the gear he stole and probably some records as well. George was always the organised sort. He probably made back-ups of his back-ups." He gestured. "And, of course, we have his little friend here." He smiled. "You've been a bit rude, by the way, Danny boy. Not introducing me to your sister here." He looked at Ro, and Danny reluctantly followed his gaze. She was staring at Holden, a sick look on her face.

When Danny turned his attention back to Faulkner, the other man had his sidearm pointed at Danny's face. "I'm not an idiot, Danny. And shame on you for trying to play silly buggers. How long have you known your sister was involved?"

"I didn't – I mean – she's not..."

"Bloody Mary leaving her here totally implies that she is."

"And you trust her?"

"Danny, if a man can't trust an East End crime boss, who can he trust?" Faulkner smiled, but it didn't reach his eyes. "Answer my question, Danny, there's a good lad."

"She's not involved, Sarge," Danny insisted.

Faulkner lowered his weapon. "I'd hate to think you were lying to me, Danny. So I'm going to assume you're not taking the piss. But we need to debrief her regardless. A bit less permanently than we did George, here." He holstered his sidearm. "I'll let someone else do it, don't worry."

"Th– thanks, Sarge."

"Of course, afterwards she is getting banged up." Faulkner clapped Danny on the shoulder and stepped past him. "Sorry lad, but we can't show favouritism in these sorts of things. You understand."

Danny said nothing. He looked Ro. She wouldn't meet his gaze.

DAY ONE

THURSDAY

Bagley-bytes 13684-3: ...Redqueen is dead. God save the queen...

+ + +

Leake Street safe house has been burned. Begin materiel evacuation and data transfer procedures.

+ + +

Getting reports from Camden Market and Walker's Court of increased Met presence, and amplified surveillance. Albion advisors on-site.

+ + +

Crouch End safe house has been burned. Begin materiel evacuation and data transfer procedures.

+ + +

Increased Albion presence reported in Tower Hamlets. Might be related to the TOAN Conference, might not. Everyone keep your masks on and your heads down.

+ + +

The Harp & Heron safe house has been burned. Multiple Met and Albion agents on-site. Catherine is in the wind. Local proceeds confiscated. Begin cTOS clean-up of all related ops.

+ + +

Blackwall Station and Dock Green have been burned. Begin materiel evacuation and data transfer procedures.

+ + +

Hobbs End and Totters Lane under surveillance. Heavy Albion presence. Begin preliminary materiel evacuation and data transfer procedures.

+ + +

Museum Station safe house has been burned. Begin materiel evacuation and data transfer procedures.

+ + +

Well, this is bollocks.

24: POLITICS

Art Coyle rubbed at his fatigued eyes and leaned back in his chair, yawning. The morning was overcast, and a light rain pattered against the windows. It had been a long, fruitless night. He'd managed to kill one of the two individuals who'd absconded with Tell's Optik, but the other was still on the loose.

Unfortunately, the hunt would have to wait. The drone had returned a few minutes ago, to recharge and reload. He rose and went to it, checking the scuff marks where the woman's shots had skimmed off its armour. There was some damage to one of the motors – a glancing hit – but nothing he couldn't fix.

He set about the task while the drone recharged. After he'd finished, he'd refill its ammunition hopper. As soon as it was ready, he'd send it out again. Tell's Optik was gone – deactivated – but the drone had caught the scent of another signal. A wireless stream, as if from a camera.

Coyle was certain now that the flat had been Tell's and had

quickly deduced that the stream was likely from a web camera. Tell had scarpered, but not without leaving a pair of eyes to watch and see who might come looking for him. He was already in the process of tracing the signal back to whoever was on the other end. Once he'd gotten a location, he would dispatch the drone and wait.

He knew, with a hunter's instinct, that the surviving operative was heading for Tell. It was what he would do, if their situations were reversed. He wondered who they were – not Albion, not the police. Someone else. The government, perhaps. Or maybe DedSec.

He'd run across the Resistance movement once before, when he'd followed a target to the States. They'd seemed largely ineffective at the time. Maybe the London branch was simply more competent. Perhaps he should ask Zero Day about them.

At the thought of his employer, he brought his display, and the tracker-app that was still running. Nothing concrete yet, but he knew he was close. He could feel it. Whatever Zero Day was planning would happen in the next forty-eight hours.

As if his thoughts had summoned them, a call-alert chimed in his ear. "Yes," he said quietly.

"Have you found Tell yet?"

"If I had, I would have informed you immediately."

"You sound upset."

"Merely tired." Coyle pinched the bridge of his nose. "Do you have anything useful to tell me, or are you merely being annoying?"

"Careful, Coyle. Remember who is in charge here."

"I have not forgotten," Coyle murmured. Rubbing his eyes,

he made his way to the window. "I believe the operation has been compromised. By DedSec."

"What makes you think that?"

Coyle looked out over the city. "Suffice it to say, I have some experience in these matters. If it is DedSec–"

"It is."

Coyle paused, digesting this. "You knew this already. Why didn't you tell me?"

"You did not need to know."

Coyle laughed. "It looks like you got that wrong then, doesn't it?"

An offended silence followed. Then, "Or perhaps we overestimated your abilities."

Still chuckling, Coyle made himself coffee. "If I had known, I would have devised a contingency plan. Since I did not, I am forced to improvise. Now that we are on the same page, however, we should discuss how best to–"

"It will be handled today."

The words came sharp and brittle, the way one might mention an unpleasant task that nonetheless needed doing, and would be done. Coyle paused, and then took a sip of coffee. "How?"

"It is of no relevance."

"I disagree."

"That too is of no relevance. What are you planning to do about Tell?"

Coyle considered throwing Zero Day's own words back at them, but decided it would be unprofessional. "I believe I've managed to locate where Tell is hiding. Once the drone is recharged and rearmed, I'll send it back out on the hunt.

Tell will not see the sunset." He paused. "Unless another unmentioned complication should rear its head, that is."

"It will not."

Coyle grunted. "That still leaves Holden to deal with."

"George Holden is no longer an issue."

Coyle hesitated. "He's dead? How?"

"It is of no–"

"Relevance, yes, fine." Coyle rubbed his face. "Then Tell is the last. And DedSec. And afterwards…"

"You will be paid the remainder of your fee, as promised." A pause. "We would encourage you to leave London as soon as possible, once Tell is dead. Things will be… chaotic, in the aftermath."

Coyle knew better than to ask the obvious question. Instead, he took another swallow of coffee and grunted his assent. Zero Day ended the call abruptly.

"Good day to you as well," he muttered. He wandered back to the window, still sipping at his coffee. He thought longingly of home, of his wife and daughter.

And he thought of Zero Day, and the threats they had made. So far, they did not seem to realise he was on their trail – or maybe they knew, but did not care.

The drone chimed, signalling that it had completed its recharge cycle. He set his coffee down and turned to rearm it.

Forty-eight hours left.

Sarah stood by the window, watching the rain fall across Whitechapel. She had a mug of tea in hand, and there was a half-eaten energy bar in her desk drawer. She felt a vague tug of excitement as she considered the day ahead. The TOAN conference was in two days, and her party as well.

No. Her revolt.

There hadn't been a proper backbench rebellion in a few years. Murmurings, stirrings, the occasional outburst. But a proper rebellion took coordination – cunning. It took the right cause, as well. Something backbenchers from all the parties could get behind. Governmental overreach was as good a reason as any.

She took a swallow of tea, watching the rain slide across the glass. It would be risky, but what was life without a bit of risk? Besides which, a politician's career was one of risk management. Doing nothing was as bad as doing something stupid. You had to be seen to do something noteworthy, else when election time rolled around, your constituency, not to mention your party, forgot your name.

"Knock-knock," someone said, from behind her.

"Winston," Sarah said, turning to greet her visitor. "You look like you've barely slept. Rough night?"

Winston looked… rumpled, which was not a word she normally associated with him. She hadn't been expecting him to pop by so early. "You could say that. Have you seen today's headlines?"

"No, I've been busy. Why?"

Winston showed her the screen of his Optik. It was a video of a body being pulled out of Regent's Canal. A photograph flashed on the display – a corporate ID: *George Holden*. Sarah sat down abruptly. "Damn it."

"You met with him yesterday, didn't you?" Winston lowered his Optik. "I saw that on the evening news. GBB was quite scathing about the inappropriateness of a backbencher inserting herself into an active investigation."

"Then I must be doing something right."

"This is no laughing matter, Sarah. You have to calm down. Let the Met do their job – hell, let Albion do theirs, whatever that might be this week." He sat down opposite her. "I'm getting pressure from the party to distance myself from you."

Sarah paused. "Really?"

"Really."

"I am definitely doing something right, then." Sarah leaned back, a speculative expression on her face. Inside, however, she was worried.

"You're taking this far too lightly, Sarah. I hope we don't wake up one morning to find you mysteriously renditioned to a black site and detained for the foreseeable."

"Well, you'll just have to come and rescue me, won't you?"

"I like you Sarah, but not that much." Winston looked at her. "I think you should back off, calm it down. We should cancel this get-together of yours and keep our heads down until we see how it all shakes out."

"By then it might well be too late," she said, softly. She frowned. "Holden used the 'C' word."

"How rude of him."

"Not that one. *Conspiracy*." She pulled out her own Optik. News reports flashed by, most of them concerned with the conference, but one caught her eye. Albion, along with the Met, were investigating a shooting near Whitechapel Station. "There was another shooting last night."

"I know. A member of the fabled DedSec, if my sources are to be believed."

"It would be, wouldn't it?" She looked at him. "You see

what they're doing, of course? With DedSec?"

"What do you mean?"

"Albion is positioning DedSec as a terror threat. You were at lunch. Remember what Cass said?"

Winston nodded, somewhat reluctantly. "Do you think there's anything to it?"

Sarah paused, considering. She and Winston had clashed as often as they'd stood side-by-side. They weren't friends, but then again they were of similar minds on many subjects. He'd been in her corner since the start of this, whatever it was, but that didn't mean he wouldn't go his own way if he thought it was to his own advantage.

Finally, she sat forward and said, "I do. DedSec are something, definitely, but they're not terrorists. Not as far as I can tell. They haven't blown anything up, after all."

"We both know there's more to terrorism than bombs."

She nodded. "Yes, but so far, they've contented themselves to graffiti and unorthodox wealth redistribution…"

"You can call it theft, Sarah. We're alone here."

She smiled. "If it were my money, I might. But it's not. The only damage they've done is cosmetic – a few propaganda bombs in inconvenient places. They're hacktivists, nothing more."

"For now," Winston said. "But you said Holden mentioned a conspiracy. Related to DedSec?"

"Not directly, no. But it's all tied in. He sent me a picture, of a man he claimed was involved in the shootings. And a number."

"So… Holden was involved?"

"That's the question, isn't it?"

"Have you told the police?"

"Not as such."

Winston sat back, a stunned look on his face. "This is not good, Sarah. Joking aside, you could be arrested for this."

"I don't think we've quite reached that point yet. Here, I'm sending the photo to you." Sarah sent the data through to Winston's Optik.

"What? Why? I don't want it!"

"Too late, already sent. Take a look at it – do you recognise him?"

Winston peered at the image, a scowl on his face. After a moment, he shook his head. "No. No bells here, I'm relieved to report."

"What about the number?"

"No."

"Do you think you could look into it for me?"

Winston was silent for a moment. Then, "Why would I do that?"

"It would mean I owe you a favour."

"Can't your assistant do it?"

"If I thought Faulkner wasn't going to be knocking on my door later this afternoon, I would. But like you yourself just said, I need to be careful."

Winston looked at the picture again, and sat back. "You think all this has to do with the shooting?" he said, in a worried tone. "An actual conspiracy?"

"There are too many coincidences piling up for it to be unrelated." Sarah tapped her fingers on the desk, thinking. "You said it yourself – something's happening. We can't see it, but it's there. Prowling in the dark. I think all of this smells like someone scrambling to hide something, and I want to know it is before it leaps out to bite us on the rear."

"If Faulkner is involved, he'll know Holden sent this to you."

"Yes."

"He might come after you as well."

Sarah nodded slowly. "I expect he'll be here before the day is out."

"What will you do?"

"Assure him I have no idea what he's talking about." She tapped at her Optik, deleting Holden's information from her device.

Winston smiled. "You know they say nothing is ever truly deleted when it comes to computers."

"Yes, but it buys us some time, I think." She looked away. "Faulkner doesn't care about me. I'm a gadfly, nothing more. Albion has bigger prey in mind."

"DedSec, you mean?"

"Alas, I was actually thinking of London," she said, softly. She looked at him. "Get me that information, Winston. It might hold the solution to our Albion problem."

Winston pushed himself to his feet. "You're going to owe me for this, you know. More than just a favour this time, I think."

"A small price to pay."

Sarah saw him out, then stopped by Hannah's door. "You heard?"

Hannah jolted guiltily, and Sarah knew she'd been eavesdropping. She turned in her seat. "I... might have, yes."

"You have access to my work files and email," Sarah said. It wasn't a question. "I need you to make copies of everything

Holden sent us and get them somewhere safe, well away from here – set up a private server or something. Whatever it is tech-savvy people do. Then scrub everything. I want nothing directly connecting us to Holden. Do you understand?"

"You think Faulkner will come for us?"

"I think Faulkner has been looking for an excuse, and we might have just given him one. If he calls, put him off. But he won't call. He'll bust in, looking to make an entrance and catch us on the back foot. Let him."

Hannah frowned quizzically. "What?"

"Let him scare you. Be scared."

"He does scare me," Hannah said.

"Good. Let him see it. You can cry if you like."

"Why?"

"Because the sooner he gets what he wants, the sooner he'll piss off. And the sooner that happens, the sooner we can find out what's actually going on."

Sarah paused. "One more thing: is there anything I should know, before the inevitable?"

Hannah looked at her. "What do you mean?"

Sarah stared back, wondering how far to push it. Wondering whether she actually wanted to know. Hannah was an excellent assistant, a positive genius at ferreting out information. She'd never asked how Hannah found out the things she did. Hannah often told her – lunches with disgruntled employees, friends of friends, she said – but such explanations never quite had the ring of truth. Normally, she let them slide. But here and now, it could sink them. "Those two reporters... the ones you vouched for, they were the ones behind that business at the police station, weren't they?"

"I honestly don't know what you're talking about," Hannah said. "I'm sorry."

For a moment, Sarah almost believed her. She wanted to believe her. "I'm sorry as well," she said.

As she turned to leave, Hannah said, "You're right."

Sarah paused. "Obviously." Then, "About what?"

"DedSec. They're not terrorists."

"You sound certain of that."

"I am." Hannah looked at her. "Whatever's going on, they're the only ones trying to stop it. I can't tell you how I know that, but… I do. They're the only ones looking out for this city right now."

Sarah knocked on the doorframe, pondering this. Then she turned away.

"No. They're not the only ones."

25: MARCUS TELL

Olly climbed the steps slowly. He was still tired, though he'd gotten some sleep in the station. It wasn't the first time he'd slept rough, but he was regretting it now. The morning was cold, and the coffee in his hands was hot. He stopped, leaning against the rail, and looked up. The source of the camera's signal was upstairs – a flat on the sixth storey of apartment residential building near the Royal Victoria Docks.

He'd changed clothes the night before, scavenging new threads from a donation bin. Nothing fit right, but that was a small price to pay. He'd washed up with supplies purchased from a Boots in the station. Mouthwash and coffee didn't mix well. Liz's Optik – his Optik now – pinged and he pulled it out, checking messages. It still hadn't synched properly with his display, but that would come in time.

The message was from Krish, consisting of emoji's and a number to call. Olly made the call. Krish picked up the first buzz. "Where the hell are you, fam?"

"Hello to you too." Olly took a sip of coffee. "I'm downstairs from Tell's flat. His other flat, I guess. What's up?"

"What's up? Are you mental? Why didn't you come back here?"

"We need to find this guy. Bagley filled you in?"

"Yeah, but–"

"Then you know everything." He paused. Then, more softly: "You know about L… Redqueen, yeah? What happened?"

"Yeah, man. It's on the telly, all over. They ain't said shit about her, but Bagley confirmed it." Krish was silent for a moment. "The cops got her body. We're putting together something to get it back… somebody to pretend to be family, maybe?"

"Sounds like a plan." Olly laughed. The sound was raw and ugly to his ears. He'd dreamed about Liz last night –the sound of the shot, and her face had been superimposed over his memory of Dempsey's. "Not that I think she'd care."

"Maybe not. But we do."

Suddenly uncomfortable, Olly changed the subject. "What about this Tell's flat?"

"Albion, bruv. They're all over it. Even found the camera."

"Shit." That meant they'd know where Tell himself was soon enough. They wouldn't be far behind him.

"It's barc mad, fam. We got everyone talking every which way. Someone, Dalton maybe, or Sabine, sent strong word – sit tight and wait for further instructions. Meantime, we're going through all that data you gave Bagley, trying to figure out where that drone came from."

"Did you tell them…" Olly began

"That you were still running around? Nah. So far nobody

but me has noticed you ain't back yet." Krish paused. "You'd best hurry though, yeah?"

"Why? Think they'll be pissed off?"

"They already pissed off, fam. Shit's about to go down." Krish hesitated. "Stay chill, Olly. And if you find anything – I mean, anything…"

"I'll contact you," Olly said. He ended the call, finished his coffee, and started up the stairs again. He put his Optik away and fished out his stun gun. It hadn't done him much good so far, but it might come in handy if Tell got stroppy. If he was even here. For all Olly knew, his quarry had already run again. If Olly were in his place, he'd have done the same.

But he hoped not. This was his only lead.

On the sixth floor, Olly crept slowly along the corridor, trying to make as little noise as possible. When he reached the door, he made to knock – only for it to swing open before he could touch it.

"Come in," someone said, from inside.

Olly hesitated, trying to decide whether to run. An older man stepped into view, a revolver held confidently in his hand. "Do not run. Come inside. Quickly now, before someone sees."

Olly swallowed and did as he was ordered. "Are– are you Marcus Tell?"

"If I am?" The old man closed the door and motioned for Olly to move through on into the kitchen. The flat was small, but classy. Like a photo from a realty company's website.

"I…" Olly hesitated again. "Look, can you get the gun out of my face?"

"No. What do you want?"

"That depends."

Tell – Olly was fairly certain it was him now – frowned. "Why were you in my flat? And where is your friend? Not attempting anything foolish, I hope."

"We were looking for you. And no. She's… she's dead."

"How?"

"A drone," Olly said. He looked at the older man. "Just like the one that shot the guy who stole your Optik a few days ago. Remember him?"

Tell frowned. "I do. Come. Sit. You look done in. I will make some tea." He lowered his weapon and gestured to a nearby table.

"Tea?" Olly said in disbelief. "We ain't got time for a brew-up, mate. That drone is still out there."

"Indeed. Do you have my Optik?"

Olly hesitated. "No. I lost it."

"Then the chances of the drone finding us are slim. At least for the moment. Sit." He indicated a chair.

Seeing no other option, Olly sat. He looked around. The décor was straight out of an old soap opera, like those his mum used to watch all the time.

"What is this place?"

"My flat. I have several. This is one." Tell put the kettle on, then sat opposite Olly. He set the pistol down on the table. "You came after me alone?" He shook his head. "The folly of youth." Tell tapped the pistol with a finger. "You are not the police. Nor are you Albion. A criminal, then?"

"No." Olly paused. "Well, maybe?"

Tell smiled at that. "Ah. DedSec."

308 _Watch Dogs Legion_

"Yeah. You know us?"

"I know some things. You are revolutionaries?"

"Resistance, innit?"

"Same difference." Tell's smile faded. "I will not ask how you came to be on my trail. I will say it is possibly fortuitous. For the both of us."

"What do you mean?"

The kettle whistled. Tell rose and turned it off. As he prepared their tea, he said, "Three weeks ago, I was... employed to assemble a number of improvised explosive devices. This I did. Now, my former employer wishes me removed from play." He set a steaming mug down before Olly. "Builder's, I'm afraid. Milk?"

Olly stared at him. "Just a drop. Go back to the bit about the explosives."

Tell sat back down. "I assume DedSec would be interested in stopping said devices from performing their function?"

"You mean blowing up? Yeah, that sounds bad."

"Excellent. I will tell you everything."

"Really? I mean, that's great and all."

Tell was silent for long minutes. Then, "I am sorry about your friend." He took a sip of tea and looked at Olly. "I would have no more ghosts on my conscience."

Olly shook his head. He hadn't been prepared for this. He couldn't really say what he had been expecting, but not this. "Tell me," he said, finally. "Start with your employer."

"I do not know their name. They call themselves 'Zero Day'. I suspect it is an alias."

"You think?" Olly paused. "Why you?"

Tell smiled. "If you are here, I'm sure you've realised that

Marcus Tell is not my real name. That the life I lead is not mine, yes?"

"These Zero Day people was blackmailing you," Olly said.

"Even so. They told me that unless I served them, they would reveal my identity to certain parties who bear me no love." Tell's smile turned grim. "I was a revolutionary of sorts myself, back in the day. There are many who would see me dead."

"And they wanted you to build bombs. Why?"

"That I do not know. I do not even know where the bombs are. Though I can guess." Tell paused. "There were others involved. A courier, from the Kelley gang – working *for* Clan Kelley, I always suspected. And a supplier, Holden."

"Holden?" Olly frowned. The name sounded familiar. Something Liz had said. "Bagley, you listening?" Tell raised an eyebrow at this seeming non-sequitur, but said nothing. "You getting this?"

Indeed, I am, Oliver. You know, you really should have come back instead of haring off on your own. Things are getting dangerous out there.

"Yeah. Listen… Holden – wasn't that the bloke Hannah was looking for?"

Oh good. Your brain appears to be working again. Yes, indeed. It seems Holden was the one providing our friend Marcus with the supplies he needed to build his toys. How convenient!

Olly looked at Tell. "Holden was a go-between, yeah? He got you the goods, white van man delivered them…"

"And then the same driver took them away, once I'd finished. A very tidy operation."

"What did Holden get out of it?"

"Money, I assume. The same thing your van man did."

"He's dead."

"I know." Tell paused. "Holden is too, or will be soon enough."

He's right, Bagley murmured.

Olly blinked. "What?"

George Holden turned up dead this morning, floating in Regent's Canal with a bullet in his head. Mr Tell is the remaining link in this particular chain.

Tell studied his face. "I was right. Holden's dead."

"Looks that way." Olly rubbed his face. "Fuck. I'm well out of my depth."

Tell smiled. "I have often felt that way myself. Especially these days."

Olly sat back, thinking. "We need to get you somewhere safe, figure out where those bombs are, and what comes next."

"I am safe here," Tell protested. "I–" He paused suddenly, and stood with a grunt. "Perhaps I spoke too soon. We're about to have guests."

"What?" Olly scrambled to his feet.

Tell set his Optik on the table. "I'm wired in to the building's security. See for yourself."

Olly did. On a black and white feed, bulky figures moved down the hall, all armed and in body armour. "Shit." He sagged back. "Albion."

Indeed. Quite a few of them, in fact. You might want to think about leaving…

"They must have found the camera, even as you did," Tell said. He checked his weapon. "I hope you have something other than that stun gun to contribute."

Olly shook his head. "I need to think."

"You think. I'll distract them." Tell went to a closet in the hall and opened it. Removing a false panel, he pulled out a rucksack and set it down on the kitchen table. Inside were a number of metal canisters.

"What are these?"

"Homemade smoke grenades."

Olly looked at him. "Bombs *and* grenades?"

"Every man should have a hobby," Tell said. He pulled two of the canisters out. "The smoke will fill the corridor, but not for long. It might not even slow them down."

"Better than nothing."

Tell smiled. "My thoughts exactly." He went to the door, cracked it, tapped the activator switch on the grenade and rolled it out the door. He did the same with the second. On the Optik screen, Olly watched as roiling smoke filled the corridor. The Albion operatives paused, fell back. Tell began to barricade the door. The old man moved quickly and methodically, as if he'd been ready for this day for a long time. "If you have an idea for how to get out, now is the time to implement it."

"How do you feel about flying?"

Tell paused. "You have a helicopter?"

"Not quite." Olly went to the window, opened it, and looked out. There were a few drones in sight – including a sturdy Ixatech model. Easily big enough for two people, the cargo drones were fairly simple to take control of, and this one zipped towards the building quickly enough. "Right, here's the plan: we take a drone down to the street, grab a car."

"A drone?" Tell asked, looking startled.

"You could always just jump."

"It was not a criticism."

Olly flinched as a shotgun roared. There was a hollow, metallic sound. "Steel door?" he asked.

Tell nodded. "Yes, but it won't hold forever. Once the smoke clears, they'll shoot out the hinges."

"It just has to hold long enough for us to get out of the window." Olly turned. "Bagley, we need a route away from here." No answer. "Bagley?" A burst of static was his only reply. As if the signal were being jammed somehow. He switched frequencies. "Krish?" For a moment, he thought it would be more of the same, then–

"Olly? Mate?"

Krish's voice was strained. Tense. In the background, Olly heard what sounded like gunfire. "Krish, what the hell is going on?"

"Don't come back here, Olly – shit's compromised, bruv. Albion–"

Krish's voice died in a blur of static. Olly cursed.

"What is it?" Tell asked, from near the door. "Is something wrong?"

"Albion. They're hitting DedSec, or at least the bit of it I know how to get to." Olly thought quickly. "You said you had *flats*, plural. Can you show me how to get to one of the others?"

Tell nodded. "Yes, but we need to move now. The smoke is clearing."

Olly turned back to the window. "It's almost here." The drone was closing in, losing altitude as it drew near the window. "Need to be well quick, though." Olly opened the window and made ready to climb out.

There was a flash, just out of the corner of his eye. And then that awful sound. *Boom*. The cargo drone came apart in burning fragments. Olly was flung back, and felt the kitchen table collapse under him. Smoke canisters rolled from the rucksack as he fell on top of it.

Tell was beside him a moment later. "What is it? Are you–?"

Olly grabbed for him. "Get down!"

Another shot, punching through the brick. Tell went flat. "No way out the window, then. We must try the door." He grabbed for the rucksack. A shot caught it – smoke erupted, and the kitchen was filled with metal fragments.

Olly yelped as one skidded across his cheek. "Forget it – we've got to get out of here…"

He stopped. Tell lay propped against the fridge, his hands cupped across his stomach. A shard of one of his own canisters was buried in his gut. Smaller fragments jutted from his face and hands.

"Fuck me…" Olly breathed.

Tell gave Olly a twisted smile. He made to speak, but then, slowly, slid down. His features slackened and his eyes went vague and clouded. Olly stared at him in incomprehension.

He was still staring when the door was blown off of its hinges and Albion operatives stormed in. He was knocked sprawling, a moment later his hands twisted up behind his back. The last thing he saw before they dragged him out, was a glint of metal through the window.

A drone, banking away and heading for home.

•••

Faulkner was standing on the back ramp of the APV, lighting a cigarette, when Danny emerged from the old Limehouse garage, Hattersley trailing in his wake. Smoke boiled into the afternoon light, and pursuit drones circled like carrion birds. Danny started towards the APV to make his report. Hattersley followed, talking a mile a minute.

"Did you see that armoury down there?" Hattersley asked, mopping at his face with a handkerchief. "They were 3D printing a whole bloody arsenal. We're lucky they didn't know we was coming."

"Yeah, funny that," Danny said. "There's cameras all over the place. You'd think they'd have had more warning."

"Maybe they weren't paying attention."

"Maybe."

Hattersley shrugged. "Hey, whatever happened, I'm cushty. Any fight you can walk away from, right?" He paused. "You're still bothered about that thing last night, aren't you? That thing with Holden?"

Danny stopped. "Wouldn't you be?"

Hattersley didn't look at him. "It's tough, man. But... you had to do it."

"Did I?" Danny stripped off his helmet.

Hattersley didn't say anything. Danny shook his head and looked around. There were uniforms everywhere. The Met was here, but positioned well back from the action. This was an Albion operation, and Faulkner didn't intend to let anyone forget it. He wondered if Constable Jenks were over there somewhere. Part of him hoped not.

Nearby, prisoners – what few there were – were being loaded into a transport, or into ambulances. The dead were being bagged up, ready to be delivered to the morgue. There were too many of the latter for Danny's taste. He was tired – no, exhausted. But every time he closed his eyes, he saw Holden.

He wasn't sure what to do. Something told him reporting Faulkner's actions wouldn't end well for him. Faulkner wasn't the sort to act on his own initiative. If he'd killed Holden, it was because he had orders to do so. Orders that could have only come from the top. And if that were the case... was that really the sort of brotherhood he wanted to belong to?

Death didn't bother Danny. Nor did violence. A soldier had to become used to both, very quickly. But there was a difference between shooting someone who had a gun trained on you, and taking out a man tied to a chair.

The army, Danny's army, didn't execute prisoners without a damn good reason. As far as he could tell, Faulkner had only killed Holden because it was expedient to do so. The technician had outlived his usefulness and, worse, was a potential liability.

He wondered – feared – what that meant for Ro. She'd been transferred to the custody suite at the base, and he hadn't seen her since. He hadn't even been allowed to talk to her, not that he knew what to say. How did one apologise for allowing one's sibling to be arrested?

Faulkner acknowledged their arrival at the APV with a nod. "They didn't put up much of a fight," he said. He sounded almost disappointed. He'd been watching the firefight through their Optik feeds. Three teams had gone in, taking the main entrance and blowing through the reinforced doors. There'd been around twenty hostiles – funny to think of fellow Londoners that way – inside. Many of them had surrendered immediately. Or tried to.

But some had resisted. 3D printed weapons could kill as easily as the real thing. Luckily, there'd been no casualties, at least on Albion's side. He thought again about how unprepared the hackers had been. Maybe Albion had caught them at the right time. Or maybe they'd been distracted. That didn't explain why the various security measures Danny and the others had located had been disabled. Almost as if someone had set DedSec up to fail.

"Still, well done, lads." Faulkner tapped ash from his cigarette. "Looks like we caught a pair of Holden's accomplices as well. They tried to set off a bomb, must have made a mistake and one of them wound up dead."

"And the other, Sarge?"

"Safely in custody and being transported back to base for interrogation."

Danny hesitated. Wanted to speak. Didn't. Faulkner looked at him for a moment, then said to Hattersley, "Go get a head count on the prisoners for me. I need to update the after-action reports. You stay here, Danny."

Hattersley glanced at Danny, but didn't argue. Danny watched him go, trying to look anywhere but at Faulkner. He'd avoided the other man as much as possible since the night before. Since the incident with Holden. But he couldn't avoid Faulkner forever.

"Cigarette, Danny?" Faulkner asked. He held out the pack.

Danny shook his head. "Don't smoke, Sarge."

"No? Good for you." Faulkner blew a plume of smoke into the air. "You did well in there, lad. Textbook."

"Thanks, Sarge."

"Few too many prisoners for my taste, though. Prisoners means paperwork." Faulkner scratched his chin and turned back to the garage. "Nice little set-up they had. Takes time to build all that. Money. Burrowed in deep like ticks. What's the one thing most organised terror groups have in common, Danny?" Faulkner went on before Danny could answer. "Money."

"Hackers, Sarge."

Faulkner laughed. "Grow up, Danny. Hackers steal pennies and piss. Everyone knows that. This sort of effort requires real money." He flicked his cigarette to the ground and crushed it beneath his heel. "And that's exactly what my report is going to say, once we've finished debriefing all these prisoners you got for me."

Danny cleared his throat.

Faulkner looked at him, a slight smile on his face. "What was that, Danny? Something to say?"

"My sister, Sarge…"

"Ah, yes. Very proud of you there, Danny my lad. It takes true dedication to the cause to throw over blood in the name of Queen and country."

Danny swallowed a sudden rush of bile. Faulkner's grin was almost more than he could bear. "Yes, Sarge."

Faulkner nodded. "Your sister has been very naughty, Danny. She's a proper little villain. Doesn't know much though, unfortunately. Otherwise the Kelleys would have never turned her over." He extracted another cigarette and tapped it on the pack, thinking. "By rights, we should bang her up in Holloway nick for a nice long stretch."

Danny didn't reply. Faulkner nodded again, as if Danny had done something right. "I'm still mulling on it, me. But you're bound for great things, my lad. Keep your nose clean, and who knows what the future holds?" He lit a second cigarette and held out the pack. "Sure you won't have one, Danny boy? Helps calm the nerves."

26: AFTERMATH

Hannah was in a café, grabbing lunch for herself and Sarah, when the news broke. GBB footage rolled across her display and she froze, unable to do anything but watch. She'd only been to the DedSec hideout in Tower Hamlets once, but she knew it well enough to recognise the building Albion had raided. And if there had been any doubt in her mind, the moment a handcuffed Krish was dragged into view, face bloodied, and unceremoniously tossed into the back of a waiting van would have made clear what had happened.

A sudden panic gripped her. She looked around, expecting to see the police or worse, Albion, coming for her. Her order hadn't arrived yet, so she hurried to the toilets. The ladies was empty so she locked herself in. Her heart was beating too fast, and for a moment, she feared she was having a serious panic attack.

This wasn't the first time a cell had been raided. There were procedures in place for this eventuality. DedSec operations were vaporous by design. Each cell in a given borough had their own way of doing things. And when one went down, the others went black until the danger passed. Forcing herself to calm down, she activated her Optik's encrypted communications app. First things first – a status report. "Bagley?"

Silence. A crackle of white noise. Then: *Hannah, I'm pleased to hear you are in one piece. That's more than I can say for some of the others.*

"That's not funny, Bagley," she hissed, pitching her voice low. "What happened?"

Albion happened. There was no warning.

"How is that possible?"

You're asking the wrong person. Actually, do I count as a person?

"Bagley!" She flinched as her own voice echoed back at her.

I don't know how it happened. All I know is that it's not an isolated incident. It's happening at various sites over the city.

"Show me."

Snippets of drone feeds peppered her display: a gang of graffiti artists in Walker's Court were rounded up by armed Albion operatives; Albion pursuit drones swept over Camden Market in pursuit of a hooded cyclist; mass arrests in Leake Street, at the Barbican Centre and the Brixton Barrier block estate.

"Enough," she said. "What now?"

I would recommend you leave the capital immediately.

"I can't." Hannah closed her eyes and bowed her head. "I can't." She felt as if the world were coming apart around her. "Sarah would wonder where I went. People would get suspicious."

By the time they figured it out, you could have a new name, a new life.

"No. My life is here. What about the others?"

Mostly keeping quiet. You know the drill – complete comms black out.

"Am I in danger?" she asked, softly.

I wouldn't have recommended that you leave if you weren't.

"How much time do I have?"

Unknown. If you're careful, they might never find you at all.

"Comforting," Hannah muttered. "Why is all this happening now? What's going on?"

Unknown. Again, I recommend you go to ground, post haste.

"I'll take it under advisement." She paused. "That information we got from Holden... has it come to anything yet?"

Ah. Now there, I might have better news for you. The man in the photo is named Art Coyle – though that's an alias. I traced the number to an obvious shell corporation with offices in a certain infamous building at the heart of the financial district.

Hannah thought quickly, as the data downloaded to her Optik. "Is... is Olly still alive?" She knew Liz was dead. Krish had told her that much, the last time they'd spoken. But if Olly was still out there...

Oliver is in Albion custody, much like Krish and the others.

"Shit. Shit, shit, *shit*." She sat for a moment. Then, in a small voice, "Is anyone left?"

A few. Enough. Bagley paused. Hannah, I'm patching you through to the café's security feed. An Albion APV just pulled up. Make yourself scarce.

Hannah was out of the bathroom moments later. She paused in the corridor. There was a service entrance – but what if they were waiting? What if they weren't here for her at all? Options and outcomes flooded her mind. One stood out, something her father had often said: the police only chase those who run.

She took a deep breath and went back out into the café. She would pick up her order and go, as if nothing at all were out of the ordinary. Then she would go back to the office and try to come up with a plan. Maybe if she were to alert Sarah as to the arrests – no. There was nothing Sarah could do about that. Nor was she likely to stick her neck out in such a fashion.

There were other ways, though. If Sarah managed to pull off her rebellion, Albion might well be pressured into releasing those it had taken into custody. She felt a flush of renewed confidence. DedSec might be down, but it wasn't out. Not yet.

Her order was waiting for her at the counter when she got back. She smiled at the barista and picked up the bag and Sarah's coffee. It was only as she was heading for the door that she realised that the server hadn't smiled back – and how quiet the café had fallen.

"I'll take that, thank you, Ms Shah," Faulkner said smoothly, taking the cup out of her hand. He tasted the drink, then grimaced. "No wonder your boss is always in a bad mood. This is awful."

"Sergeant Faulkner," Hannah said, with forced mildness. Underneath, her heart was pounding. Why was he here? What did he know? She tried to think – could Krish have given her up? She didn't want to think so, but there was no telling what Albion had done to him.

Faulkner set the coffee back on the counter and gestured to the door. "Shall we?"

"Are we going somewhere?"

"Outside. For a quick chat."

"I don't think we have anything to say to each other, do we?"

Faulkner's smile faded. "It wasn't a request." He gestured and she felt hands grip her upper arms tightly. Two Albion operatives in full tac-gear stood to either side of her. She looked at them and then at Faulkner.

"Oh," she said, in a small voice.

Sarah was in her office, talking to Moira Jenks, when an alert interrupted her. She held up a finger, silencing Jenks, and answered the alert. A message from Winston, just three words: *You owe me.* She sat upright and clicked the attached file. It wasn't much, but what was there painted a picture. Sarah had always had a talent for putting together puzzles and what Winston had found was possibly the last piece of this particular one.

"What is it?" Jenks asked, playing with her Optik.

"The answer to a question." She thumped her fist on her desk and laughed, low and loud. Winston had worked more quickly than she'd dared hope – then, he'd had the photo for help. "One that's been bothering me for some time."

Jenks suddenly sat up. "Bloody hell," she said. "They just hit DedSec!"

Sarah looked at her, the words not quite registering. "What? Who?"

"Albion! That shit, Faulkner – he just led a full-on raid, in Limehouse. They've arrested like fifteen people..."

"They can't do that," Sarah protested. "Albion doesn't have permission..."

"They're bloody acting like they do." Jenks sounded stunned. "And that's not the only one – I'm getting alerts from CID... there are more raids scheduled for today, right now.

The Guv wants every uniform to report in, something about providing a police presence…"

Sarah snorted. "More like the Met got shut out, and he wants to pretend he's in on the operation before someone starts asking awkward questions." She sat back, frowning. If Albion had received permission for such an operation, that meant things were moving faster than she'd anticipated. "This moves up the timetable somewhat." She looked at Jenks. "What are you going to do?"

Jenks shrugged. "I can read the writing on the wall as well as you, ma'am." She scratched at the scab on her cheek. "The Met's not in charge anymore. It might not be official yet, but it will be. And I don't fancy serving under an arse-wipe like Faulkner."

"If anyone asks, we'll say you're still assigned to protection duty," Sarah said, with a chuckle. But there was no real mirth in the sound. It wasn't a laughing matter. She switched through her display, looking through the newsfeeds until she found coverage of the Limehouse raid. A smiling Nigel Cass was being interviewed by a GBB reporter.

"Smug creep," Sarah muttered. She switched feeds, looking for something less offensive.

Albion was conducting a multi-media blitzkrieg – bombarding the airwaves with propaganda, even as GBB showed footage of their successful raids. Sarah shut off her feed with a disgusted sigh and ran her hands over her head. "This doesn't change anything," she said after a few moments. "It just makes the climb a bit steeper."

Jenks frowned. "Not giving up then?"

"No. But I might need to re-evaluate my current strategy."

Sarah rose. "We'll need to move quickly. Get ahead of all this somehow." She checked the time. "Hannah should have been back by now."

"My fault, I'm afraid, ladies." Faulkner stood in the doorway of her office, a smug smile on his face. "Surprised to see me, *Ms* Lincoln?"

"Not as such, *Mr* Faulkner." Sarah turned, putting a smile on her face. "Might I ask what you've done with my assistant?"

"She's in the corridor, with one of my men."

"Why?"

"She's a person of interest in an ongoing investigation – and before you say it, yes, our current remit allows for this particular investigation, as it's related to an active terror threat."

"DedSec," Sarah said.

Faulkner tapped the side of his nose. "Got it in one. I knew you were clever." He glanced at Jenks. "You're out of uniform, constable." Jenks made an obscene gesture in reply and he grinned. Faulkner's gaze switched back to Sarah. "We suspect your assistant has some ties to known subversive organisation DedSec."

Sarah paused. "And why do you suspect that?"

"Need to know," he said, clearly relishing the words. And suddenly, she knew he was lying through his teeth, without a shadow of a doubt. This was an act of spite, nothing more. But the end result was the same. Hannah would vanish into the labyrinthine bowels of Albion's organisation, like the others she'd heard rumours of. She couldn't allow that.

Yet, she hesitated. What she had was valuable. More valuable, perhaps, than Hannah. The sort of cudgel that could possibly be used to beat Albion senseless – if she didn't waste it. Even as the thought occurred to her, she felt a flush of shame – and the flicker of an idea.

Decision made, she cleared her throat. "I know who he is, you know."

Faulkner paused, a quizzical look on his face.

"I know who he is," Sarah repeated.

"Who?"

"The one Holden sold the drone to."

Faulkner tensed. "I don't know what you think you're talking about, but–"

Sarah overrode him. "You know damn well what I'm talking about. Holden sold something – a weapon – to someone else. Someone who decided to use that weapon to kill others. If that were to become common knowledge, well… our Mr Cass might have a bit more difficulty getting his foot in the door, mightn't he?"

Faulkner stared at her. "You don't know anything."

"I started to wonder why you didn't want us to see the Limehouse facilities. And then I realised… it wasn't you. It was Holden. He knew that any official visit would reveal that something was missing. So he came to try and intimidate us – me. And when that failed… when someone in Albion figured out what was up… he came looking for protection."

Faulkner smirked. "And?"

"And I know who he sold the drone to."

Faulkner's smirk flattened. "Tell me."

"No."

Faulkner took a step towards her. Jenks moved in front of her, and he stopped. He looked past the constable. "Don't be a bloody idiot. You don't want to be on the wrong side of us. Not now. All your little games up until now… that can all be forgiven. If we worked with bloody hill chieftains and warlords, we can work with a Labour politician."

Sarah nodded. "What do I get in return?"

Faulkner sneered. "You get not to get arrested here and now."

"Not good enough. Hannah walks."

Faulkner's sneer faded. "She's a terrorist. Or at the very least, terrorist-adjacent."

"That's total crap and you know it. This is just you trying to get your own back, because I've been making you look a right pillock lately. Not you needed much help in that regard." Faulkner clenched his fists, but she could see the gears turning in his head. She kept talking. "You don't have *anything* right now. You've hit a few hacktivist hives. Good for you. But when people learn that Albion sold a weaponised drone to a murderer, all that good PR goes right in the bin."

"What are you proposing?"

"A trade. Hannah – and a clean slate, between you and me. In return, I'll give you what I know. Eminently fair, I think"

"What do you know? What have you actually got?" he growled.

"A name. And an address."

"And if I say no?"

"Then the press will know what I know the moment you leave this office. It goes without saying they'll fall on it like ravenous hounds, and pretty soon Albion will be in the crosshairs of every pundit, muckraker and politician in Whitehall. And Nigel Cass will have you to thank."

"I could arrest you."

"Not going to happen. Yes, you could arrest my assistant. You might even arrest my personal security here. But you can't get to me. Not yet. Not without a bloody good, totally watertight reason. You're hoping to find something to hang me with, but the truth is... you have nothing, and you know it."

Faulkner grunted and looked away, plainly debating with himself. Sarah sat back down and began to arrange her paperwork. At her gesture, Jenks sat down as well. They held the cards now. Faulkner had to choose between petty satisfaction – and job security.

Faulkner turned back. "Deal."

DAY ZERO

FRIDAY

Bagley-bytes 13698-4: Okay, things look bad, I admit it.

+ + +

Today's big news, besides the imminent extermination of DedSec London, is the TOAN Conference. Met, Albion and more out in force, so anyone still planning on crashing that particular party needs to be on alert.

+ + +

Related to yesterday's unfortunate occurrences, things are hotting up further afield in old London town. It's no longer just the East End feeling the heat. Met officers in full riot have been spotted mustering near both Kensington and Chelsea field bases. If you're in residence, clear out. That means you, Dalton.

+ + +

No, Terry, they're definitely not following you. In fact, if an unmarked van offers you a lift, you should definitely take it. I insist.

+ + +

On the subject of unmarked vans and Wandsworth, we've learned that prisoners are being transported from Albion's Tower Hamlets facilities to Nine Elms Docks. That includes DedSec members. Just a heads up.

+ + +

Everyone else... it might be time to think about relocating. London is getting a mite dodgy.

27: BREAKOUT

Danny made his move just before dawn on the day of the TOAN conference. It had taken him until then to come up with a workable plan, and to gather his courage enough to enact it. Hattersley was on duty, which made things both easier and harder.

The Tower Hamlet South base was stripped bare of personnel, thanks to the conference. Albion was on full alert, every set of boots on the ground barring those on essential duties. Danny was supposed to be part of a sweep in Limehouse, but he'd begged off, calling in sick. Faulkner wasn't going to like it, but – well, Faulkner wasn't going to like what happened next either.

Thankfully, he was distracted. Faulkner was busy overseeing the latest raids – and the media frenzy that surrounded them. He was in a bad mood as well, despite everything humming along like clockwork. Something had gone wrong somewhere, though Danny wasn't sure what. Maybe it was just the fact that Cass had pulled two out of every three Albion operatives out of the field in Tower Hamlets for a special detail. A special detail Faulkner obviously wasn't a part of.

Whatever the reason, Danny was glad of it. The fewer people in the base, the less chance there was of things going wrong. Not that he expected things to go right. Hope for success, plan for failure – that was his motto.

He approached the custody suite as if he didn't have a care in the world. The layout of the back of the warehouse was simple enough. The custody suite was at the end of an improvised corridor of steel grating and chain link fencing, overlaid with a network of gantries and drone berths and interspersed with electronically controlled gates.

The suite sat at the centre of several such corridors, each branching off in a different direction. Behind the suite, near the loading bay doors, were several parked APVs, their bumpers aimed at the doors. Danny's exit strategy hinged on stealing one.

This time of day, there'd only be one person on duty and a response team on call. Even so, he'd have to be quick. There were cameras everywhere. The minute he made his move, it was all but certain someone would scramble the response team and Albion SOP was to come in hot.

There was a raised metal platform set off side of the cells, where the duty guard sat. Each of the suites had a closed circuit camera installed, feeding back to a bank of monitors on the platform. There was also a main control panel. The suites had digital locks that could be opened singly or all at once from the panel. The benefit of the panel was that you didn't need a code – you just flipped a switch and all the doors unlocked at once.

Being assigned to guard duty was boring. Danny had done it a time or two, but there'd never been anyone in the cells. It was different now. The cells were full, some of them with more than one person. Danny couldn't hear them, but he could feel them, feel their fear, their resignation. He didn't like it. It only solidified the choice he'd made.

As he crossed the floor towards the platform, Danny saw that the loading bay doors at the rear of the warehouse were closing. He could hear trucks moving out. He climbed the stairs and said, "We get a delivery?"

Hattersley turned in his chair. "Danny, matey. Come to join me in my purgatory?"

"Figured you could use some company. What's with the trucks?"

Hattersley indicated the monitors. "They were taking out the first load of overflow."

"Where are they going?" Danny asked, leaning over Hattersley's chair. He spotted Ro immediately. She wasn't the only one in her cell – there was a young man there as well. Some DedSec punk, he figured.

"Wandsworth. Nine Elms Docks." Hattersley put his hands on top of his head and leaned back in his chair. "Remember all those fucking barges Albion bought about three months ago? Somebody decided to turn them into mobile bases – drones, gun emplacements and custody suites in the holds."

"Why?"

"Safer, innit?" Hattersley shrugged. "Faulkner – or somebody higher up the chain – wants the suites cleared."

Danny paused. "They're expecting more prisoners?"

"That's the word." Hattersley looked at him. "Me, I figure it's got to do with that TOAN conference today. Lots of protests. Lots of unwashed wankers looking to get arrested."

Danny grunted and let his hand slip towards his sidearm. He didn't want to shoot Hattersley, but he might have no choice. The thought of it churned in his gut. "When's your shift end?"

Hattersley checked his Optik. "Ten minutes, give or take. Why?"

"Because that means we've got ten minutes until someone notices you opened all the cells," Danny said, raising his sidearm and pressing it to the back of Hattersley's head.

Hattersley stiffened. "Danny? Mate, what are you playing at?"

"Open. The. Cells," Danny repeated, softly.

"You can't do this, man," Hattersley said, not looking at him.

"My sister, yeah? Got no choice. Open the cells."

"You won't shoot me … ?"

Danny paused. "No. I won't." He stepped back. Hattersley turned, a look of relief on his face. Danny slid behind him as he rose, and brought the solid weight of his pistol down on the back of Hattersley's head. The other man crumpled silently. Danny looked down at him for a moment, and then stooped, took both his sidearm and his Optik. It only took a few moments to unlock all the cells. He was down the steps and at Ro's cell a moment later, Hattersley's assault rifle in hand. He hauled it open. "Right. Time to go."

"Danny?" Ro sat up, and so did her cell-mate. "What are you doing?" his sister asked.

"What does it look like I'm doing? I'm getting you out."

"You'll get in deep shit."

"And?"

"They might shoot you."

Danny stopped and looked at her. "I say again – and?"

She gave a crooked smile. "Just checking. Bruv." She looked at her cell-mate. "You coming?"

The kid stood. "What about the others?"

"I've unlocked all the cells," Danny said, looking him up and down. "You're the one they got yesterday over near Canary Wharf, aren't you?"

"Er yeah, that's me. Olly."

"Danny." Danny looked at his sister. "Ro, help me get the other doors open. We've only got a few minutes. We need to get everybody out, and to the APVs." He looked at Olly again. "DedSec, right? Means you know computers and that?"

Olly frowned. "Yeah?"

"Merry Christmas." Danny tossed him Hattersley's Optik. The lad caught it with a dawning look of glee. "Think you can make use of this?"

"Oh yeah."

"Good." Danny joined Ro in opening the cells. "Everyone out, we don't have much time." There weren't many left – a dozen. Not all of them were DedSec. "Right, people! This is a prison break." He ignored the barrage of questions, the suspicious looks, and said, "If you want to come, follow us, or stay here – don't matter to me."

"Where are we going?" Ro asked.

"APVs at the back. We get one of them moving, we can get out of here." He gestured. "Everyone follow me. Be quick. We've only got a few minutes at most…"

An alarm began to blare. Danny turned.

"Scratch that. Let's go!"

•••

It took Olly a few moments to crack the encryption on the Optik and download his customised app suite. By the time he was up and running again, alarms were going off. He looked at Ro. "Your brother isn't exactly the stealthy sort, is he?"

"Danny's more of a door kicker." She looked at her brother. He was up ahead, leading the way. "This is your plan? We run?"

"Technically, we're driving," Danny called back. "The APVs are just up ahead. We just need to – shit!" He leapt back as shots pinged off the metal grating around them. People dropped flat, yelling or screaming. Half-crouched, Danny swung his weapon around and up, returning fire. At first Olly couldn't tell what he was shooting at. Then he heard the telltale whine of motors.

The bulky shape of a riot drone hurtled by overhead. As it sped along, it dropped smoke canisters. Coloured haze filled the air, making it all but impossible to see. People were coughing, crouched against the sides of the corridor. Through blurring vision, Olly recognised one of them. "Krish?" he coughed.

"Fam, that you?" Krish grabbed him by the shoulders. "Shit, man, I thought they'd wasted you!" He pulled Olly close, nearly cracking his ribs in a hug.

Olly pushed him away. "Good to see you too." He looked up as Danny made his way back to them. "What's going on up there?"

"Riot drones. Three of them – one up ahead is armed. Rubber bullets, but that doesn't mean shit close as it is. Between us and the APVs. Other two are spotters. They'll pop smoke and keep us corralled while the response team closes in." He looked at Olly. "You do anything about that, DedSec?"

"Depends on whether this system is running on cTOS," Olly said. He held up the Optik, squinting at the screen through the stinging smoke. He found what he was looking for soon enough. He tapped the screen and there was an echoing clang as every gate in range automatically locked. "Right, that should hold them for a bit."

"What about the drone?" Ro asked.

Olly shook his head. "Got to be in sight of it. Hard to do anything when it's shooting at you, though." He looked at Krish. "Any ideas?"

Krish gestured. "Gimme." Olly handed him the Optik, and Krish tapped at the screen. Olly blinked as his display was suddenly crowded by multiple visual feeds. "That's the security feeds for everything in here." He grinned at Danny. "For a military contractor, Albion don't know shit about security."

"Good thing for us," Olly said. He could see armed men moving through the chain link corridors on all sides. The response team had split up to cover more ground and cut them off. "We're about to be surrounded. They can open the gates manually. I can lock them again, but it's not going to stop them for long."

"Then we'll have to fight." Danny handed his sister a pistol.

"Now we're talking," she said, as she checked the weapon's magazine.

Olly shook his head. "Maybe not. Gimme your Optik."

Danny looked at him. "What? Why?"

"I can take out the other two drones while Krish keeps the

response team pinned down. That leaves the last drone for you two. Think you can handle that?"

Danny looked at his sister. "He for real?"

"Must be if you locked him up," she said. "Give it to him. I don't give us good odds otherwise." She started pushing her way towards the front. Danny handed over his Optik and followed. Olly took it and looked at Krish.

"Right. You know what to do?"

Krish nodded. "Think this will work?"

"We'll see. Just keep them off our back."

"Yeah, man." With a tap, Krish activated the sprinkler systems, filling the warehouse with sheets of water. It mixed with the smoke, making a greasy haze on the air. An instant later, the alarms cut out with a strangled squawk.

Olly waited for the drones to come back for a second pass. When one got close enough, he took aim with his Optik and snagged it. A moment later, it was banking left and heading back the way it had come, popping smoke across the warehouse. He took control of the second a few moments later. Through its display, he spied Danny and Ro moving towards the third. It waited for them, hovering in the open space leading to the parked APVs like some malign wasp.

Danny drew its attention, firing short bursts that splashed across its frontal armour like droplets of water. The drone followed his movement, returning fire. Rubber bullets punched into the floor and wall around him. Ro stepped out of the corridor and fired her pistol with more enthusiasm than skill. The drone whipped around, responding to the threat, and Danny took it down, blowing out its motor and sending it hurtling to the floor.

Olly sent the remaining two riot drones back towards the Albion operatives struggling with the gates. Searching the on-board directories, he realised they were armed with tear gas canisters as well as smoke. Grinning, he gave them new orders. He looked at Krish. "Time to leave, bruv."

"*Past* time," Krish said. "I've locked them out, but they're already trying to reset the whole system. More drones coming online as well."

Between them, they got the rest of the prisoners moving. Danny was already behind the wheel of one of the APVs, and its engine roared to life. Ro had his rifle and was gesturing frantically for everyone to get aboard. Krish headed for the back, and Olly climbed into the front. "What about the doors?" he asked.

"What about them?" Danny asked.

"They're still shut!"

Danny laughed. "That's their fucking problem. Rosemary – get your arse in here!"

"Don't call me that," she snarled, squeezing in beside Olly. "Everyone is in – let's go if we're going to go!"

On his display, Olly saw banks of tear gas filling the makeshift corridors, and Albion operatives coughing and cursing as they shot the hinges off the gates and broke through. Then he was flung back into his seat as Danny threw the APV into motion. As they hurtled towards the doors, Olly tapped at his screen. At his direction, the remaining APVs grumbled to life. They rolled from their berths and sped towards the loading bay doors, alongside the one they'd commandeered but they got there first. Metal buckled and tore as the armoured vehicles punched through, and out.

Danny followed them a moment later. Olly heard a sound like rain and realised someone was shooting at them. "Hang on," Danny growled, dragging the APV around and crashing it through a chain link fence and onto a side street. "Where to?" he asked, looking at Olly and Ro.

"You don't know?" Ro asked, staring at him.

"Hey, I got us out – now pick a direction…"

28: AFTERSHOCK

Sarah Lincoln sat in her empty dining room in her Whitechapel home, watching a replay of footage from the mass of raids that had occurred yesterday evening and late into the night. Police officers and Albion operatives – it was hard to tell one from the other in the jerky footage – smashed in doors, dragged out "dangerous subversives", hauled them towards waiting vans or just clubbed them down in the road in front of the cameras. She finished her coffee and refilled the cup, again.

"Don't you think you've had enough?" Hannah asked, from the doorway.

"No," Sarah said, softly. Then, "The others?"

"Winston was the last to leave. The streets are in utter chaos."

"I expect so." Sarah took another swallow of wine. She finished it, considered having another and then put the glass aside. She stood. "Any word from Jenks?"

"Not yet."

Sarah had sent Jenks out to find out, well, anything she could. Not that she expected there to be anything. No one seemed to know what the hell was going to happen next, though it was plain that Albion had mobilised in force to flood the streets ahead of the TOAN conference. Mass arrests were being reported. Other private security firms were also vying loudly for the government's attentions, and Nigel Cass himself was reportedly claiming a great victory for the forces of law and order. He was going to get what he wanted, and there was very little she could do about it right now. Winston and the others were scared into uselessness, and she didn't blame them.

She was scared too, as scared as she'd ever been in her life. Something monstrous had been let loose and she knew already that getting it back in the bottle would be a titanic struggle.

She wandered out of the dining room, already planning her next move. Or trying to, rather. Her home was a relatively modest terraced house in Varden Street. It had been expensively decorated, by a professional interior designer. She went to the kitchen and looked through the sliding doors at the superbly appointed garden space at the rear of the house. The air was hazy with smoke. The breeze was carrying it east, from the river.

Of late, she had the feeling that there was a hell of a lot going on that she couldn't perceive. Currents of power were shifting. But to where? And to whom?

"What now?" Hannah asked. She'd followed Sarah, quiet as a mouse.

Her boss studied her. Finally, she cleared her throat and said,

"Did they know it was going to happen? Did they… get out?"

"I don't know what you're talking about."

"We both know that's not true."

Hannah turned. "How did you convince Faulkner to let me go?"

Sarah paused. "I… gave him something he wanted."

"What?"

Sarah studied her assistant. "Why does it matter?"

Hannah met her gaze without flinching. "I think I have a right to know."

Sarah turned away. "It doesn't matter now. That particular bullet has been fired."

Hannah grabbed her arm. Sarah stopped. Looked down. Then looked up at Hannah.

The young woman didn't let go. "Sometimes I wonder why I stay," she said, softly. "People ask me all the time how I can work for someone like you."

Sarah was silent for a moment. "And what do you tell them?" she asked, finally. She fixed Hannah with a cold eye. "What is your answer to that question, Hannah?" She let some of the anger she was feeling creep into her voice. She was angry that Hannah could be so ungrateful. Angry that she was hiding something. But mostly she was angry that everything seemed to be spinning out of control, and there was nothing she could do about it.

Hannah let her go. "I think… I think you mean well. But I think somewhere along the way you forgot why you got into politics. It's become an end unto itself."

Sarah stared at her. Then, she laughed, low and long. She shook her head and looked away. Hannah's words stung.

Maybe there was some truth there. Maybe Hannah was just naïve. Both could be true.

"Things are going to get worse now," Hannah continued. "They've been getting pretty bad for a long time, but now…"

"Now the fuse has been lit," Sarah said. She took a deep breath. "There's no going back from this. We can only go forward." She looked back towards the window, trying to decide what sort of politician she was going to be.

A scattering of ash, carried by the breeze, fell over the garden. Decision made, she turned back. "You want to know what I told Faulkner?"

Hannah said nothing. Sarah told her. Then, she turned and left, giving her aide some privacy.

Olly looked out the window of the grimy corner café, watching the new Albion checkpoint being constructed across the street. "This is so bad," he said. The café was empty, had been closed down for months. According to Ro, it was a Kelley business, now shuttered and just waiting for the day they burned it down in order to collect the insurance money.

The interior smelled like stale coffee grounds and rotten bananas, but it was tolerable. They'd come in the back, looking for a place to wait out the confusion. Unfortunately, things didn't seem to be getting any better.

Albion was all over the city now. They were looking for something, but Danny couldn't tell them what. The fugitives had abandoned the APV as soon as possible. Krish and the others had scattered, as per DedSec protocol. Olly had told them he was planning to do the same. And he would, as soon as he found Liz's killer.

"I can't believe we're doing this," Danny said. "We should be getting out of the city." He sat across from Olly in the same booth, watching his former comrades in arms set up their checkpoint. His ACR assault rifle was on his lap, concealed under a newspaper, and he was stripping it down and rebuilding it without looking at it. It seemed to soothe him, though it made Olly nervous.

"Feel free," Ro said. She sat at the counter, her elbows resting on the countertop. She gestured to Olly. "Me and him got unfinished business."

Olly nodded. "Me and your sis had a good talk while we were banged up. We're both looking for the same person. And from what she says, maybe you are too."

Danny grunted. "And who might that be?"

"The bloke going around shooting people with an Albion murder-drone." Olly watched Danny's expression change from annoyance to confusion to interest. He looked at his sister.

"Holden," he said, flatly.

She nodded. "Now we know why your boss killed him."

"Shit." Danny sat back, rubbing his mouth. "Faulkner knows. That's why he had me looking into the death of your pal, Colin."

Ro nodded. "Colin was the common thread. He's the one who delivered everything. If anyone knew where this guy was, it was Colin."

"Every vehicle these days has GPS," Olly said, looking back and forth between them. "If it hasn't been tampered with, it'll have a record of every stop he made."

"Including wherever he dropped off the drone. Shit." Danny

rubbed his chin. "So where's the van?" He looked at Ro.

She shook her head. "The night Colin died, they took the van somewhere out of the way, stripped it and set the rest on fire. There's no way we can get that information now."

Olly ran his hands over his head, trying to think. There had to be a way. He wished he could call for help. But he knew better than to even try to contact Bagley or anyone else. When a member of DedSec got arrested, they were cut off.

"We know what he was delivering, at least." He looked meaningfully towards the horizon, where dark smoke still rose in towering columns.

"He wouldn't have done it knowingly," Ro said. "Colin was a twat but he wasn't a murderer." She knotted her hands together. "Maybe he found out. Maybe that's why they killed him."

"I don't think so," Danny said. He looked out the window. "I've seen shit like this before. Not here, but overseas. Somebody is cleaning up all the loose ends."

"That includes us now," Olly said. Everyone fell silent, thinking about this.

Danny gestured. "Yeah. Albion just needed an excuse – an enemy. The best enemies are nebulous, innit?"

"Nebulous?" Ro asked.

"Word-a-day app on my Optik," Danny said. "Anyway, DedSec can be anything – nobody knows shit about you, right? So if that tosspot Nigel bloody Cass says you lot are terrorists, who's to say different?"

Olly nodded. "Go on."

"An enemy is only as good as their actions – nobody cares about propaganda bombs, or street murals. But hacking drones to turn them into sniper devices…" Danny trailed off.

"And then you hire somebody to eliminate the witnesses, so nobody knows the truth."

"Albion was behind all this?" Ro said, disbelief in her voice. She looked at Danny, but he could only shrug and look away.

"I don't know," he said. "I thought…" He trailed off and shook his head. "I was wrong though. What I've seen? Yeah, I could believe it."

"Doesn't matter," Olly said. "We need to – wait." A call-alert had popped up on his display. It was a number he didn't recognise. He looked at the others, and then, warily, answered. "Hello?"

"Olly?" A young woman's voice, audibly nervous.

Olly frowned. "Hannah?"

"You're still alive. Thank goodness. Where are you?"

"I'd rather not say, love."

"Are you still… in the city?"

Olly paused. Then, "Yes. Why?"

"I know who killed Liz, and. I know where they are."

He frowned. "What do you mean?"

"I'm sending it through now."

Data flooded his display. A name, a face – and an address. His hands knotted into fists. "Coyle," he murmured. "Hannah… thanks."

"Don't thank me yet. Albion know as well. You might not have time." Hannah paused. "Good luck, Olly." She ended the call.

Olly leaned back. "Bloo-dy hell," he breathed.

"Who was that?" Danny asked, leaning forward.

Olly shook his head. "Doesn't matter. I know where he is."

"The assassin?" Danny asked.

"Yeah."

"So what's the problem? Let's go get him." Ro cracked her knuckles.

"Albion knows too."

Danny paused. "That explains some things. I bet that's what Faulkner was busy with today. Trying to mount an op to hit this guy. Ten to one, he's heading there right now."

"Then we need to get there first," Olly said. "We catch this guy, maybe we can get him to talk. We could take down everyone involved in this, clear DedSec – hell, clear ourselves. And we stop him from killing any more people."

"I'm in," Danny said. He looked at his sister.

She sneered. "I was in like ten minutes ago. Keep up."

Danny looked at Olly. "We're in."

"Well that's a relief," Olly said, laughing. He paused. "Only missing one thing."

Ro looked at him. "What?"

"It's just… in DedSec, we use these masks. Usually when it's something big, you know?" He sat back. "We make our own. Rite of passage, innit?"

Danny reached into the gear he'd scavenged from the APV and tossed something to Olly. Olly caught it and looked at what he held. "A gas mask?"

"Practical *and* stylish." Danny pulled out two more and tossed one to Ro. "May as well be prepared, right?" He began pulling things out of the bags – body armour, grenades, extra magazines for the ACR rifle and the Albion-issue P9 pistols.

Olly stared. "That's a lot of iron."

"Probably going to need it," Ro said. She slid her P9 into

the back of her waistband. "What's the plan?" She and Danny looked at Olly.

"Why are you asking me?" he protested.

"Because I'm a grunt and she only knows how to hit things." Danny checked the ACR. "You're the one in DedSec. By default, that makes you in charge."

Olly frowned. "Fine." He looked at the mask in his hand. "Okay. I'm in charge."

"Great. So what's the plan?"

Olly pulled on the mask.

"We improvise."

29: THE PINNACLE

"The Pinnacle?" Ro said. "He's in the fucking *Pinnacle*?" She sat in the back of a stolen transit van with Danny and Olly. Olly had hacked the van and they'd used it to navigate the increasingly blocked-off streets. It had still taken them longer than any of them liked, and they'd lost most of the day avoiding checkpoints.

"Makes sense," Danny said. He checked his rifle over again, moving his hands over the weapon without looking at it. "One of the tallest buildings in London. And it's at the heart of everything. If I were a sniper, that's where I'd set up."

"And it's mostly empty, since the crash," Olly said, tapping at the screen of his Optik. "Of the forty-one floors, over half are currently unoccupied. This guy Coyle is renting one of the uppermost storeys. Claims it's a business, lot of equipment moving up, but nothing beyond that."

"He's probably been here a few weeks," Danny said. "Checking the lay of the land, making sure he had access to the right equipment. These guys – operators – they're like fucking ghosts. Nobody knows they're there until they do the job."

"Met many of them then?" Ro asked. She meant it to come out curious, but it sounded acidic. Danny frowned.

"Not for sure. But… you hear things."

Ro leaned back, arms crossed. Impatience brewed in her gut. She wanted to do something, to hit something, but so far they'd just sat in the back of a van parked a few hundred metres from the Pinnacle's entrance on St Mary Axe. Around them, from what Ro could tell, the city was tearing itself apart.

Spontaneous protests were springing up everywhere, mostly in the form of flash mobs and street parties. Albion and the Met were doing their best to disperse these gatherings, but for every one they stamped on, two more sprouted elsewhere. Olly had implied that DedSec was behind some of these, but Ro suspected he was just putting on a brave front. He didn't know for sure any more than she did.

Danny and Olly kept talking, chewing over the problem. Ro closed her eyes, tuning them out. She wondered what she would do next, if they made through the next few hours in one piece. She couldn't go back to the Kelleys, even if she'd been inclined to do so. Faulkner had never gotten around to debriefing her, but that didn't mean much where Mary Kelley was concerned. She and Billy would assume Ro had talked, and they'd top her if they got the chance. Maybe Danny was right and they should leave.

But not forever. Just long enough. Then she'd come back and settle up. She owed Billy Bricks a slap, and Mary Kelley as well. And Faulkner, come to that. She glanced at Olly and wondered if DedSec were looking for new members. She wasn't any good with computers, but she could learn. And she could fight. Something told her they were going to need fighters soon.

Danny snapped his fingers in front of her face, startling her. "Oi, you listening?"

"Yeah," she said, swatting his hand aside. "You two are talking bollocks, when we should be going in there. Building is empty right now, yeah?"

"Yeah," Olly said. "Most everything inside closed early today. Might be some people in the offices, security, that sort of thing though…"

Ro shrugged. "Nothing we can't handle. We know where we're going. Let's go."

Danny shook his head. "And do what?"

"Punch the fucker in the bonce, what else?" Ro said.

"And then what?" he pressed. She made to retort, but realised he had a point. She settled back with an impatient grunt.

"We grab him," she said, after a moment.

Olly stiffened. "Not him. The drone." He looked at them. "We need the drone. Think. It's like Colin's van, it's got a GPS. That thing will have a record of everywhere it's been, everything it's done. If we take the drone, we've got him."

"*And* we keep him from using it again," Ro said, nodding. She gestured to the Optik in Olly's hand. "So do it."

He frowned. "I need to be close to do it. In sight of the damn thing. And even then, it's not certain. Especially if its shooting at me." He looked at Danny. "If we could get to the floor below him, I might be able to do it. But we'd need to distract him. If he sees what I'm up to, he'll just send the damn thing after us."

"I can do that," Ro said.

"Do what?" Danny said, staring at her. "You're not going in there."

"Fuck that noise. You want him distracted? I'll distract him. Come to that, I'll take him down." She leaned forward, eager now. "He's using a drone to do his dirty work. How tough can he be?"

Danny looked at Olly. Olly shrugged. "I mean... you got a better plan?"

Danny sagged. "No. And we've got no time to come up with one. Faulkner is probably already on the way." He looked at Olly. "If it comes to it, I'll keep them off of you as long as possible. But if they show up before we get out, I can't promise we'll walk out of there. If Faulkner knows what he's dealing with, he'll come in shooting."

"That might make it easier for us," Ro said. She saw the look on Danny's face and smiled. "Cheer up, bruv. Maybe you'll get to tell Faulkner what you really think of him."

Danny snorted and looked at Olly. "Think you can get us in the building?"

Olly nodded. "We need to go now though."

"Then let's do it," Ro said, standing and throwing open the back of the van. She looked around. The narrow street was mostly empty, except for a few parked cars, but in the distance she could hear sirens and the faint crackle of loudspeakers. Riot drones swept by overhead, racing towards some unseen confrontation.

Danny checked his radio as they crossed the street towards the diamond shaped archway that hung over the front entrance. Glazed glass made a shadowy mass of the interior, and the revolving doors were shut. "Nothing on the frequency yet. Too much going on. But if they're not already on the way, they will be soon."

"We'll be quick." Olly had his Optik out as they reached the doors. He brushed his fingers across the screen, doing what Ro couldn't tell. Some hacker bullshit that might as well be magic as far as she was concerned. "Doors are on a timer. The mechanisms automatically lock when they shut it down for the day. But... ah. Give it a push."

Ro pushed one and was rewarded by a slow revolution. She glanced at the others. "Right. Top floor, then?"

"I'm sending the schematics to your display," Olly said. "Fire routes and service stairs are highlighted – just in case."

Ro blinked as the schematics for the building suddenly overlaid her vision. She hadn't often used that function of her Optik, and it was somewhat disorientating. She shook her head and pushed through the revolving doors.

It was quiet inside. Polished chrome columns rose to either side of the entrance. Long reception counters ran along the walls to either side of the security gates that allowed entry into the building proper. Olly motioned for them to wait and went behind the counters. After a few moments of hurried work, he said, "Right. The security system has been deactivated and the CCTV is looped."

"That was quick," Ro said, impressed despite herself.

Olly shrugged. "Not exactly MI5, is it? The system hasn't been updated since they converted it to cTOS. A baby could crack it."

"Take your word for it. What now?"

Olly extended his hand. "After you."

"Wait a sec," Danny said. He pulled out a grenade and

a length of wire. He used a roll of duct tape to attach the grenade to the side of the counter, and stretched the wire from the grenade's pin to the other side of the security gate. "Flashbang," he said, as he worked. "Someone tries rushing through, it'll buy us some time."

"How many of those do you have?" Ro asked.

"A couple. Not enough." Danny pulled out another. "I'll set some more toys as we go up, though." He smiled and she thought that he seemed happy for the first time since he'd come home.

Ro felt a sudden twinge of regret. She looked at Danny. "Thanks, by the way."

"For what?"

"Coming to get me."

He shook his head. "Didn't do it for you. You imagine what Mum would do to me if I'd left you there?" He grinned as he said it, and when she punched his shoulder, she pulled the blow. Only just, though.

"Shithead."

"I love you too," he said.

"You two done?" Olly asked. "Because there's a killer upstairs, waiting for us."

"Luckily he don't know that," Ro said. She shifted the P9 in her waistband so that it was out of sight. Two lifts sat opposite the entrance, to either side of a long corridor. "I'll take the lift," she said, heading that way. "You two take the stairs."

"He'll see you," Danny objected.

She hit the button and turned. "We want him to, don't we?" As the doors opened, she stepped back into the lift and waved goodbye to her brother and Olly.

"Better hurry, lads. We're on the clock."

Red sky at night. Coyle gazed out over the London skyline, looking west. He could not help but wonder at the purpose of it all. And there was a purpose, however oblique it seemed from the outside. He'd begun to pack earlier and clean the empty offices, obliterating all physical traces of his presence. Once he was finished, he would begin moving his gear downstairs, to where his car waited. The only thing he couldn't easily move was the drone. He hated to abandon it. It was just as well that he had other plans for it.

He smiled, pleased that his gambit had succeeded, if only at the eleventh hour. He was fairly certain he had isolated Zero Day's signal, and that meant he could find them. Each call they made to him had brought him one step closer, and now he was certain he needed only one final contact to acquire a target and bring this affair to a satisfactory conclusion. Or at least, to make the attempt. Coyle was no fool, to proclaim victory before the final blow was struck.

He finished the last of his supplies, and disposed of the rubbish. The building was empty, having been evacuated earlier, during the excitement. Albion and others patrolled the streets, but he would have no difficulty getting past them.

He checked the drone, in preparation for what would likely be its final flight. As he was reattaching the ammunition hopper, he heard an alert chime. The sensor network he'd installed after moving in had detected something. He brought up the CCTV feeds on his display, but saw nothing. Acting on a sudden suspicion, he switched to his own cameras and saw that someone was in one of the lifts, ascending to his floor – a young woman, dressed for the street, rather out of place in this upscale environment.

As he retrieved a pistol from his bags, he considered his options. He could kill her in a moment, obviously. But he found he was curious. So instead, he waited. When the lift chimed and the doors slid open, he smiled politely. "May I help you?"

"You Coyle?" she asked, in brusque tones. East End, he guessed. A faint lilt to her voice, hinting at Caribbean antecedents.

"That rather depends, my dear. Who are you?"

"Someone looking to do some business with you," she said. "We've seen what you can do with that toy of yours, and we want you to do it for us."

"And who is us?"

"Clan Kelley, yeah?"

Coyle frowned. "Really? How did you know where to find me?"

"Tracked the GPS on Colin's van, didn't we?" She tapped the side of her head and circled the room like she owned it. "Wasn't hard."

His frown deepened. On the face of it, perfectly reasonable. "So why did you wait so long to pay me a visit?"

"Wanted to see what you were up to." She spotted the drone and stopped. She gestured. "That it? That the thing that shot our Colin?"

"Yes. I hope he wasn't a friend of yours."

"Just a driver," she said, but he could hear the lie in her voice. "Ten a penny, them. Out of curiosity, who hired you to do it?"

"I'm sure you understand that I cannot divulge that information."

She shrugged. "Fair enough."

"How do you know my name?"

"We know a lot?"

"By 'we' you mean Clan Kelley?"

"Who else would I mean?"

He studied her for a moment. "You're a bad liar." He raised his gun.

"Woah woah, wait, wait…" She raised her hands.

He paused. Alerts flooded his display. Every motion sensor he'd planted was going off at once. He checked his private feed and saw a flicker of light from downstairs. He knew a flashbang when he saw one. Figures in black were pouring into the foyer, moving up the stairs, taking the lifts. He counted twenty at a glance. "Albion," he murmured. "How unexpected."

She smiled. "Someone must have grassed you up."

"I wonder who," he said.

"Not me," she said quickly. "I don't want to get caught any more than you do."

"Mmm. Then you won't object to me activating my security team."

"Team?"

Coyle extracted his Optik from his coat pocket and tapped it. There was a sudden flurry of clicking as a dozen of his spiderbots scuttled into view. Each was armed with a homemade firearm, no two alike. They scurried past her, moving towards the elevator shaft.

"The fuck?" she said, watching them.

"Idle hands are the Devil's playground," Coyle said. "They won't keep Albion back forever, but they will buy enough time for escape."

"Well, let's shift it then," she said.

Coyle raised his weapon. "I didn't say 'we', now did I?"

"Is that any way to treat a future business partner?"

He laughed. "The pretence was amusing at first, but I'm tired of this game. Who are you really? And why are you – what?" He turned as the drone suddenly twitched in its berth. He activated his display. Data spilled across his vision. Warnings flashed. Someone was trying to crack the firewall. They were trying to hack the drone. "Ah, so that's it…" he began, pleased to have figured it out.

He heard the scuff of a shoe on carpet, and realised his error even as he turned back. A distraction. Of course. Coyle caught the punch on his forearm and swung his weapon around. She backpedalled, throwing herself behind a stack of boxes as Coyle fired. She scrambled towards the kitchenette as Coyle tracked her. She slid behind an island countertop and out of sight. Coyle didn't pursue her.

"I don't want to kill you," he called out. "I will, if you insist, but I'm pressed for time. As are you. I doubt you have any wish to be caught by Albion."

Keeping one eye on the kitchenette, he retrieved his Optik and activated the drone. It took him only a few moments to locate the intruding signal. One floor down, directly below. He smiled and gave the drone its orders. As it lifted off and sped towards the open window, he turned back to the kitchenette. "You made a good effort, but not good enough."

Silence.

Coyle frowned and started towards the last place he'd seen her, his pistol extended. "Tell me just one thing – did Zero Day send you?"

"What the fuck is a Zero Day?" she snarled, lunging forward, swinging the wooden cutlery drawer at him. He fired even as she brought the drawer down on the gun in his hand, tearing it from his grip. She came at him fast, fists low. He caught a punch in the side and returned it with interest. They moved in a tight circle, trading blows. She was skilled – trained. And she had the advantage of youth. He swatted her fists aside and scanned the floor for the gun. When he spied it, he made a dive.

She came after him, but not quick enough. He scooped the pistol up and rolled over, aiming at her face. She froze, eyes wide.

Coyle smiled. "Goodbye, whoever you are–"

There was a ding from the lifts. They both turned, startled.

The lifts opened and canister grenades rolled out, spewing smoke. Coyle and his attacker dove for cover, even as the first Albion operatives stormed the floor.

30: FREE FIRE

When the first of his boobytraps went off, Danny didn't flinch. He glanced at the lifts, and then back at Olly. "How's it coming?" They sat on an empty floor, surrounded by glazed windows, looking out over the city. Dozens of free-standing cubicle partition walls were stacked in piles around them. Directly above them, Ro was facing off against Coyle on her own. Danny tried not to think about it.

"I need more time." Olly was sweating, fingers flickering over the screen of the Optik, ribbons of code unspooling across the screen.

"We might not have it. We've got company."

"Albion?"

"Who else?" Danny rose and went to the lifts. The thought of facing Faulkner wasn't a pleasant one. Especially with nowhere to go. "Any way you can lock these down?"

"Not right now," Olly said, not looking up from his screen.

Danny grunted. "Guess it's up to me, then." Setting his ACR aside, he started moving the partition walls around, arranging them into improvised entry control points.

As he worked, he became aware of a faint clicking sound emanating from the lift shaft. He considered asking Olly about it, but didn't want to distract him. Instead, he pried open the lift doors with his survival knife. As he did so, he could hear the whine of the shaft motor as the car rose from the lower floors. Someone was coming up.

A flash of movement above him caught his attention. He looked up – and nearly lost his head. The shot was deafening in the confines of the shaft and he jerked back, ears ringing. A small scuttling shape leapt down from within the shaft and clattered towards him, weapon firing. "Olly – get down!" Danny cried, as he threw himself backwards over one of his improvised berms.

He scrambled towards his weapon, snatching it up even as the spiderbot crested the berm. The pistol attached to its chassis barked, shattering a window behind him. Danny took aim and returned fire. The machine came apart in a spray of sparks and metal shards. He didn't have time to celebrate however – another one leapt out of the shaft, weapon firing. Danny ducked down, and glanced back to check on Olly, who was lying flat nearby. "You okay?" Danny called out.

"Yeah, but I think we got trouble."

"Tell me something I don't know." Danny fired, but the spiderbot was moving too fast, scuttling for cover. He could hear gunfire from the floors below, and wondered how many of the sodding things there were.

"Not those. I think Coyle figured out what we were up to. He just sent the drone out."

Danny felt a brief flare of panic. If Coyle knew where they were, what had happened to Ro? "Where?"

Olly looked at him. *"Here."*

Danny made to speak, when he saw a black shape sweep past the windows. He swung his weapon up and fired, stitching the windows. Olly covered his head as Danny fired. The drone kept moving, banking. There was a crack of thunder and a window exploded, filling the air with glass. Danny staggered back, still firing. Another crack, another window exploded. He concentrated on the drone, trying to predict where it would go, firing as he moved.

"We've got to find some cover," he shouted, as the drone veered away. He heard the clicking of the spiderbot behind him and spun, driving the stock of his ACR down on top of it with a crunch. The machine tried to move away and he fired down at it, destroying it. He turned, looking for Olly. He spotted him crouching behind a berm. "Olly? Up. Let's move!"

Olly climbed to his feet, eyes on the windows. "If I can just get it in range…"

"It'll blow a hole in you the size of a football. Come on."

"Where to?"

"Upstairs," Danny said. "If he's figured things out, Ro is in trouble." He hit the door to the stairs, slamming it open. Olly hurried after him, and Danny kicked it shut. There was a boom even as it closed and the door was all but torn off its hinges, the metal dented inwards by the shot. "Go!" Danny said. Olly nodded and started up, taking the steps two at a time. Danny hesitated. Shouts from below warned him that someone was coming up. He braced himself against the rail and pulled out his last booby trap – a stun grenade.

Danny popped the pin and dropped the grenade straight

down. "Grenade out!" He turned away as the charge went off – light and noise filled the stairwell. Danny hurried after Olly, ears ringing.

Olly was waiting on him at the next landing. "I heard shooting," he said.

Danny shouldered the door open without replying, his thoughts only for Ro. He flinched back as bullets marched up the wall beside the door, filling the air with plastic dust. He fired back blind, and jerked his head towards one of the cubicles that filled the floor. "Go – I'll cover you." Without waiting for Olly to reply, he stepped out of the stairwell, still firing. A quick glance told him everything he needed to know – six men, in fatigues and armour opposite him, another man – Coyle – caught in between. And near him, Ro. Hunkered down, trying to avoid getting caught in the crossfire.

When the magazine ran dry, he ejected it and slapped in a fresh one without lowering the weapon or slowing down. He only released the trigger when he joined Olly behind a cubicle partition. "Ro's still in one piece."

"More than I can say for us," Olly hissed. "Look!"

Danny looked up and saw a familiar black shape hovering before the windows. "Shit on it," he growled, and raised the assault rifle.

"Wait," Olly said. He had his Optik out, aimed at the drone. Danny looked back and forth between them.

"You get it?" he asked.

"Not yet." Olly hunched forward, engaged in a code-war with the drone. If he slacked up, or mistyped even one number, the drone would follow through with its current programming and blow both him and Danny into a fine red mist. "I need time," he hissed.

Danny looked at him, and then at the drone. He took a breath and shouted, "Cease! Fire!"

The gunfire stuttered to a drawn-out halt. Silence fell. Torn papers and dust sifted through the air. Danny peered around the edge of the partition. "That you, Sarge?"

No reply. Danny cleared his throat. "I just want to talk."

"Is that you, Danny?" Faulkner called. "You disappoint me, lad. Thought you had more sense. There's a good lad, I said—"

"Oh, piss off, Sarge," Danny replied.

Olly watched Faulkner's face through the split-screen CCTV feed as he worked. The Albion operative looked angry – more, he looked worried. "That's no way to talk to your superior officer, Danny."

"You're not my superior any more, Sarge. I'm out."

"You with them DedSec lot now, Danny? Is that the path you want to follow?"

"Better them than you, Sarge."

Faulkner looked at his men and gestured. Olly showed the feed to Danny, who frowned and nodded. "You're not planning to try and flank me out are you, Sarge? Because I'll hear that donkey Mueller coming a click away."

Faulkner hesitated. Looked up and saw the cameras. Danny laughed at his expression. Faulkner raised his weapon. Olly switched to a secondary view as the shot took out the camera. "I can still see you, Sarge," Danny taunted.

"As can I," Coyle called out.

"That you, Coyle?" Faulkner said. "It's been some time. Croatia, wasn't it?"

"Zadar. I wondered if you remembered."

"Hard to forget. Whatever you're being paid, Albion will double it."

"In return for what?"

"Kill these DedSec pricks with that fancy toy out there."

"I have been trying. They're quite obstreperous."

"Try harder," Faulkner said. "Danny – I'm giving you until Coyle here figures out where his interests lie. First one to choose the winning side gets amnesty. The other gets a shallow grave."

"What about my sister, Sarge? What about Olly here?"

"Sacrifices must be made, Danny. DedSec are terrorists. Can't let that sort run free." Faulkner paused. "And your sister is a criminal. But I'll show some kindness… you lot surrender, you might walk out of here alive."

Danny looked at Olly, who shook his head. "What about the drone?" Danny murmured. Olly shook his head.

"Need more time," he grunted. The drone had been designed to resist hacking attempts. Worse, it could enact proactive defence protocols – such as targeting the hacker. Which it was now trying to do. But if he could just – "Ha!"

The drone waggled its fans and veered off, repositioning itself. Danny breathed a sigh of relief. "You have control?"

"No, but I managed to change its attack parameters." Olly shifted his display, looking through the drone's sensors. It was moving away from the building, looking for targets that didn't exist. It didn't solve the problem, but it had bought them some time. "And I locked our pal Coyle out. At least for the moment."

Danny nodded. "Coyle?" he called out.

"Where is my drone going?" Coyle replied.

"Away," Danny said. "That means the odds are tipping."

"Not in your favour, Danny," Faulkner interjected. "Unless you've forgotten how to count. Five of us, one of you."

"Three, fuckstick," Ro called out, from somewhere across the room.

"Four, technically," Coyle added. "I have no interest in your kind offer, Faulkner. I only want to get out of here. London has lost its lustre for me."

"Sounds like the odds are about even, Sarge," Danny said. He gestured and Olly nodded, and began to crawl towards the next set of partitions. He wished he had a weapon, even a stun gun – something. He was the only unarmed person in the room.

Except he wasn't unarmed. He slid into a cubicle and lifted his Optik. Though the sniper-drone was proving obstinate, there were other, easier targets to be had. If he could nab one or two of them, it might make the difference. Through his display he could see the Albion goons shifting position, spreading out. Faulkner was remaining where he was, still talking. They were all trying to buy time. But what was he waiting for – ah.

Olly picked up a piece of paper, crumpled it, and tossed it at Danny. Danny looked at him. Olly pointed to the partition between them and the lifts, and mimed knocking it over. Danny frowned, but nodded. He scooted behind another and gave it a kick.

The partitions toppled like dominos. The way was clear moments later, and Olly took aim. The lifts gave a squealing chime as Olly locked down the panels. Danny cleared his throat. "No one is coming up the lifts, Sarge. And I'm covering the stairs."

"It seems we're at an impasse," Faulkner said. "We'll get reinforcements up here eventually. One way or another. How many spare magazines you got, lad? One maybe two? Three at most, I expect."

"Got my rifle, Sarge."

"So do we, Danny. No matter how you slice it, lad, you're outgunned. All we have to do is keep you penned up and wait." Faulkner raised his voice. "That goes for you too, Coyle. There's no way out. Be sensible."

"Tell me, Faulkner – did *you* murder Holden?" Coyle called.

Faulkner didn't reply. Coyle laughed. "I thought so. Must have come as quite a shock, him selling Project LIBRA out from under you. No wonder you're here, looking to add my head to the pile. Cass won't be satisfied with anything less, from what I remember of him."

Danny looked at Olly and mouthed a question. Olly shrugged. It didn't surprise him that Coyle and Faulkner knew each other in some way. Coyle had to have had some familiarity with Albion to know about the drone in the first place – he might even be working for them. That would explain why Faulkner was here – to make sure Coyle didn't talk.

Olly cycled through the camera feeds, watching the Albion operatives spread and draw closer. One was creeping towards Ro. Olly leaned back. "Ro – look left!"

On his display, he saw Ro pivot, the pistol in her hand rising. He heard it bark, saw the flash on the feed. The Albion goon retreated hastily. Danny nodded to him in thanks. "I'd stop moving around, Sarge. It's only going to get somebody killed."

"Cost of doing business, Danny. We all know what we're getting into when we sign the contract." Faulkner was signalling again. Olly didn't know what the gestures meant, but he could guess. An alert chimed on his display – he'd caught a signal. A passing riot drone. He motioned frantically to Danny as he called the drone and gave its programming a tweak.

It crashed through the window a moment later, popping smoke and blaring underground hip-hop from its loudspeakers. Danny rose and fired smoothly. Someone cried out, and Danny started advancing, loosing quick bursts as he went. Olly scrambled after him. The drone circled the floor, the air from its fans knocking over partitions and sending Faulkner's men scuttling for cover as smoke filled the space. Danny pivoted and one fell, clutching at his leg. Olly realised Danny was shooting to wound.

Coyle, however, wasn't. Through his display, Olly saw him rise and fire. An Albion operative spun, the bullet catching him in the neck. Coyle vanished, already moving. "Fall back, fall back," Faulkner roared. He fired, and the riot drone bucked, bleeding sparks. Albion regrouped, and Danny was forced to duck down. Olly slid to a halt beside him. Smoke was everywhere, and Olly blinked back tears.

Someone crashed towards them – Ro. She dropped into a crouch nearby. "What now?" she shouted, trying to be heard over the loudspeakers. The music caught off with a strangled squawk as someone put a bullet into the drone's CPU.

"Good effort, lad," Faulkner growled, from close by. "But

we're between you and the lifts, and if you try for the doors, we'll put you down." A radio crackled, and Danny looked to his own. A short burst of voices. Reinforcements, Olly knew. There'd be more drones, more guns. More than they could handle. Danny shook his head.

Olly was about to speak, when Coyle beat him to it. "I'm out of patience, Faulkner. I think it's time you left. Danny, or whatever your name is – unlock the lifts."

"Why would we do that?" Danny called.

"See this?" Coyle looked up, towards one of the cameras, and held up something long and thin – like a cigar made of metal. "You think I don't have contingencies in place?" He raised the device, indicating the red LED button on top. "A bit old fashioned, I know. But then, so am I."

"The fuck is that?" Ro asked.

"Detonator of some kind," Danny said. He raised his voice. "You've got this place wired, then?"

"Someone recognises the classics," Coyle said, keeping the cubicles between them. "I've secreted explosives throughout this building. I've now activated the timers. I let my thumb off the trigger, they go off early." He raised his voice. "Can you hear me, Faulkner?"

"I hear you," Faulkner replied, loudly. "What do you want?"

"I should have thought that would be obvious. I want you and your men to pull back. Immediately. Or we'll see how much structural damage this delightful edifice can sustain without collapsing." Coyle paused. "You have three minutes."

"I've got people all over the building," Faulkner protested.

"I'd hurry then."

Faulkner grimaced, and he glanced at the cameras. Then he

gestured and his people began to pull back, heading for the lifts, carrying the wounded with them. Olly released the lock on the lifts as they reached them. Faulkner was the last to go. As the doors closed, he paused. "There's no way out of here. You might as well surrender." Olly wasn't sure who he was talking to, Coyle or them.

Coyle answered for them. "Two minutes."

Faulkner cursed, and was gone. Olly checked his display, watching the lifts descend. "They're going," he murmured. "Keep him talking while I figure us a route out of here."

Danny peered around the edge of the cubicle. "They're gone. Just us now. May as well pack it in, because we ain't going nowhere."

"You're either brave or stupid," Coyle said, out of sight.

"Bit of both," Danny said. He glanced at Olly. "Can't get a bead on him," he whispered. "We need to draw him out."

"I'll go," Ro hissed. Danny tried to grab her, but she was too quick. She slipped away, into the labyrinth of cubicles.

"Keep him talking," Olly said. He flicked through the CCTV feeds, trying to find a vantage point that would show them Coyle. Danny cleared his throat.

"What was this all about, then?" he said. "If you weren't working for Albion, then who? What was the point of all this?"

A moment of silence. Then a laugh. "You really don't know anything do you?" Coyle called out. "Not a damn thing."

"Enlighten us."

More laughter. "It won't matter soon enough. Once I regain control of my partner, I'll settle this affair for good." Coyle paused. "You might even thank me for it, given what's coming…"

"Wh– what's coming?" Danny asked.

Silence. Danny looked at Olly. Olly could only shake his head. An alert flashed on his display and he stiffened. "Shit."

"What?"

"I've lost control of the drone." Olly made to stand. "He's bringing it back!" He heard a shout and a crash, followed by a gunshot. Danny surged out into the open, yelling his sister's name. Olly started to follow him when he heard the sound of glass shattering. The drone had returned. "Danny, look out!"

Olly lunged, tackling the other man to the floor. There was a crack, and Ro cried out. Olly looked up and saw the drone hovering over the cubicles, its weapon smoking. As he stared, unable to look away, it turned towards him, barrel tracking him.

"Oi! Over here," Ro shouted. A chair bounced off the side of the drone, and the machine spun. Danny shoved Olly aside and rose, his rifle spitting fire. Sparks burst from the drone's underbelly, raining down onto the carpet. The machine spun in a wild circle, motors whining like a wounded animal. It started to retreat and Danny pursued, firing steadily, emptying the magazine into it.

It teetered, wobbled and finally crashed down with a shriek of abused metal. Danny ejected the spent magazine, slapped in a full one, and fired again, blowing out the drone's CPU. He turned. "Ro? Rosemary?"

"Here," she called. Olly and Danny hurried towards her. She sat with her back against a cubicle, her face and shirt spattered with blood. She held something in her hand. Danny bent, a look of concern on his face, but she waved him off. "I'm fine. Not mine."

Olly looked past her and saw Coyle – or what was left of him. Danny turned. "Was that you?"

"No. Truly. Something… somebody else took control in those last few moments." He paused. "Shit – the detonator…"

Ro held up her fist. She held the detonator, her thumb on the switch. "Took it from him. Nearly got topped doing it." She put a finger through a hole in her jacket. "There an off switch for it, or…?"

Danny took it from her, gently. "It's wireless. We just need to interrupt the signal."

"Or find something to keep it from activating," Olly said. "Still got some of that tape in your bag?" Danny nodded.

"Think so."

Olly bent to retrieve the bag, then suddenly stopped. "Woah. Anyone else feel that?"

"Feel wh–" Ro began.

The boom of the explosion reached them a moment later. It was followed by another, and then another and another. All from different directions, all around the compass point – but especially to the west, towards Parliament and the TOAN conference. Flares of light and fire rising over the nearby buildings, reflected in the glass and chrome. Cavernous rumbles, far louder than any summer thunder. Then the first shockwaves rippling out across the area, maybe the whole city. The building shook itself, trembling again and again as it rode out the blasts. Outside there was the constant sound of falling glass and debris. Alarms blared from near and far.

Olly straightened slowly, terrified eyes wide. "Fucking hell…"

"What *is* that?" Ro said, scrambling to her feet.

"Explosions," Danny said, in a hollow voice. "Got to be." He looked at Olly. "Maybe that Tell bloke wasn't the only one making bombs."

Olly watched the hellish blossoms of fire and smoke sprouting up across the capital, turning the twilight into a living nightmare. He closed his eyes. Opened them. Grabbed the tape, and made sure the detonator wouldn't go off accidentally. Then he looked at the others.

"I don't know," he said. "But we're gonna find out."

LATER

Bagley-bytes 45700-0: ...

+ + +

Welcome to Checkpoint London.

+ + +

Hope you survive your stay.

EPILOGUE

Olly sat in the café across from the gates to Victoria Park. No longer a pop-up, it was practically an institution these days. London had changed while he'd been gone. Albion checkpoints were everywhere, and the city felt like it was at once locked down tight and ready to explode at any moment. Some things remained the same, however. Drones filled the skies, and people filled the streets. It was still London, despite the changes.

Still home.

He sat back and smiled as Hannah slid into the booth. "Welcome back," she murmured. "The others...?"

"On the way." He, Danny and Ro had split up, after Coyle's death. Hannah had helped them get out of the city, out of Faulkner's reach. They hadn't seen each other in a year. Despite only knowing them a short time, Olly found himself missing them. He leaned towards her. "How are things?"

"As good as can be expected. Worse than they ought to be."

"I saw. There's an anti-immigration protest in Brockwell Park."

"And others scheduled for the rest of the week." She looked him up and down. "You look different. Beard, button down shirt … you look like a farmer."

"Cheers. Beards confuse facial recognition software. Change the shape of the face, or something." He looked down at his clothes. "And I am a farmer. Or at least I was working on a farm. Up in Yorkshire." It was better than being a courier, but not by much.

"I wondered where you'd gone." She looked around. "Krish went to the Shetlands."

"You're having a laugh."

She spread her hands. "I don't know what to tell you. He likes it up there." She frowned. "I don't think he's coming back."

"A lot of them won't," Olly said, softly. "It's different now. Since Liz. Dalton…"

They both fell silent, thinking about those last few hours a year previous. The bombing of the TOAN conference and related sites around London. The attempted bombing of Parliament. The subsequent collapse of DedSec London. So many had gone missing – arrested or killed, like Dalton and Liz. Others had been shipped off to Albion-owned black sites. But not everyone.

Despite this, DedSec was, for all intents and purposes, dead. Even Bagley had gone mostly quiet. Olly had kept his hand in, following the news. Shifting cryptocurrencies into ghost accounts, building up a war-chest, though he wasn't sure why. He'd heard whispers that others were doing the same. DedSec was gone, but that didn't mean you couldn't fight back. Though what form that fight might take, he couldn't say.

For weeks – months – after he'd left London, he'd expected Faulkner to pop up, and arrest him. He'd kept an eye out for surveillance, but detected nothing. That didn't mean they weren't watching him, but he'd improved his old camouflage apps while in hiding. He'd spent sleepless nights scrubbing Oliver Soames from every database and server he could think of, and then done the same for Danny and Ro. As far as Albion was concerned, they'd never existed. Like Coyle.

Like Liz.

There'd been nothing in the news about either of them, though he hadn't expected it. Especially Coyle. He'd tried to dig up information on the assassin but found only whispers – hints. Whoever he'd been, he'd definitely been working for someone. Someone who'd also hired Tell, maybe Clan Kelley too. Someone named Zero Day, according to Ro. But none of his investigations had amounted to anything.

Olly scratched his chin. "I heard Sarah Lincoln on the radio this morning, tearing strips out of Albion. Nigel Cass and his bootboys ain't gonna like that."

"They never do."

"The way I hear it, she's positioning herself for the next leadership election."

Hannah just smiled. Olly chuckled. "Friends in high places." He paused. "I never thanked you for helping us get out of the city, afterwards." Albion had been everywhere in the days after the bombing. London hadn't been safe.

Hannah made a dismissive gesture. "I had to do it for my own safety as much as yours. But you're welcome." She smiled again. "I did what I could to get everyone out." She paused. "If you were wondering, between the breakout and that business with Coyle, Faulkner wound up being reassigned."

"I'm surprised he didn't wind up with a bullet in his head."

"Word is, he might be back in Cass's good graces, though. And back in East London."

Olly grimaced. "Wonderful. There's one bloke I don't ever want to see again."

Hannah was about to reply when the door to the café opened. Danny entered, Ro following in his wake. They didn't look much different to when Olly had last seen them. Danny had shaved his head completely and wasn't wearing a uniform. Ro was dressed like a stockbroker and had grown her hair out. Olly waved, and they joined him and Hannah.

Danny smiled. "Sorry we're late. Had to visit Mum."

"Is she … ?" Olly began.

"Nah, she's fine," Ro said. "Glad we're back."

"Glad we're talking," Danny said. He looked at his sister and nudged her with his fist. "Better than last time I came home."

Ro laughed. "Yeah." She looked out the window. "Our ends have seen better days, though."

"That's why we're here," Olly said. He looked around. "That's why we came back."

Indeed. And just in time, too.

Olly smiled as Bagley's voice filled their ears. "Bagley… long time no see." He paused. "Well, talk anyway."

I am pleased to see you all in one piece and in fighting shape.

They all traded looks. Olly cleared his throat. "I'm guessing you were the one who brought us back?"

Sabine was the one who issued the command to regroup. For my part, I am simply grateful.

"So let's get to it," Ro said. "Why are we here?"

In the aftermath of the bombings, things got worse in London. People disappeared. DedSec scattered. The Signal Intelligence Response Service, Albion, the Kelleys, plenty of other chancers – they all but divvied up the city between them. There was no one left to stop them.

Olly leaned back. "But…?" he said, softly.

But there are still those who wish to fight back. And they need help.

"I thought you said DedSec was gone," Danny said.

It is. It was. But it can rise again. With help.

Olly smiled and looked at the others. Slowly, one by one, they nodded in agreement. He leaned forward, arms crossed on the table. "Well then, I guess you better bring us up to speed, then, huh?"

Welcome back. Welcome to the Resistance.

ABOUT THE AUTHORS

JAMES SWALLOW is a *New York Times, Sunday Times* and *Amazon* #1 bestselling author of over fifty books, and a BAFTA-nominated scriptwriter. He is the creator of the Marc Dane action thriller series, and has written for franchises such as *24, Star Trek* and several high-profile video games. He lives and works in London.

jswallow.com
twitter.com/jmswallow

JOSH REYNOLDS is the author of over thirty novels and numerous short stories, including the wildly popular *Warhammer: Age of Sigmar* and *Warhammer 40,000*. He grew up in South Carolina and now lives in Sheffield, UK.

joshuamreynolds.co.uk
twitter.com/jmreynolds